The Snow Houses

To Cate~
May you always
listen to the snow
fall.

Linda L. Cecil

May, 2022

This is a work of fiction. Names, characters, places, and incidents are either the product of this author's imagination or are used fictitiously. Any resemblance to an actual person(s), business establishment(s), event(s) or place(s) is entirely coincidental.

Cover design by Rebecca Cantrell

Acknowledgements

I am grateful to many friends and family members for their advice, feedback, support and encouragement through these past two years; you know who you are and I am eternally thankful to each of you. I honor my daughter, Brenna, whose love of writing and artistic vision of all things of the heart are, and simply always will be, a true inspiration to me. Lastly, I am indebted to my husband, Joe – whose opinion I value above all else in all things – for his wisdom, warmth, and unwavering belief in me. He is my true champion.

Snowflakes are one of nature's most fragile things,
but just look what they can do when they stick together.

- Vesta M. Kelly

Prologue

Saturday morning came in hot and the sun glinted off the gravel-pocked wide bumper of our beat-up Ford F150 truck Mama had fondly named The Beast. It wasn't much to look at, but it was functional, sturdy, and, above all, safe. Mama liked safe things. I knew this because her life had been anything but.

The plan was for us to be on the road by midmorning in order to reach Amarillo before nightfall. After placing our small cooler with water and sandwiches on the seat between us, then making sure her pistol was safely secured under her front seat, we were ready to head out. Mama planned for no longer than a three-day turnaround, one day to Amarillo, next day the drive to Emmit to pick up my sister, Sage, then another to get back home to Lona.

Mama had gotten the okay from her boss to take both Monday and Tuesday off since she'd gotten that big promotion. I didn't know too much about it except that she'd been working a long time on some project when she found a bunch of problems and was able to save one of our local ranching businesses a bunch of money or something.

She was humming to herself and I knew she was excited and happy about our little trip. We both were. I don't know which of us was happiest, though, Momma because she got her girl back, or me because I just got a sister.

"Did you remember to put the hose out?" she asked.

"Oops," I said, jumping out of the truck and running around to the side of the house to retrieve the hose Sammy, my friend who lived down the road, would need to water our flowers. I didn't even notice the small black sedan as it pulled into our driveway.

It took me a few minutes to hang up the hose and when I came back around to the front porch, I saw Mama face to face with a woman I didn't recognize. She was about Mama's height but heavier with a lot of black eye makeup and bright red lips. Her tight sweater, shiny skirt and high heels seemed almost comically out of place here on our plain gravel driveway.

She pointed agitatedly towards Mama, then back toward her car, and I saw Mama shaking her head as if to reinforce that whatever it was that this woman was saying, Mama wasn't going for it. I couldn't make out anything from where I stood, so I took a few tentative steps forward, not sure if I should come closer to them or if I would be intruding. Mama looked at me, then gave a slight shake of her head so I moved back to where I had been on the porch, still straining to hear the conversation. Snatches of "you'll be sorry," and "she means business," wafted up to me in a voice I didn't recognize. I saw Mama hold up her hands and say, "I think this conversation is over," as she turned to come back towards me. Just then the woman screamed at her "I don't give a SHIT what you think, Shari Stevenson!" "Leave us ALONE!"

Mama turned back to her, steel in her voice as she said "you have about five seconds to get off my property, Veronica Valdez, or I'll have you arrested for trespassing. Do you understand me?"

"Arrested?" Veronica sneered, "by who?" "You don't have *any* cop friends in this town anymore! You just wait, Shari! You have no idea who you're messing with, *juera*!" as she got into her car and slammed the door, spraying gravel as she tore down and out of the narrow driveway.

I didn't know what to say, I was so dumbfounded by what had just happened. Mama was visibly shaken but immediately came to me and folded me into her arms.

"Don't worry, honey" she said, stroking my hair like she did whenever I was upset, her troubled eyes scanning up and down both sides of the road. "She's just an angry, jealous woman."

"But what's she so mad about Mama? What did she mean by 'you'll be sorry'? And what does that mean, *juera*?" I was scared.

"It's a long story, honey, something that happened way back when we were in high school. A little about what's happening now, too, it sounds like. And don't worry, *juera* means 'white girl.' How's about I tell you more about all this once we get on the road?"

I wondered what she was thinking, she was so clearly upset, but at the same time trying to calm me down. Just when I started to press her for more, she turned toward me, placed both of her hands firmly on my shoulders and, in a bright, but now less-than-cheerful voice, said "Get in The Beast, lil' lady, and lets you and I get the hell out of Dodge!"

We had barely pulled onto the frontage service road that takes you to the freeway when I realized I had forgotten the album I had made for Sage. So when I threw my hands up, shouting "WAIT! Mama!" it startled her so much that she almost ran off the road, quickly steering to the side and shoving her foot on the brake, the old truck bathed in a flurry of gravel and dust.

"KC! *WHAT?*"

"Mama, I forgot the album! I need it! Can we go back and get it?"

It was really just a makeshift plastic binder of old photos of Mama and me that I thought Sage and I could go through on our trip back home to Lona. I filled it with all the photos I imagined she would want to see, from when I was a little baby, to our ex-hamster, Zeus, to the garden Mama had tried growing in the rock-hard clay behind our house.

"Oh, Lordy, KC! Let's just let her see it when we get back, ok?"

"But Mama I NEED to get it! *Pleeeeeease?*"

She sighed as she put on her blinker, glanced in the rear-view mirror and pulled a U-turn, heading back home. Pulling up to our front porch, I quickly jumped out of the truck before she even had a chance to come to a complete stop and ran into the house to retrieve the album, not knowing that would be the last time I would ever see Mama alive again.

1 RUNNING BETWEEN THE RAINDROPS

Back when I was a kid, I loved spending time down at Sammy Pino's house, especially in his kitchen. His mom would always, and I mean any God-given time of the day, have a big pot of green chile on the back burner of her old gas stove. Not a stew, not a soup. Seriously, just plain ol' chopped-up green chile, seeds and all. I can still picture Mrs. Pino, barely five feet tall, deep creases etched into her warm, brown face, black and gray hair pulled into a small tight bun at the nape of her neck, one plump arm planted on her apron-covered hip as the other stirred and stirred that big pot. Then came the homemade tortillas. Pat, pat, flip, pat, grill on the heavy cast iron skillet, flip again, slide out onto a large chipped plate then start another one. I'm sure she could do it in her sleep. And they didn't last long, not with five hungry boys in the house, and, most of the time, me. Sammy showed me how to take one of those warm tortillas, slather it with a heaping spoonful of green chile, a sprinkle of garlic salt, then wrap it up and eat it. If you liked spicy food like me, it was heaven.

Our little town of Lona is smack dab in the middle of New Mexico, located about thirty miles south of where Interstates I-25 and I-40 meet, best known for its abundance of the state's official vegetable and, in Mrs. Pino's household, green chile. Rich with fertile fields that crisscross the land where the Rio Grande River and its acequias keep most areas well-irrigated, the majority of residents here either work for the University of New Mexico's Branch College or have their own stake in our small farming community. Well, everyone except Mama and me.

Houses are scattered all up and down our rural two-lane road, some right on the edge of the road, some set far back up on the hill. Ours is somewhere in between. Mama called our rambling adobe house "our country getaway," though no one ever visited us and, as far as I knew then, we weren't getting away from anything. Mama inherited it after her parents passed away, Grandpa recently from a heart attack and Gran several years earlier from cancer. The townspeople used to whisper that Edna Stevenson was a lusher.

When I asked Mama what that meant, she just shook her head and said that some people oughtn't be throwing stones when they lived in glass houses. Mama had a way of explaining all sorts of things that, whatever your question, she always made her answer more interesting.

Like how one of her old friends from Texas asked how she was liking "all that crazy desert heat," Mama would just talk about how the Rocky Mountains stretch all the way down to right about where we are. Mama loved talking about how it rains a lot in the summer when all the clouds bundle up every afternoon and it pours down for maybe fifteen minutes or so, then stops. And how we almost always get snow in the winter.

But, if you ask me, we really do get all that crazy desert heat. Maybe not like Death Valley heat, but hot enough. And muggy in the summertime...whoooo, muggy. I remember one afternoon a couple of summers ago, Mama and I were out on our front porch trying to cool off in the shade from the porch's wide cover since our swamp cooler was on the fritz. Again.

A bunch of big dark thunderclouds had gathered above us, cramming together like they'd all been invited to a big party in a little house, and once they got there, they weren't sure what to do, so they just kept pushing in, more and more, one on top of the other. Anyway, I remember we were just sitting out there on a couple of old plastic

Woolco chairs, drinking iced tea, not saying or doing much of anything. It was hot as hot could be, so hot even the flies just kind of laid around, too draggy and listless to do much of anything themselves. All of a sudden, out of nowhere, there was this huge, walloping *craaaack* of thunder that made us both jump out of our skin. Then it became really quiet. Too quiet. Like you knew something was going to happen but you didn't know what so you just waited, anticipating. After a few seconds, those dark clouds just opened up and started pelting down rain. One minute, two minutes, faster and faster. Three minutes, building up, harder, faster. Four minutes, louder, faster, *louder*. I looked anxiously over at Mama. Raindrops were pinging and zigzagging off everything they landed on, pouring down so hard you couldn't see ten feet in front of you. Louder. Faster. *Louder*.

Then it stopped. Just like that. Like someone had reached up into the sky and flicked off the rain switch. The sun began to slowly peek out from behind the edges of a big black cloud that was already high-tailing it toward the mountains, and everything was all wet and clean and quiet again. I looked at Mama and she looked at me and we smiled. Just like that, New Mexico rain.

"Mama," I ventured, "wouldn't it be cool if we could hear snow fall, too? I mean, is that even possible?"

"Hmm," she paused a few seconds before speaking, looking out over the wet yard. "Well, rain's heavier than snow, of course, so when it hits something, like the roof or the windows, it makes a sound, kind of like it's shouting 'Here I am! Listen to me!' Then all the raindrops buddy up together, and the more they do so, the louder and louder they get. And pretty soon, there's more shouting and splashing and craziness, then all of a sudden, it ends and all those fancy raindrops who thought they were

3

so special shouting and beating against the window, well, they're all gone. Just soaked into the ground or running down into some old culvert pipe.'

'But snow, well now that's another thing altogether. Snow doesn't need to shout, in fact, it doesn't need to even make a sound. It's so light and soft, and, well, *content*, you know? It doesn't need you to hear it when it decides to show up. It just kinda floats on down. And when it does, it gathers with all its other little snowflake friends and, then, without making a sound, they decide to stick to each other. And then some more snowflake friends join in, and well, pretty soon, you have this whole big quiet snow party going on."

I thought about rain friends and snow parties. "So do you think snow is better than rain?"

"Depends," she said. "When all the farmers around here need the rain to take care of their crops, then rain is probably better right then. But the snow gathers all winter long, and then it melts in the spring and when it melts it fills up all the lakes and rivers and even fills up that ditch out there," she pointed out towards the road.

I looked out towards the road, still thinking. "But, I kind of *want* to hear the snow fall down, Mama. I mean, not all crazy like the raindrops, just curious what snow *would* sound like, you know, if we could hear it?"

"I guess that'd be pretty cool," she said, absent-mindedly twirling a strand of her long white-blonde hair around her finger. All of a sudden, she stopped, frowning at it, then quickly tucked it back behind her ear. I felt a twinge. What had she thought about just then? Or seen?

"What's the matter, Mama?" I asked.

"Nothing, honey, why?"

"I don't know, you had a funny look on your face just now."

"Oh, nothing. Really. I mean, well, actually, I guess I was thinking about the rain and stuff and it reminded me of something your grandpa told me a long time ago. Something about running, and raindrops, and I guess it just kind of popped back into my head."

"What popped into your head?"

"Well, as I remember, he was talking about a guy he used to work with, his partner at the bank, maybe? Anyway, I think he said something like 'Marvin's so damn lucky, he can run between the raindrops and never get wet,' and at this she put on her most solemn face, "and then he also said, and I remember this clearly, 'Shari, things don't usually turn out that way for us normal folks.'"

I thought about running between raindrops. "Are *we* normal folks, Mama?"

"Well, sure, but I think what Grandpa meant was that a person can hope for something to happen, but no matter what you do or no matter how hard you try, sometimes you just can't *make* it happen."

I could sense something sad about her as she spoke, so I said encouragingly. "I think you could make *anything* happen, Mama."

"Oh, KC, from your lips to God's ears," she smiled, reaching over to pull me into a hug. "You always say the nicest things to me. Where do you get all that yummy love, I wonder?"

"From you, Mama," I said earnestly, and a quiet, knowing smile passed between us.

"But," I pressed on with our earlier conversation, all thoughts of running in the rain now forgotten. "What do you think it would sound like, Mama, I mean, if snow did have a sound?"

"Well," she said brightly, thankful for the diversion. "For sure it'd have to sound really beautiful, you know? Or happy. Like if you could hear an angel's wings fluttering, or if you could hear a dog's tail wagging, that's what I would like to think snow falling would sound like.'

'But," she concluded. "As far as which is better, the rain or the snow, I think the snow is still way better. Even if you can't hear it."

Mama was just good that way.

2 WATER UNDER THE BRIDGE

Sammy and his brothers used to take turns tight-rope walking across the dilapidated abandoned wooden footbridge that crossed the fast-moving irrigation ditch that flowed behind our two houses and through most of the north valley of our little town. This irrigation ditch, or acequia, serviced all the crop fields, the endless rows of green chile, corn and alfalfa, and pretty much any other crop the farmers in this area could grow. Ever since the county people came out a couple of years ago and built a new bridge closer to the turnoff to the Simpson's farm, no one used this old rickety one anymore. And since it was so close to the road anyway, people just bypassed it and used the easier route to cross the ditch. It was already past being of any good use and had fallen into a state of deep neglect and disrepair. Mama wrote letters and made phone calls to all the townspeople she thought might be in charge to come out and dismantle, or at least, block off, the bridge so no one could use it, but to no avail. Mostly, they just told her it was low on the priority list. But Mama kept calling and writing until one day, a blue county truck pulled up next to the bridge and a guy with a clipboard and a camera walked up and down the sides of the canal and the bridge, making notes and taking pictures. Mama watched his every move, satisfied something was finally going to get done.

But the days turned into weeks and then into months and nobody came back. I think she just got tired of all the calling and letter-writing, so one day she just marched up to the courthouse downtown, pushed open the door to the mayor's office and demanded to see anyone who could come out and take care of the old bridge. Forty-five minutes later, she headed back out of the building, red-faced and furious. They not only weren't going to come out and block off the bridge, they didn't even have it in their system as it even being a problem and didn't have any plans to do anything, regardless of how much she explained the danger it posed.

So, as easy as Mama was with most things I did, she had one absolute rule, and that was for me to stay far, far away from that bridge. I used to think she thought it was haunted or something, because whenever she looked at it, her face would grimace into a frown and her eyes would tighten up like she was seeing something scary, or at least something she didn't want to see, something she didn't want me to see. So I mostly stayed away. Mostly.

If you ask anyone around here, there's an old tale about a ghost woman named La Llorona. Depending on who you talk to, she could be anything from some wild crazy woman who floats along the ditch banks late at night, moaning and wailing for her lost children, to a ghost woman whose footsteps disappear in the quiet snowfall as she softly makes her way through the night, to just a plain old woman walking along the bank who was just trying to scare her children into being good and from playing near dangerous water. Sammy's version was the best: he said she's over ten feet tall and skinny with long black wild hair and you have to be really careful not to look into her one big, bulging eye or you'll get dragged, screaming and wailing, into the ditch to join all her other lost, drowned children. He swears that he once saw La Llorona floating along the edge of the very ditch bank where Mama's dreaded bridge is. I asked Mama about it and she just pooh-poohed the whole story, but I could tell she was thinking about it and how she might possibly use this new Sammy information to further keep me away from that bridge.

For kids like us living out in the country with not much to do in the summer, floating down the water on inner tubes while watching water skippers skitter across the surface was a rite of passage. But because I was expressly forbidden to go near the bridge and, just forget ever going *in* the water, I'd sit on the bank and watch Sammy and his brothers having all the fun while they did their best to get me to ignore Mama's warnings.

But Mama also said that a girl could do anything a boy could do, probably ten times better, so I reasoned that the challenge of me getting across that beat-up old bridge was as good a reason as any to prove her right, even if I knew it was wrong.

It wasn't strong, but the top plank was just wide enough that one could tiptoe across it, and I sat watching five harebrained boys pushing each other to make it to the other side where they could jump off into soft mossy ground below and claw back up the other side of the embankment. Sammy made it the first time he tried, laughing as he jumped off, daring me to come across.

I was hesitant but didn't want to be considered childish, though it was just Sammy and his brothers and their opinions didn't actually count. The uneven boards creaked and groaned as I took the first step, even with my light weight. I thought for sure, now, of all the times I'd wanted to cross it, this time, right when I got over the middle, was going to be when I'd be flung into the water below and prove Mama right after all. Well, right about it being dangerous, that is. I waited, trying to decide if it was worth it as Sammy yelled from the other side.

"Whatsa' matter, you a 'fraidy cat?" he called out. "Bet you too scared, huh? Ok, just crawl across then, just like a little baby!" he and his brothers all laughed, as if that was the funniest thing they'd heard all day.

9

Right then I decided there was no way I was going to let Sammy Pino or anyone else tell me how or how not to cross that old bridge. I took a deep breath, balanced my skinny arms out like a propeller, and sashayed my way across the boards like I was The Queen of Sheba, never looking down at the fast-moving murky brown water, nor even breathing, until I was safely on the other side. I jumped down onto the grass, ran back up and quickly crossed over, this time even faster than before as I shouted out to them, "so who you callin' a 'fraidy cat now?"

We kept that up until we got bored and just kicked around at the edge of the water for a while until I heard Mama calling my name. Not wanting her to see me so close to the bridge, much less *on* it, God forbid, I sprinted up to the edge of the road and zipped through the weedy, overgrown vacant lot next door, forcing myself into a slow walk as I made my way around the corner and back into our yard from Sammy's side. I don't know who I thought I was fooling, though, especially not Mama, because the look on her face as I casually strolled around the corner of the house said it all, my triumphant bravery quickly dissipating under her withering look.

"So where were *you*, young lady?"

'Oh, just hanging out with Sammy and his brothers," I tried to sound casual, but my labored breathing was betraying any attempt at composure.

"I know that, but *where* were you?"

It was useless to lie to Mama. Maybe I was just a bad liar, or maybe she could tell just by looking at me, but it didn't make any difference. She just knew.

"At the old bridge."

"KC! I've told you a thousand times to stay away from there! What don't you understand about no?" When I saw her lips purse together into a thin line and her eyes harden, I knew she was finished talking and that was my cue to head to my room.

I didn't know until years later that Mama had history with that old bridge and that was why she was so adamant that I not go near it. Floating on inner tubes down the canal was a summer ritual in Lona that pretty much every kid participated in at one time or another, back then and still to this day. Often there could be as many as ten kids on it at any given time and this particular day it was Mama, her best friend Karen Simpson, and a couple of the other local girls, Veronica Valdez and Cindy Bustos. Mama didn't really hang out with them since they were a couple years older than her, but they just happened to be floating down that same afternoon as Mama and her own friends.

Everyone knew, well, I mean any kid from around Lona who was floating down the canal knew, to get out of the water way before you got even close to any of the large round culvert pipes that ran beneath most of the country roads out in our area. The old abandoned bridge was about 100 feet before you reached the first culvert pipe, so it served as a visual reminder to get out of the ditch when you got to it. You just knew.

That fateful afternoon, Mama and her friends lost track of where they were and just floated on past the old bridge, laughing and goofing off and not paying any attention to their surroundings. Mama, being the one in front, suddenly realized the danger, but too late as she, screaming and flailing, got sucked into the wide aluminum pipe that ran under the road. The other girls behind her quickly saw what was happening and scrambled to the bank, barely getting out before they, too got sucked inside. Mama futilely clutched and grabbed at anything she could find as she was propelled by the current through the long, corrugated pipe, but it was useless because the inside was covered with thick moss, too slick for her hands to grasp.

Karen ran the thirty feet to the other side of the road that crossed the ditch. "Shari! Shari! Oh my GOD, Shari!" she screamed, scrambling down the bank and halfway into the rushing water, holding onto a crooked branch of willows to steady her as she peered into the large pipe.

Turning up she shouted "Veronica! Help me! Please!" but Veronica was nowhere in sight. Within a few seconds, Mama came sputtering out, grabbing onto Karen's outstretched hand. Karen pulled her up and onto the muddy grass, both of them coughing and choking out water, just as Veronica peered over the bank at them.

Karen turned accusingly up toward her, her voice seething with fury.

"Why the *hell* didn't you help us?" she screamed at her. "You were RIGHT THERE!"

"She looks okay to me. I'm leaving," Veronica replied. Her eyes, cool and indifferent, briefly touched on Mama's stricken face then quickly looked away as the two drenched girls carefully stepped their way up the side of the ditch. When they got to the top, Mama searched around, but Veronica and Cindy were already headed back down the other ditch side, dragging their tubes along, not looking back.

Needless to say, the old bridge was officially off limits.

3 STILL WATERS RUN DEEP

Mama was born here but moved away when she was in high school. I didn't know why she left in the first place but I do remember seeing her now, sitting out on our front porch some evenings, looking out to where the crows and the sparrows would gather on our scrubby front lawn and big old tears would be running down her cheeks. But knowing Mama, I figured those tears were because she was just so happy to be home.

The sign on the side of the highway as you came into town still said "Welcome to Lona, pop. 2,272, The Biggest Little Town in New Mexico." When she arrived back here in Lona (pop. 5,449) that cold spring day of 1986, she rounded it up to an even 5,450, although technically it was 5,450 and a half, since she was already four months pregnant with me at the time. Ever since they opened the community college on the south side of town back in 1975 Lona had really grown, but it's clear that old sign is going to remain the faded, bullet-riddled 2,272 for as long as it stands sentinel on the edge of the road, regardless how many people actually live here now.

I was born on Mama's birthday; she always said that someone in this world was smiling on both of us that special day. Aunt Penny and Uncle Doug came down from Alaska to meet me and Aunt Penny stayed with us for a couple weeks afterward. Since there was no other family to speak of, Mama welcomed their help and companionship. She'd always liked Penny and the feelings were mutual. Of course, I wouldn't officially meet either of them until years later, but Mama spoke so fondly of her that I just knew I would love her as much as she did when I finally did.

Early on, Mama needed to find a steady job in Lona, which proved difficult for a single woman raising a child. Even though she had inherited Grandpa's house, there wasn't much money left over to live on once the taxes and bills were paid from the meager till she had saved up. Grandpa also had a small life insurance policy, which Mama promptly put into a savings account, refusing to touch it, even though we could've used that money. And since the irregular parttime hours at the diner weren't conducive to having a babysitter, she began looking into a job where she could work from home. Mama had done pretty good in her high school math classes, so when she approached Dennis Buchner, an old friend of her father's, he was more than happy to hire her to manage his customers' accounts for his business, JB Associates. It provided bookkeeping and accounting service to a good portion of businesses in Lona, El Rio, and also to all the small ranches and farms up and down the Rio Grande Valley. Though he had two other bookkeepers working fulltime, when Donna, the youngest, informed him she was getting married and moving to Austin he realized that hiring Mama just made sense. They established a great working relationship; her attention to detail and her prompt delivery of the perfectly analyzed accounting sheets at the end of every week took a huge load off Dennis's work. He was happy to have her, and vice versa. Besides, she said she was tired of working as a waitress, mostly because she worried about leaving me home alone too often.

Mrs. Chavez down the road babysat for me most of the time when I was little; she didn't have children of her own and Mama always said she was the nicest person she'd ever met here. Once I started school, we didn't see her as often, and now, I don't even think she'd remember me, it's been so long. Sammy and his brothers used to say her and her

14

husband kept real live bats in their garage and she'd kill them and cook them for dinner; I asked Mama if she believed any of that and she just shook her head and said "remember what I said about glass houses, KC."

I do kind of remember one thing, though, something I hadn't thought of in years, and that was Mrs. Chavez's snow globe collection. I could see them lined up on every shelf, every table, everywhere throughout her small, tidy house. I'd never seen anything like them and even though Mama told me not to ever touch them, one day while I was playing in the den, I noticed this one globe with a little green frog sitting atop a bridge. It was larger than the other ones and I remember wondering why in the heck anyone would put a frog on a bridge inside a snow globe. Then my curiosity got the best of me, and as I reached for it, it slipped through my fingers, shattering onto the hard tile floor. Mrs. Chavez came running in from the kitchen, and, seeing me frozen there staring at the floor, she abruptly stopped, looking at me so strangely I got scared. Then, just as quickly, she came right over, scooped me up, and gave me a big hug. She wiped the tears off my cheek like it wasn't such a big deal after all and I felt a little better. But I can tell you one thing, I never touched those snow globes again.

Working from home allowed Mama and me to spend all our time together, well, mostly, until I started school, then we just made do with the little time we had on evenings and the weekends. But it seemed we were both happiest just sitting on our front porch, me by her side, reading, or talking about the birds or the mean kids in school or the nice teachers. Oftentimes she'd dial the radio in the kitchen to her favorite country music station and we'd listen to the twang drift through the screened window. I was too young to understand her work business, but she bought me a little blank accounting book so I could pretend I was just like her. Each afternoon after school, I'd jump off the bus and run up our long driveway and she'd be standing there, waiting for me on the porch with a big smile and an even bigger hug. After a snack and a quick rundown of my day, we'd go into the den and sit side-by-side at the long desk, her face stern in concentration as she worked over the ledgers, and mine equally concentrating over mine. Our work couldn't have been more different, because next to her neat, clean handwriting, dutifully written in perfect rows were my curlicue- and scribble-filled images of flowers and horses and butterflies dancing aimlessly from page to page.

Most times I was okay with being alone. As long as I had my drawing books and paints and brushes, I was happy. Other than the regular school-day humdrum, I was always excited to show her what I'd drawn, or what I was planning to draw, or even just sit out on our old front porch and talk about what I was drawing. Mama was good that way, always nodding yes, or smiling patiently as I'd show her each page I'd been working on. She acted like I was the next Georgia O'Keefe, she thought I was that good. Secretly, though, I was most happy just sitting with her, just me and Mama, listening to the birds, watching the sun rise.

As if she thought she had the time and patience, Mama decided to start a garden behind our house. She, to no avail, attempted to keep our sparse collection of tomatoes, squash, jalapenos and one long row of beautiful pink hollyhocks from dying, but it was clear, at least from the vegetables, that we weren't going to be future farmers of any sort. She tried to grow herbs also, but no matter where she planted them, the hot sun would bake them into a crisp so she gave up on those, too. There was other stuff, like poison ivy and such, but mom kept it out of our yard pretty well. I was officially the water girl since we didn't have any type of built-in sprinklers, so every day, I'd get that sprayer started up on the hose and water everything.

Mama said I was born with a green thumb but I didn't see that. I just knew that I didn't want them to die and they made Mama happy when she saw how big they'd grown and actually were getting the little flowers, which meant the fruit of our labors was on the way. I was always happy when Mama was happy, even if that wasn't often.

We never talked about my father so I didn't know much about him, other than that Mama would just say he wasn't a part of our lives anymore. Evidently, he was as far down on her interest pole as one man could get. But I guess the longer you go on not talking about something, the easier it gets to just not talk about it, so the subject rarely came up anymore. Besides, now that I'd just turned thirteen, it seemed like I always had more important thirteen-year-old things to worry about than those of a father I'd never even known.

Probably the closest I ever really got to knowing anything about him was that April morning when Mama got that call. I was in the living room drawing when the phone rang. I ran into the kitchen and unhooked the green wall phone's receiver. Holding it to my ear, I dutifully said "Stevenson household," listening, as a woman's voice I didn't recognize asked for Shari Davenport. 'Um…Davenport?' I said, just as Mama snatched the receiver from my hand and promptly thrust a pointed finger toward the living room.

Hushed tones from the kitchen. Fragments of "What? What do you mean? She *what?*" was all I could decipher from where I was glued to the wall's edge, furtively peeking around the corner, trying to gather what I could from this confusing conversation. Not wanting to be seen, I edged closer to the kitchen, just enough to hear her voice stammer into the receiver "So, w…w…wait, does this mean I really get Sage? Oh my God! It's really true? My daughter is coming home?"

I must have let my held-in breath out just at that same second, because right then she turned towards where I had been hiding and saw me standing there, blank-faced, transfixed. The alarm on her face was unmistakable. Quickly composing herself, she said into the phone "Look, I'm going to have to call you back in a bit. Stay there. Yes, I'll call you right back." She hung up and stared at the receiver a few seconds before slowly turning towards me. "Honey, we need to talk."

4 JUERA

Shari Stevenson was somewhat of a curiosity among Lona's predominantly Hispanic residents. Except for her big, dark brown eyes, she was a blank canvas, eyelashes and brows that looked almost as if they had been dipped in snow. Her pale hair was so light it looked almost white as it fell in thick waves across her shoulders and down her back, and she also had the lightest of ivory skin that her mom kept shaded from the merciless summer sun. And boy, was she tall. At 5'5" in fourth grade, she towered over everyone, even the boys, so from the time she was little, this strange girl was the subject of much curiosity --- oftentimes people just stared at her, not sure what to make of her.

As she got older, she learned to keep to herself with few, if any, real friends. In junior high it seemed most of the boys thought she was cute, though much too tall. And some of the girls, especially the popular ones, simply resented her uniqueness, which only added to the aloneness she often felt. Not shy, but extremely wary, Shari's reputation started early, many thinking her snobbish and standoffish, when she was really just trying to not stand out at all.

Once in fourth grade, a boy came up to her and asked, "Hey Shari, do your feet stink?"

Surprised at the attention, but immediately defensive, she answered, "Of course not! Why?"

"Because you're always walkin' around with your nose up in the air" he laughed, running off.

Her father, Dan Stevenson, was Lona's only banker. His small establishment was actually tucked into a small brick building between the town's bowling alley and post office so it seemed there were always people constantly hanging around outside the big glass window that said Lona Bank and Trust painted in cursive gold and black letters. Shari always tried to avoid that stretch of road in town, knowing the kids knew she was the banker's daughter, which only added to her aloofness.

Her mother, Edna Stevenson, died when she was thirteen. Cancer, though many townspeople, well, *townswomen*, to be exact, often gossiped that she died from drinking and how sad it was for poor Dan Stevenson to be raising those two young kids alone.

"Don't listen to them honey," he would tell Shari when she'd press for more information. "They don't have a blessed thing better to talk about so they make up what they can and pass it around like a bag of potato chips just to see who'll grab onto a handful."

Her brother Doug was two years older and enjoyed his football, girls and partying. Handsome, smart, and outgoing, he had no trouble making friends, not always the best kind, but he was still just one of those kids everybody seemed like. Where Shari spent many lonely nights crying herself to sleep, painfully aware of her undeniable differences, yet yearning to somehow fit in, Doug blossomed and thrived, oblivious to her teenage misery.

As high school came around, though, things seemed to get a little better. The boys in her class started catching up to her in height and started taking a real interest. She was vaguely flattered by this unfamiliar attention but stayed wary and distant, as if to protect herself from her torturous adolescence. Regardless, Shari being the object of attention became a bother for Doug because most of the guys who fawned over her were fellow football or basketball players and having them eyeing his sister was a becoming a distraction.

Time helped her finally find a good friend, Karen Simpson, a fellow outskirts-of-Lona outcast who constantly worried about her weight and frizzy hair. Where Shari was tall, Karen was not even five feet, yet, the two of them became inseparable, spending their weekends hanging around the Tastee Freeze just like all the other town kids, hoping to at least *look* like they were fitting in.

One of Lona High School's popular girls, Veronica Valdez, was crazy about Doug. She tried everything to get his attention, and everyone in school knew that Veronica was one of those girls who usually got what she wanted, so Doug's disinterest in her was a constant source of frustration.

Because the high school's population was so small, every single girl in the entire school was in Shari's Home Economics class that first year. Not just the other little freshmen like herself. Everyone. And, as luck would have it, Veronica, a junior, was her designated table mate, so there wasn't much Shari could do. And, boy, Veronica took her pent-up frustration out on Shari as if it was her fault that Doug didn't pay any attention to her. No matter what the assignment was, Veronica would make it worse, either by forgetting one part and then blaming it on Shari, or feigning surprise to the teacher when the cake didn't rise because someone had forgotten to put in baking powder. And because the rest of the girls pretty much saw Veronica as the leader of their pack, Shari saw no possible way to make this any better. She had hoped that Veronica's crush on Doug would soften her resentment toward her, thinking that if Veronica pushed her too hard, she'd know it would lessen her chances of being with him. Again, to no avail.

"I heard in class today that Veronica asked you to the Sadie Hawkins dance," Shari mentioned one evening after dinner.

Dad raised his brows over his nightly newspaper, "Isn't that Clint Valdez's girl?"

"Yeah, why?" Doug asked.

"Oh, no special reason," Dad replied, but Doug persisted, saying "Do you know them?"

"Well, I know Clint. He comes in to settle his ranch accounts every month. I was just curious because I thought his daughter would've graduated last year."

Shari shot her brother a surprised look, since Doug was a senior and Veronica was a junior.

"I don't know, Dad. I'm pretty sure she's only 16 or 17," he said. "How can you graduate that young?"

"Well, I don't know for sure, but I know she's listed on his loan paperwork and as memory serves me, she'd be almost 19 by now. But none of our business, I guess. I shouldn't have said anything and neither will you," Dad warned with a sharp glance. He raised his newspaper, dismissing the conversation entirely.

Pulling Doug away from Dad's earshot, Shari hissed under her breath "You're not actually going to *go* with her, are you?" she asked, incredulous.

"Maybe. What's it to you?'

"Well, she only treats me like crap any time she's around me is why."

"Just ignore her, everyone else does."

"She's in my Home Ec class *and* my typing class. I *can't* ignore her. The only class she's not in is Accounting. I'm going to ask around."

"Well, I'm not surprised she's not in accounting, ha! I mean, aren't you the only girl in that class anyway?" he teased. "Besides, do you really think YOU'LL be able to find out anything just by asking around? Keep your nose out of it, Shar, she's got a temper."

As soon as she could, Shari finished the dishes and ran to the den, taking the phone and its long cord around the corner into the hall closet.

"Karen, you are NEVER going to believe this!"

The dance came and went and Doug and Veronica became a couple, if you can call driving around in Dad's old truck back and forth on Friday nights a couple. It was kind of like Doug wasn't sure he even wanted to be called a couple, now that he had it in his mind that Veronica was really two years older than him. But it didn't take long, given the penchant for teenagers to talk, especially Veronica's so-called closest friends who knew her back story. Pretty soon the entire Lona high school class body knew that Veronica Valdez had actually flunked two years when she was in grade school in Santa Fe and was really eighteen, going on nineteen years old.

Funny thing, though, the teenager gossip line. Shari swore Karen, who swore MaryBeth, who swore Danny, to ultimate secrecy about Veronica's real age. So of course, over the next few weeks, everyone in school knew. And Veronica was hellbent on revenge when the end of the gossip line reached her and she found out it was Shari who started the whole thing.

The first incident took place in front of the library, which was a long low building directly across the street from the main entrance into the high school. Shari was waiting for the school bus and Veronica came up behind her, shoving her to the ground so hard that Shari landed with an OOMPH on the pebbly blacktop road squarely between the buses' two huge front tires just as it had started to take off. The alert driver quickly slammed on the brakes and clamored down the steps as several kids ran over to help her up. Shari got up, hurt and shock on her face, and quickly looked around to find where Veronica had gone but she was nowhere in sight.

It didn't take long for word to get around school what had happened. That evening Doug, who rarely even said as much of a muffled "hey" when he'd see Shari in the school's hallway, came into the kitchen after football practice and sat next to her at the table.

"I heard what happened," he said solemnly, and Shari could read real concern in his troubled eyes.

Even though she could feel the tears well up, she just said "I'm all right."

"Ha! Knowing her, she was probably wishing the bus was moving faster when she pushed you down."

"But why do that? I'm so sick of her being so mean to me! I've never done anything to her!"

"Well, you *are* the one who told the whole world about how old she really is," he reminded her. "Of course she's pissed off. But I'd really, *really* stay away from her if I were you, little *juera* girl," he chuckled, narrowly dodging the spoon she propelled at him.

Avoiding Veronica Valdez proved easier said than done, because the following day at school, rumors of what happened the previous afternoon had already started to swirl through the hallways. Veronica tried to kill Shari Stevenson. Shari Stevenson threatened Veronica with a nail file. It was all ridiculous teenage gossip, but nevertheless, it eventually made its way to Principal Adams' office and both girls were called in the following afternoon.

Of course, Veronica's version was far from the truth as she explained that she had accidentally bumped Shari and that she must have just lost her footing or something. Shari denied this, telling him exactly what really happened. Neither girl budged from their stories and by the time they emerged red-eyed and puffy-faced from his office a half hour later, both went their separate ways.

But for some reason, whatever happened in that office that afternoon, Shari and Veronica forged an unspoken understanding – maybe they were under threat of expulsion, or community service, no one really knew – but between the two of them Veronica vaguely implied she wasn't going to sabotage every move Shari made and Shari accepted the fact that in order to keep this fragile truce going, she wouldn't badmouth Veronica to Doug anymore. Then that summer, the mishap near the old bridge happened and things were never the same again.

5 SWEPT AWAY

It wasn't any surprise to anyone when Shari eventually decided to leave and go live with her Aunt Mae and Uncle Jim in Texas. Her Dad had seen how cheerless she had become and realized that Lona wasn't being kind to his only daughter. He hoped her being around a woman might help her navigate the inevitable difficulties of being a teenager, so his sister Mae was more than accommodating when he called and proposed his idea to her.

Emmit, Texas was a good fit. Shari finished the next two years of high school, got a job as a waitress in Dixie's Diner, and didn't once look back to Lona.

One day a group of Texas State Troopers came into the diner and settled into a large booth on Shari's station. One in particular, Mike Davenport, took a keen interest in Shari and before long, made a habit to make sure he would get her as his waitress whenever he came in.

"You sure have pretty hair," he commented one morning as she set down his coffee, ready to take his order. When she didn't respond, he continued. "I can't tell if it's silver or white, but it's just plain pretty to me."

"Um, thanks," she said warily, unsure of what more to say. Her hand immediately went up to her hair, an automatic habit borne from years of merciless playground taunts. She knew all too well her unusual hair was often the topic of conversation but still tensed whenever someone made a comment about it. When she was born, the doctors ran all sorts of tests, thinking it might be albinism, or a lack of the pigment melanin, but her skin color was, though extremely light, perfectly normal and her eyes were the same deep chocolate brown as her father's. It was just the hair. It was finally concluded that it was plain ol' hereditary, although neither her mother or father could identify anyone in their families who had such light, almost white hair.

"What can I get for you?" She kept her eyes downcast, waiting on his response.

"Well, that depends," he teased. Then, seeing how she was blushing and not lifting her eyes to meet his, he said, "Ok, ok, I'll have the #3 with bacon and a side of pancakes."

"Um, well, okay, I'll go put this right in," she said, still focused on her notepad.

"Hey, look up for a minute, pretty girl with the white hair."

She slowly raised her gaze and saw the unmistakable interest in his eyes.

"I'll...I'll be right back with your order," she stammered, hurrying away from the table, swearing she could hear his soft laugh.

When his food was ready, she brought it to him, again not looking him in the eye, as she arranged the plates of bacon, eggs and pancakes in an arc in front of him. She could feel him smiling at her and as she started to turn, he touched her arm.

"Hey, I won't bite. Seriously. I just want to know your name. I'm Michael, Mike, Davenport," he waited, still smiling at her.

"Shari."

"Just Shari?" he teased.

"Shari Stevenson. I'm, um, will there be anything else?"

"Dinner?" he asked, this time more seriously.

"I, I don't understand" she said, confused, as she looked down at the huge breakfast sitting in front of him.

"Will you have dinner with me?"

They met that Friday evening at Jeremiah's Steakhouse over in Cloverdale. It was closer to Aunt Mae and Uncle Jim's house and an easier drive for Shari. She was nervous because it was the first real date she had ever been on and when she said as much, Mike was incredulous.

"You're kidding, right? Someone as beautiful as you?"

After their third dinner together in as many weeks, Shari was smitten. She thought Mike was funny and smart and everything the boys back in Lona weren't so it didn't take long for her to reveal all the teenage heartache and frustration she had bottled up inside. It was as if she had found someone, for the first time in her life, who liked her for who she was, not just for how she looked.

Mike was the only child of Mina and Tom Davenport, the third-largest landowners in all of West Texas and when he chose the life of public service over overseeing their vast land holdings, Mina Davenport was angry and upset.

"Tom! How can you just sit there and say nothing to him?" she challenged, clearly aggravated when her husband refused to get involved in Mike's career decision.

"For crying out loud, Mina! He's twenty-four years old! Let him make his own decisions for once in his life!"

"But he has everything he could possibly want here! Why on earth would he want to go put his life on the line every day, dealing with criminals, and druggies and felons?"

"And don't forget all those dangerous speeders," Tom lightly goaded her.

"Oh, just forget it! You don't even *want* to help, do you?

"Help what, Mina? Change his mind so he's doing something *you* want him to? How fair is that?"

Needless to say, when Mike first brought Shari home to meet them, Mina's reception was lukewarm at best. Tom found her warm and engaging, as did she with him, but nothing Shari did seemed to thaw Mina out. Mike's shifts as a State Trooper often kept him away from town and she ran each time the phone rang, praying it would be him. Weeks turned into months and then on the night of her twenty-third birthday, he knelt down and proposed to her.

It wasn't until Sage was born a year after they married and had moved from Mike's tiny apartment into an equally tiny house, that Shari realized the only key to Mina's cold heart was going to be this beautiful baby girl. Where Mina had been consistently chilly and distant toward Shari, she melted whenever she was around her only grandchild. In time, they forged a tenuous relationship where Mina could spend more time with Sage and Shari could finally feel like she was a valid part of Mike's family.

Their lives became somewhat routine, though happy. Shari quit her waitressing job to take care of Sage and Mike started climbing the ranks within the State Police. One night when Mike was on a three-day patrol of two West Texas counties, the phone rang about 9:30.

"Hello?" Shari said, not recognizing the number on the phone's caller ID.

"Is this Shari Davenport?" a male voice said.

"Yes, who's this?"

"You don't know me, but I know your husband. Here's the truth. He's a dirty a cop and he's involved in some shady shit."

"What? What do you mean?" Shari said, instantly afraid.

"You just tell your husband he's going down." Then the caller hung up.

"Wait! Wait!" she shouted into the dead line. She quickly dialed Mike's service phone, but it went straight to voicemail. Then she dialed the station, only to be told that Mike wasn't on duty that night.

"Not on duty?" she said disbelievingly. "He left for work hours ago!"

"I'm sorry ma'am, he's not scheduled 'til this Saturday."

"Saturday! Are you *sure*? He said he would be coming *home* this Saturday!" Shari exclaimed, now clearly upset and worried.

Scrolling back through the caller ID, she found the unknown caller's number and pressed the redial button. Listening as it rang several times, unanswered, she thought to herself, anxiously, who *was* that? What did he mean?

Growing more upset by the minute she was finally able to get ahold of Mike's best friend, Eddie Martinez, who confirmed to her the dispatcher's information that Mike wasn't scheduled to be on duty until Saturday.

"Well, do you know where he is?" Shari was nearly shouting.

"I honest to God don't know, Shari. Seriously. Let's just calm down a bit and let me ask around and see what I can find out, okay? I'll call you right back."

"Please, please Eddie, tell me I'm not going crazy! And hurry, ok?"

She sat on the couch for the next 30 minutes, paralyzed with fear that something had happened to her husband, imagining him lying in a ditch, covered with blood, unable to reach his phone.

It wasn't until about an hour later when the phone rang again, this time Eddie hurriedly whispered into the receiver, "Shari, you've got to get out of the house! You've got to go get Sage and get out right now!"

"WHAT? Eddie, what do you mean? What's going on? Where's Mike?"

"I can't tell you right now, just DO it Shari! RIGHT NOW! You're in danger!"

"But, but, I don't know where to go, Eddie!"

"Meet me at your aunt and uncle's house as soon as you can and I'll explain everything! Just GO!" he said, quickly hanging up.

Pulling into their driveway fifteen minutes later, she saw Eddie's state patrol car parked alongside Aunt Mae's Subaru. Quickly unbuckling Sage from her car seat, she hurried up the steps as Uncle Jim rushed her into the house. Eddie was sitting next to Aunt Mae who was softly crying into a tissue.

"Oh, Shari! I'm so sorry!" she cried.

"He's dead! He's dead, isn't he? Oh my God what happened? Eddie, what happened?"

Eddie stood up and came over to where Shari was still rooted, her arms clutching her squirming toddler. He gently took Sage from her arms and handed her to Uncle Jim, who went over and sat next to Aunt Mae, then turned back to Shari, placing both his hands on her shaking shoulders.

"No, Shari, we don't know anything. We can't find him."

"Wha...what?" Shari stammered. "Eddie, you're not making any sense! What do you mean, can't find him? Why? What happened?"

Eddie dropped his hands and motioned for her to sit down at the kitchen table. "We believe he's in a lot of trouble, Shar, he was caught in a police sting tonight, trying to sell almost a kilo of cocaine."

"I...I...I don't understand! Mike doesn't do drugs!"

"I'm so sorry, Shari. He's been under surveillance for about six months now. I couldn't say anything about it until we had proof. He's been recorded on camera taking drugs from the evidence lock-up room and selling them to a local drug dealer."

Her head spinning, she held onto the edge of the chair as Eddie helped her sit down.

"Eddie, this doesn't make any sense! Why did you say I had to leave my house?"

He looked at her directly and said, "Because we believe you're in danger. Sage, too. These people not only don't have their drugs or the money they paid, but now Mike's disappeared. They'll stop at nothing for revenge. Look, do you have somewhere else you can go?" he said, turning questioningly to Aunt Mae and Uncle Jim.

"You'll just stay here with us, sweetie!" Aunt Mae exclaimed as she came over and gave her a big hug.

"No! Not here!" Eddie said emphatically. "You are all in danger, and if Shari moves in here, it will be a target on all your backs."

"Well, where will we go? We need to find Mike! What if something's happened to him?" she wailed; her entire world shattered in a matter of minutes.

"I just don't know what to tell you," he said, shaking his head. "But I do know one thing, these people will stop at nothing. *Nothing*," he emphasized. "I tell you what, let's get you and Sage settled into a hotel room for tonight and let me talk to some people. I'll figure it out and we'll take it forward tomorrow, ok? I promise, Shari, we'll get this worked out."

"Has anyone contacted his folks?" Shari asked.

"I haven't. I wasn't sure if you wanted to be the one to tell them or what."

"You should probably call them since you know all the specifics, Eddie. Plus, they know you like a son. I just don't know what I could say that would soften the blow for them."

She gave him the number and went to pick up her sleepy Sage. "Hush, sweetie, hush," she whispered, hoping her words didn't belie the absolute terror she was feeling inside.

After a restless night's sleep in an unfamiliar hotel room, Shari was jarred awake by a loud knocking on the door. She lay paralyzed on the bed, not moving an inch, looking over at the still-sleeping Sage. After the next, louder, knock, she carefully got out of bed, trying not to wake her. She tiptoed over to look out the peephole, shaking with relief as she recognized the familiar face of Tom Davenport, Mike's father. She quickly slid the chain over and unlatched the lock, letting him step inside the darkened room. Just as he did, he was shoved heavily from behind and he flew down into the room, hitting the hard wood floor with a loud thud.

"Whaat...?" was all Shari could squeak out before something heavy hit the side of her head and she blacked out.

She felt, rather than saw, a razor-thin shaft of bright afternoon light slicing through the crack in the curtains. Disoriented, she tried to sit up. She felt something warm running into her eyes and put her fingers up to touch the moisture, gasping as she realized it was blood. Groaning, she gripped the side of the desk to stop her from falling over as she looked wildly around the room.

"Sage!" she called, "Sage!!!!" seeing the empty bed and the crumpled body of her father-in-law on the floor. Sage was gone.

The ambulance whisked both of them to the hospital where Tom was treated for blunt force trauma resulting in a severe skull fracture and was put in the intensive care unit for treatment and observation. Shari's x-rays showed no concussion so, after suturing her head and determining no further injuries, she was released to a waiting police officer, who promptly brought her to the police station where she was put into an interrogation room. The police were stoic as they took her story down. Mike was, after all one of their own, and now he was missing, his wife hurt, his father nearly beaten to death and his baby daughter was nowhere to be found.

Her hands wrapped around the coffee cup, Shari lifted it to her lips, unable to sip, as she bleakly looked around at the unfamiliar faces. Tears welled up in her eyes each time she allowed herself to think of the situation. Sage was gone. Sage was *gone.*

"Shari! Oh, Shari, there you are! Oh my God! And Sage!" Shari stood up, turning toward the familiar voice of her mother-in-law Mina as she came through the door and around the table to give her an awkward hug.

"Has there been any word at all?" she asked, stepping back and eyeing Shari anxiously.

"No, nothing." Shari said, her words hollow and flat.

"We'll find both of them, I know we will! And Tom, Tom's going to come out of this, and, well, everything is going to be just fine!" Mina smiled, a little too brightly, in Shari's opinion.

"How do you know that, Mina? Huh? Just how in the hell do you know all that?"

"Well," she sniffed, "I'm just trying to be positive."

"I'm sorry. I didn't mean that. I'm just so tired and I don't know what to do or think anymore."

"Let me get you something to eat. You probably haven't eaten all day," Mina surprisingly offered, then looked down at her pinging phone, "Oh, never mind, I have to get this," she said, hurrying out of the room. Minutes later the lead detective, Martin Davis, came in and sat across the table from Shari.

"I wish we had better news, Mrs. Davenport," he began.

"Don't! Don't tell me she's dead!" she sobbed, unable to contain the fear and sorrow that had been building up for hours.

"No, no, we don't think that. But I don't know how to say this. I'm so sorry, but…. It's Mike. They found his patrol car about an hour ago. There's no sign of him. I'm so sorry."

She dropped to the floor, her head spinning, unable to process what she had just been told. "Mike? Gone? Wha…why…?" Then, "Oh my GOD! Is Sage…? Did he…?"

"No, no, it doesn't appear that she was with him. But we do need to bring up the possibility that she might have been kidnapped."

"KIDNAPPED? WHAT?"

"Mrs. Davenport, these people your husband were involved with, the majority of them work through a network that covers pretty much all of West Texas, maybe further. They're bad folks and this is part of their method of operation. And the problem is, if they have taken her, we have no way of knowing where. We have every resource available working on this. I don't know what else to tell you at this point, other than it might be a good idea to go home and get some rest."

"I'll wait," she whispered, barely able to speak. "I'm not going anywhere without my daughter."

35

"You're welcome to bunk here, but I can't vouch for how comfortable it'll be. Marcy can get you set up if you'd like."

It seemed ages since Shari had slept, even though it was only twelve hours ago that she had opened her hotel room to her father-in-law. Twelve long hours since Mike and Sage were gone.

"What happens next?" She'd never been more afraid in her life.

"Well, we've got everyone on this. If we hear anything, I promise you'll be the first to know. But for now, I suggest you get some rest."

She followed the female officer back to the bunk room and sat on the narrow bed's edge, knowing sleep would be impossible. A light knock on the door startled her and she rushed over to open it.

"Mrs. Davenport, can you please come back out? We've just received a phone call."

Heart pounding, Shari followed the officer to the front office where two other officers and another gentleman dressed in a suit were standing, silently looking at her as she came in.

"Mrs. Davenport," the man said, "I'm Agent Robinson, FBI. We are so sorry to hear about your husband. We've got everyone looking for him. But also, we need to let you know we've had a female agent monitoring your home phone and you received an anonymous phone call that the caller told us they have your daughter. They've demanded a ransom."

"Where? Where is she?"

"I'm sorry, the caller didn't say, they just instructed us to drop off twenty thousand dollars in Pike Park by midnight tonight."

"Twenty thousand! I don't have that kind of money!"

"Well, actually, they didn't mention you, Mrs. Davenport. The caller specifically said to send Mina Davenport, alone, with the money."

"Mina? What's Mina got to do with this?"

"We don't know, ma'am, but we've contacted her and she's coming back in."

Twenty minutes later, Mina rushed back into the station, her face red and flushed.

"Mina, they...they've taken Sage..." Shari crumbled into the chair.

"What? Where IS she?"

"We don't know, and... it's Mike. Mina, no one can find him."

Mina's face went pale as she tried to process Shari's words. "What do you mean, you can't find him? And what about Sage? What the *hell* is going on here?"

"We found his patrol car, ma'am," Agent Robinson interjected, "but there was no sign of him. He's not answering his radio or phone, either."

"Well, he couldn't have just disappeared so I guess you boys have your job cut out for you, don't you? And if I'm not mistaken, the three of you sitting here are three more who should be out looking for him, correct? So, what the hell are you still doing hanging around here?" she bellowed to the room.

Within four hours, Mina had gone back to the ranch, pulled money from her safe, and was driving toward Pike Park, a small bag full of the ransom money tucked in her trunk. Two undercover officers were following at a safe distance, when she suddenly slammed on her brakes and pulled to the side of the road. They passed her slowly, then pulled up and around, quickly making a U-turn. But by the time they got back, her car was gone. They immediately drove to Pike Park where the ransom pickup was to be and found no people or vehicles in sight.

"Dispatch, we've lost our subject. Repeat, we've lost our subject."

Mina pulled into a narrow alley three blocks from the remote park and turned off her headlights. Within a couple of minutes, two young men appeared with Sage between them, hesitantly moving forward toward her car. She got out just as Sage broke free from their grasp.

"Nana! Nana!" she cried, running the short length of the dark alley, propelling her small body into Mina's outstretched arms.

"You better not have touched a single hair on her head," Mina stared at them over Sage's head buried into her middle. She unlocked the trunk, pulled out the bag, and laid it on the ground in front of them.

"We did just like you said, ma'am," the taller one said, quickly picking up the bag and moving back to stand next to the other.

"It's all there, ten for each of you, now get out of my face," she said, her voice steely.

Buckling Sage into the front seat, she turned to them again, her voice threatening "and know this, one word, just one slip-up, and you are both dead, do you understand?"

"Where's Mama?" Sage whimpered. "I want Mama!"

"We're going to go see her now, honey. But remember, we can't say even one word about this, ok because we don't want those bad guys to come and take you away again!"

"But I can tell Mama, though?

"NO!" Mina said so forcefully that big tears immediately welled up in Sage's eyes.

"I'm sorry, peanut," Mina softened. "You just can't tell anyone anything right now, *especially* your mom."

"Can I tell Daddy then?

"No, honey, not even Daddy."

Tom Davenport was upgraded to stable, then serious, then was eventually sent home. And Mina, of course, had only the best home care available for him. When he asked about his son, however, she was intentionally vague, only giving him the scant police reports and saying he was still missing. She was worried that if he thought Mike was gone, he'd somehow figure out her plan. There were no messages, no information, and no phone calls. But, even though my grandmother knew the truth, my mama was becoming suspicious as she thought back to when things had begun to unravel.

Increasingly involved in stealing and selling illegal drugs had put my father in an impossible position and he knew Shari was having real doubts. His latest theft from the police evidence room and his shortsighted idea to sell it back to the very criminals he had busted cinched the fact that he was now a marked man, putting his life, and Mama's and Sage's, at stake.

Desperate, he approached his mother, and, after hearing his story, she agreed to help him come up with a plan. He was to turn off his radio and "disappear" for a week. She hired two associates to find a way to get Sage away from Mama, and, as it worked out, the perfect opportunity arose when the detectives decided it would be best for them to go to a hotel room for their own safety. She had no idea, of course, that my grandfather would come to the hotel room to check on Mama and Sage that next morning, but the plan was already in place by that time and there was no way to stop it. Once they had Sage, they did exactly as she instructed.

She also had no way of knowing that the bad guys would make good on their threats. My father's body was found two weeks later by a couple of hikers coming down a remote trail in Caprock Canyon. He had been strangled with his own service belt, his hands and feet bound and a rag stuffed into his mouth.

But the details of his death, just like everything else in the Davenport's world, were carefully kept out of the papers, and, by the end of two months, no one really even thought anymore about what had happened to Officer Mike Davenport. Life in this small Texas town plodded on.

There's a saying in West Texas that if you've got enough money, you've got enough of everything. That evidently included the ear of the local courts and judges because it wasn't even a week after Mina had Sage back at her expansive ranch and had initiated charges against my Mama to have her declared an unfit mother.

The authorities said Mama knew about the drugs Mike had been stealing from the evidence room. They said she most likely helped him because they needed the money the illegal transactions brought in. They even said she was a bad mother. Worst of all, when my father died, grandma took immediate control of his accounts that he had always kept separate from Mama's, and even though there was no concrete evidence proving that she was even involved, Rocket Docket McFadden, Emmit's only trial judge, and close friend of the Davenports, was able to get her deemed unfit. Somehow, grandma made the case that Mama, through her lack of maturity, had not provided proper guidance, care, or support for young Sage. She also tried to prove that she neglected her daughter by her full awareness of Mike's illegal activities.

Mama sold everything she could to raise enough money for a lawyer, who initially told her it would be a slam dunk and that she'd have Sage back within a week, but that turned into a couple months. Each plea he set up to see the judge for another trial was turned down and went unexplained, his questions unanswered yet again, and another technicality prevented any of his motions to go forward.

In the end, it didn't matter. Certain key evidence mysteriously disappeared. Eye witnesses suddenly changed their stories. Judge McFadden sided with grandma and declared Mama unfit to raise Sage, and because Mike Davenport was gone, he granted Mina and Tom full custody. His decision was final, so Sage went to live with her grandparents, just like Mina had planned all along. So, no matter what Mama did, she just couldn't find a way to get Sage.

Moving back to Lona was probably the one hardest thing Mama ever did. And the best. No one in Texas knew she was pregnant with me and she kept it that way. And, as far as anyone in Lona knew, she was just another single pregnant woman. After I was born, it took her only six months working, first at the diner, then at JB Associates, to save up enough money to hire her own local attorney, one who was also certain they could get her custody of Sage. They began working on a strategy, but each time he filed a motion, it was dismissed for lack of evidence. Year after year, no matter which way they went, Mina Davenport was there to stop them at every turn.

And each time, Mama vowed to come up with yet another strategy, another way, another reason to get her daughter back. But no matter what she did, and no matter how hard she tried, she just couldn't make it happen.

Then simply, finally, Sage turned sixteen. When they went to the last of a long series of court appearances, Sage stood up and voiced her opinion on where she wanted to live.

Sage was coming home.

6 IN THE CLEARING

After Mama finished talking, I was quiet, not knowing what to say. Even though she had glossed over some things and probably left out a lot of the others, I was old enough to understand that this was pretty serious.

I have a sister. Somewhere out in Texas, I have a *sister*. And my father, the father I'd never known a thing about—why didn't you tell me, Mama, I thought fleetingly—died before I was even born. It had been exactly thirteen years ago that Mama had left Texas to come back home to Lona, went back to her maiden name, and raised me, as unknown and anonymous to my sister, my father, and his family as they've always been to me.

"Are you okay?' she said, watching me anxiously.

"Sort of, I guess. I mean, I just, I just don't *know*, Mama! I mean, all this…I, I don't know what to say! I have a *sister*! And my *dad*! Why didn't you *tell* me, Mama? You don't even know why he died?"

"I couldn't, honey. I couldn't say anything. And no, I don't know any of the circumstances of his death. And that's the truth, I promise you."

"Don't you *want* to know?"

Mama hesitated before she spoke. "Yes and no. I mean, yes, of course I've always wondered what really happened to him. I guess his bad ways just caught up with him. You know, KC, I truly loved him at one time and he *is* the father of my two beautiful girls. But the way everything turned out back then with Sage and the courts and your grandmother and all, I just can't help but believe that him being around would have made it all even worse. So, another part of me doesn't want to know about anything that involves him. Ever."

I thought about that. Ever seemed like a pretty long time. "What about grandma and grandpa? Do they know about me?"

"Your Grandpa Tom died almost three years ago, and he was always a good man, so at least I knew Sage would have someone kind in her life." she continued. "A good friend of mine, Shelly Martin, used to work for them on their ranch. She was a gal I worked with at Dixie's Diner, then she went to work for them as a housecleaner. It was the only way I ever got any news about Sage, but she quit after a couple years, saying that Mina, well, your grandma, was an angry, vindictive woman, so I lost my only connection. But, no, they don't know about you, honey, and I've tried to keep it that way."

"Why?"

"Because I've always been afraid they would come and try to take you away from me too, just like they did with Sage."

"But Mama, how could you just let her stay there?"

"I didn't get a *choice*, KC! Everything was against me. Lord knows how hard I've tried over the years, but your grandma was always one step ahead of me."

"But Sage is still coming home, right? I mean, we can still go get her, right?"

"I hope so, honey, and I'm going to do everything I possibly can to make that happen."

"Like what?"

"Well, I've already called your grandmother. She has Sage now, but since Sage has told the courts that she wants to live here, it's pretty much a done deal. Plus I've also told Aunt Penny and Uncle Doug all about it."

"But," I looked at her apprehensively, almost afraid to ask the question burning in my mind. "Does *she* know about me, Mama?"

"She does now, honey."

It took a couple of months for Mama to get all the paperwork in order and the day was set, Saturday June 14. School was out and the summer stretched before us. We spent most of the day Friday rearranging my little bedroom into one that was now going to be shared by two. Two sisters. I had a *sister*.

It's not that I ever really felt alone here, just me and Mama, even though we didn't have any relatives around to speak of. Mama's mama had died when she was young and her dad died while she was still living in Texas so I never knew either of them. And her brother, my Uncle Doug, moved to Eagle River, Alaska, to start a vending machine business almost twenty years ago. That's where he met and married my Aunt Penny, and then they met me when they came back to Lona to help Mama after I was born and to finally get us settled into Grandpa's house. After all the lawyers and tax people were able to come to a decision on how Grandpa's assets would be distributed, Uncle Doug and Mama both got money. Uncle Doug invested his portion in his business and everyone agreed Mama should get the house.

I begged Mama for any details, any photos of Sage, anything at all, but she didn't have any, save for one small, grainy black and white one that she opened up her wallet and handed to me. I gently held the dog-eared and faded photo up, squinting at the smiling little girl with the white hair and big dark eyes. In my mind I had envisioned that she would look just like me so was surprised how different we obviously were.

"She was almost three years old there," Mama smiled, looking over my shoulder at her oldest daughter's image. "Kind of reminds me of you, don't you think?"

"Did I used to have blonde hair, too, Mama?" I asked hopefully.

"No, yours has always been the beautiful brown you have now. You have your dad's coloring."

"That's okay," I said, and just for a second, I tried to conjure up a picture my father, but I was far too excited to give it much real thought so I just said "It doesn't matter, 'cause she's coming home! Sage is finally coming home to her Mama!" I exclaimed.

"And to her sister," Mama said softly, tears brimming in her eyes.

7 COWBOYS AND ANGELS

Jude Lightfoot pulled up the last of his three fishing lines, humming softly, even though the hooks had the same plump worms as when he'd thrown them in. He frowned up towards the road as a black sedan whizzed by. "Damn kids," he thought to himself.

It was hot this time of year, hotter than he remembered it for June, but that was ok with him. He had no plans before this and no plans after. Well, except maybe a nice long shower and a couple beers.

Folks in Lona knew Jude, or at least *of* him and his movies. They were mostly B-rated Westerns, but he had his one big break when he was sixteen and cast as the endearing, yet goofy Bobby Hooper in the offbeat and wildly popular television comedy Hooper's Home.

He was born here in rural El Rio, just ten miles outside Lona up in the foothills. His father, Daniel Lightfoot, a full-blooded Navajo Indian, secretly married Marion McAlister on the very same ranch Marion's family had owned for over 100 years. Against the staunch wishes of his parents and pretty much his entire clan, the marriage had its problems from the beginning, especially given the cultural differences, and everything eventually took a toll. After their divorce when Jude was seven, Marion had other ideas, one of them being to "get out of New Mexico and get into civilization," as she called Los Angeles. Her father's ranch was held in trust and supplied her with a modest income, so that's where they landed, just the two of them, in a tiny two-room hotel/apartment in east LA. Jude's father moved to the reservation with his family and died two years later with no contact whatsoever once Jude and his mother left New Mexico.

A somewhat shy, soft-spoken kid, Jude really never fit into the southern California beach vibe his mother had envisioned; it just wasn't his thing. When she left for work, he would get up in the morning and walk outside to the complex's fenced-in pool area, morosely taking in the empty, dirty pool and the tattered plastic lounge chairs littered around the cracked deck. Even though summer stretched before him with the promise, well, *hope*, of long days playing or riding his skateboard, he yearned to be back on Grandpa's ranch, back with the cows, and the stars and the river and trees. He would lie in bed at night, listening to the constant and monotonous sounds of the traffic, the sirens, the "city-ness", and pretend he was anywhere but this place he hated. He naively envisioned a life where he could be a real cowboy, one that actually rode a horse and rounded up cattle and slept under a canopy of stars next to a flickering campfire.

So that fall when the chance to play Johnny Mac in the 5th-grade theater department's play Howdy Cowboy was posted on the school's bulletin board, Jude ran home, darting up the two flights of concrete stairs two at a time, excited as he burst through the front door.

"Mom, *Mom*! I'm going to try out for a play at school."

"A play? What kind of play?"

"It's called Howdy Cowboy and this guy, his name is Johnny, it's him and he's a cowboy, a *real cowboy*, Mom!"

"Well, maybe he's a real cowboy but, Jude, you're not an actor. You've never even once said anything about acting. Do you have any idea what it takes?"

"I don't care, Mom! I want to be a *cowboy*!"

She was doubtful at first, especially because she realized it meant having to drive him to and from rehearsals on time she didn't have, but, in the end, she finally agreed. But surprisingly, it turned out Jude was a natural. By early high school, he was in nearly every production offered and his shy demeanor all but disappeared when he was on stage. Acting became his passion, and it wasn't long before his acting coach recommended him for a local toothpaste commercial. That led to a spot on another commercial, which in turn led to him being cast in the community theater's production of Annie Get Your Gun, to rave reviews.

Now Marion was a full, onboard stage mom and Jude's schedule took precedence to most things in their lives. At sixteen, he was accepted into the prestigious Hollywood High School Performing Arts Center, where his natural good looks and native American heritage caught the eye of an up-and-coming director, Branson Butler, and he was cast in his first real western as Chief Grey Eagle in the fairly successful movie, Johnson's River.

Hooper's Home came along the next year and though it wasn't a beloved Western, casting young Jude Lightfoot was an easy decision and subsequently made him a surprising new star. Although he studied his roles with a meticulous vengeance more than most, the comedic role he was playing made him feel like something was missing and his frustration grew, almost to the point where he was ready to drop out of the series.

That's when he met Annie, a makeup artist three years older than Jude with a smart-ass mouth and beautiful eyes.

Jude waited until it looked like she was headed for the break room.

"Hey, so, you're Ann, right?" he said, catching up to her.

"Annie, but yes" she eyed him, not slowing her pace.

"I'm Jude, Jude Lightfoot," he said, offering his hand.

"Are you KIDDING me?" turning around to face him, incredulous.

"Well, um, what do you mean?" He was taken aback by her seeming hostility.

"Seriously, Jude, everyone in this entire building, in this entire city, knows who you are!"

She strode up to him, stopping a foot in front of his face. "Do you really think I don't know who you are?"

"I...I.... uh" he was tongue-tied.

"Look, if you're getting ready to ask me for my number, I don't date people I work with...especially younger guys, even if you *are* Jude Lightfoot," and she huffed away without another word.

Wow, he thought to himself with a smile. She's perfect.

"So, let's pretend I'm *not* Jude Lightfoot," he said, catching up to her again. "Let's say I'm just a guy asking a pretty, interesting girl out. We don't even have to call it a date, just coffee. What then?"

It took two months of his constant badgering for her to finally agree to meet him for dinner. She was a quirky, funny and beautiful girl and Jude was smitten. With her no-nonsense approach and her dedication to his work, he reconsidered his role and realized the worth of perhaps staying on with Hooper's Home after all. His career flourished and by the following year when it was clear they had become the new 'it couple,' teenage hearts were breaking all over Hollywood.

But regardless who you were, the acting business was often merciless when it came to having any sense of a personal life, and young Jude and Annie's situation was no exception. All of Hollywood wanted to know who this Annie was and what was to become of young Jude

Lightfoot. In order to find even the smallest island of privacy, he eventually purchased a bungalow off of Cahuenga Blvd. in a secluded gated community and he, his mother, and Annie moved in.

Their marriage that following New Year's Eve was a simple Justice-Of-The-Peace affair, although the sneaky paparazzi were waiting in full force as they made their way out of the courthouse to cameras and microphones thrust in their faces, the blush of matrimony quickly fading amongst the melee. It did eventually become easier as Annie worked long days right alongside Jude, spending their nights wrapped in each other's arms, but as Jude's career was skyrocketing, Annie's was beginning to falter. It wasn't that she wasn't good at what she did; she was one of the best young talents around. But small things started happening. Late to work, long lunch hours, missed appointments, until finally, her boss called her into her office one afternoon.

"Annie, what is it? You're not up to the task lately and I can't keep covering for you."

Only Annie and Jude knew about Annie's depression. It had started when she was a teenager in an emotionally abusive home environment. By the time she was twenty she was combining Zoloft with alcohol, which only compounded her already destructive world and Jude found himself at a complete loss how to help her. One evening as they laid next to each other in the dark, she propped herself up on her pillow, her gaze level.

"Jude, you're just starting this amazing career and I can't let you keep taking care of me all the time. It's just not fair to you."

"But I love you. That's what you do. You take care of the people you love."

"Can't you see? I'm *nothing* anymore! I can't work, I can't sleep, I can't even take care of myself, much less you or a career!"

"Let me worry about my career," he said, smoothing the damp hair from her forehead. "We're going to be fine; I promise."

"But I'm so sad all the time, Jude. I just don't know what to do. I can't stand taking that medicine. It makes me sick and I don't think it's helping anyway."

"Hey, do you want to go somewhere? I mean, like a vacation? Or maybe we could go out to Grandpa's ranch? We could spend as long as you want there!" It had been years since he and his mother had left New Mexico and Jude longed to have Annie love his childhood home as much as he did.

"What would I do out there? Jude, it's been almost a year now. If the doctors can't help, what on earth makes you think the middle of nowhere could?"

"Well, you could paint, or you could…"

"Stop it, Jude! Oh, never mind! Just leave me alone!!!" she shouted, burying her face into the pillow. Jude was helpless.

Work became an increasingly tricky affair for Jude, especially if any of the roles took him away from Los Angeles. Marion was generally helpful, but she had little, if any, understanding of Annie's depression.

"I guess I just don't get it, Jude. I mean, I know how much you love her honey, but what does she have to be sad about? She's got everything any young woman could want!"

"Mom, it's not that easy, the depression thing. It's worse for her."

"Well, when I was young, if you got depressed, you just worked through it. That's just what you did. I don't want to sound unfeeling, honey, it's just that, well…" she trailed off, seeing the pain on Jude's face.

"It's not working for her, Mom. The doctor says it can be worse in some people than others. And I'm worried about her. I thought maybe we could go to the ranch for a month or so, just us. What do you think?

"What's more important is what does *Annie* think?

"She's not exactly on board with the idea," he said, thinking of their previous conversation in bed.

"Have you thought of maybe just changing the scenery here instead? What about going out to the Del for a week or so? That way you two could spend a little couples' time together without me hanging around all the time."

Jude knew that was magnanimous of his mother, but just nodded silently.

"We'll see. I'll bring it up when she's feeling a little better."

The next morning Annie came into the kitchen, almost dancing, her hair freshly washed and even a little makeup on her face.

"Morning!" she said brightly.

"Well, good morning to you, sunshine!" Jude returned, clearly surprised.

"So, we're going to Hotel Del?" she trilled. "I would *love* to do that, Jude! How fun that will be! I'm packing today so we can go any time you're ready!"

Mom, Jude sighed to himself. Well, at least her spilling his secret turned out well, so they set out for Coronado Island Saturday morning. The marine layer was still thick on the coastline as they made their way down the San Diego Freeway, and they were both in high spirits as they crossed the bridge and headed out to the island. Hotel Del Coronado was a charming, historical beachfront hotel that catered to some of the most famous people in the world, boasting an esteemed reputation for offering complete privacy to its many prominent guests.

After settling into their spacious room, Annie changed into her bathing suit, turning first one way, then the next in front of the full-length mirror.

"What do you think, honey? Still got it?"

"Still got it, babe, you're gorgeous."

She smiled tentatively, giving a thumbs-up but he couldn't tell if it was a smile of gratitude or doubt. When she laid down on the bed, he was confused. "Aren't we going to the beach?"

"I'm a tiny bit tired, so I'm thinking I'll get a little nap in before I come down, okay? Maybe 45 minutes or an hour then I'll come down to the beach and meet you."

He nodded hesitantly, "Ok, but I'm going to check on you if you're not down by 2, ok?"

"I'll be there," she promised, yawning as she tucked herself under the comforter.

Jude went out to the beach, walking up and down the wide sandy shores where guests were sipping on their pina coladas and sodas. It was a beautiful afternoon and Jude eventually found himself about a mile down the beach, further than he had planned to go. He looked at his watch and realized it was nearly 2:30.

Crap, he thought, turning around and walking quickly back toward the hotel. As he got closer, he could see red and blue lights flashing near the front entrance to the immense hotel. Sensing something wrong, he started running, faster and faster until, out of breath, he stopped at the edge of the long stone wall separating the hotel grounds from the beach.

"Hey, what's going on?" he asked a young man who was also standing nearby, watching the commotion.

"Don't know, just saw them take a woman in the ambulance."

Jude's heart fell as he started pushing through the throng of onlookers. He was forcefully pushed back by a security guard just as he got to the front of the crowd.

"Back, fella!" he ordered.

"No! I think that might be my wife!" he screamed, clutching at the guard.

"Sorry, I can't let anyone through," he responded, pushing him back.

Then his eyes lit up, "Hey, aren't you Jude Lightfoot?"

Jude shoved him hard, hard enough that he was momentarily thrown off-balance and fell to his knees. Jude quickly ran past him and sprinted up the wooden stairs leading from the beach to the hotel grounds.

"Hey, asshole!" the guard shouted after him, then, standing up, barked something unintelligible into his two-way radio as Jude ran toward the cadre of police cars stationed in front of the hotel.

"Sir, please, sir!" he pleaded with the first policeman he came to. "Please! I think that's my wife! Please, you've got to help me!"

Just then a strong arm pulled Jude aside. "Mr. Lightfoot? Sir? I'm Stan Marker, Hotel Manager. Sir, I'm going to need you to step inside. Please. There's been an incident."

"What the *fuck* do you mean, an incident? What the FUCK happened here?"

"Sir, I'm sorry, but I'm going to insist you step inside."

Fuming, Jude shook off his arm and followed him inside the lobby to where the manager motioned to a small office off the lobby. They went inside where he quietly closed the door behind Jude.

"I'm sorry, Mr. Lightfoot, but it seems there was an, uh, incident involving your wife."

"What do you mean? What happened?"

"We don't know for sure, but..."

"WHAT DO YOU MEAN??? Where's Annie? Where are they taking her? I need to be with her! I need to see her!" Jude lunged toward the door, but the manager quickly intervened.

"I'm sorry, Mr. Lightfoot," he said as he touched Jude's arm. "I am truly sorry. Your wife, is, um... I'm so sorry, Mr. Lightfoot, but your wife is gone. She's passed away."

The room started to spin, slowly at first, then picked up speed, just as Jude fell to the floor, his eyes seeing nothing but blackness. Stan caught him just as he missed the edge of the desk, then pulled him up into the nearest chair, holding his arms back so he wouldn't slump forward again.

With one hand he reached over and pushed the phone's intercom. "Nellie, please come into my office. Quickly. And bring Dr. Thompson with you."

For weeks, Jude barely remembered waking up each morning, or falling asleep each evening, it was all such a blur of deep sadness, pain, and profound loss. Annie's parents had flown in from Indiana to get Annie and take her home for the funeral. Marion had taken care of the press releases, and the memorial there in L.A. She hired extra security to keep onlookers away. She fielded all the calls from his producers, his coworkers, his friends. She made sure the phone calls were screened and that no one was allowed near Jude for the time being. She took care of everything, from publicly denying gossip-mongers, to making sure the incessant helicopters circling above his house were ordered away by threat of a lawsuit. She took care of it all.

Even the autopsy report.

The coroner said Annie's cause of death was an accidental overdose of prescription drugs. When the official results came back a couple weeks later, Jude was sitting in the den reading when his mother came up to him. There had been rumors, of course, but Jude couldn't believe that Annie could ever consider taking her own life. His brain simply couldn't process that irrevocable choice, that absolute mistake, that horrifying possibility, although the questions hung like heavy wet curtains around the room.

Looking back, things that had been so blurry before, so difficult to understand, were slowing starting to make sense. The times Annie would decline going out to dinner with their friends. How she kept even her closest girlfriends away. When she'd go for two or three days without eating. Or how their guest room had become her only real escape from the world, and, Jude thought sadly, from him.

"Honey, she was sick. I apologize for not understanding better from the beginning."

Jude eyed his mom, searching her face, seeing the raw pain in her eyes.

"I know, Mom. But it's not anything you did. It's not. I don't know what else anyone could've done. Except me, I guess. I should've been there. I should've been there to help her. I think it's my fault after all, Mom."

He had spent that terrible afternoon with Annie, sitting for hours next to her in the morgue, watching her perfectly calm, beautiful features. Annie was gone forever and Jude had never felt more alone.

8 COLLATERAL DAMAGE

His mom thought a change of scenery would be good, getting away from all the sadness, not to mention the incessant caravan of people slowly driving by his house at all hours of the night and day, trying to catch a glimpse of the shattered Jude Lightfoot. And she was right. Ever since the funeral, Jude came to realize that he had to get away, though to what or to where, he hadn't a clue.

Marion had inherited her late father's beautiful, secluded place, The Triple R, which stood for Rocky River Ranch, twenty-five acres of fertile land, including water rights bordering the tiny village of El Rio out in New Mexico. When his life turned upside down, his grandfather's ranch and its promised seclusion seemed a natural place to return.

It was just going to be a couple months at first, but those two months turned into six, then into a year. And as quickly as Jude Lightfoot had risen to stardom, he just as quickly faded out of the limelight. But then that was just as he wanted, he thought. Even his agent had stopped calling with any offers or projects, just forwarded his monthly royalty checks when they came.

The Triple R wasn't really a working ranch anymore; though sometimes he would get requests from townsfolk to hunt or fish with him on his property, which he readily accepted, not for the company, but because he just liked hunting and fishing. Marion, Miss M to their meager staff, was now the head of everything to do with the ranch that Jude just wasn't interested in. Two ranch hands, Otis McDormand and Nico Jimenez, kept the day-to-day operations moving smoothly and lived in the bunkhouse off by the corrals, even though it'd been years since the ranch had seen any cattle.

Jude would occasionally drive his pickup truck into Lona for food and supplies, or to get feed for the ranch's two horses. Pulling into the parking lot, he rolled down the window and climbed out of his truck, giving Tucker, his black lab, a hands-up, signaling him to sit still in the seat until he came back.

Dennis Buchner, one of the local businessmen, was standing on the top step talking to Dave Chavez, the feed store owner. Both turned as Jude climbed the wooden stairs towards the store's front porch.

"Hey, Jude," Dennis smiled. "Haven't seen ya around for a while. How's it going?"

"Good, nothing new," he replied, turning toward Dave. "Just need about six bales of alfalfa and a couple bushels of corn if you don't mind."

"Sure thing. No problem. And, hey, glad to hear things are good out there. Getting warm already, huh?"

When Jude didn't reply, Dave continued, clearly wanting to make small talk. "Hey, whatever happened when that new phone guy came out to your place a while back? Word has it he got a real run for his money."

Cell phone service had always been sketchy out on the ranch; just not enough phone towers or coverage, so Jude made the decision to install a land line in the main house. The problem though, was that the 120-year-old adobe home had walls that were over two feet thick and the rookie phone installer was befuddled with, first, the fact that it was Jude Lightfoot who lived there, and second, that he couldn't figure out how to drill far enough to get through the thick walls. He brought first one bit, then changed it to a longer one, then finally took a pick and hammer and tried to dig out the hard clay brick. Just when he thought he was through, a large section of the wall broke off and fell to the polished Saltillo tile floor, cracking three large tiles.

Jude, who had been in the den at the time, came running into the kitchen to see what had happened. Upon seeing the rubble on the floor and the shock on the rookie repairman's face, Jude broke out into uncharacteristic laughter.

"Sir, I'm so sorry! I...I...was just trying to get through the wall, and....and... I, oh gosh, I'm so sorry, Mr. Lightfoot!"

"No, seriously," Jude tried to catch his breath between the laughter, "it's ok, dude. This place needs a little updating anyway," as he bent to help him pick up the pieces of what was left of the damaged kitchen wall. Needless to say, the phone didn't get put in that day or any day after and, surprisingly, Jude didn't miss it as much as he thought he would. It was one less connection to the outside world he didn't need to worry about.

But Miss M wanted her wall and floor fixed yesterday, so one of his errands this Saturday morning was to finally get materials so he could do just that. His mother rarely complained and was always patient, but when it came to her house, he knew there was no one more meticulous than Marion Lightfoot. Jude kept finding the little notes she had left around the house to remind him to get the kitchen repaired so he knew he really needed to just cowboy up and get it done. Lona's only hardware store was just down the road from the feed store and he had hoped to run into the feed store get what he needed, then move on to the hardware store then head home. And he for sure wasn't in the mood for small talk.

"So, what, the whole town knows about it?" he asked irritably.

"Well, they don't mean any harm. And maybe not the whole town, but you know how folks 'round here talk," Dennis said amiably.

"Oh yeah, for sure I know that" he said, brushing past both and heading into the store, signaling an end to the conversation.

He thought better of it, and, turning back said "Sorry, boys. It's just that..."

Dennis held up his hand. "No worries, Jude. You've had a helluva ride, son. Go on, get about your business. It's all good here."

As he was driving out of the parking lot, he decided to take the longer way back to the ranch this time, out past the edge of Lona on the small side road that ran alongside the alfalfa field he had seen from the highway coming in. He pulled off the narrow country road, crossed up and over the irrigation ditch, then parked next to the small lake just past the end of the road. He pulled out his tackle box and three fishing poles which he always kept in his truck, just in case, he thought. Escobar Lake was one place he hadn't had a chance to fish yet so he took his time setting up his poles and settling down in his camp chair to relax. Tucker ran rampant up and down the banks of the little lake, joyfully cutting loose as he splashed through the mud and the muck that lined its soft, silty banks. Jude must've dozed off because he was startled awake by Tucker's licking his face, leaving a sloppy layer of brown mud. "Aw, geez, Tuck!" he said, though he wasn't angry in the least. "Ok, buddy, let's get these lines in," he said, pulling them in just as a black car whizzed by on the road past the ditch.

He loaded up all his gear then played fetch with Tucker for the next thirty minutes or so before they drove back up the road towards El Rio. "Beautiful," he sighed to himself as he casually meandered along the road through the dappled shadows, admiring the huge cottonwood trees that formed a heavy, thick canopy. Coming around a bend, he glanced to his right at a wide swath of corn standing sentinel in perfect green rows, one after another, horizontally planted such that he became slightly mesmerized as he drove by. In an instant, he jerked the steering wheel to the right when he realized a young girl had suddenly appeared up ahead in the middle of the road, wildly waving her arms for him to stop.

He slammed on the brakes, pulled over and jumped out, running up to her as she was screaming and crying and pointing toward a house at the end of a long gravel driveway. He tried to take in the scene of her, maybe fifteen or so, skinny as a rail, the front of her shirt covered in blood, big eyes wild with fear.

"What *happened*? Where are you hurt?" he exclaimed, reaching out for her, but she turned and started running toward the house, pointing and screaming back to him, "Not *me*! My Mama! Someone hurt my Mama! You've got to help her!"

Jude ran, following her up the driveway, and saw a woman lying on the ground next to the open door of a truck, her entire upper body red as blood seeped out of a small hole in her chest. The young girl knelt beside her, trying to hold up her head, which kept falling limply to the one side. She looked up at Jude beseechingly and with such heartache and fear that Jude was frozen in a standstill. Then she started wailing again, jarring him out of his trance.

He knelt down and gently pried the girl away, trying to get a better idea of how bad it was. Feeling the side of the woman's neck for a pulse and realizing there was none, he took off his shirt, rolled it into a ball and carefully placed it under her head. "Sweetheart," he said, trying to calm the girl down, "Let me...." but she wrenched away from him and threw herself back down, tucking her thin arms under her mother's lifeless body, holding her tightly. He immediately pulled out his cell

63

phone and punched in 911 but realized he couldn't get a signal. Frustrated he jumped up. "Stay right here!" he shouted. "I've got to call for help! I can't get a signal! I'm going to go down to the end of the driveway to see if I can, ok?"

He ran, holding his phone up in the air, dialing, then redialing again, the emergency number. As he got near the road, he realized Tucker was still sitting in the truck, his nose pressed to the driver's side window watching him. Jude ran up, opened it, and Tucker jumped out, happily wagging his tail. "Tucker, come!" he commanded, finally getting a signal on his phone.

Just as the 911 operator's voice came on the line, he realized Tucker had taken off towards the tree and weed-filled lot next to the house. "Tucker! Come, boy!" he commanded, and then, out of the corner of his eye he noticed a shadow, a person maybe? slip from behind a large cottonwood tree and fade behind the rest of the trees, disappearing. Tucker came loping back, clearly disinterested in whatever had caught his eye.

"Sir," she repeated, "Sir, can you hear me? Can you tell me your address?" the operator asked.

Jude looked around wildly. "I don't KNOW where I am! Somewhere on that road from Escobar Lake that leads out to El Rio, the back road! Please hurry!"

"Are you on State Road 415?"

"I DON'T KNOW!" Then, remembering where he had turned off from the main road, he said, "there's a little fruit stand right where you turn to get on this road. Mark's? Markel's? Something like that. I'm just past the old bridge!"

"Markie's Market? Yes, ok, sir we are sending an ambulance right away. Please stay on the line, sir," but he had already lost reception as he darted back up the drive.

Jude ran back up to the girl and her mother, and knelt back down again, unsure what to do.

The cops and ambulance arrived within ten minutes. As the EMTs carefully loaded Shari's body onto a stretcher and put her in the back of the ambulance, Jude and KC stood there, watching silently, helpless to do anything.

The cop came over to them after the ambulance left. "I'm Officer McMahon with the Lona Police Department. Can you tell me what happened?"

"My Mama! S-s-s-someone shot her and…and…it's all my fault! I…I…." KC twisted her body into Jude's, burying her face in his chest.

Jude wasn't sure how to respond, so he hesitatingly put his arms around her thin shoulders, trying to calm her down. Her sobs wracked her entire body and all he could do was try to comfort her as best he could. "I'm not sure, sir," he said, looking over the top of KC's trembling head. "I was driving down the road when I saw her just standing right in the middle of the road, waving her arms and screaming, and covered with blood, so I had to stop. That's when she told me her mother was hurt, so I just ran up the driveway and found her laying here."

Another high-pitched wail from KC pierced the clear morning air.

"I'm sorry, miss, but can you please come over here and sit with Officer Jenson?" He motioned to the uniformed female officer standing by him. She came over and gently unraveled KC from Jude's arms, steadying her as she walked her over to the open door of the police car.

Officer McMahon turned back toward Jude, eyeing him suspiciously.

"She was already gone by the time I got here, sir," Jude offered first. "I think her daughter must've witnessed it, but I'm not sure."

"Well, I'm going to need to have you both come down to the station," he said, looking around again at the scene. "Officer Jensen! Can you radio in and get the Sheriff out here? I don't want anything or anyone messing this up."

"Can I move my truck off the road first?" Jude asked.

"Leave it where it is," came the gruff remark.

"What about my dog?"

"I'll make sure it gets taken to your house."

9 THE COMPANY OF STRANGERS

The Lona County Courthouse Complex was a small affair, as far as buildings go. Still, it housed not only the courthouse in the main section, but also the police headquarters and jail on one end and on the other end, the town's only law office. Sitting by myself in a row of chairs close to the receptionist's desk, I could hear her whispering into her phone, something about Mama's murder. "Murder? *Murder?*" I could feel a hard ball in my stomach as I swiped at the tears that kept sliding down my cheeks.

I stared hard at her just then, squinting my eyes and furrowing my brow and really *stared* at her. I felt that if I stared long enough and hard enough, she was going to just look up at me and say "Oh, honey, this was all just a big mistake." Then Officer Jenson came up to me, kneeling in front of my chair.

"KC," she said gently, "we need to ask you some more questions if you're ok with that."

I nodded my head miserably and followed her down the hall, looking back once more toward the receptionist still on the phone, with a last, futile glance.

The rest of the afternoon was spent in a broken-hearted blur, Jude in one room and me in another with Officer Jensen. I knew Mama had a gun and told her exactly where they could find it. She called it in and they had, right where I said it was, under the front seat of our truck where she always kept it when we were going on a trip. She was really nice, I thought, in fact she kind of reminded me of Mama when she'd look at me so kindly, and it started me bawling all over again.

"KC, you said that someone shot your mom and then you said it's all your fault. What did you mean by that?"

Tearfully, I retold her everything I could remember. No, no one was in the driveway when we came back to get the album. No, Mama didn't come into the house with me. Yes, I got the key, unlocked the front door, ran inside to get it then ran back out when I heard the shot. Yes, Mama was lying on the ground next to the open door of the truck. No, there wasn't anyone else around. Wait, I think there was something over by that big old cottonwood tree in the vacant lot next door. No, I don't have my own phone. No, I just ran out toward the street when I heard that truck coming down the road.

"Ok, KC, I understand. Can you tell me exactly what you saw over in the vacant lot?"

"I, I'm not sure what it was. Maybe a big black dog? I couldn't really tell, and, and...well, everything was happening so fast and I was... I mean, my mom was, I was trying....and...I..I..." Emotionally spent, I slumped over the table, sobbing into my arms. "This is all my fault!"

Officer Jensen came around the table and sat down next to me, her hand lightly touching my arm. "Honey, it's *not* your fault. There is no way you could've known this would happen. Please don't think that, ok? KC, what makes you think this was 'all your fault'?"

"BECAUSE IF I HADN'T MADE MAMA GO BACK AND GET THAT STUPID ALBUM, NONE OF THIS WOULD'VE HAPPENED!" I shrieked.

Later, when they were done questioning us, I was brought out to the front desk again and saw Jude waiting on a bench. He got up and walked towards us. "What now?" he asked Officer Jensen, looking at me somewhat skeptically.

"Well, we'll need to get her to her next of kin," Officer Jensen said. "Do you know how we can get ahold of them?"

"*Me?*" Jude asked incredulously. "I don't even *know* her! I only met her a few hours ago!"

"Oh, no worries, Mr. Lightfoot. If we can't contact anyone, we'll keep her here temporarily until we can set her up with a foster home."

"My....my Aunt Penny and Uncle Doug," I whispered. "I want to go with them. Please don't make me go away." I stared at her beseechingly, not even knowing what going to a foster home meant.

"Ok, honey, let's get ahold of them and have them come pick you up, ok?"

"I...I...I can't call them. I don't have their number. It's in Mama's... I mean, my Mama has..." I faltered.

"It's ok, hon," Officer Jensen said. "Where do they live?"

"Somewhere in Alaska."

Exasperated, she turned back toward Jude. "Mr. Lightfoot, is there *anyone* you know here in Lona who might be able to take care of her for the time being until we can get this sorted out?"

"No, I, um, don't know too many people here," he said, somewhat sheepishly. "I pretty much just stay out on my ranch."

She smiled, both knowingly and sympathetically, then turned back to KC. "Well, let's see what we can do about getting ahold of your aunt and uncle, KC, ok? Meanwhile, we'll get you set up, just temporarily mind you, with a nice family."

"NO!" I shrieked, grabbing her arm, pleading with her. "Please... please don't send me away!"

"Look," Jude interrupted, "maybe there's another option. But first let me see if I can get ahold of her aunt and uncle."

Jude was able to find Aunt Penny and Uncle Doug's phone number by calling Mama's boss. When he gave it to Officer Jensen and she made the call, they were both shocked and heartsick when she informed them about what had happened to Mama.

"I'll be on the first plane down there," Aunt Penny tearfully told her. "I think one leaves for Anchorage at 4 p.m. so I can be there Monday afternoon. Officer, can you put KC on the phone please?"

"Aunt Penny!" I wailed into the receiver, "She's gone! Mama! Mama's gone!"

"I know, sweetheart. I'm so, so very sorry and so sad… shush, honey, don't worry, honey, we'll be down as soon as we can, ok?"

"When? When will you be here?"

"In a couple days, honey. We'll make plans today and be there by day after tomorrow, I promise."

"Please hurry, Aunt Penny. I…I'm scared."

"KC, I'm…" Penny said, her voice clearly distracted as she was trying to make sense of what Doug was trying to say to her in the background.

"Aunt Penny?" I couldn't understand what she just said.

"I'm sorry, honey, I'm just trying to think things through. Look, I'll be there soon. I'll come down first because Uncle Doug is saying now that he'll need to get a few things buttoned up here first, but don't worry, ok? We'll be there as soon as we can."

"Aunt Penny… wh…what about Sage?" I asked hesitantly, remembering her for the first time.

"Once we get down there, honey, we'll go pick up Sage and bring her home."

Officer Jenson got on the phone after we were done and I heard her say "Yes, no, don't worry, we've got it covered. Yes, I'll have our receptionist give you all the numbers and details. Yes, thank you. Again, I'm so sorry about your sister-in-law. Yes, ok, goodbye."

She turned toward me and Jude. "Ok folks, so what're we gonna' do? Jude, you mentioned there might another option?"

"Well, I was thinking maybe she could come out to the ranch with me for a couple days until her relatives get here," he offered, then, seeing the raised brows of everyone in the room, he quickly added. "I mean, she could stay with us, me and my mom. She's just like a grandma and all, so I'm sure it'd be fine for a couple days."

Jude figured I could come out to his ranch and stay for a day, maybe two at the most, until Aunt Penny and Uncle Doug could get here. But when he called his mother, she clearly had other plans. Listening to him explain what happened to Mama and finding out I had no family here, she didn't think twice. "She'll stay with us for as long as she needs to," she said without hesitation.

"But, Mom! She's just a kid! We haven't had kids on the ranch since when I was young!" he protested, determined not to let any hopeless reminders of Annie and her and his future children never getting the opportunity to live on the ranch deter him.

Unfazed, his mother just said "Well, it's about time, isn't it? And, besides, she's not exactly a little kid, Jude. She's a young woman, one who's just lost her mother and we need to, no, we *must* help her." She was unhesitatingly convinced I'd be better off out at the ranch than any other place and it soon became clear that she usually got her way, regardless of what Jude thought.

Sitting on the edge of the bunk bed in the police headquarters later that afternoon, my heart hurt so much I felt like I couldn't even breathe. I couldn't believe Momma was gone. I mean, I knew it, but I just couldn't *feel* it. In fact, I couldn't feel anything but pain. This only happens to the people down the street, or to your teacher's nephew, not to us. Not to Momma.

Officer Jenson came in and offered me a turkey and cheese sandwich with chips, but I wasn't hungry. At dusk she came back in and announced that Mr. Lightfoot's offer for me to stay out on his ranch with him and his mother until Aunt Penny and Uncle Doug could get here was approved. I realized I didn't have much of a choice, so I dully nodded my head as I watched her leave.

So it was sort of settled, then. I was to stay with Jude Lightfoot and his mother on his ranch in El Rio for the next few days until Aunt Penny and Uncle Doug could get here. The police released Jude's truck to him, and on the way out to his ranch, he asked if I wanted to stop by our house and get pajamas, or clothes or whatever I might need. The thought of coming up our driveway and seeing where Mama died overwhelmed me and I just shook my head no. "Well, I could go in and grab a few things for you," he said, clearly understanding my pain, but also knowing I'd have to have at least a few things to get by. "I'll just park way down on the side of the road and you can wait in the truck, ok?" I nodded. Parked on the side of the road, I couldn't help but peek up to see our truck still parked in the driveway. Someone, probably the police, had closed the doors and there was yellow police tape in a big circle around it. I stared at it, it seemed smaller somehow, and, if any truck could be called lonely, this was the one. Lonely and quiet. And sad.

I jolted back just then at the sound of Jude walking up to where I sat. Evidently, they must've given him the keys to our house because I could hear him jangling a key chain that sounded just like Mama's. He'd come back with a kitchen garbage bag full of clothes and I silently groaned when I saw my favorite stuffed bear tucked under his other arm. "Figured you'd want this," he smiled brightly, handing it to me as he slid into his side. Irritated at his optimism, I pretended not to even notice he'd plucked it off my bed and included in what he figured were my must-haves. I took it, squeezing it in tightly next to me.

Once we got out to the ranch, I met Jude's mom, Marion, or, as she preferred being called, Miss M. She came out onto the porch just as I was trudging up the steps, and immediately wrapped her big arms around me and pulled me close like she'd known me my entire life. I wasn't sure what to do so I just stood there, arms limp at my side. She smelled like a combination of lilacs and cooking oil and I realized I just wanted to stay right there, wrapped tightly in her warm embrace for as long as I possibly could. She finally let me go, then lifted my chin with her warm hands, studying my face carefully. "Honey," she began, but stopped as tears spurted from my eyes. "Well, shoot," she said, looking back at Jude, "let's just all go inside, ok?"

She hovered over me all the way to the guest room, clucking to Jude to bring my meager belongings inside, asking what I wanted to eat, showing me where the bath and towels were.

That night, alone in an unfamiliar place, around unfamiliar people and all alone, I cried myself to sleep for the first time in my life. All I could think about was Mama. I woke up the following morning and just laid there in bed, not moving. Surely this whole thing had been just one big nightmare. I willed my puffy eyes to stay closed as I imagined myself lying in my bed at our little house. I could hear Momma in our kitchen, making breakfast, softly humming along to a country western song coming from the little radio that sat on top of our fridge. Just then, in that simple memory, nothing hurt. I could only hear and see and feel my Momma.

Then I heard Miss M knocking softly on the door, asking "KC, are you awake, honey? I've brought you some breakfast," and tears flooded my eyes yet again. I didn't say a word, hoping she would just go away and leave me to my misery. Of course, she didn't, opening the door a few inches and peeking in on me. I pretended to be asleep, although I guess some people just *know* when you're pretending. "Ok, honey, well, here's some toast and jam. I know you're probably not very hungry but I think you should try to at least eat something."

She set the tray on the small dresser next to my bed and I could feel her looking down at me. Part of me wanted to jump up and have her hold me again like the night before on the porch, but I felt like I was betraying Mama so I kept my eyes tightly shut, not saying anything. I actually hadn't eaten in almost 24 hours, so when she quietly left the room, I peeked over at the thick slab of homemade toast and jelly and my belly rumbled. Quickly, I jumped out of bed, took a big bite and jumped back in, pulling the covers as far over me as I could. It took only about 30 seconds for me to want more. How could I ever be hungry again, I wondered, as I took another bite, laying there thinking about Mama and how much I missed her.

A storm had blown through Eagle River, Alaska that same night that had left Uncle Doug and Aunt Penny's town in tatters. Their small house withstood the brunt of it, but the old water line coming in from the street didn't and they were faced with a major problem. Aunt Penny called the next day to tell me the bad news.

"Honey, it's going to take a bit longer that I thought," she said after describing all the water damage. "I've got to wait until we can get this under control and your Uncle Doug has to go figure out the damage to the vending machines around his region so it might be a week or so before I can get there. Uncle Doug will need to pick up his new truck then, too. I'm so sorry, honey. But it sounds like you're in good hands for now, right? Can you hang in there for a bit longer?"

"I'm guess so," I said glumly. "It's just that I'm so lonely, Aunt Penny."

I laid awake every night that first week, thinking first about Mama, then Sage, then Mama again. I spent the first couple of days in my room, just off the ranch's spacious kitchen, but after the first few days under Miss M's careful watch, I started to guardedly make my way out to the veranda each morning, hoping to not have to see anyone or talk to anyone. Miss M always had a covered plate of something warm and delicious waiting for me on the little table next to my bedroom door, but my appetite eluded me most of the time.

The detective came out to the ranch almost every afternoon those first few days. Personally, I think he was really just coming out to check up on me. I'd obligingly come out of my room for the duration of his questions, then go right back when he left. One afternoon, Jude stopped me in the hallway, touching my arm as I passed by. "KC, I know we hardly know each other. I've never really had a chance to tell you how sorry I am about what happened to your mom."

I could feel the tears well up in my eyes as I looked at him. "Thanks," I mumbled, then hurried back to my room to be alone.

Things continued this way for a little over a week until one day, Miss M stood outside my closed door, rapped loudly, then announced that I was to come out of my room immediately. I had been writing in my little journal I'd kept since Mama had gone away so I closed it and carefully tucked it under a stack of neatly folded clothes. "I'm ok," I called out to the closed door. "I don't want to."

"Well, you have no choice. I need you immediately!"

I got up and opened the door a couple inches, cautiously peeking out and saw her standing there, a ball of black and white fur in her hands.

"I need someone to hold onto Tucker's new little friend," she smiled, holding out the squirming pup towards me. I couldn't help but smile as she thrust the little pup into my arms. "What's its name?" I asked, trying to keep the wiggling puppy still in my arms.

"Well, Jude and I thought maybe you could name her. She's the only one that's left of the litter, cute little thing."

From then on, I didn't feel such a need to stay closed up in my room. I'd named her Salva, mostly because it just sounded nice, not realizing its meaning at the time. Salva kept me awake and busy most of the time, anyway, so it was as good an excuse as any to get out into the yard and play with her.

In my way, I was grateful to both Jude and Miss M. They treated me like family and I found myself looking forward to seeing them each morning.

I didn't realize how big the house was, nor the yard, nor the stables. Mine and Mama's house could've probably fit into the courtyard of this one. One afternoon a few days later, Jude caught up with us, moving into a casual stride, keeping up with Salva and I as we were heading back from the stables. He said "Hey, KC, I just found out that your Aunt Penny and Uncle Doug will be here this weekend. Isn't that great? She said the plan is that once they fly into Albuquerque, they're going to first drive over to Texas to pick up Sage then come here right away. I guess you and your sister will be moving in with them into your, I mean, you and your mom's... I mean back to your house." He fell silent.

I don't know how I felt about going back home without Mama being there. Jude must've read my thoughts then, because he immediately collected himself and said, "Now, if you don't want to go with them, you can always stay here, but just so you know, they are your legal guardians now and I'm not, so you might have to work that out with them. But your sister will be with them, too, so I'm sure you'll want to be with her and your family."

"Family," I thought desolately to myself. There was no family without Mama.

11 MORE BETTER, LESS WORSE

Sage Davenport stood stock still, a statue waiting on the expansive porch next to two large suitcases, a duffle bag and a small backpack as Penny and Doug pulled into the long circular driveway that spanned the front gardens of Mina Davenport's stately mansion.

"Wow," Doug whistled under his breath, taking in the colossal structure.

"Yeah," Penny agreed. "Now this is what you call *big* money."

A tall blonde woman came out to the porch just as they were walking up the wide steps.

"Hello, I'm Mina," she said, looking at them appraisingly. "And," she said, extending her arm, "this is Sage."

"Hi Sage, I'm your Aunt Penny," Penny offered her arms in an embrace, but Sage turned away, staring out into the garden of roses and bluebells.

"Sage! Where are your manners?" Mina admonished her, then, turning back to Penny and Doug, "I'm so sorry. This has all been almost too much for her I'm afraid. Would you like to come inside?"

Penny and Doug followed Mina inside to the cool air-conditioned foyer, both rendered speechless, trying to keep their reactions neutral as they took in the vastness of the grand staircase and the 18-ft high wall of windows played out before them.

"Mrs. Davenport, we're so sorry about all this," Doug finally offered. "Yes," Penny added, "We can only imagine what Sage is going through."

"Well, thank you, but, please, call me Mina," she said, then "I still can't understand how you two can *possibly* think it's a good idea to take her from the only home she's ever known and then move her out to the wilds of New Mexico."

"It's only four hundred miles, not the end of the earth. Besides, you can visit her any time you want." He then cautioned, "and it's not an *idea*, it's a fact. You know why we've come for Sage. With Mike's... well, when Mike..." he stopped, seeing the pain shoot across Mina's face. He cleared his throat, then continued. "I mean, with Shari being awarded full custody, then finding out that she had named us as Sage's legal guardians in her will, well, frankly, I don't think there's much left *to* understand. And remember, Sage is the one who made the decision to live with her mother."

"I know that, it's just that I don't think Sage realizes what a big change this is going to be. Plus, she won't know *anyone* there." She turned and looked directly at Doug, ignoring Penny, "And neither do you, from what I understand, except maybe for that other woman?" she asked, her feigned concern not missed by anyone.

Penny's eyebrows shot up. "What other woman?"

Doug cast a sharp look toward Mina. "No one important, just someone I used to know in school."

"I understand it was more than just a *someone*," Mina scoffed. "Weren't you two planning to get married or something? Or, wait, didn't I hear she ran off with some guy you went to school with?"

"Enough, Mina, where are you getting all this? Besides, it's ancient history. Come on, Pen, we're leaving." Penny eyed him curiously, but Doug was clearly avoiding her glance, so she filed that little fact in her mind to deal with later.

Mina came over to where Sage was standing and gave her an awkward half-hug. "I'm sure going to miss you, honey," she said, but seeing how she stubbornly refused to return her affection, she dropped her arms down to her side and turned toward Doug and Penny.

"Well! I guess that's it for now, then!" she exclaimed brightly. "I'm sure you'll let me know when you get to New Mexico safely because I do *so worry* about my girl." Penny noticed Sage wince slightly at Mina's words so she gently took her arm and guided her toward the door.

"We will, I promise," she said, as they walked out into the late afternoon sun and got in the vehicle, the three of them driving out of Emmit, Texas and heading toward their new life, whatever life so precipitously held for them all in New Mexico.

Sage sat quietly in the back seat of Penny and Doug's Suburban, even though Aunt Penny chattered away, trying to keep things positive and upbeat. Asking Sage questions about school and friends. They'd made it about fifty miles outside Emmit when Sage put up her hand and simply said "Enough. Stop. I don't want to listen and I don't want to talk."

Aunt Penny gave her a half-hearted smile, then said "Well, of course, honey, you don't have to talk if you don't want to. We totally understand, right Doug?" looking over at him encouragingly. He kept his eyes on the road, not saying a word.

She frowned slightly at him, then turned back in her seat towards Sage and said kindly "Just try and rest then, ok? We'll get this all figured out soon enough."

The next couple of hours rolled by and by the time they reached Amarillo, it was time to call it a day and find a motel. "Anyone hungry?" Penny asked hopefully, looking back at Sage, who just shook her head no.

"I am," Doug said, pulling off the interstate and onto the small frontage road. "It looks like that Hudson Motel over there has a vacancy and I see a Denny's next to it" as he drove in the direction of the hotel's big red and white sign. They waited in the car for him to come out with the keys and as he pulled around the side of the hotel, unlocked the door and started unloading their things, Sage looked around, then turned back to them, declaring "I want my own room."

"Well, no, I got us a suite with one bedroom and then a pullout couch in the front area," Doug said firmly. "Two rooms are too expensive."

"I want my own room," she repeated, looking at him levelly.

Aunt Penny quickly intervened. "Sage, honey, that doesn't make any sense, and besides, we don't have that kind of money, I mean, not like..."

"I'll pay for it myself, then," Sage snapped, pulling out her purse and wallet. As she opened her wallet, she took in a quick, angry breath. "What the HELL? Where's my credit cards? Where's all my money? What did you do with my money?" she swung around toward Aunt Penny accusingly.

"What? I didn't do *anything* with your money, Sage! Why would you even think that?"

"Um, well, *duh*... I guess because my wallet is EMPTY!" she shot back, looking quickly away when she saw the pained look spring into Penny's eyes.

"Hey, just wait a damn minute here" Uncle Doug interjected. "She didn't take your money. I didn't take your money. No one here took your money. So, you best rethink what you're accusing us of, young lady and watch what you're saying."

"Well, it's gone and I..." a look of realization dawning over her. "Dammit! I *KNEW* she was going to cut me off!"

"Sage! Enough of the language already!" Doug admonished. "*Who* cut you off?"

"My grandmother! She's making sure I don't get a penny from her, just because I wanted to live with my mother instead of her! This is how she's playing her crappy dictator game! She *never* changes! I'm calling her right now!" She yanked her cell phone out of her purse and angrily pushed the buttons. With dismay, she held up the phone, realizing it was dead. "Whaaaaat!!!!! I HAVE to have my phone!"

Seeing how spun up Sage had become, Penny came up to her and planted her hands firmly on Sage's shoulders. "Sage," she told her, taking one hand and gently lifting Sage's chin up. "This is going to all work out. I promise you. I am so, so sorry your grandmother is doing this. But you're with us now. We will, and I promise this, we WILL work this out."

"But, but, now I don't have ANYTHING!" Sage cried, slumping down to her knees on the small concrete walkway outside their room. Her sobs shook her entire body, so Penny knelt down next to her, looking up at Doug and motioning for him to take the rest of their luggage in.

"You have us, honey. I know you don't know us and I know this is all new and scary, but I promise you we already love you. We are all family now and we will do whatever it takes to make you happy."

Defeated, Sage just shook her head back and forth, silently looking up at Penny with Shari's mournful brown eyes.

Jude and Miss M brought me to the church and, judging from the cars in the parking lot, it looked like every single person in Lona was there. Jude gave my hand a quick squeeze as I got out of his truck. "You'll be fine, KC," he said as I waited next to the steps leading up to the front of the church. He went around to the other side of the truck and helped Miss M out and they made their way into the church. Miss M pressed a soft handkerchief into my hand as she passed by me, dabbing at her eyes with her own. "Love you," she mouthed quietly.

I was anxious about meeting Sage. When I first saw her getting out of the back seat of Aunt Penny and Uncle Doug's truck, I was startled how much she looked like Mama. Even though I had seen the baby picture Mama showed me, it was now even more clear how totally unalike we looked. She was tall, almost as tall as Mama was and had her same nose. She also had Mama's thick, white-blonde hair. But the thing I remember most were her big, dark eyes, Mama's eyes, which right now were looking at me with a guarded mixture of cool reserve, sadness, and what I could have sworn was some kind of restrained anger.

Just then Aunt Penny came around the back and, with a brave look, held out her arms. "Well, here you two are!" she exclaimed brightly. "Sage, this is your sister, Karalyn Celeste, KC this is your sister, Sage." I groaned upon hearing my birth name; no one ever used it anymore and I was surprised to hear it myself. Mama told me that she planned to name me Angel but she finally decided upon Karalyn, because one of her closest friends when she was growing up, Karen, was the only one who Mama felt ever really knew her and had always been there for her. One day after third grade had begun, I stormed into our house and declared that I wanted to change my name. I wanted to be called Rose. Or Maria. Or *anything* but Karalyn. Karalyn With The Pointy Chin. Karalyn The Skinny Pin. I was sick of the teasing. So when Mama suggested KC, that was all it took.

I looked shyly up at Sage, but she had already turned away from me. I figured she was either too shy herself, or too distraught over Mama, but I still felt the sting of dismissal. Aunt Penny smiled nervously back and forth between us for a moment, then took our hands as she shuffled us into the church, one on each side, Uncle Doug coming up behind. I peeked at Sage every so often as we were walking up the aisle to our seats, but she just stared straight ahead.

As we made our way up to the first row that had a purple and gold "Reserved" sign hanging on the end, Aunt Penny motioned for us to follow her and sit down. As if we weren't already the center of attention, the four of us, the only family Mama had left, gave even more reason to whisper, these four forlorn souls sitting all alone in the middle of the long pew, especially with all the other ones behind us full to the edges.

Mama's will specified that she wanted to be cremated. The service was short; we weren't churchgoers and Lona's churchgoers pretty much knew that. But Betsy Iverson sang Amazing Grace so beautifully and befitting of Mama it made me cry even more. Sage stared at Mama's ornate urn the entire time, never crying once, just staring at it as if she could see inside, see the mother she never really got to know.

Aunt Penny put her arms around both of us as the pastor finished with a solemn "Amen." We stood up and followed them out of the church. Once outside, neither Sage nor I knew what to do as person after person came up to us and either hugged us or squeezed our hands, then hugged Aunt Penny and Uncle Doug with quiet words of comfort and condolence.

The ride to the cemetery was short and we were all deep in our own thoughts. The graveside ceremony was short; just myself, Sage, Aunt Penny and Uncle Doug, Jude and Miss M, and a sprinkling of the townspeople Mama knew or had been friends with.

Uncle Doug talked about when him and Mama were kids and how close they had been and how he had teased her on this or that and everyone chuckled. Then he spoke of how much he was going to miss her and what a good mother, sister and person she was. Aunt Penny kept dabbing at her eyes, darting looks between Sage and me, then back to Doug. When Mama's urn was finally lowered into the ground, a keening wail erupted the silence, one so sad and anguished everyone stopped and looked around to see where it had come from. It was then I realized it was me who had made that mournful sad cry. I missed Mama so much. Just then, Sage looked back at me, as if she was seeing me for the very first time, her dark eyes flashing in anger. She whipped around, pointing her finger right at me.

"Shut up! Just SHUT UP! This is NOT ABOUT YOU!" she screamed.

Startled at her anger, I immediately ran to Aunt Penny's side.

"Sage!" Aunt Penny said sternly. "What has gotten into you?"

"This! This whole thing!" Sage shouted. "This is WRONG! My mother should be here now! We shouldn't be putting her in the ground! No one should be crying or singing or laughing or ANYTHING!"

"Sage, honey, calm down," Aunt Penny soothed, "let's just get home and get settled down, ok?" but Sage just jerked her arm away and ran towards the car.

Aunt Penny took my hand and pulled me close, seeing my confused and hurt expression. "It's ok, KC. She'll be ok. This is just hard on everyone."

"But why is she so mad at me?" I asked, my voice quivering on the verge of fresh tears.

"She's mad at the world right now, honey. She's not mad at you, I promise." Aunt Penny turned towards Jude and Miss M. "I can't tell you how much we appreciate all you've done for us."

Jude nodded, watching me carefully. "Are you ok?"

"Um, yeah. Thanks," I mumbled. Miss M came up to me and hugged me tightly. "We're here for you," she said and I knew she meant it.

The ride back to our house, Mama's house, was quiet. No one said a word after Sage's outburst at the cemetery and I couldn't wait to run inside and just hide away in my room, my old room which I now had to share with this girl who hated me.

Aunt Penny and Uncle Doug had done their best to keep everything the way it was, only moving Mama's things out of the bedroom they now called theirs. Twenty minutes later Sage finally opened the bedroom door and looked inside.

"That's your bed over there," I offered, pointing to the bed, my old bed, next to the window. I had switched beds back before Mama died, back when our hopes were high in anticipation of Sage coming live with us. It had the better view of the garden and was closer to the closet and bathroom and I, well, I just thought it'd be better since she was older and stuff. She silently put her duffle bag and backpack on the end of the bed, took off her sandals and dress and pulled out a pair of shorts and a t-shirt. She never looked at me once, just put them on and laid down atop the comforter, closing her eyes, shutting me out. "Do you want anything to eat?" I asked hesitantly. She turned toward the wall without saying a word.

The next several days were pretty much the same, I'd try to make small talk, Sage wouldn't respond. One morning Aunt Penny came into the kitchen where Sage was sitting at the table reading a magazine. "Sage, honey, why are you treating your sister this way? She's just trying to be your friend," she asked earnestly. "You need to be kinder to her, to all of us, because we're all in this for the long haul."

"What do you mean *why*?" she flashed back. "Don't you *get* it? I wanted to come here to be with my *mom*! I don't *know* any of you, I *hate* this place, and now my mother is *dead*."

"But, Sage, she was KC's mother, too," Aunt Penny said quietly.

"Sure, and I didn't even know her! KC got to spend all these years with her and I got NOTHING!" She slammed her hand down on the table then jumped up and ran to the bedroom.

It took almost a full two weeks for Sage to finally say something to me. I had gotten used to her silence so one afternoon when we were sitting together on the couch in the den, not talking, watching a Family Ties rerun and she casually asked if I had any DVDs, I was simultaneously startled and surprised. "Um…. sure! We've got *tons*! Mama and I …." I could see her eyes tense up, "I mean, we've got….um, there's a lot of Westerns, a bunch of comedies, some romance, stuff like that." I was careful not to tell her that most of the movies we had were pretty much just ones Mama liked.

"What about horror movies? Thrillers? Anything like that?" Again, I didn't want to explain that most of what we had were Mama's taste, so I just said, "Nah, I've never been much into scary movies."

She seemed ok with that, but I almost felt like I was being judged somehow. "How about *Independence Day?*" I offered, knowing that was one of the movies Mama wasn't exactly happy that I got, but it was exciting to watch; even Mama liked it.

"I got this one for my birthday last year," I said, hoping she'd think I've been watching this type of movie for a while. I was almost fourteen, after all.

"When's your birthday?" She asked abruptly.

"Actually, it's in a couple weeks, on the 7th. Why?"

"I don't know, just curious, I guess. When was Mom's?"

I didn't want to say anything right then. But something in me felt a deep connection to Mama right in that instant, and I said simply, "same day as mine." I thought for sure she'd go into one of her moods and stomp off into the bedroom, but she just shrugged and didn't say any more.

We spent the next two hours engrossed in the movie, not speaking. There were a couple parts that were so funny Sage even laughed out loud, but then quickly looked at me and got quiet again. But it was ok, I thought. At least she wasn't moping around or completely silent. Aunt Penny came in, looking like she was about to say something, then stopped, smiled, and walked back out. She came back in after a while with a big bowl of popcorn and set it down between us on the couch. A good move on her part, since she knew we'd have to start sharing our lives at some point and this was probably as good a start as any.

Jude and Miss M stopped by later that afternoon to drop off a few things I had forgotten to pack when I left the ranch. I heard a vehicle coming down the driveway so went out on the porch to see who it was.

Recognizing his truck, I smiled and waved; it was good to see them both. Miss M got out and gave me a big hug. "So happy to see you honey! How're you doing?" "Oh, ok," I said, "how about you? How's Salva doing?"

"Well, I think she's missing you. But at least she keeps Tucker busy. Maybe you can come out and see them both sometime?"

"I'd like that," I said then turned as Jude came up to me, smiling, holding up my favorite red sweatshirt and the large, overstuffed purple bear.

"Thought you would want these back," he said as I quickly grabbed the bear, hiding it behind me before Sage could see it. "Um, thanks," I said, suddenly shy around him. Then, seeing them waiting expectantly, I offered "do you want to come in for a while? Aunt Penny's out in the garden and Uncle Doug's in town, so come in while I go find her." I had to track Aunt Penny down because she was on the far end of our yard, trying to stretch the garden hose toward the stand of pink and red hollyhocks lining the fence. "I wouldn't bother with those, Aunt Penny!" I called out. "Mama says they're wild and don't need too much water anyway." She looked back towards me somewhat exasperated, then smiled. "Ok, well, at least now I know. What's up?"

"Jude and Miss M stopped by to drop off some stuff I left there."

"Oh, good! Did you ask them in?"

"Yes, they're in the kitchen."

When we came back in from the garden, Sage and Miss M were sitting at the table, talking animatedly about something while Jude leaned against the counter, watching and listening intently.

"I see," Miss M smiled at Sage. "That's really interesting! Have you thought of doing something with that, I mean, like selling them or something?" I felt a quick rush of jealously and was surprised I felt so irritated. Sage rarely talked to anyone, so seeing her so engaged in a conversation with people I knew and loved really bugged me. I looked at Jude but he, too, seemed rapt in the conversation.

"Hey folks!" Aunt Penny chirped. "So nice to see you! Iced tea?"

"Nah, we're actually on our way into town to get some supplies," Jude said. "Didn't mean to impose or anything."

"No imposition! Stay for dinner! Doug should be home soon and I put a pot of green chile stew on earlier, so it's no trouble at all."

A small part of me wanted them to stay, really, but another part, a part infused with a bright and unexpected surge of resentment, simply didn't want them sitting here talking to Sage. I know it sounded petty, but these were *my* friends, not hers. "They're busy, Aunt Penny," I quickly interrupted, "Besides, I'm sure they have better things to do, right, Jude?'

He looked at me with a mixture of confusion and concern, trying to read my face. "Um, yeah, yeah... we've got a lot to get done this afternoon. But thanks, anyway," he nodded toward Aunt Penny, his eyes still on me. "Maybe another time."

They left shortly afterwards and I went into my room. Sage came in and flopped down on her bed, now all conversational with me. "Wow, I can't believe I was just talking to *Jude Lightfoot*! Oh my God! He's like, *super* cute!"

So *now* she's talking to me, I thought to myself, completely irritated. "You weren't really talking to him, you were talking to Miss M," I said a little too sharply. "Besides, he a lot older than you, Sage! You're only 17!"

"Only by four years! Who cares? What's he like? I mean, is he nice, mean? What's his story?"

I begrudgingly told her the little I knew of Jude's past Miss M had divulged to me, but I felt protective and somewhat traitorous even talking about him and later regretted saying anything at all. "He's had some tough things happen to him, Sage, so don't go mentioning any of this to him, ok?"

But Sage was intent on finding out everything she could about Jude. "Well, sure, everyone's heard stuff about him and how his wife committed suicide and all that. I do know how to read, KC. What I *meant* was, is he like, easy to talk to, is he nice to dogs, what's his thing?"

"Easy to talk to, loves dogs. Satisfied?"

"Geez, thanks for the all that valuable information," she said sarcastically. "Don't you want to go visit his, or I guess, your, sort-of dog out there?"

"I will sometime. Why?" I could see where this was going.

"Well, I was thinking maybe I could go with you. I've never been on a real cowboy ranch."

"Sage, it's not a *real* cowboy ranch. They don't have a bunch of cows or cowboys or anything like that. It's just an old ranch he inherited from his grandpa or something." The last place I wanted to take Sage was out to Jude's beautiful ranch, so if I could make it out in a negative light, that's what I was going to do. "Besides, you hate dirt and horses and all that anyway," I reminded her. "Didn't you and your grandparents used to live in like a fancy mansion or something?"

"*Our* grandparents," she reminded me, "had a huge house, but I never really liked living there once Grandpa died. It was big and cold and so far out of town there was nothing to do but hang around the grounds. I was alone most of the time. Well, unless I was in school, of course. They had horses but the stablemen took care of them and I wasn't allowed to go down to the stables by myself. I actually really wanted to learn to ride a horse, and Grandpa was going to teach me, but Grandma said that I was too young."

"What were they like?" I asked. This was one of the first real conversations we'd had and I was genuinely curious about them, plus relieved not to be talking about Jude anymore.

"Well, for one thing, they had a ton of money. They had all sorts of people working for them, housekeepers, yard guys, a cook, you name it. I don't even remember all their names, there were so many around all the time."

"I mean, were they nice? Were they old?"

"Of course, they were old, dummy. They're grandparents! Grandpa was almost seventy when he died a few years ago. Some kind of stroke or something like that, I think. Supposedly he had been in some weird accident or something a long time ago. Got hit on the head and he was 'never the same,' according to Grandma."

"What about her, your grandma?"

"Well, *our* grandma, she's something else, for sure. She's tall and pretty, I guess, but she can be really mean. If someone ever crossed her, man, she'd make them pay."

"What do you mean, 'pay'?"

"I mean, like one time I went with her into town so she could pick up her dry cleaning and the lady there said she apologized but one of Grandma's blouses had gotten caught in their machine and got a small tear in the sleeve. KC, I swear that tear was about as big as my pinkie fingernail but Grandma acted like the entire blouse was in shreds. The owner offered to compensate her for the blouse, but Grandma was furious. She started yelling at her how incompetent she was and that she shouldn't have a business if she couldn't do it right, and how she was going to make sure no one in Emmit *ever* came into her shop again, and so on and so on. I was so embarrassed. Another time the guy at the car garage left those little paper mats that they put down on your car floors so they don't get dirty when it's being fixed and when we got in to go home and she saw them, she immediately got out, reached back in the window and started honking the horn. Off and on and off and on until they came running out of the bay. She screamed at them, pointing into the car, saying stuff like "what kind of place is this that you're so incompetent you can't even remember to take these trashy mats out when you're done? The guy was all embarrassed and came over to take them out and I remember her staring him down saying something like "you will never, ever touch this car again or you will never, ever work in this town again." It was awful. Awful.'

'Yeah, and problem was, she was that way with *everyone*. Well, not with me, of course. But most people were afraid of her and I think they probably thought I was like her too, just being her granddaughter. But I didn't care. Some of the girls at school thought I was a snob, but I seriously just didn't care. At first, I was worried about coming out here. I mean, I was afraid I might even miss her, you know? But when we got to that hotel and I realized she'd taken away my credit cards and my money and she turned off my cell phone service, I wasn't worried any more. I figured if she could do that to me, she didn't really love me anyway."

"Wow," I said, not able to think of how to respond. I'd never been around anyone who was ever *that* mean in my entire life. I was always absorbed in Mama's love and so a little part of me just wanted to go over to Sage and give her a big hug. But all I said was "Well, what about your dad?"

"I never really even knew him, and, besides, KC! Why do you keep saying "mine" all the time? He was *your* dad, too."

"I know, I guess, but I never knew him. Or them. It's always just been Mama and me like, *forever*, and, I don't know, I just wondered, I guess."

I immediately regretted saying that as I saw the pain shoot into her eyes. "I'm sorry, Sage. I didn't mean to... I mean, I didn't......" But I could see she was done talking as she got up and stomped out of the room, ignoring my apology. I called after her "Well, I hurt too, you know! I never got to know him, or my grandparents, or even *you* until now!"

I don't know if she even heard me over the slamming of the bathroom door.

13 HIDING IN PLAIN SIGHT

There wasn't anything at all moving forward on Mama's death. Murder, I guess, but even now, I still can't seem to say it out loud.

Detective Alvarez, Al to his friends, called the house every couple of weeks to let us know the status of the investigation. Which was pretty much nothing. Each time Aunt Penny would look at my hopeful face as she hung up the phone, only to see it fall when I'd see her expression.

They had found a single 9mm caliber bullet casing in the weeds on the side of our driveway. But that was about all the evidence they'd been able to come up with. That and a single shoeprint in the dirt area around the old cottonwood tree, the one I had thought I'd seen something when Mama was shot. A crime scene specialist took plaster casts of the shoeprint and all Detective Alvarez could tell us was it matched the tread of a size 10 Reebok running shoe. I tried to tell the police the best I could, but I couldn't actually remember seeing a person at all, much less if it was a man or a woman. In fact, it could've been a dog, for all I knew, I told them. But by the time they had finished grilling me for information that day, I was pretty sure I hadn't seen anything at all.

The autopsy report stated her death was by one bullet directly to the heart, which wasn't a surprise to any of us. I told the police that day I had heard only one loud shot. One shot that took Mama away forever.

It seemed like the detective interviewed everyone in our small town so of course everyone knew everything about this case. Mama didn't have any enemies, wasn't in any financial trouble, didn't have a shady ex-boyfriend, and wasn't hiding anything from anyone, anywhere. Well, except me. I guess she did have her secrets after all. But that wasn't anything anyone local would know about, except maybe Uncle

Doug and Aunt Penny, and they had been all the way up in Alaska. Besides, they'd be the last ones to want anything to happen to Mama. It was almost as if whoever did this materialized out of thin air, shot Mama, then materialized right back into thin air and was gone. But then there was the Reeboks. And the bullet casing.

One afternoon Detective Alvarez came to our house. I saw him through the kitchen window as he was coming up the driveway carrying a large manila folder and ran to get Aunt Penny.

"The detective is here, Aunt Penny! I think he found something!" She hurriedly took off her gardening gloves and smoothed her hair back from her face. "Give us a little time, ok, KC? Where's Sage? Maybe you two can go do something else while I'm talking to him?"

"Why? Why can't we be there too?"

"I need to go over a few things with him first then I'll fill you in, ok? He's actually here because *I* called him."

"Why? Why did you call him? Why can't I listen, too?" I whined.

"No, KC, not now, ok? Just give me a few minutes alone with him." She sent me a pleading look as she went to answer his knock. I trudged unwillingly down the hall into our bedroom where Sage was lying on her bed, listening to music with her headphones on. "What's up?" she said, taking them off as she saw me flop down on my bed, frowning up at the ceiling.

"Nothing. Well, something. That detective is here and Aunt Penny won't let me stay there and hear what he has to say."

"Why not? It's something new about Mom, I'll bet. I'll go see what I can find out," she said peeking out our door then tiptoeing down the hallway towards the kitchen where soft voices could be heard.

Thirty seconds later she was back in our room, defeated. "Ugh! She *knew* I was eavesdropping. How does she do that, anyway? God, that woman has a sixth sense or something!"

"Well, she did say she'd tell us whatever happens."

"Oh, right, she'll tell us what *she* wants us to know, you mean."

When we heard his car pull out down the driveway, we both got up and started out the door, but Aunt Penny was just coming in.

"Ok, girls, here's what's going on. I want you to know I called Detective Alvarez because I found something when I was cleaning out your mom's stuff in her closet." She looked at me, as if asking permission to continue. When I didn't say anything, she proceeded "and that's when I came across a box with some letters and stuff in it." She held a small sagging cardboard box on her lap as she set down on the end of my bed and both Sage and I clamored over to see what was inside.

"Letters? What kind of letters?" Sage and I looked at each other, then back to Aunt Penny.

"Well, I don't know, exactly," she said, looking at me again as she considered the hodge-podge collection of papers. "We can't touch them right now because he's sending out a guy to pick them up so they can brush them for fingerprints and then I guess there's some chain of command thing he has to follow so I can't let you even touch the box. But there's other stuff in here, too. Like a couple old picture frames with no photos in them, a round plastic thing that I thought kind of looks like a teething ring or something a baby would use, that kind of stuff. He said once they've done the initial processing, they'll return the personal things and keep just the letters for now."

I had begun to think nothing was ever going to become of Mama's case and this new piece of information brought up not only a pang of sadness, but also a new, heightened sense of urgency to find her killer. "Can't you at least tell us what the letters said? I mean, just a little bit?" I pleaded.

"I can't, honey. It's not that I don't want to, it's more that I just don't want to upset you. These were all were pretty mean-spirited, whoever wrote them."

"But maybe we could help," Sage offered, nodding her head towards me then back to Aunt Penny. "I mean maybe us looking at them too, we might see a clue or something that you guys missed. Can't we just take a peek?"

"I can't even do that, hon. I'm sorry," Aunt Penny said, looking back and forth at us. "What I do know is that some of the notes are written on Post-Its, some just look like they've been scribbled on the back of a newspaper, and it looks like some of them are typewritten letters. But, just between us, from what I could tell I'm pretty sure they all came from the same person."

"Who?" we said in unison, eyeing the haphazard stack with suspicion.

14 CHICA

Veronica Valdez didn't like surprises. So, when she heard that Doug Stevenson and his wife had moved back to Lona to take care of his orphaned nieces, she was irritated at both the flash of intense anger she felt at his memory, along with the surprising anticipation she felt in possibly running into him.

They hadn't left things well in high school, especially after his back-stabbing little sister Shari had to go and tell the entire Lona High School student body that she had failed second and third grades. It wasn't that she was unintelligent or anything, she just had a hard time reading and understanding things. By the end of first grade her parents realized there was something wrong because she had such difficulty comprehending what she was hearing from her teacher. Her frustration, even as a young child, was clearly evident in her lack of progress at school, so with the help of her teachers and a couple of therapists, young Veronica was eventually diagnosed with a combination of dyslexia and hyperkinetic impulse disorder. With the proper therapy over a year and a half, she did well and it was recommended she retake her second-grade year as the best way to ensure her continued progress in school.

Her father relocated the family from Santa Fe to Lona in 1972 for his new job as ranch manager. Since it was the beginning of fifth grade the move ensured a clean slate, socially speaking, for Veronica. So, as far as anyone was concerned, she was simply another twelve-year old going into sixth grade, and the fact that she was really fourteen was never brought up again.

Well, she reminded herself, not until Miss High and Mighty Shari Stevenson had to go and mouth off. Veronica blamed Doug for telling Shari in the first place and, although he repeatedly denied it, she never really believed him. It rankled her every time she thought about it back then and it still bugged her to this day. She remembered the embarrassment of walking down the high school's hallway, trying to avoid the scornful glances of her classmates. Even those she considered her closest girlfriends were somewhat hesitant around her, especially when they thought she was now two full years older than them and probably a lot more mature and experienced than she was letting on.

She figured breaking up with Doug Stevenson was one of the easiest boyfriends she'd ever dumped. Well, maybe not exactly dumped. Technically, he had dumped her. One night after they'd had a what she thought was a pretty great make-out session in the back seat of his father's truck, he told her that he wanted to cool things off a little.

"What do you mean, 'cool things off a little?'" she challenged him, but felt the slight fear in her voice as she spoke. "Like break up? Or what, exactly?"

"I mean, I just think we should chill a while. Maybe take a few weeks off, and, you know, it's okay if you want to start seeing someone else, get to be with some older guys, that kind of stuff."

Alarmed, she shot back, "*No*, Doug, it's *not* okay. And that's *not* how this is going to go down. You are totally messing with the wrong bitch if you think otherwise. I guarantee you'll *never* get another date in Lona if you think that's how it's gonna be."

"I just meant that it might be better if..." he stammered.

But she kept on her rant, "In fact, Doug Stevenson, if it weren't for me, you'd still be jerking off in your room every weekend."

"That's bullshit and you know it."

"It's my word against yours."

"Fat chance of that."

101

"Well, then, I guess we'll just let everyone make up their own minds, won't we." she said with mock sweetness, "Let's see just who they'll believe once I get my side of the story out."

She didn't care how cute he was or how he kissed or even how he taught her things to do that she would've never thought to do. *No* guy was going to treat her like that and get away with it. 'Yeah, I'm totally done with this loser', she thought later that evening, 'his loss, totally better off without him.'

Graduation and, more importantly, the after-graduation parties, was only three weeks away and Doug still kept his distance. She tried to pretend he didn't exist but there was something that always brought her back around to thinking about him. Seeing him in the hallways at school, watching him flirt with Tammy Armijo in history class, fooling around with his buddies at the Tastee Freeze on Friday night, all of it just made things worse. He rarely even acknowledged her anymore and, secretly more hurt than infuriated, she knew she had to change her tactics. So she put her sights on Greg Baca, a guy she knew Doug never really liked anyway and was always dumping on because he thought he paid way too much attention to his little sister.

'This will be perfect. I'll show *him*,' she thought to herself, although in the flurry of exams, graduation exercises, and, of course, the parties, she never really found the opportunity she needed to hook up with Greg. It seemed that whenever she was looking for him, he was either in the library studying, which she never felt the need for, or rushing off to his after-school job, which she had way better things to do. 'That's going to change, and soon,' she vowed to herself.

Veronica and Greg first met in 6th grade when he and his family moved from Albuquerque the same year she and hers did from Santa Fe.

His parents had divorced and his mom wanted to be closer to her sister and her family, so that's how he ended up in Lona. But he wasn't exactly popular or anything so she gave him little, if any attention back then, favoring the likes of the Doug Stevenson crowd throughout her high school years instead. Even though Greg was smart and quiet, he pretty much faded into the teenage woodwork, finding friends with the uncool crowd of kids, kids who included Shari Stevenson, in his mind, the most beautiful girl in the world.

The day Shari Stevenson moved to live with her aunt and uncle in Texas was probably the worst day of his high school life, and, being the quiet person he was, no one ever really knew the extent of his feelings. The only good side of it was that Doug Stevenson and his jock friends finally stopped harassing him.

Greg wasn't a big guy, nor a strong guy, but he knew he was smart. He always wanted to be a doctor, even when he was a little boy, but with limited family money and no prospect of college on the horizon, he was forced to take small part-time construction jobs or working at the market as a bagger during the summers to try and save money for nursing school. His cousin Danny eventually got him a job after graduation in the same department where he worked at the Lona Medical Clinic running lab samples back and forth between the clinic and the lab. It just so happened that Veronica Valdez had recently been hired there as the new receptionist.

"Hey handsome," Greg heard behind him one morning while he was at the coffee maker in the break room. He turned to see her standing beside the counter, one hand perched seductively on her hip and a sexy smile on her lips.

"You've been here over a week and you haven't even *once* said hi to me, Greg Baca," she pouted.

"I...I...I didn't think you recognized me."

"Of course, I did," she purred. "How could *anyone* not recognize someone so handsome?"

Getting over Doug hadn't been easy, but Veronica was on a mission. Greg Baca was an easy target, so to speak, and it wasn't long before they were dating exclusively and soon any memories of Doug were pushed to the very bottom of her heart. Especially after graduation when she found out he had up and moved to Alaska, of all places, to start a vending machine business. Out of sight, out of mind, and, she hoped, out of heart.

To his surprise, Greg found himself smitten with Veronica. Even though he always thought she wasn't actually his type, he also never would've thought someone as popular as she would ever want anything to do with a nerd like him. He remembered the teenage angst he'd always felt around her and her popular group of high school friends. He even remembered feeling sorry for her when the rumors spread around about her skipping two grades of school. So, this was all a novel and heady experience for him. He could hardly believe his good fortune and quickly jumped into their relationship with little, if any, precaution for his heart, the two of them seeing each other nearly every single night, whether at her apartment or the back seat of his car.

One afternoon almost two months later, Veronica came up to Greg just as he was getting out of his car from his latest lab run.

"Hey, hon, can you take a break?"

"Sure," he said. "What's up?"

"Well," she said, looking around the lot. "Can we go for a coke or something?"

"I can't right now. What is it? I mean, what's going on? Is everything ok?" he asked apprehensively.

"Um, ok, well, look… I was, um, well, I was hoping we could go somewhere in private, but, well, I'm not exactly sure how to tell you this, but…. I'm, um, I'm pregnant."

"What? *Pregnant?*" He couldn't believe he'd heard her right.

Seeing the disappointment on her face, he caught himself. "I mean, that's great! Really!"

"Are you sure?" she asked, trying to read his face for any hint of regret.

Veronica and Greg recited their marriage vows in a hastily put-together wedding a month later. Greg's mother was none too happy and made it clear throughout the small ceremony by constantly glaring over at Veronica and then turning and whispering to her sister, Lupe. Later, after the ceremony was over and they were all heading into the café for dinner, Greg pulled his mother aside.

"What was that all about, Mom? Geez, I mean talk about rude!"

She just gave him a knowing smirk and said "Just wait, *mijo*. You just wait."

Little Veronica, or Ronni, as they called her, was born nearly seven months later and son Rico came a year and a half after that. Juggling two small kids and a job wasn't exactly what Veronica had envisioned for her life, but the money was needed until Greg could complete his coursework to get his Associates Degree in Nursing at Lona's branch campus of the University of New Mexico. Things became a process of settling into her life with her son and daughter, a husband who worked endless hours at the clinic, and a boring, unfulfilling job. She eventually started taking classes on her own in medical technology and became a certified phlebotomist, though she was never truly satisfied.

Time with her girlfriends out at Paco's Bar became about the only thing that made her happy and she made it a point to meet them two or three times each week. To Greg's mom's credit, she was a doting grandmother and was always more than happy to watch the kids, even when Veronica would call at the last minute, sometimes late in the evening and ask if she could drop them off.

Greg was so engrossed in his career he didn't have time to realize how dissatisfied his wife really was. Though increasingly unhappy, Veronica knew that Greg was a good provider, and she was proud of how well they thought of him at the clinic and how he got regular promotions. Between their two jobs, they made an ample living and Greg was more than generous with her and the kids. They wanted for nothing. When they bought their first little house over on 1st Street, she didn't ask where the money came from, knowing his parents had pitched in a good portion of the down-payment.

Once the kids became teenagers and nestled into their high school years, friends, and dating though, Veronica knew something had to give. Their divorce came during Rico's junior year in high school. Ronni had already moved out of the house and when Greg decided to move to Albuquerque, Ronni moved in with him and Rico stayed in Lona with Veronica. She went back to her maiden name and life went on for everyone in their own private ways.

But in Lona, nothing was ever discreet or private, regardless who you talked to. Shari Stevenson's recent murder, still the talk of the town, was no exception and it was no surprise when Veronica's friend, Cindy Bustos, called late one afternoon a couple weeks later.

"Guess *what*?! Doug Stevenson is moving back to town!" she said breathlessly.

"*What*? Why?"

"I heard him and his wife were named as the girls' legal guardians or something, and that they're going to move into her old house." Everyone in town of course knew what had happened to Shari Stevenson, how she had a secret daughter out in Texas that no one had known about, and about how her younger daughter had moved in with that actor guy out in El Rio after her mother was murdered.

"Wow, that's some crazy shit," Veronica said. "Craaaaaazy."

"Yeah, and I heard they're hiring some fancy lawyer out of Las Cruces to take over the case."

"Is that so?" she asked. "Why? Do they know anything new?"

"Nothing I know of. Hey, wanna meet us around nine at Paco's tonight?"

"Sure, see you later," she frowned, hanging up the receiver, deep in thought.

15 EASIER READ THAN DONE

Detective Alvarez had talked to pretty much everyone Mama knew, and had gone through all her bank accounts, her credit statements, her phone records, everything, but hadn't come up with a single decent lead. There was one little blip that showed up on their screen for her credit card regarding a charge for $149.64 for a leather gun holster, but when Uncle Doug showed him his and let them know Mama had given it to him for his fiftieth birthday this past year, that lead evaporated pretty quick.

He was helpful in one area, though. And that was regarding the box of letters and notes Penny had found in Mama's closet.

After his technician meticulously brushed for fingerprints and photographed each piece of paper in the box, Detective Alvarez turned to where Aunt Penny and I were sitting at the kitchen table, watching him expectantly. I had begged her incessantly to let me stay and listen to what he had to say and she finally just gave up, telling me not to expect much.

"I'm thinking it might be best to send all these to a forensic handwriting analyst in Albuquerque," he explained. "It might take several weeks, though, so we'll have to sit tight until we get more information."

"Ok, but what do *you* think of them so far, I mean, can you tell me what any of them mean?" she asked pointedly.

"Well, without going into a lot of detail, what I *can* tell you is I think the letters are most likely from a woman because of the style of writing," he explained, holding one out for her to inspect.

The page he held up read simply:

SHARI

YOU ARE RUINING EVERYTHING

LEAVE US ALONE

"Well, this doesn't show much," Aunt Penny declared. "I mean, what does it mean? Is that your personal or professional opinion?"

"I really can't say much more, Penny, not even my personal opinion on this. I'm sorry."

He went on to explain that department policy was that no one could discuss their initial findings on the letters, nor any of the Post-Its or other items as they each had sensitive information that he wasn't allowed to divulge at this time.

"What do you mean, 'sensitive'?" Aunt Penny persisted. "What kind of information? I read each and every one of those and I didn't see anything but a few rambling threats from some crazy person."

"I'm sorry, I just really can't get into that right now," he repeated, gathering up the papers. "You're going to just have to trust the system."

"Well, I sure hope someone can tell us something sooner than later," she huffed, clearly irritated, as he and his assistant headed out the door.

"I promise we'll contact you know the minute we know something," he offered. She just stared at him and closed the kitchen door.

My curiosity got the best of me.

"Aunt Penny, what was in the rest of the letters and notes you read? I mean, you went through the whole box, so he knows you saw them all."

"I honestly couldn't make any sense of them, honey," she said genuinely. "At first I thought it was just a bunch of notes and stuff your mom'd been working on. Maybe stuff from clients, or, well, I don't know. They just didn't make sense. I didn't really even think much about them until Detective Alvarez took such interest in them. Now I kind of wish I had paid more attention."

"Could you tell if the rest of them were, I mean, was someone mad at my mom?"

"Seriously, they were just a bunch of notes, hon. And maybe a couple invoices, or bills. That's what made me think they were part of her work. I just flipped through a few of them, saw that most of them looked like stuff from the Lona Medical Clinic, stuff like that. The only thing that was suspicious was the one you just saw. But I still didn't think much of them at the time so I boxed them back up and then put the box away."

"But," I pressed, "what do you mean? What... what did they actually say?"

"KC, look, all I can say is there were a few others in there that sounded a little bit threatening towards your mom. I couldn't tell, though, because none of them were signed or anything."

"Threatening how?" I couldn't imagine anyone ever being so mad at my mom that they would want to hurt her.

"Just kind of telling her to back off, I guess, like that first one. It's hard to decipher them. Let's just let the detectives do their jobs, ok?"

But Penny was admittedly more concerned than she let on and, a few weeks later, went to Doug and sat next to him on the couch. "Can I talk to you a minute?"

"Sure. Everything ok?"

"Well, I've been thinking a lot about the case, Doug. We've got to go outside Lona," she said, then, seeing Doug's face tighten, she quickly continued. "It's not that I don't think these guys are doing their jobs, it's just that now, after all this interest in that box of stuff in Shari's closet, I'm wondering if this is all above their heads. I mean, I'm wondering if they have all the resources they need."

"Resources like what?" Doug asked.

"I don't know. I guess it just seems like no one has a clue what happened and we haven't gotten any closer to finding out what happened than we were the day it happened."

"Ok, what do you suggest, then?"

"I'm thinking of calling around to see if there's anybody here in New Mexico that might specialize in crime, you know, maybe a private investigator, or lawyer, or whatever."

"We already have the detectives and cops, Pen, plus you know how much I think of Al, and he's doing ok, right?"

"Doug, he hasn't done *enough*, in my opinion. He didn't even interview Shari's boss, that Mr. Buchman guy, until I mentioned it. I know Al's your friend and all, but really? I'm going to look around. No offense, Doug, but we need more help on this."

"Ok, I guess that'd be all right. I just don't think we're going to get anywhere with it."

She didn't respond, just looked at him. Sensing there was more, he searched her face. "You still seem bugged with something. What is it?"

"Well, I've been thinking about what Mina said when we were in Texas picking up Sage. About that 'other woman', and well, I'm just curious. What'd she mean to you?" Penny noticed a slight tightening of his eyes. Was that fear, she thought?

"She was just a girl I dated in high school, that's it, no more. End of story." He started to rise, signaling an end to the conversation.

111

"Wait, a minute, Doug," she put her arm on his, stopping him from getting up. "I'm just curious. What did she mean by that business with you and her planning to get married? Is that true?"

"No! I never asked her to marry me. Hell, we were just kids, Pen."

"But why would Mina think you were getting married, then? I mean, how would she have even known any of that?"

"I dunno. Maybe Shari mentioned something to her way back when. You know how gossip gets going. Just drop it. That woman means absolutely nothing to me," he said emphatically.

Penny wasn't so sure.

Jamison Roybal pushed open the glass door of his small law office, a one-lawyer affair located at the far end of a low-slung strip mall in the far southern New Mexico city of Las Cruces.

"How's your sister doing, Marci?" he asked his receptionist as she was coming in from her lunch hour.

"She's better, thanks. I think she'll be coming home from the hospital tomorrow."

"Happy to hear that. If you need anything at all, let me know," he said earnestly.

"Thanks, Mr. Roybal. I really appreciate that."

"You know you can call me Jamie, right?"

"I know. Thanks, Mr. Roybal."

Jamison, Jamie to his friends and family, and Mr. Roybal to his colleagues, had always wanted to be a lawyer, even when he was a child growing up. His father had been a county judge and his mother a court reporter, so the legal system wasn't new to him nor his two younger sisters. Getting through law school in Denver had been a challenge and he didn't pass the bar until his third try, but, ultimately, he did and started practicing in the Denver area for a hip new firm, Simpson, Simon and Deetz.

His first two years out were the basic expectations of any newbie, mostly grunt work, a few easy civil cases, just enough to cut his teeth. It was when the Ferris Daniels case came along that everything changed, irrevocably, in Jamie's life.

He was assigned the unenviable task of research, and, only working with the two primary lawyers, he went through the discovery process and presented his findings to them each afternoon. Always a stickler for detail, he made the perfect investigator, because nothing got past him. And when the lead lawyer broke his leg in a skiing accident, Jamie was the logical next person in line to take up the slack.

Word around the legal circles from the prosecutors was this was a slam-dunk and Daniels was going to fry, but Jamie had his doubts. Even when forensics proved that the tiny blood specs on his boots were an exact match to Miss Cooke's, he still suspected there was more to the story. Mr. Daniels was easily one of the most transparent, distraught, frightened clients Jamie had ever worked with and though some of his colleagues suggested he was being played, he felt, deep in his gut, that the guy was innocent.

All the evidence was mounting against him and he had to come up with something, anything, to help his client, but was at a dead end and the trial date was coming up fast. He and the lead attorney sat with Daniels day after day, grilling him, trying to extract any tiny, however-insignificant piece of information he could give them that might help his case.

Exhausted, Jamie finally told him things didn't look good at all and to prepare himself for the worst. That's why when Daniels came to him late one afternoon with a story so sensational, even he had to think Daniels might be guilty after all. He told Jamie that he thought the real murderer might be a guy his sister used to date whom he'd let stay with him temporarily. The guy had only stayed with him for a few days, but it was over the same time frame when the murder had taken place.

"But where were *you* that night?" Jamie asked.

"I was home, in my apartment, the entire evening."

"And you didn't see or hear your friend come and go? Not a thing?"

"No, and we weren't really friends. I didn't hear a thing."

"Do you realize how this makes you look?" Jaime was incredulous.

"I know all that! God knows I've been over this in my mind a thousand times, but I also know I didn't do it."

"Well, let's hope for a miracle between now and next week."

Jamie spent the next three days reviewing again and again the evidence at hand. One evening as he was sitting in his office about ready to call it quits for the night, something about the crime scene photos kept poking the back of his mind. He spread them out over his desk again and meticulously pored over each, one by one, scrutinizing every single angle, the lighting, the entire scene, when, on the last photo, he stopped, sucking in his breath. His heart racing, he pulled the desk lamp down and closely inspected the photo with the magnifier. "How could we have missed this?" he thought excitedly, then hurriedly went through all the other photographs again. None of them showed what he had just discovered, which was just a tiny glint of something shiny, right there, nearly hidden on the edge of the woven chenille bedspread. He immediately called the police and obtained permission to revisit her apartment, taking the officer with him inside. They went directly to the bedroom, where Jamie bent down at the footboard of her bed and there, almost completely hidden, he saw the small set of keys snagged on the heavy woven fabric of the bedspread, caught between the mattress and the footboard, dangling about a foot above the carpet.

The detectives were able to trace the keys back to a man named Titus Percy, a known cocaine addict with a felony conviction for assault.

The jury came back with their verdict in a record three-hours' time, unheard of when it came to capital murder cases. Percy was sentenced to life in prison without the possibility of parole.

Jamie Roybal became a legal hero and he blossomed in the case's wake. Simpson, Simon and Deetz offered him a promotion in the Denver firm, which he kindly, but promptly, turned down, his sights set on setting up his own practice back in New Mexico.

Roybal Law soon became a staple business in the Las Cruces area and Jamie had a steady, fulfilling career.

"Mr. Roybal, line two" he looked up distractedly from his current case's brief and punched the button. "Thanks Marci," then, "Jamison Roybal, how can I help you?"

"Um, yes, Mr. Roybal, my name is Penny Stevenson. I live in Lona and my sister-in-law was murdered almost three years ago. Can you help us find out who did it?"

"Um...I'm not a detective, Miss Stevenson."

"Mrs., if you don't mind, but does that mean you can't help us?"

"I'm not saying I *can* help, but, well, give me a quick rundown on the case first, ok?"

Penny relayed everything she knew up to this point about Mama's murder. She told him about the letters and notes she'd found in Mama's closet and how Detective Alvarez had taken them in for processing. After she was finished, she waited silently for an answer on the other end of the equally silent line.

Jamie had heard about the case up in Lona, but he also knew it was full of holes and fraught with poor policework. It had been years with no real leads. "Geez," he thought to himself. "Do I really want to get involved with this?"

"Mr. Roybal?" Penny questioned, "are you still there?"

"Um, yes, I am, I'm sorry. I was just trying to think this through. I understand what you are asking, Miss, I mean, Mrs. Stevenson. It's just that, well, like I said, I'm a lawyer, not a detective."

"But I've read all about you! I saw how you solved that case with that professor guy up in Denver, what with figuring out the keys and all that. That's why we need you. We followed that case from the beginning and we all were sure he did it. Then you, you figured out the impossible! You did that because you kept at it and that's the kind of person we need now. You're the only one who *can* help us!"

"You've got to remember, I was part of a team, ok? But let me see what I can do. I'm not promising anything but I do know a good investigator here in town, so maybe I can get together with him and see if he might be interested in helping you out, ok?"

"Oh, yes! Yes, Mr. Roybal! I can't tell you how much this means to me and my family."

"Ok, so tell me again really quick who the main players are here, ok?"

For the next twenty minutes Penny went over the case in detail. When she got to the facts revolving around Mina and Tom in Texas, Jamie groaned, interrupting, "Wait. Wait a minute. Are you talking about Mina and Tom Davenport? THE Davenports?"

"Well, um…yes, I guess so, I mean, I don't know any others." Penny said, a little worried now. "What difference does it make?"

"They're only the most well-connected, wealthiest ranching couple in West Texas, is why, I mean." Then, "I heard about Tom, I'm sorry," he said, exasperated. "Look, this could be tricky."

"Well, I never knew him, but thanks anyway. I know Sage thought a lot of him. But Doug and I met Mina when we picked up Sage and even though she's kind of put-offish, I know she will be the first one to stand up for us. She's promised to help out in whatever way possible and has said time and time again that money is no object."

"Money's always an object, Mrs. Stevenson," he reminded her. "But let me see what I can do. I'll get back to you in a couple days if that's good?"

"Yes, of course. Thank you, Mr. Roybal."

"You can call me Jamie."

After hanging up, he called Patrick Lassiter, Pat to most, probably one of the last great lawmen in New Mexico and relayed his conversation with Penny to him.

Patrick Lassiter spent twenty-seven years as a Texas Ranger specializing in investigations and felon apprehension. After retirement he moved to New Mexico, accepting a Special Investigation Reserved Officer position with the New Mexico State Police in Las Cruces.

"Good to hear from ya, hombre. How the hell are ya? Heard how you handled that case up in Denver a few years back. Mighty proud if I do say so myself."

Embarrassed but secretly enjoying the surprising attention from a man he'd known and respected more than half his life, Jamie continued, "I know it sounds crazy, Pat, but what're your thoughts? The Stevensons don't have a thing to go on, or so it seems."

"Well, I got that one figured out, for sure. I've read all about it. That bunch of boys up in Lona are all talk, thinkin' they can handle this by themselves. Hell, they probably couldn't even tie their own bootlaces cuz they'd probably have em' on backwards to begin with," Pat surmised. "I'll tell ya, I've been around enough to know a screwed-up investigation if I ever saw one. But, hell, they're still a good bunch of guys. You spring for breakfast tomorrow morning and I'll hear you out. Not promisin' a damn thing, though, so keep that straight."

Jamie smiled into the receiver. "See you in the morning."

They met at the Cruces Diner and spent the better part of an hour going over Shari's case.

"It's a bit tricky, though, I'll tell you straight up now," Jamie said, after outlaying all the information he had been able to get from the Lona detective working the case.

"Why's that?"

"Well, I'm sure you've heard of the name Davenport? Mina and Tom Davenport?"

"Hell, yeah, who hasn't? Least, that is, in Texas, I guess. Probably one of the meanest women I've ever had the displeasure of meeting. Tom was right enough, I reckon. Always makes ya wonder how two such different people end up together."

"Well Tom's gone now of course, but they're Shari Stevenson's in-laws."

"Christ Almighty," Pat whistled. "I had a run-in with their son, Mike, several years ago. He was a bad one."

"Small world, for sure," Jamie said. "All I know for sure is something stinks about this case. I want to take you out and talk to someone sometime soon, the guy who was there when it happened. Well, not right when it happened. He showed up right after it happened."

"Now don't that sound suspicious," Pat said. "I reckon we go take a trip up to Lona and pay this yahoo a visit too. What'd you say his name was?"

"Jude Lightfoot."

"What the hell? Now ain't this world full a' surprises today! *Jude Lightfoot?* Well, I'll be damned! Know him and knew his granddaddy. Good man. Had a nice little spread out in El Rio. Man, did we have some damn good times back in the day. Miss him a lot."

"Jude and his mother, Marion, live out there on that same ranch now, have for a few years from what I understand. Lost his wife, so he decided it was best he came home I guess."

"Yeah, I read about all that way back. Sure has had some tough licks, that kid. Well, hell, I'm liking this case more and more."

Two days later, Patrick and Jamie sat on the long front porch of the ranch, Miss M fluttering back and forth, busying herself pouring them iced tea.

"A little more iced tea?" she asked, motioning only to Pat, Jamie noticed, smiling.

"Oh, no thanks, ma'am, but that sure was good," he answered as she was already pouring more into his glass.

"Oh, call me Marion, Mr. Lassiter! And just a spot more, then I can go get busy in the kitchen getting dinner ready," she smiled at him, adding, "Jude should be out in just a minute or two."

She finished pouring then stood there, expectantly, but he just smiled back and didn't say any more so she turned and went inside.

"I think someone's got a little crush on you," Jamie winked at him.

"Nah, I've just always had that effect on the ladies," Pat nodded towards the kitchen, just as Jude came walking out, a big smile on his face and arms stretched wide.

"Well, well, if it isn't Sherlock Holmes in the flesh!" he came right up to Pat and gave him a hearty hug.

"Well, I'll be damned!" Pat stood up. "Dang, you weren't knee high to a grasshopper last time I saw you!"

"Grown a bit for sure. How ya doing, Mr. Lassiter?"

"Oh, Good Lord, call me Pat. Fine's can be, I reckon. Geez Jude, how long's it been? Too long I reckon. Hey, now, I was sure sorry to hear about your wife. Real sad story," he said sincerely.

Jude's eyes were downcast as he said, "Thanks, I…I'm….well, it's been tough. I was sorry to hear about Candy, too."

"Yep, that woman was one of a kind, that's for sure. Goddamn cancer. But enough of all this cryin'. Hey," he said, turning back toward Jamie. "This here's Jamie Roybal, Doug and Penny Stevenson brought him into this mish-mash."

"I guess that's true enough," Jamie agreed as he stood up to shake Jamie's outstretched hand.

Pat smiled patiently at them like he was ready to referee a tussle, then turned to Jude. "I know this isn't gonna be a regular job, but Jamie here tells me you have a little info we might be interested in."

Nothing like getting right to it, Jude thought. "Sure, do you want to talk here or go inside?"

"Here's fine."

For the next couple of hours, Pat, Jude and Jamie went over everything Jude could remember about that day. Pat grilled Jude, pushing him to remember anything, any little detail he could remember.

"Did you see or hear anything out of the ordinary? Any little thing at all?"

"No, but I was just trying to help KC. She was so upset, and rightly so of course, but she was crying, and there was blood everywhere, and then the sirens, it was just a crazy time."

"Has anyone interviewed the little girl?"

"Well, she's grown up in the past few years, for sure, so I wouldn't exactly call her little anymore. She's gotta be 15 or 16 by now."

"Young lady, then," Pat said. "What's her story?"

"The cops took down all her side of the story that afternoon, I know. She's come out to the ranch a few times, but she's pretty shy and never talks about what happened, at least not to me. And I don't know how much Detective Alvarez has been in contact with her or her aunt and uncle, Penny and Doug Stevenson. You'll no doubt want to talk with them, too."

"Were they there, too?"

"No, actually, they lived in Alaska when it happened."

"Well, hell yeah I want to talk to them, can you set up a meeting with that lil, er, young lady, pretty soon?" He nodded towards Jamie, then stood up, put his large hands on the table for emphasis, and looked both Jamie and Jude directly in their eyes, his voice getting low and quiet.

"Ok now both of you listen *real* close, ok? Once I get the green light from my buddies at the State Police Office, I want to interview every single family member and every single close friend Miss Stevenson ever had, just to rule them out. I want you to talk to her boss, what's his name? Dennis? Find out who she worked with, if there were ever any issues, anything. Talk to everyone who's known her or worked with her or played with her or danced with her. Once we got 'em eliminated, we can start tightening the noose on this sonofabitch. I want to see a record of every phone call, every credit card receipt, and every single email she either sent or received. I want IP addresses for everyone involved. I want cell phone numbers and I want internet searches. Get those letters and notes from the Lona yahoos; use my name if you need to. I want to see whatever they have on this case. I want it all. Do you two understand me?"

Jamie and Jude nodded in unison.

"Er, um, so what exactly do you want us to start with?" Jude asked hesitantly.

"Well, I want to start with the daughter, KC. Can you set that up?'

"Sure, I'll get right on it. I haven't seen her for a while, but I'm sure she'd be willing to meet with you any time you want."

"And Jamie, you sir, you get the fun stuff. Contact Mina Davenport and set up a meeting, pronto. I can drive over there when need be. Then I want you to get me a list of every person who came into contact with Miss Stevenson in the couple months before she died. Every plumber, every grocery clerk, every single person, comprende?"

"Um, Pat, so, um, just asking, where you planning on being while you're here in Lona investigating?" Jude asked.

"Why, right here on the ranch, goober. Where'd ya think?"

Miss M secretly smiled to herself from her perch inside the kitchen door.

17 A WORK IN PROGRESS

Sage and I had forged a passable relationship, nothing I'd envisioned in my early eagerness for a sister, but, as far as two totally different teenage girls living under the same roof could be, it was okay. We had a routine where we helped Aunt Penny and Uncle Doug in the mornings around the house and yard, me mostly working in the garden with Aunt Penny and Sage mostly in the house and Uncle Doug out trying to get their vending machine business name out to local companies and stores. But we were all doing our own things, even though the reality of Mama's death still hung silently over each of us in our own ways.

One of the hardest things I had to do was go back to school that fall. Sage and I rode the bus that picked us up at the end of our driveway every morning at 7:15. Sage always took the very first seat available, even if there was someone sitting next to her, so oftentimes I just made my way to the back where Sammy Pino and his brothers were already taking up the entire last two rows. The bus made its way along the winding country road, picking up everyone from the runny-nosed elementary school kids all the way up to the cooler high school kids too young to drive yet along the way. By the time we got up on the main road and into Lona, the bus was full. Because Lona High School was located on the far south end of Lona, our drop off was the last on the line.

I was in 9th grade and Sage was a junior. Being that it was my first year in high school, I was nervous to begin with. I'd spent the entire Sunday afternoon before trying on outfits, trying to decide if I should wear a skirt and top with my new shortie boots which were all the rage that year, or maybe the black tights and the long purple knit sweater. Mama never let me go out of the house with any kind of tights on unless whatever top I was wearing completely covered my butt so I finally had a few to choose from, thanks to Aunt Penny's generous birthday gifts. It seemed that all the girls were wearing shorter, and more low-cut clothes than ever and even though I hadn't ever really been that interested in fashion before, this year was different. It wasn't that I wanted to stand out more, I just didn't want to be so *plain*, especially now that I had Sage walking next to me each day. Each outfit I put together was quickly taken off and thrown on the bed as I searched for an even cuter, better look. After the fifth ensemble, I finally settled on a pair of black jeans, black knee-high boots, and a green plaid sleeveless blouse that I hoped played up my brown eyes. I turned anxiously from our long bedroom mirror towards Sage.

"Ok, what do you think about this one?" I asked hopefully.

"They all look okay to me," she responded, yawning.

"Well," I pressed. "I mean, do you like this better than the skirt and top? Or was the purple sweater better?"

"Like I said, they're all fine, KC. They all look great on you."

I wanted so badly for her to be, well, more of a sister. I knew she didn't have to ever think twice about what she was wearing, and, surprisingly, I wasn't jealous in the least bit. On any given day, Sage could casually throw on a pair of worn blue jeans and a t-shirt, add a cool belt and look like she was ready for a magazine shoot. But of course, I didn't inherit her natural beauty, that height, that hair, that resemblance to Mama. Even though Mama always used to say that no matter where you were in life, no matter what you had, to always remember there was always someone out there who had a little more than you and someone who had a little less. There was always someone who was a little prettier than you and someone who was a little less fortunate in the looks department. I sighed, hanging up the last of my pile of clothes and putting my shoes and boots away under the bed.

Mama was good that way, but right now, I just wanted someone to tell me to wear the purple sweater.

That first morning Sage, thankfully, patiently waited for me to get off the bus so we could walk in to the small complex of low-slung buildings together. All eyes were on us as we made our way across the parking lot and up the steps to school. Well, actually, all eyes were on Sage. But she never turned her head, not once, not even when some guy let out a low whistle or when another quickly elbowed his buddy to get him to look Sage's way. She couldn't have cared less.

Throughout that first year, I think she only hung around me out of guilt. Or maybe it was because she never really took the time to cultivate her own friendships. I had my friends from previous years, and I'd often walk with them to our common classes, but, for the most part, it was just me and Sage. We were both fairly good students; I had to study a little harder than her but I was better in art and English than she, and she was better at math.

The problem though was that where drawing, or writing in my journals brought me a lot of satisfaction, nothing really seemed to make Sage happy. It wasn't that she was so terribly *unhappy*, she just hardly ever smiled. No matter what I tried to get her interested in, she would roll her eyes, or fake an exaggerated yawn, or plain just tell me no and to leave her alone.

Most often, I thought she was just passing time with me, waiting for something bigger or better to happen to her. It seemed I was still a child in her mind. And there was always something in her invisible line of sight because she had a way of looking out at nothing, and I would just wish I had a place somewhere in that head of hers.

But time is a great healer, they say. Plus having an Aunt Penny in our world. Aunt Penny, frustrated with how we constantly weren't seeming to get along, would cheerfully suggest one thing or another, always to be met with Sage's uninterested eyes. She was determined, however, that Sage and I become friends and so each day she worked on us in her own Aunt-Penny ways. Sometimes she'd just casually say something like, "hey, I need someone to run down to Markie's after school and get me some eggs and bread. Will you two go for me?" Or, "who wants to earn a few bucks weeding the garden?" Or, "it would be so cool to go into town Saturday to see that new dress shop. Who's interested?" Every idea she came up with involved putting Sage and I together to make it work, and against all odds, by the beginning of the following summer Sage finally started coming around.

It wasn't ideal, but at least she didn't treat me like a pain-in-the-ass kid so much anymore, and once I found out she liked certain movies, or certain this or certain that, she was better at spending time with me.

"What's in those books you're always looking at?" she asked one afternoon.

"Oh, just some drawing stuff. Want to see?"

"No, not my thing. It's just that you sure spend a lot of time looking at them."

"One of these days when I save up enough money, Aunt Penny says she'll take me into Albuquerque and get the supplies I need to start my own painting."

Her entire demeanor perked up. "Albuquerque? Cool! I want to go, too, ok?

"Um, sure. It'll be fun. If it ever happens. I've got to earn some more money first."

Two days later, Aunt Penny came into our room and announced we were driving to Albuquerque on Saturday for lunch and a girl's day shopping.

"Oh, and we'll stop by and get your artist stuff, too, KC, if you want to." She winked at Sage.

I looked back and forth between them, trying to decipher the unspoken communication I'd just witnessed.

"What's going on?" I asked suspiciously.

"Well, nothing much," Aunt Penny said, still smiling, "Unless you want to call it an early birthday gift."

I jumped up and threw my arms around her. "Oh, Aunt Penny! Thank you! Thank you so much!"

"Well, don't thank me, thank your sister. It was her idea."

I was speechless. I quickly turned back toward Sage and saw her tentative smile.

"That's super cool," I told her. "Thanks, I mean, really," and then I just went right over to her and hugged her too. She didn't exactly hug me back, in fact, she acted kind of awkward about the whole thing, but she didn't exactly *not* hug me back, either, just a small token pat on my back, then pulled away. But that was enough for me.

That Saturday morning, as promised, the three of us piled into Mama's old truck and headed to the mall in Albuquerque. It wasn't far, only about 40 minutes or so, but the day was a clear, cloudless blue, she had her oldies in the cd player, and I was looking forward in great anticipation to our little outing. Even Sage was in a rare good mood. Aunt Penny had purposely chosen the truck instead of Uncle Doug's suburban, saying "Just easier for me to drive than that big ol' SUV," she'd explained, but I think Sage and I both knew better.

Aunt Penny couldn't sing worth a darn and Sage and I giggled as we listened to her unabashedly belt out Madonna's "Like A Virgin" as if she were up onstage herself.

"What? You two think you can do better?" she smiled at us, clearly happy we were having a little fun, even if it was at her expense.

"Not me," I said promptly. "I can't sing anything!"

"Me neither," Sage added, then turned toward me, "I've heard you sing to yourself in our room. I think you have a pretty good voice."

Wow. Two nice things from Sage in one week. "Aw, well, it's easy when you think NO ONE IS LISTENING," I said with feigned indignation. She and Aunt Penny just laughed.

The drive took a bit longer than we had planned because, coming into Albuquerque on I-25, there was a huge traffic backup. Rather than waiting in the long line, she took the first available exit, and we soon found ourselves in an area of the city with lots of big, older buildings that were clearly for businesses other that shopping. I could see the Bernalillo County Courthouse sign and next to it a huge parking garage.

"Um, Aunt Penny, I think the mall is back the other way," remembering the times I had come into town with Mama.

"Gosh girls, let me get turned back. I just thought we'd be able to get past the traffic and get back up on the freeway." She was clearly frustrated, but she had never been here before, so it wasn't really her fault when we found ourselves on one one-way street after another, going further and further into downtown.

"Crap!" She hit the steering wheel with her hand in frustration. "Ok, KC, do you have any idea how to get back up to the freeway?"

"Mama used to come this way whenever we went to the zoo. Maybe turn right at the next light?" I asked, hopefully, not really remembering the exact way. "I think you're heading the right way, but I'm not like a hundred percent sure or anything."

"There! There's the sign for the freeway!" Sage shouted suddenly. "Turn left here!"

Aunt Penny quickly maneuvered over to the left-hand lane and ran through the just-turned-yellow traffic light. A large SUV blew his horn at her and flipped her the bird as she whizzed through the intersection. She promptly flipped him the bird back then quickly looked over at us. "Oops, sorry about that…" but we were all laughing so hard we didn't even see the smaller truck pull out in front of us until it was too late.

The impact spun Mama's truck around and into a circle, landing exactly backwards in the same lane we were in. It happened so fast that none of us even said a word until Aunt Penny shouted "Oh my GOD! Are you girls ok?" as she looked at us, sitting there in shock. "I'm ok, I'm ok," I said, and Sage chimed in "I'm fine, too, Aunt Penny. Are you ok?"

Luckily, it wasn't as bad as it looked. We got out and the guy in the small truck Penny had just hit got out and ran over to us, yelling "Are you all ok? Is anyone hurt? Oh my God, I'm so sorry! I didn't even see you!" He was young himself, probably not even twenty yet, his face a mixture of worry and distress as he looked at us, then back at his damaged truck.

"My mom is going to KILL me," he moaned. "I am dead meat!"

"Honey, we're all fine, and don't you worry, no one's going to kill anyone. Are *you* okay? Let me just call 911," but no sooner had she said that than we heard the sirens coming our way so someone else must've called it in already.

Once the police arrived and made sure no one was injured, they took their reports and spoke to a couple who said they had witnessed the entire thing. As it turned out, the young man had also become disoriented trying to make his way back from downtown and was looking at his phone for a GPS signal when he inadvertently ran a stop sign on the side road coming out and we hit him. There was a deep dent in the front side of his truck where we collided, but The Beast hardly even had a scratch except for a tiny ding on the heavy bumper. Neither of us needed a tow truck, so once the cops had us move our vehicles out of the road, we got ready to leave. But the poor guy looked so dejected it was almost comical. In fact, Aunt Penny felt so sorry for him that she went over and told the police officer she wasn't going to press charges or anything, but the officer said that it wasn't up to him, advising her to get all the insurance information down and contact her insurance carrier for further instruction.

"Ok, but I'm not pressing charges anyway," she said loudly, trying to assure the guy it was all going to be ok. "What's your name, honey?" she asked, coming back up to our little trio.

"Rico, ma'am. Rico Baca. I had to come to Albuquerque to take care of a traffic ticket I'd forgotten about and I got lost and…"

"No problem, really, hon, we sure got lost ourselves!" Aunt Penny said sincerely, then, "Ok, well, here it is, Mr. Rico, I'm Penny Stevenson and I don't want you to worry about anything, got it? Here's my insurance information and you can give me yours. We're not hurt. You're not hurt. It's all ok. Do you need to call anyone? Do you want *me* to call anyone?"

"No," he looked dejectedly at his phone. "I already texted my mom. She's on her way."

"Do you want us to wait here then? We can, it's no problem at all."

Sage elbowed me, then looking over at him said enthusiastically, "Yeah, *no* problem at all!"

Both Aunt Penny and I turned to look at Sage, curiously. What's that all about, I wondered. I could see she was staring at Rico, totally enthralled, her large eyes beaming luminously toward him.

"Well, I guess it'd be ok if you wanted to wait around till my mom gets here," he said then turned and looked shyly at Sage. "I mean, you don't really need to, but that'd be fine."

"Ok, we'll wait right here with you until she gets here, ok?" Aunt Penny said but she and I had somehow become instantly invisible to both of them.

We all sat down on the edge of small concrete wall next to the roadside. Sage and Rico chatted nonstop and Aunt Penny and I made small talk to pass the time. Thirty minutes later a car pulled up behind his truck and a woman jumped out, running towards us. "Rico! Mijo! Are you alright?" She ran up to him and grabbed him, looking him up and down before she turned angrily toward Aunt Penny.

"What did you *DO*?" she hurled at her.

Rico quickly interrupted, "Mom, nothing! It was *my* fault! I ran a stop sign and Penny...I mean, Mrs. Stevenson..." She put her hand up in front of his face. "Not another word, Rico! Shut UP!" She spun around to where we were standing. Then a dawning of realization washed across her face. "Penny? Penny *Stevenson*?"

"Uh, yes, I... I'm Penny Stevenson, um, do I know you?"

"Penny Stevenson, as in married to *Doug Stevenson*?"

"Yes, Doug's my husband. And *you* are?"

"Veronica Valdez. I knew Doug in high school," Veronica said, regarding Penny with a cool and calculated gaze.

"Oh! So it's you! Okay, wow, it's crazy to meet you like this!" Penny offered Veronica her hand, accompanied by a generous, but cautious smile. Was this the "other woman"?

Veronica hesitantly took her hand and gave it a limp squeeze, taken aback by Penny's friendliness, but curious as to why Doug would be talking about her. "Me? I mean, I wouldn't think he would've even remembered me after all these years."

"Oh, sure," Aunt Penny continued. "In fact, you came up way back when we were in Texas picking up Sage," she motioned over to where Sage, Rico and I were standing. Veronica's eyes tensed up, but she quickly covered her surprise when Penny turned back to her, jumping on the chance to change the subject. "Right, yes, um, I'm so sorry about your sister-in-law. That was real sad news around Lona."

"Yes, for all of us. But thank you for saying that. It's been a hard time. Sage, KC, come over here a minute, ok? This is Rico's mom, Mrs. Valdez. She knew your Uncle Doug from high school."

The three of us awkwardly came over to where the two women were standing and I could feel a weird vibe coming from Rico's mother. It was like she really wanted to leave, but something was keeping her rooted in her spot. And I couldn't shake the feeling that I had seen her before. Where? I wondered.

"Anyway," Aunt Penny continued, "your son is such a nice, respectful young man and there's no worry about this ol' truck's bumper, so don't even think on that, ok, Rico?"

Rico still looked as if his life was over that very moment, but when Sage said "yeah, it's hard to hurt something that sturdy, kinda wish it *was* damaged so Aunt Penny would finally go get a new one," they all laughed, well, all except me and Veronica. I loved Mama's truck and it instantly irritated me that Sage would so easily cast it off.

"Well, us girls have got to get going or we won't have time to shop for our birthday girl here, so, I guess we're gonna' head on out," she said. Rico immediately turned to Sage, asking "so it's your birthday?"

Sage turned back to me, saying, "No, it's my sister's birthday" and gave me a sweet smile. My momentary irritation gone, I could've hugged her right then but didn't want to embarrass her. He gave me a quick "well, happy birthday" then went to get in his truck. He twisted back around after opening the door and said "maybe we'll run into each other in town." But I knew that wasn't meant for me as I looked at Sage's happy face.

Veronica got into her car and, before driving off, gave us a slight wave, unsmiling as she drove off. Aunt Penny vigorously waved back and Sage and I did our own little version of a wave but it was a strange encounter, especially when I looked over at Aunt Penny's face, deep in thought.

Once we finally found the Coronado Mall, we spent the next couple of hours walking around the different stores, sometimes going in, mostly just browsing. Sage spied the Macy's and led us in like a drill sergeant, Aunt Penny pulling up the rear. We dutifully followed her around the huge department store since she seemed to know where everything was anyway. Finding nothing that interested her, we ended up on the second floor of the mall, right by the arts and crafts outlet so I picked out a few things I needed to get started on a watercolor painting

I'd been wanting to experiment with. Lunch was at a little New Mexican restaurant Mama always loved across from the mall and we left Albuquerque and headed home, full and happy.

"Everything ok, Aunt Penny? I asked as we made our way up onto the freeway.

"Oh sure, sure. No worries. Just a little tired, I guess. Haven't done that much shopping in years!"

But I could tell something was wrong, so I pressed on. "What were you and Rico's mom talking about Uncle Doug?"

"Nothing important. I was just curious how she knew me and she was just curious that I knew her, I guess."

"How do you know her?"

"I don't really *know*, know her, I just remember your uncle talking about some gal he knew in high school is all. What a small world, huh, to have run into her like this?"

"Excuse me? We ran into her son, first! Literally!" Sage laughed and we smiled. "And I, for one, am happy we did," she continued. "He's super cute, huh?"

There were so few times that Sage ever really smiled that I had to let it go and agree with her. It seemed to me that every guy Sage met was "super cute," just like Jude was "super cute" and the weatherman on Channel 7 was "super cute," so I just nodded my head, not saying anything.

"What," she eyed me, "you don't think so?"

"No, it's not that. Yeah, he's cute, I guess. But you think Jude's cute, too," I reminded her.

"Absolutely, ridiculously cute!"

I don't know why that bothered me so much but it did. Was everything always about Sage?

"Anyway, I'm going to find everything I can about Rico Baca when we get home!"

"Just be a little careful, Sage," Aunt Penny said. "I was trying to be nice when we were talking with her after the accident, but I'm not entirely certain your Uncle Doug would appreciate you snooping into all that."

"I don't care about *her*," Sage emphasized. "I'm just interested in *him*."

"But Aunt Penny, why wouldn't Uncle Doug want anyone to snoop into his past?" I questioned her.

"KC, you sure ask a lot of questions! Let's just let it go for now, girls, ok?"

I did let it go. For that day. But I was certain I was going to find out what I could about this questionable woman and how she knew my uncle.

18 BIG CHILL

Sage and Rico did run into each other the following week. We'd gone with Uncle Doug into town to help him fill some of the vending machines and as we were finishing up at the gas station on Dunbar Street, Sage jumped up, excitedly, waving "Hey, Rico! Over here!" as she saw him walking on the other side of the road by the barbershop. He smiled and waved back, looking for traffic as he loped across the road and came up to us.

"Hey," he said, the huge smile still spread across his face. "Whatcha' guys up to?"

"Not much, just helping out my uncle." Sage smiled back.

Invisible again, I asked, "So did you ever get your truck fixed?"

"Nah," he said, his eyes fixed on Sage's. "Found out it's got a little more damage than we first thought. Man, that ol' truck of yours sure did a number on it! My mom's making me earn the money to pay for the repairs. I'll be driving it like that for the next twenty years."

We all laughed. Then Sage said, "Well… maybe you could help us out. Uncle Doug is always needing someone to help him move his vending machines, so he could probably use someone big and strong, you know, for the lifting and stuff."

Rico blushed at this, but sounded enthusiastic "Sure! I mean, I could really use the extra cash. So, should I call him, or what?"

"No, I'll talk to him when he comes out. Or, if you aren't doing anything, why don't you just hang around here with us until he's finished and you can talk to him yourself?"

Uncle Doug came out of the station about ten minutes later, pushing a large empty dolly towards his truck when he noticed us all waiting there.

"Oh, there you girls are. Was wondering if you'd left me for a better deal over at the Tastee Freeze." Then, spying Rico, his face went pale and he stiffened, saying "ok, girls, let's get going now."

His gruffness wasn't lost on any of us and Sage spoke up first. "Wait, wait, Uncle Doug! This is Rico and...."

"I know who he is, Sage. Come on, let's go."

"But, wait! I told him you might be able to use some help with your machines and stuff so I asked him if he might want to help you out."

"Sage, I don't need any help. And I said let's go. Now."

"But...I don't understand! He's just looking...."

"Sage! This isn't any of your business. I said let's go. *NOW.*"

Sage and I both became silent as we saw Rico's confused face, not knowing what had just happened or what he'd possibly done to make Uncle Doug so mad.

As we got in the vehicle, Sage furiously slammed the door and turned accusingly toward Uncle Doug. "That was crappy! You don't even *know* him!"

"Mind your mouth, Sage, and I'm not going to tell you again. Mind your own business!"

"Well, he *is* my business! I like him and he likes me and we've met a couple times to just hang out and...." She could see Uncle Doug's stoic, angry face staring straight ahead as he drove out of the parking lot. I was surprised at Uncle Doug's reaction but even more surprised because I didn't know Sage had met with Rico at all. Not that she would tell me anyway, but I pretty much thought I knew her comings and goings so I felt a little cheated by not knowing this information. Regardless, the three of us didn't talk all the way home, and when we pulled into the driveway, Uncle Doug got out, slammed his door and went into the house, leaving Sage and I alone to go in.

"Ugh!" She simpered. "I don't know what's wrong with him! It's like he's mad or upset or something with Rico and he doesn't even *know* him!"

I had to agree but knew it was best to keep quiet when Sage started on a rant. Just then I remembered Aunt Penny's reaction to Rico's mom when we were in Albuquerque, and wondered if there was more to the story than either her or Uncle Doug were telling us.

"So," I said, changing the subject of Uncle Doug's rude brush-off as we kicked off our shoes and sat on our beds, "I didn't know you've been seeing Rico."

"Not actually like a date or anything, KC. Just hanging out. I was going to say something but you got all after me a while back when I was saying I thought Jude was cute so I didn't want to make you mad again. And big deal about that anyway. So I thought he was kinda cute. I could tell you were bugged when I mentioned we go see him on his ranch, am I right?"

She was right. I hadn't wanted her to go with me to see Jude when Miss M had asked me to dog-sit for an afternoon out at the ranch a couple of months ago. So I made up a story to both her and Aunt Penny that Tucker had to have a small lesion removed so was in a cone and was making a fiasco of everything he was around so she thought maybe I could come out and keep him and Salva occupied while she got some of her much-needed projects done. Technically, she had asked if both Sage and I might want to come out, but I told her Sage wasn't feeling well and couldn't make it so Aunt Penny had said it was fine for Jude to pick me up and take me out there one day when Sage was supposedly in town.

Now I know she was with Rico. It didn't really make me feel bad or anything, other than I just wished she would share that stuff with me. Like sisters do. Or are supposed, to anyway. When Jude had picked me up that afternoon, I found myself giddy with anticipation. After Mama died and things started to get back to a semi-normality, I didn't have much of a reason to go out to the ranch very often. We were all invited for a big Thanksgiving dinner last year, though, and Jude dropped off little gifts at Christmas that Miss M had crocheted for all of us, but, other than the occasional meeting at the grocery or post office in town, I hadn't seen him at all.

Not that it mattered to him, I was sure, because I was just another silly teenage girl in his eyes, even though I was almost sixteen. And there weren't any guys at school I was interested in. Well, ok, maybe that guy in Chemistry who sat in front of me and always made it a point to turn around and say hi whenever I'd sit down. He was okay, I guess.

But Jude was the one guy I always came back to. Was it because he was there when Mama died? I couldn't be sure. Sometimes that day seemed like it was years ago and sometimes it seemed like it was just yesterday. Whenever I'd think about him, it rarely included that horrible day, though, so that must be a good thing.

"A silly crush. He's not even remotely interested," I silently reminded myself as I listened to him chatter along the whole way out to the ranch. All I could offer was an occasional 'mmm' or "yes." And I don't even remember getting there, I was so happy sitting this close to him in his truck, for once without Tucker lodged in between us.

Once we got inside the kitchen he put his bags on the table and, turning to me, asked "All going ok with your sister and all?

"Um, yeah, it's ok. She's still not all that talkative with me or anything. But, yeah. Things are okay."

"Yeah, well, I get that. Sometimes, well, most times I don't much feel like talking, either."

I immediately felt a pang of sadness for him, knowing all he had been through in his life, so quickly changed the subject.

"How's Salva? I'll bet she's getting big."

"She's a small horse! Seriously, KC! How long's it been? You haven't been here in *forever*."

I felt a small thrill when he said that and smiled inwardly. Just then Miss M came bustling in. "Oh, KC! There you are! And haven't you grown up! Why, you're nearly as tall as me!" Which wasn't saying much. Miss M was maybe 5'3 at her full height. Sage is the one who inherited Mama's tall stature. Along with her beautiful blonde hair and big brown eyes. And, well, everything beautiful, it seemed to me.

"Wait till you see Salva! Come on, dear. She'll be so happy to see you!"

I didn't want to leave Jude but had no other choice as he had already finished putting his things away and was dialing someone on the phone. I reluctantly followed Miss M out to the barn and, as we came around the corner, I was immediately pounced upon. Good lord, Jude was right. Salva was HUGE. After a few minutes getting reacquainted, we went to find where Tucker had gotten off to and I pretty much had the rest of the afternoon tied up. I'd occasionally look around to see if Jude was anywhere close, but it was just me, the dogs and the rest of ranch.

When it was time to go home, Miss M came out and said she'd be taking me home whenever I was ready. I felt instantly deflated as I'd been anticipating the ride back home with Jude. But Miss M was the kindest person I knew next to Mama and Aunt Penny so my nose getting slightly out of joint lasted only for a few seconds or so and we headed home. I almost asked her where Jude was, but figured one, it wasn't any of my business, and two, she'd see right through me and then I'd for sure die of embarrassment because I knew she'd mention it to him.

Once she dropped me off, I trudged off to my room, not paying any attention to anyone, just wanting to be alone. Sage was already there and could see I was bugged about something as I flopped down on the bed.

"You ok?"

"FINE," I said a little too sharply. Sure, I thought to myself, it was all fine and good and she was seeing Rico and all, but what about me? I knew Jude was too old for me but there was just something more about him I wanted to know. I lay there feeling sorry for myself.

"Well, *fine* right back to you," Sage retorted. "I'm going to get dinner anyway.'

I felt my stomach grumble so really had no choice but to lick my imagined wounds and head down the hall to the kitchen behind Sage. Uncle Doug was already sitting at the table and Aunt Penny was just finishing ladling out her homemade chicken tortilla soup. New Mexican cooking had opened all sorts of culinary doors to her and her limited cooking skills. She was having a ball trying out all the new recipes and since August was green chile harvest time, one of the gals down at Markie's had shown her how to roast them on a charcoal grill, then put in Ziplock bags and freeze. We've had something with green chile in it every night for the past two weeks, it seemed. But none of us were complaining, it was all that good.

"Any word on the new machine going in at the gas station?" Aunt Penny asked Uncle Doug.

"Gonna take it over next week. Maybe the girls can help me out?" Sage stabbed a glare at him and I was silent. After how he'd acted at the gas station over Rico, we were both still angry but it was clearly lost on him. He looked back and forth at both of us and just said, indifferently, "Or not, up to you girls."

I was quiet the rest of dinner, sipping on my soup and only half-way listening to Aunt Penny and Uncle Doug's conversation. After a while, Sage got up, rinsed off her bowl then put it in the dishwasher.

"You up for a movie?" I asked, hoping to take my mind off Jude.

"No, I think I'm going to go for a walk. Need to get away from you-know-who for a while. Wanna come?"

"Sure," I said, quickly rinsing my own dishes then catching up to her as we headed out the door. Maybe now I could tell her how I really felt about Jude. I tried to reason with myself that, surely, she'd realize I'm a really *old* almost-sixteen-year-old and that even though Jude is older than me, it didn't matter, right? And, well, I don't know what I was thinking. What actually *was* I thinking? Mama used to always say I was older than my years, so what did that make me? Seventeen? Eighteen? Old enough for Jude to be interested in me? Too young for him to even give me a second look? My thoughts flitted back and forth as we walked down the driveway and out to the road. Maybe she'll give me some advice, I hoped, thinking how I could start the conversation. We made our way south and soon found ourselves headed toward the old bridge.

"So," I began, "I was wondering what you thought about…"

"I'm so fricking *mad* at him, KC," she interrupted, suddenly turning towards me, not even hearing what I'd said. "It's like he won't even give Rico a chance."

"I know," I agreed, any hope of a Jude conversation dashed. Even though I was the one who's always been wanting Sage to connect with me, I had to sit back on my feelings yet again and allow her to continue.

"It just so *unfair*! I wonder if Aunt Penny knows anything? I mean, surely, she can see how Uncle Doug gets all weird about all this. I'm just going to ask her tomorrow when he's gone."

We sat down on the edge of the first plank, letting our legs dangle over the churning water. We didn't talk, just watched the water churn by and, for a fleeting moment, I could almost hear Mama's voice telling me to get back home. But Sage was quiet so I took the chance and began again.

"So, Sage, what do you think of Jude? I mean, of me and Jude? Well, I mean, do you think he's too..."

"KC! LOOK!" she shouted suddenly, jumping up and running toward the center of the bridge, pointing excitedly down into the water.

"What?! What is it?" I too jumped up and ran over to where she was, searching the water for whatever she'd seen.

"I don't know! I think it's a dog, or some kind of animal! Hurry, KC! We've got to help it!" She turned and ran to the other side of the bridge, yelling "I can't see it now! It must have floated away! Oh, God, I hope it's not going to go all the way down to that big pipe!"

"I don't see anything," I said, my eyes hunting back and forth for anything that looked even remotely like an animal. "Sage, are you *sure* you saw something?"

"KC! I *know* I saw something! We've got to help it get out!" She ran the short distance to the other side of the road that crossed the culvert pipe and started making her way down the edge of the slippery grass that lined the bank of the ditch.

"Sage, be careful!" I yelled to her, following her as best I could, stumbling and grabbing at whatever I could to keep myself from falling into the water.

Sage was already down at the edge of the water, holding tightly onto a thin clump of willows, stretched as far out over the water as she could, peering back into the dark culvert. "I can't see it! KC! What should we do?" and, just as she looked up at me, she lost her grip and fell headfirst into the water.

"Sage!" I screamed as she went in, trying to reach her. She quickly surfaced, thrashing and flailing as the strong current was dragging her away.

"Help! Help me, KC!"

I clawed my way up the bank and ran down the bank so I could get in front of her. I had to run down the bank about thirty yards before I spied a small outcropping of rocks down at the edge of the water so I stumbled down the bank's edge and positioned myself on the edge of the biggest one, just as Sage came towards me.

"Grab my hand, Sage! Grab it!" Our outstretched hands connected just in time and I pulled her towards the rocks, using them as a shield against the fast current. I could feel the impact of her body hitting the rock and she screamed out in pain.

"Oh my God! Sage, Sage! Hold on!"

She screamed again as I wrestled her against the current, pulling her halfway out of the water and lodging her between two large rocks.

"KC! I think I broke my leg!"

"What? Hold, on, Sage. Just hold on a minute, ok? Don't move! I need to get us back up to the top."

I pulled her arm around my shoulder and dragged her up the slippery bank, her wincing in pain with each step, her left leg dangling at a dangerous angle. Once we reached the top, we threw ourselves down onto the ground, gasping for air.

"Sage! Oh God! Ok, stay right here, I've got to go get Aunt Penny! Are you ok if I leave you here?" I searched her stricken face.

"Yes, but, KC! What do you think happened to that little animal? I mean, I don't want it to drown!"

"Sage, *forget* the animal!" I yelled at her, then, seeing her stricken look, I softened. "It's gone, but I'm sure it'll get out when it gets a chance, ok?"

"Are you sure? I mean, well, ok, ok, I'm sure you're right," she said, biting her lip and I could see the pain etched across her face.

"Don't move!" I yelled back to her as I took off running for the house. Minutes later, Aunt Penny, Uncle Doug and I hurriedly made our way back to where Sage was sitting on the bank.

"Oh, Sage, honey! What happened?" Aunt Penny ran over and sat beside her. She barely touched Sage's swollen ankle as Sage winced in pain.

"Well, that's not good." Uncle Doug said gruffly. "What the hell happened?"

I immediately said "We thought we saw something in the water and when we tried to find it, Sage slipped and fell in."

"We're going to have to get you to the doctor, honey," Aunt Penny said. "Doug, will you run back and bring the truck? I think it'll have to be the emergency room, this late."

An hour later, while Aunt Penny and Sage were in the exam room, Uncle Doug and I sat in the waiting room, not speaking. I was worried about Sage and, frankly, I didn't really even *want* to talk to him, especially not after how he'd treated Sage over Rico. When they finally came out about, Sage was steadying herself on a pair of crutches, clumsily shuffling along, her left leg in a cast up to her knee.

"What? Oh, Sage!"

"It's ok," Aunt Penny said. "It's a pretty bad break, though."

"Can I help?" Uncle Doug offered, getting up and moving toward them.

"No!" Sage seethed at him and he stopped, looking sheepishly at Aunt Penny. "I've got this, Doug, thanks" she shot him a pleading look. Sage ignored him as they limped by and out the door to the parking lot.

I went over to help, but Sage determinedly moved past me, too. I was unsure what to say.

Tentatively, I said, "It'll be ok, whatever it is, Sage. I'm sure of it."

"Oh, what do YOU know?" she whipped around, pointing her anger directly at me.

"I... I was... I'm just trying to help." I was stunned and hurt by her response.

Aunt Penny stopped, holding Sage on one side and reaching for my arm. "It's ok, KC. She's just hurting and upset right now. Plus, it wasn't exactly great news from the doctor." Then, to Sage, "And, Sage, *enough.* You two've gotten too far to backtrack now, so please don't act like this."

"But TWO MONTHS ON CRUTCHES?" she wailed. She stopped, then turned back to me. "I'm sorry, KC. I'm being such a bitch. I'm just so *mad.* At EVERYTHING! Will you get me my phone? I want to call Rico." She cast a withering look in Uncle Doug's direction.

"It's okay," I assured her, "I'd feel the same, too." I also cast a meaningful look his way and went to find her phone.

Because of the severity of the injury to her leg when Sage crashed into the boulder, not only could she not place any weight on it, the x-rays showed a possible ankle joint injury which might require surgery. The doctor wanted to wait until the swelling had gone down and then schedule her to go to Albuquerque for an MRI the following day, which, of course only added to her frustration. By the time we got her home and situated, Sage was in a dark mood. It wasn't helping that Aunt Penny, trying to make her comfortable, fretted off and on the rest of the evening. Honey, don't sit there, Sage, honey, don't lean that way. Sage, you'll fall over if you don't sit up. She hovered until Sage, huddled into the recliner with Mama's old denim quilt tucked around her, just rolled her dark eyes at me and mouthed "shit."

Surgery wasn't necessary after all, but, nonetheless, the rest of that winter was a dizzying maze of doctor's appointments and physical therapy for Sage. It was her senior year of high school, and where most of her classmates were busy with senior activities, finals, prom, and graduation – she was content to not be "part of the scene" anyway, so this setback with her leg was just another blip on her irritation radar.

Probably the only bright spot during that entire time was me getting my driver's permit. Now that I was old enough to drive, Aunt Penny occasionally let me drive The Beast around, but she insisted on taking Sage to and from her physical therapy appointments in town.

Long days turned into even longer weeks, and by the beginning of March, Sage was able to move around on her own, so one chilly afternoon we begged Aunt Penny to let us go into town. Rico and Sage were a thing now and he had stood by her side throughout both the physical and emotional struggles. But this particular afternoon, I just wanted to spend time with Sage alone, so was surprised when she agreed. Aunt Penny had let me drive Mama's old truck back and forth to see Jude and Miss M several times so I simply convinced her it wouldn't be a problem driving into town.

"Well, ok," she said, standing on the porch and anxiously looking up at the heavy gray clouds. "Just be super careful, KC. It looks like a storm might be coming in."

We stopped first at the Tastee Freeze, even though there was hardly anyone there because it was still pretty cold outside and I guess no one was yet in the mood for ice cream. We drove around town for a while, getting bored, and were heading back home when I suddenly pulled over to the side of the road.

"I have an idea!" I declared, putting the truck in reverse, pulled a U-turn, and headed back towards town.

"What?" Sage eyed me suspiciously.

"Just wait, you'll see." I had a plan.

It wasn't really a cave, but I liked to think it was. My friend Connie and I found it way back when we were in sixth grade and thought we had found a secret treasure. It wasn't much more than a huge dug-out hole back behind the abandoned Simpson's Junkyard on Elm Street, left over from what was probably some type of in-ground storage or something. It was covered up with a couple sheets of plywood, and we spent many fun afternoons just hanging out there, just the two of us, talking about mean girls and cute boys. The last time I had visited it was a few years ago, and even though I was older by that time, I still remembered how much fun we'd had back then. Thinking that maybe I could recapture that feeling again, and even though I felt a little absurd, I had gone ahead and cleaned it out a little, sweeping up the dirt floor and brushing away the cobwebs. It wasn't the same, of course, being there by myself, so I eventually just stopped going altogether.

But right now, I felt an immediate, inexplicable urge to show it to Sage.

I pulled into the bumpy lot, parking the truck and quickly hurried around to the passenger side to help Sage out. She struggled with her crutches for a few seconds then unceremoniously threw them into the back with a huff. "I think I'm about done with these."

"Are you sure? I mean, I can help if you want me to."

"No, really. I'm getting along ok without them. I'll be fine. I actually haven't used them much these past few weeks anyway," she said, her eyes scanning the abandoned lot. "So, what the heck is this place?"

I had tried to imagine what Sage would think of it. Would she think it was as cool as I did? Could we make this something we could both share? I wanted so desperately to have some kind, any kind, of connection with her and, despite Aunt Penny's endless attempts to paste us together, I felt I would always be the naïve little outsider sister in her mind.

But just as we had made our way about halfway across the lot, I stopped abruptly. *What was I thinking?* Suddenly seeing this whole thing through Sage's eyes, I instantly realized how ridiculously childish she was going to think this was. Panicked, I quickly turned around and held my arms out to stop her.

"Wait," I said, seeing her surprised face at my hasty turnabout. "Hey, Sage, you know, I was just thinking... this probably isn't such a good idea after all."

"What do you mean?" she eyed me curiously then strained to see into the lot behind me.

"I...um...well, I mean, with your leg and all...I...look, let's just do this another time, ok?" I desperately wanted to leave, wondering to myself how I could've so foolishly thought showing her my old childhood fort was an even remotely sane idea.

"KC, my leg is fine! I can walk on it perfectly well now! No, I want to see what you wanted to show me," she started to push past me.

"Sage, *seriously*," I pleaded, reaching for her arm, but she was already ambling past me.

I caught up to her and lightly touched her shoulder.

"Sage," I said quietly. She stopped and turned, watching me carefully.

"What's wrong, KC?"

"Well, it's just that..." I stammered, forlornly looking toward the weathered swaying plywood pieces covering the fort then back to her. "I mean, nothing's *wrong*, it's just that, well, it's just this old place, it's kind of like a cave, really, where I used to hang out with my friend when we were younger and we, well, we thought it was so cool back then and it was so secret and we spent all our free time here and I was just thinking it'd be cool for you and me and then, I mean, and now, well, we're so much older, and, well, I know you'll just think it's silly, and...well..." I knew I was babbling but I was already committed. "I guess, I mean, I just thought...." I trailed off helplessly.

"Thought what? Really, KC, geez, give me some credit! Do you think I ever had cool stuff when I was growing up? Think again, believe me. I. Had. Zero. Fun. The closest I ever got to anything exciting was going with Grandpa to the horse races. Grandma would've killed him if she knew he took me. And besides, so what if we are a little older now. At least let me see it first, ok? And maybe let *me* decide if I think it's silly?"

Resigned, I plodded dejectedly ahead into the vacant lot and over to the dilapidated fort, Sage hobbling along behind. She eyed the plywood suspiciously as I reached down and took hold of the edge of one of the larger pieces, pulling it up and over. Sage stepped closer to the edge and cautiously peered down into the hole.

"What *is* this place?" she frowned back at me, immediately hesitant and suspicious.

I knew it. I just *knew* it. God, what I wouldn't give to restart this day. It was all I could do to not let that cruddy piece of plywood fall back over the hole and just march back to the truck and leave. But now that we were here, I didn't have much choice but to go ahead and let her see.

"Well, ok, and don't freak out or anything, but we have to climb down in it first and then you'll see what I mean."

153

"Down inside *there*?" she said incredulously. "I'm not going down there, KC!"

"Good!" I said with relief, turning around and starting back toward the truck. "So, let's just get going and we can..." I turned back. Sage hadn't moved.

"But," she said, still eyeing the hole. "Maybe I could just watch *you* go down," she suggested, clearly not what I was hoping she'd say.

"I mean it, Sage, let's not even do this. I am seriously *fine* if we just leave right now."

She was watching me intently. "KC, what's *wrong* with you? First, you were all excited to show me this place and now you're trying to high-tail it out of here. Are you worried about my leg? Because don't. What's really going on?"

I was miserable, but realized just then that now maybe she wasn't thinking it was as totally awful as I first thought. "Ok," I ventured. "But whatever you do, please, *please* don't make fun of me, ok?"

"Promise," she said, still looking down at the opening.

"Ok, just hold on a minute while I go down. I need to check it out first then I'll come back up and help you get down," I said, switching on the small flashlight I had brought with me from the truck.

The hole was about fifteen feet in diameter and about ten feet deep with an old, but sturdy wooden ladder attached to the small rocky ledge leading down one side. I turned backwards and started to make my way down, the flashlight held tightly in my armpit. On the last step, I jumped the rest of the way down and landed with a soft thud.

"See, nothing to it!" I called encouragingly up to Sage, but she was shaking her head, still staring into the semi-darkness below.

"KC, are you kidding me? What if there're spiders or snakes down there?"

I swung the flashlight in a big arc, showing that there was nothing but dirt.

"Come on, it's all good! I already cleaned it all out!" I climbed halfway back up the ladder to help her, "just come down and you'll see there's nothing bad down here." I stretched up my hand. "Here, I'll help you."

Hesitantly, and with me guiding each foot to the next step, she carefully picked her way down the short rocky wall and when she got to the bottom she turned and looked around.

"Wow, it really is kind of cool down here."

"Really? You think it's cool?" I was pleasantly surprised.

"No, goofball, I mean it's kinda *chilly* down here." She pulled her sweater closer about her shoulders.

"Well, sort of, I guess, but you get used to it."

I pulled a slim matchbook from my jeans pocket and started lighting the dust-caked candles that years ago I had tucked into the little niches that Connie and I had dug into the hard dirt walls.

"Ok, now don't get scared, but I need to pull the top back over us." I reached up, just as I saw the first few flakes of snow starting to lightly drift down.

"Dang it, Sage. It's starting to snow."

"So?"

"So, we should probably head back, don't you think?"

"Why? Are you afraid to drive in the snow?"

"No, not at all. But I'm sure Aunt Penny is having a fit right now, thinking of me driving in this weather."

"Just a little longer, KC. I'm actually kind of liking this place."

"Ok, then, but I still need to pull the top over us then, ok?" I immediately reassured her, "Not all the way. I promise, but if I don't, you can't really see the candles or get the full effect," I explained to her, already clumsily sliding the heavy plywood over the opening, leaving just a small area exposed where the snow came fluttering inside.

She didn't say another word. There, in the darkness with just the gentle twinkling of the candles, and the light snowflakes floating down then wisping out as they landed on the soft ground, something magical happened for both of us. Sage looked around, fascinated, as the candlelight softly flickered off the uneven walls.

"Wow!"

I didn't say anything, just let her enjoy it, my earlier fears forgotten as I watched the change in Sage.

As her eyes adjusted to the candlelight, she began to move around the small area.

What's this?" she said, lifting a small object from one of the cubbyholes in the wall and examining it.

"Oh, that's just an old pottery vase that Connie made. She must've left it here a long time ago. Sage, I know this is maybe on the kid side of things, but I've just always thought it was a neat place, kind of like a secret place no one knows about that's all mine, ya know? I mean, yeah, it's probably silly and all to think that way, but it just makes me, I don't know, feel *happy* to be down here, you know? Away from everybody and everything. Especially after Mama...I mean, well...."

Sage quickly changed the subject. "Does Connie ever come down here anymore?"

"No," I laughed, glad for the diversion. "Her family moved to Illinois years ago so I'm sure she doesn't!"

She turned around, sweeping her arms in a wide arc, and for just a moment, I could see a younger, happier Sage, her face radiant, a girl I know she could have been in a different world.

"I like it, KC. I mean, yeah," she said as her eyes swept the semi-darkness, "we're probably a little old to be hanging out in a fort, or whatever you call it I guess, but this is different. It's like, well, it's like just ours... no one else's... no grandma, no Connie, no one, just us. Just us sisters, KC. Just you and me."

I almost fell over. Sisters. And just like that, for the first time since she had come to Lona, Sage had finally found something that made her happy.

21 THE SNOW HOUSES

That following summer I turned seventeen and got a job at Markie's
Market working three days a week stocking merchandise. It didn't pay a
lot, but allowed me to save up a little in my meager college savings
account that right now consisted solely of my grandpa's life insurance
policy. I was hoping to go to the community college for a semester then
maybe transfer to the main campus in Albuquerque next year and Aunt
Penny and Uncle Doug promised to match whatever funds I could save
so I put every paycheck right into savings.

After graduation, Sage spent most of her time between Rico,
helping out around the house when she could, her leg completely healed
now. Uncle Doug had finally, though reluctantly, agreed to let both her
and Rico help him out with his business and, surprisingly, Sage was a
fairly happy worker. I'm guessing because her and Rico got to spend all
their time together now. But we made it a point to go to the "fort" at least
once a week and it became not so much a silly remembrance of
childhood fun, but more of a safe place, a place we could just hang out.
Well, for the most part, that is. Even though we had become much closer,
I would occasionally see something sad in her eyes. Every now and then
I'd catch her just staring at a candle, not saying anything.

"You ok?" I would ask. And she would always just smile her sad
smile, nod and keep staring.

We found we could easily dig out a few more small niches in the
sides, each long and tall enough to hold a candle, so there was always
enough light down there. The roof was so old and the wood rotted and
cracked that there was actually enough light without the candles but they
just made it look more interesting.

"Hey, Sage," I asked her hesitantly one lazy afternoon when we were sitting on a couple of pillows we'd saved from Aunt Penny's Goodwill pile, neither of us saying much. "Have you ever wanted to bring Rico down here?"

Surprised, she answered "Rico? Of course not! Why would you even think that?"

"I don't know, it's just that, well, you two are getting so close and all and I just thought..."

"Well, you thought wrong. This is kind of *our* secret place, remember?"

"Well, yeah, I get that. I was just wondering, you know?"

"Well, stop wondering. I like things just the way they are, got it?"

And I was fine with that. Once I understood how much Sage had undoubtedly missed out on growing up around Grandma Mina, it was easy to see why she was so at peace with our little hideaway. It was as if she could be a kid again in a way. And Aunt Penny never once questioned where we went, giving us a lot of freedom to come and go. I think she was just mostly happy that we were finally getting along so she didn't want to rock the boat.

"Ladies," she said one day while we were finishing up breakfast. "I have a proposition for you."

Immediately suspicious, Sage said "What kind of proposition?"

"Well, I know you're both busy with all you've got planned for this summer, but I was wondering if maybe you two might be interested in helping Mrs. Chavez up the road clean her house once in a while?" Doris and Alvaro Chavez lived about three houses up from ours. I vaguely remembered her from when I was young but couldn't quite place why. Something about bats, maybe? Aunt Penny had met both of them one day while she was at Markie's grocery as they were struggling to get his wheelchair off the back of their car and ended up offering to get their weekly groceries for them. Mr. Chavez had had a stroke and was relegated to a wheelchair and it was all Mrs. Chavez could do to take care of him. She told Aunt Penny she could either pay to have that nurse lady from town come in and help once a day, or pay to have someone clean her house, but not both. The nurse won out, so, when Aunt Penny approached Sage and I we were both interested in this novel idea.

"So, what will we actually be doing?" I asked, not sure what was the right way to bring it up. I was trying to figure out how I'd do whatever was needed yet still keep my job.

"And how much is she going to pay us?" Sage. Always direct.

"Well, I think just helping with housework, and we didn't exactly talk about money," Aunt Penny ventured, "but I'm going to assume she'll do something. I'm thinking how about you two just go over there, help her clean up and then see what she does. If she doesn't pay you anything, don't worry. Just come back home and then the next time she calls I'll mention to her that you girls will probably need some compensation for helping her out. What do you think?"

Sage tried to look disinterested but it wasn't working because when she looked at me, she could tell we were both thinking the same thing. "Hell, yeah" she mouthed to me, just out of Aunt Penny's line of sight.

That seemed fair to both of us so we nodded our heads in agreement and headed out the door.

"Remember, though, she's old, doesn't hear very well, and she may have trouble telling you what she needs done, ok?"

Sage and I walked down the road to the Chavez's house, me doing most of the talking as more and more memories came back, mostly about how when I was a kid, we all heard the story that Mrs. Chavez kept bats in their garage as pets and she cooked them in a stew that she took down to the veteran's home. I told Sage all this as we walked along and by the time we got to their house, we had built up such a fascinating story in our minds that we were both a little scared to ring the doorbell.

But we were both wrong because, when we walked up the steps, the front door flew open and Mrs. Chavez came out with a big smile and outstretched arms, folding us into her big bosom as if we were her long-lost children.

"Oh, girls! Just look at you, all grown up!" she exclaimed, holding us out at arm's length, looking us up and down.

"I can certainly see your mom in you," she said kindly to Sage.

"And from what I hear of you, young lady" she said, turning to me, "you and your mother were like two peas in a pod. Girls, I cannot tell you two how very sad we were to hear of her passing. It seems like just yesterday she was dropping off my dry cleaning for me."

Sage and I both winced. We rarely spoke of Mama, and hearing her name brought up fresh pain, even after all this time. Not looking at Sage, I just nodded and mumbled an incoherent "thank you."

"I'm sorry," she said quickly, seeing the look on our faces. "Let's just go in and take a look around, shall we?"

Coming into her small living room was like walking back into time. I remembered playing in this room when I was little and, as I looked around, I remembered how Mrs. Chavez used to take care of me when Mama had to work. And now, as I looked around at the walls, I remembered how all of them were covered with shelves holding the most unusual collection of every kind of glass snow globe you could think of. Giant ones, tiny ones, ones with cats inside. Others with castles. I was fascinated then and I was fascinated still. The afternoon sun glinted off each round orb like starlight so the entire room simply shimmered with light. Sage and I stood there looking around, mesmerized.

"I know it looks all pretty and shiny right now," Mrs. Chavez smiled, watching our reaction. "That's because I spent all day yesterday dusting these off since I knew you two were coming by."

"Wow," I said, "I don't remember there being so many!"

"Over a hundred now," she said, proudly. "I've been collecting them since I was little. They're all like my little babies. I collect lots of stuff, not just these and I can tell you, there's only one time I can remember ever breaking anything so you can see they're all pretty special to me." I cringed when she said this, a vague memory of glass shattering jumping into my mind, but all she did was wink at me, all but forgetting what happened when I dropped that frog orb all those years ago.

Sage ventured, "Um, I guess we're not sure how you want us to help?"

"Well, believe me, I know how busy all of you young people are these days, but I really need someone to help out with the heavy stuff, maybe once a week, if you're ok with that. Mrs. Pino down the road --- do you remember her? Anyway, she still insists on helping out with groceries and such. I just do not know where that woman gets her energy, that's for sure, because I sure don't have the get up and go I used to. It seems everything aches anymore and … gosh, I'm going on and on, aren't I? Anyway, just dust and vacuum and mop the kitchen floor. I can do pretty much everything else. Do you girls think you might want to help me?"

"Sure!" we both nodded enthusiastically, any thoughts of bats or stew completely gone now.

"Ok, then, I guess I'll see both of you Friday afternoon about one?"

Fridays became our favorite day of the summer. That was because not only did we get out of our routine for a while, at the end of each afternoon spent cleaning, instead of cash Mrs. Chavez would give us each some little knick-knack to take home. She clearly collected more than just the snow globes, so sometimes it would be a random ceramic animal, others a little glass vase; it changed each time and we looked forward to the end of each day of helping her. Silly as it seemed and even though we could've used the money, Sage and I both decided this was way more fun.

We made a pact that whatever she'd given us went straight into the fort so it wasn't long before the walls were chock full of all the knick-knacks we had crammed in next to the candles.

One particular Friday several weeks later when we had just finished cleaning up the kitchen area and were getting ready to head home, Mrs. Chavez walked in, a thoughtful look on her face.

"Girls, I've got something very special to show you," she said, hands behind her back as we looked at her then to each other, questioningly.

"One for you," she handed a round glass orb to Sage.

"And one for you," she smiled, handing me an almost identical one.

"How pretty!" Sage exclaimed as she turned the glass orb upside down, shaking it, then right side up again, as the tiny snowflakes inside fluttered all around, finally settling down over a miniature Ferris wheel with tiny people lined up to get on.

I did the same, and as the snow settled in mine, I saw a beautiful cathedral with tiny pine trees lining its path emerge in the orb.

"This is beautiful!" I exclaimed, as Sage, too, nodded in awed agreement.

"Well, girls, these two are very special to me," Mrs. Chavez said solemnly. "They were my mother's and she used to call them her snow houses. After she was gone, I started collecting them myself, and, well, you can see where that's gotten me," she smiled wistfully across the room at her vast collection.

"Why do you call them snow houses?" I asked.

"Well," she said as she walked over to a bookshelf and pulled out a small, tattered book, holding it out for us to see. "I loved this book when I was young, it's called The Little Eskimo. Mother read a lot to me, but this was my favorite, I guess, mostly because we lived here in New Mexico where it's warm and she lived up there with all the snow and the igloos, and such, and well, I just loved it. I wanted to be an Eskimo when I was little, it was all so enchanting to me, that life...the snow, everything. We read this book so many times I think I had each page memorized!"

"I remember that book from when I was little, too." I said. "But I thought it was a little boy Eskimo?"

"I'm talking about the book that was out when *I* was little, and believe me, that was a long time ago," she smiled. "I don't think that one ever really said if it was a boy or a girl, just a little Eskimo. Anyway, even if it did, I always just believed it was me."

She looked at us then quickly put the book away. "Gosh, I'm rambling, girls... sorry about that. Anyway, so to answer your question, KC, in the Inuit Indian culture, an igloo is also known as a snow cave, or a snow house, really just a shelter made out of blocks of snow. It's simply amazing to me how someone can take something so light and fragile as snow and then build it into something so strong and protective, you know? Anyway, I guess Mother just liked 'snow house' better than 'snow cave', so that's the name that stuck. But I really think she started calling them snow houses because of me and the book. Even now, whenever I look at these," her arm swept the room, "I still often pretend I'm there, right in the middle of each snow house, getting ready to ride the Ferris wheel, or go into the church, or hug Santa as he makes his way through the forest to deliver his big bag of toys. She only had three of them back then and every once in a while, she would let me hold one as long as I was really careful because they're so delicate. I just loved them. I always have."

Mrs. Chavez sat down on the sofa, dabbing at the corner of her eye with the edge of her flowered apron. Sage and I looked silently at each other then back to her, not knowing what to do or say.

She softly blew her nose and continued, "One day when I was little, I picked up her Christmas Snow House. It was the oldest of the three and a little bigger. It slipped from my hands and crashed to the floor, shattering into a million tiny pieces. I was very young, you see, and so afraid that Mother would be angry or upset that I didn't know what to do. I knew I wasn't supposed to pick it up unless she was around so I just stood there staring at the floor, the water starting to seep towards our big rug. All those tiny little snowflakes. I was sure they were going to melt as I fell to my knees and started bawling. Mother came running in just then, her eyes quickly taking in the scene and me standing there, crying like a baby, and, in one quick movement, just came right over to me, scooped me up and hugged me tight. I didn't know what to do! I was so sure she was going to be angry. But she wasn't. So I just hugged her tighter, too."

'She didn't say anything at all. Just kept holding me. Then, when I had the courage to look at her face, I could see those big tears rolling down her cheeks."

'Mother, I'm so sorry!" I wailed, "I was just looking at it and, and, it, it just fell and it's all broken now, and I'm so sorry!"

'Then Mother bent over and picked up the little Santa figurine that used to be inside the Christmas Snow House, turning it around as if examining it for cracks. "Honey, it's ok." She sniffled. "It's okay honey."

'We cleaned up the mess together, and, after that, not another word was said about it. She didn't worry so much anymore about me picking the other two up, although I rarely did. Mother died years ago, but I later learned from my father that that Christmas Snow House was her favorite and was the first one her own mother had ever given her, the same year she died."

Sage was solemn, as was I, not sure what to say to Mrs. Chavez as she reminisced.

I hesitantly offered mine back to her, saying "They're so beautiful. Thank you for sharing them with us." "No!" she held her hand up, "They're for you to keep. I've had these two on my dresser for many, many years but I think they'll be in a happier place now with you girls."

'You know, I never did get over breaking her most precious one, but I eventually realized, years later, that the other two were just as important, if not more important, because they were all I had left to remember my mother."

"Kind of like me and KC," Sage said quietly.

I hadn't ever said anything to Sage about that day Mama died and she had never asked. It was almost like if we didn't talk about it, there would be no room for the hurt to find its way into the already-small space between us. Sometimes I don't even know how I feel, it's still so unreal to me. I know Sage felt a deep sadness for losing the one chance she had to get back with Mama and I didn't want to constantly reminisce about how wonderful my life with Mama was because I didn't want to hurt her feelings. Neither of us wanted to break this fragile bond we had forged. I don't even allow myself to think about it much, either. Because when, on those very few times I do relive that horrible day, I just get sad all over again.

The day started out with perfect weather and Mama and I were both in high spirits, each in our own ways, of course, anticipating going to get Sage.

Once Mama had everything set in the truck, we headed down the road. When I realized I had forgotten the photo album I'd made for Sage, I begged her to turn back so I could get it.

I remember running into the house to get the album. Just as I reached for it on my nightstand, I heard a loud bang, well, louder than a bang, I guess, more like a sharp blast. It didn't occur to me that it was a gunshot until I relived it later, telling what I could remember to the police officer at the station.

But I remember it startled me, so, grabbing the album, I ran back to the front of the house and across the porch. I couldn't see Mama right away so looked around. Out of the corner of my eye I remember seeing something moving behind the old cottonwood tree in the empty lot next to our house, not sure what it even was. I thought for a split second it was a huge black dog or something, but then when I looked again, nothing was there.

Coming around the front of the truck, I saw Mama laying on the dirt gravel of our driveway, her arms and legs splayed awkwardly, her face up, eyes open. I quickly ran over to her, kneeling beside her, just as I saw the blood spurting from her chest.

I remember screaming and screaming, "Mama! Mama!" then looking around wildly again to see who was there. It was eerily quiet but even then, I just *felt* like someone was watching us.

Sobbing, I propped up her body as best I could almost to a sitting position, putting my hand over the hole in her chest, trying to stop the bleeding, but it just kept coming.

If it hadn't been for the loud hum of a vehicle coming down the road, I probably would've passed out right there and then as I held Mama's head in my lap, crying and moaning and rocking her limp body back and forth as her blood soaked through my hands and onto my jeans and t-shirt.

Hearing the truck's engine, I gently laid Mama down, jumped up, and ran down the driveway, wildly waving my arms to draw the driver's attention. I remember running into the middle of the road and him stopping his truck right in front of me and jumping out.

I remember us both running back up to Mama.

I remember screaming.

"Sage, get up!" Aunt Penny knocked on our bedroom door. "We need to be to your doctor's office by 8:30!" Sage's leg was completely healed and today was her last physical therapy appointment. Aunt Penny felt it would be better if just she and Sage went, but Sage asked if I could drive her instead.

"I guess so," she said hesitantly. "Just be careful, ok?"

"I'm always careful! Don't worry about us, we'll be fine," I said, but I was slightly surprised that Sage had asked me to go. Although we had become much closer, I still never felt like we were completely in unison with each other. Even the times when I thought we were surely making a breakthrough; something would always cloud over her and she'd withdraw back into one of her moods. But I took what I could, however small the steps.

"Do you like driving the truck?" she asked as we drove along the highway into town.

"It's ok, I guess, it's transportation. Why?" I asked her, curious.

"Oh, I don't know, it just seems so old and creaky. I can't wait until I can start driving again, too. It's totally unfair that you're younger than me and having to drive me all over the place."

"You'd be driving me around right now if it weren't for your leg." I reminded her.

"And I hope it won't be this rattletrap! I'm still surprised Aunt Penny held on to it and didn't just sell it." She paused when she saw the hurt look in my eyes. Mama's truck was like a warm security blanket for me; I would never part with it.

170

"I'm sorry, KC. I wasn't thinking. I was just trying to...." She trailed off.

"Nothing to worry about," I reassured her and she smiled gratefully back at me.

The small clinic where her appointment was housed day surgery, outpatient services, physical therapy and a pharmacy, so I wasn't surprised to see the full parking lot. Since we were running behind, I dropped Sage off and went to find a parking spot. As I circled around the lot with no luck, I realized I'd have to go to the back side of the building if I wanted to find one, so I maneuvered the truck around and drove down the narrow alley towards the rear of the building.

Just then a black car came around the corner of the building, nearly running head on into me. We both stopped as it was immediately clear neither of us was going to be able to get past each other. But since I had already traveled almost to the end of the building, I assumed the person behind the tinted windows would back up the few feet needed so I could get around. The car just sat there, so I rolled down my window and waved my hand just a little, thinking they'd realize they needed to back up. Still the car just sat there, engine running.

"Oh, for Pete's sake," I thought to myself, irritated. "*Really?*" I put the truck in reverse and, looking in my rear-view mirror, realized that yet another car had started down the alley behind me, blocking my way. They waited about five seconds before giving a short horn burst. I put my hands up in the air to show, hey, it wasn't me and I didn't have any control over the situation. Another honk. I finally got out, turning to the man in the car behind me and yelled out to him, "I can't get past the car in front of me, sorry."

He got out, red-faced, and marched past me and up to the car, angrily waving his arms in the air. As he got about five feet from the driver's side, the window rolled down and I could see a vaguely familiar-looking dark-haired woman, close to my age, reach out a bright-red nail-polished hand and flip him the bird. He clearly wasn't in the mood as he shouted to her "Move your damn car, lady or I'll move it for you!"

She rolled her window up, reversed her car and backed up. The guy huffed back past me, giving me a look like it was all my fault, slamming his hand on the side of the truck as he went by.

"Hey!" I yelled at him but he was already getting back into his car.

As I made my way into the rear parking area, I kept an eye out for the black car but didn't see it anywhere so assumed she must have gone out the other side of the building. I found a parking spot and waited there until Mr. Nice Guy had parked and left. Once the coast was clear, I got out, locked the truck and headed toward the front, where Sage was waiting for me, clearly irritated.

"Where *were* you?" she asked.

"Sorry, there was a little traffic jam in the alley. Are you done already?"

"Sarah says my doc got called out on an emergency so I had to reschedule."

"Well," I said, trying to alleviate Sage's obvious bad mood. "Then that means we have free time. I don't have to go in today, so what do you want to do?"

Her bad mood instantly forgotten, she smiled at me and I smiled back because we both knew what we were going to do as I drove towards our fort. By this time, we had made a small shelf out of bricks and old pieces of plywood we had found lying around the lot so we could have a place to keep Sage's portable CD player and her favorite CDs and also some of my books, but most importantly, we had constructed a little area with carved-out holes in the walls that held our two precious snow globes. Well, snow houses, now. Ever since we brought them down here, it seemed like snow houses just fit for some reason. I don't know why, but it was kind of like an unspoken shrine to Mama and, short of praying to them like one would to the Virgin Mary, which we, of course had never done, we kept that part secret, even to each other.

It seemed like Mama, in her own special way, was always with us. Me, well, because I'm the one that lived with her. I just *knew* Mama.

But Sage, Sage only had the wish of Mama.

Like the time she was holding her snow house and all of sudden it slipped from her hands. She grabbed for it as it fell, but, miraculously, it landed on the edge of her pillow and just rolled off into the soft dirt, completely fine. She reverently picked it up and held it close as we both exhaled in relief, watching the snow inside begin to float down and settle over the tiny Ferris Wheel.

"God! I can't believe I just dropped it! I think mother is watching over me, I swear, KC."

"Maybe she's watching over both of us," I said gently. "You know," I continued, watching as the last of the snowflakes had fallen inside the globe, "When I was little, Mama used to say something kinda cool about snow."

"What's that?" she said.

"Well, she said that you can't actually *hear* the snow fall, but that if you *could* it would sound like angel's wings fluttering or a puppy's tail wagging."

"Oh, gosh! I *love* that! I've never even thought about what snow falling would sound like," Sage said. "It would have to be something pretty special, knowing her, to say that. Well, what I *think* she would have said, anyway."

"She loved you, you know," I said quietly. "And she never, ever, stopped trying to bring you home."

"I know, and really, KC, I'm good. It's all good," she said, gently placing her globe back up in the niche.

We spent the next hour or so just hanging out. In the beginning we had been worried that the rain and snow would destroy anything we put down there. Even though the thick plywood cover, swayed with age and water, was just big enough to cover one section of the fort's opening, we knew we had to figure out a way to keep our things dry below. Once Sage suggested we tack a heavy tarp over the top, but all we could find was a big blue one in the shed by our house and neither of us wanted to call any attention to our little hideaway. So, I suggested why not just put it under the plywood, which we did. But, of course, we soon realized that wasn't the best of ideas, because the first time it rained, the tarp collected the water in a big pool. When we tried to pull the cover off, we knew the water was going to fall out of the tarp and ruin all our treasures below.

Sage went back to the truck and grabbed and old garden hose Aunt Penny left in the back.

"KC, find a knife or something I can cut this with!" she commanded.

I ran to the edge of the lot and looked around at the junk laying there, spying a piece of an old metal shingle and ran back with it.

"Will this work?" She looked at it doubtfully, but took it anyway and began sawing a five-foot piece of hose off the roll.

"What are you going to do with that?" I couldn't figure out what she had in mind.

"Just watch," she said as she knelt down and put one end of the hose into the pool of water. Then she bent over the other end of the hose and took a deep breath. I couldn't believe she was going to try and suck all that water out herself.

"Sage... I...." Just then she spit out a mouthful of water and quickly put the end of the hose on the ground. Miraculously, a small trickle, then a full stream, of water started flowing out the hose. It wasn't long before all the water was gone.

"Wow! Where'd you learn how to do that?" I was impressed.

"I saw Grandpa do it. One time the little electric pump that takes the water from the rain barrel out to the garden failed, so he just got a piece of hose and did this same thing. Easy peasy, nothing to it." But we knew we still had to solve the water dilemma before the next monsoon rains came.

"We could put the tarp on top, then cover everything with weeds and such so that no one will see it," I suggested.

"Too much work to do that every time," Sage reasoned. "I think we're gonna need a new roof."

Finding something large enough to cover our fort proved difficult. As we wandered around the junkyard, though, something caught my eye.

"Hey!" I yelled out excitedly to Sage, "come look at this!"

She ran over to where I was standing, looking down at what looked like an old metal road sign.

"Do you think this'll be big enough?" she asked eyeing it, not as convinced as me.

"Well, there's only one way to find out," I replied, reaching down to lift up one corner. "Help me lift this, ok?"

Sage went around to the other side, and, between the two of us, we were able to drag the heavy piece of metal over to our fort and slide it over the hole where it more than adequately covered the opening. Looking down, it was hard to read because it was so dirty, but you could just make out the faded words:

Fort Unity

5 Miles

Ahead

"Wow, well, I guess this will work just fine," Sage said. The sign's wording was perfect. A silent thought passed between us as we realized the old sign's relevance and we just smiled at each other.

After we got it somewhat in place and had settled back inside, I told Sage about my encounter with the cars in the alley at the clinic, both the girl and the man.

"It was weird, but the girl looked very familiar to me, I just can't place her." I said.

"What'd she look like?" Sage asked.

Long hair, dark, brown eyes, and…oh!" It suddenly occurred to me why she was so familiar. "You know, she actually reminds me a lot of Rico's mom!"

"Really? Hmmm, well, he does have a sister. I think her name's Renee, or Ronnie, or something like that. But she doesn't live with them. I think she lives over in Albuquerque with her dad. How weird that you ran into her here."

"Yeah, and it was almost like she knew me. I mean, why else wouldn't she have just backed up and let me pass? It was like she was challenging me to a car duel or something."

"Well, I haven't ever met her, I just know of her by what Rico tells me. He says she's a real pain in the ass but then what brother wouldn't say that, ha!"

"Or sister?" I said softly, only half-kidding.

"I've never *once* said you were a pain in the ass!"

"Well, maybe not in so many words…"

"Oh, geez, KC. Forget it, ok?"

"It's no big deal, it's just every now and then I get the sense you'd sometimes rather not be around me."

"I used to feel that way all the time, to be honest."

"Not anymore?"

"Nope. We're good. Seriously," she turned toward me, her face illuminated by the candles. "KC, I know I'm not the easiest person to be around," she said quietly. "And sometimes I don't even like myself. But you, gosh, *everyone* likes you. You're kind and funny and strong and, well, you're better at being a good person than I will *ever* be. And I don't know how I could've gotten through all this crap with my leg if you hadn't been around to help me. So, there."

Wow, I thought to myself. I didn't know what to say. This was something about me that just didn't fit. Me, funny? Strong? I've never been really good with compliments so I tried to change the subject.

"Um, well, thanks, I guess… I mean, so, anyways…. how's things going with you and Rico?"

"Fine. He got a job over at Wilson's for the summer, just helping bale hay and stuff like that. It'll last until September then he's thinking of enrolling at UNM's satellite campus here for a semester to see if he likes it or not and if he does, he's going to transfer to the main campus in Albuquerque and live with his dad."

"What does he want to study?

"Not sure. He's thinking maybe eventually he'll try getting into law school. He just wants to get out of Lona, I think. Besides, his mother still treats him like a kid. He can't wait to get out of her house and on his own. I've actually thought about maybe doing the same thing. I mean, I don't know what I'd study or anything, but it'd be cool to be with Rico if he goes. Maybe we could even get an apartment together. But Aunt Penny and Uncle Doug don't have the money for *that*, nor would she even let me, I'll bet."

"But Sage, Grandma Mina has TONS of money. I know if you just asked her, she'd be more than happy to pay for at least your tuition."

"She's always told me that she has some trust or something like that set up for me." She eyed me, saying "and I'll bet you'd be in on that now, too. But I actually don't know if I even want to ask her, after how she treated me when I first came out here. She's so damn controlling and that'd be just one more way that I'd be under her thumb again. I don't even hardly talk to her if I can help it."

I sympathized with her, but was a little envious nonetheless, that she had that ready income and I was saving every penny I had from my meager paycheck. For some reason, Grandma Mina never accepted me as her biological granddaughter. I had pretty much gotten over that a long time ago because she rarely even contacted Sage anymore either, but it still hurt.

I also knew I had an opportunity to get into school for that creative art internship my journalism teacher had recommended me for. I already applied for it but I hadn't told Sage or even Aunt Penny or Uncle Doug anything yet and wasn't sure when I should.

"So, what about you?" she asked, changing the subject. "You still have that crush on Jude?"

I felt an immediate twinge in my gut. Sage knew I liked him but she also knew I didn't want to talk about it because he was clearly too old for me and clearly not interested.

"Sage, he doesn't even know I exist," I finally said.

"Well, you sure don't give him any reasons to *know* you exist, either. I mean, when was the last time you were out at the ranch? Or even talked to him?"

"I haven't been since I went out with Aunt Penny a while back. You know that."

Jude had asked us to come out and talk to him and a new detective about Mama's case. It was hard, sitting there, trying to answer questions to things I really just wanted to forget about. But he was sweet and encouraging and even put his arm around me a couple times when he realized I was having a particularly hard moment. I don't know if I was much help, as everything I told that new detective guy, who, incidentally reminded me of some old cowboy actor, had already been repeated and repeated again for the past couple of years to the Lona police and detectives. I really didn't see any reason to keep going over the same things, but Jude said Mr. Lassiter was really good and so I figured if Jude trusted him, then I would, too.

But right now, I didn't want to talk with Sage about Jude. What I really wanted to talk about was her and Rico, so I tried to maneuver the conversation back to them.

"So, you and Rico ever...you know?"

"Kissed? Duh of course."

"No, I mean…."

She blushed, which was saying a lot for her.

"Not exactly, I mean we've, well, you know, but not really *that* yet."

"Yet? So, does that mean you *are* going to?"

"Well, probably, KC. Geez, enough with the questions!"

"I know, but, well, it's just that, I don't know, I guess I kinda feel like I'm sort of losing you, and I just found you…"

"Aw, c'mere." I nudged towards her and she put her arm around my shoulder, pulling me in close. ''I promise, you'll be the first to know if we do."

I sighed to myself, knowing I wasn't so sure of that, but enjoyed the sentiment anyway. If Sage wanted me to know something, she'd tell me. It seemed that the two of us were always just a line or two away from getting in sync with each other. I don't know if it was because neither of us fully trusted the other with our feelings or what, but I did know that if Sage wanted to keep something a secret, no amount of coaxing was going to pull it out of her, regardless if she felt closer to me now or not.

We spent another fifteen minutes talking then figured we needed to get back home and explain to Aunt Penny about Sage's appointment being rescheduled.

I thought about Jude all the way home.

Jude, Jamie and Pat sat around the ranch's big dining room table, large and small stacks of files and paperwork spread out in a fan in front of them.

"This doesn't make any sense," Jamie frowned, pulling the top sheet off a stack of haphazard papers. "Why would Veronica Valdez have sent Shari letters? And some of them less than three weeks before she died?"

When they first interviewed Veronica, she repeatedly denied having anything to do with the notes and letters. It was her son Rico who found one that hadn't been sent yet and brought it to Jude's attention. After analyzing the writing and confronting her with their newfound evidence, she capitulated and admitted she had written them, but had absolutely nothing to do with the murder.

"But she never said exactly *why* she wrote the letters, did she?" Pat ventured. "I mean, we still ain't got a good solid reason for her sending them. I swear, that gal could hem and haw her way out of a can of beans if she had to. We ain't got nothin' even close to an explanation."

"Maybe she still has something for Doug?" Jamie ventured. "And she's been divorced from Greg Baca for a while now, right?"

"Yeah, but these are from years ago," Jude reminded him. "And we can't be sure exactly when they were even sent to begin with. Maybe she's just a vindictive, bitter and angry woman with a score to settle? It'd be one thing if we had something on her, but her alibi for that day seems water-tight."

"What about the rest of her family?" Pat asked them. "Her ex is in Albuquerque and she's got two kids, a boy and a girl. And Sage has something goin' with the boy, right?"

"Yes, from what KC has told us, Sage has been seeing Rico for almost a year now." Jude offered. "The daughter, Ronni, lives with her dad in Albuquerque. You know, now that I think about it, it was kind of odd, because at our last meeting KC mentioned she was pretty sure she saw her here in Lona a few weeks ago."

"Doin' what?" Pat asked.

"I guess she saw her in the parking lot of the clinic. She wasn't sure it was even her, but evidently Sage confirmed it was her after KC described her. Do you want me to go talk to her?"

"Let's wait on that a bit, too. I'm most interested right now in the mother. You say Veronica told you she was in Albuquerque the day of the shooting?"

"Yes, we pulled her cell phone records and it shows one call at 8:30 a.m. that morning to her ex-husband, one at 8:43 a.m. to Ronni, both of them originating here in Lona. The third call came from her cell phone when she was at a place called Mindy's Boutique on Montgomery Avenue in Albuquerque and that call came in at 12:16 pm. to her daughter again, who was also in Albuquerque. The Medical Examiner says Shari was killed somewhere between 12:15 and 12:45, so that would've been impossible for Veronica to get back to Lona from Albuquerque in that time frame.

"That still doesn't account for the letters."

"I know, it doesn't make sense to me either."

"Ok, so Veronica has a ticket for now, but I still say she's good for it. How're we doing with talkin' to the in-laws?"

Jamie had dispiritedly been waiting for that question. "Well, I'm trying to pin down a time when I can drive out there and talk to Mina Davenport. She's always got something or another going on and seems like she has a good reason to dodge me every time. I'm not sure what to do about it."

"Hell, rookie, you just want me to do it? Me and Mina Davenport go back a *looooong* way."

"How's that?" Jamie asked. "I mean, did you know her from here or when you were in Texas?"

"Son, West Texas was my home for near on thirty years. Never saw anyone even half as bad as when Mike Davenport came on the force. All bright-eyed and bushy-tailed with a talk like you've never heard. Ladies' man, too, a real player. I didn't like him from the first time I met him. Something slippery about him. Surprising he wanted to be in law enforcement, given his background. You do know they're like only the wealthiest ranchers in west Texas, right? Damn, I sure wish I had even a tiny bit of what they have. The first few years he was the golden boy. Everyone thought he could do no wrong, he kept his nose clean, he had good collars, no problems whatsoever. Then little things started happening on his watch. We heard he'd had a problem with some junkie downtown so had to bring him in and "accidentally" left him sitting in the back interrogation room, handcuffed to the table leg, for over four hours, crap like that. It was like, if he didn't like someone, they knew it because he wasn't going to let them forget it. Then other times, evidence would go missing, mostly small stuff, but eventually things like a gun and some pot went missing. He had an explanation for everything and since he was such a "good guy," not much ever came of it. I always wondered about the gun, though. Heard they eventually located it and such, but, still. Then things kinda settled down, I guess. Anyways, I'm ramblin' here, sorry."

"No, it's interesting stuff," Jamie said and Jude vigorously nodded his head in agreement.

"Ok, well, so after I left the force and moved out here to New Mexico, I kinda lost track of what was going on out there. But Petey McAlistar called me a several years ago, this would've been after Mike and Shari had gotten married, and told me he'd heard through the grapevine that Mike had gotten involved in some kind of gang activity, not him of course, but catching em'. Turns out one of them became a confidential informant and it wasn't long before ol' Mike got his fingers caught in the proverbial cookie jar, if ya know what I mean."

"So was that when he ended up dead?" Jude asked.

"No, I think that crazy lady karma must've just jumped up and bit Mike's rich ass, ya know what I mean? He got caught stealing a half kilo of cocaine then tried to sell it. Turns out the guy he was selling it to was an undercover, and, so now, who *knows* what she did with his sorry ass..."

"Too bad Shari got caught up in all that," Jamie said. "Man, I guess Mrs. Davenport, Mina, really had it in for her that she was able to get custody of Sage and all. I don't get it."

"Don't get it? Hell, it only takes one hangin' judge in your back pocket and you got the world on a string. Poor Shari didn't have a chance, sad to say. Ol' Mina never lets anyone get the best of her. Never did, never will. I think her figuring out a way back then to get sole custody of her granddaughter was her way of just flippin' the bird to the whole entire Texas State Police Department. And to Shari, too, bless her heart."

"Well, I guess it all worked out for the better," Jude said, then when he saw the surprised looks on Pat and Jamie's faces, "I mean, not for the better, that's not what I meant. It's horrible what happened to Shari and I'm honored that you guys think I can help out in some way. Really. But what I mean is, at least Sage is here and Mina didn't try to get custody of KC."

"Well, so ya want me to go out to Texas myself?" Pat asked. "Or do you want to go, Jude? We can head out this weekend and be back before Sunday chicken dinner?"

"Nah, I can't. I've got plans this weekend."

"Wait," Jamie interrupted. "I think I've got a better idea of how we can talk to Mina Davenport."

"Like what?" Jude asked.

"Well, I'm thinking what needs to happen is we need to talk to Mina Davenport on our turf, not hers."

Pat nodded his head enthusiastically. "Yep. Yep, that might work. Get her outta her comfort zone and we might have a fightin' chance to get some answers."

"How do you plan to do that, Jamie?" Jude asked. "I mean, from what I can gather so far, she's pretty crafty."

"I'll have to do some digging. But my thought is, maybe we can dummy up some paperwork involving Sage's custody and such. Something that has to be done specifically here in New Mexico, not Texas. That way, we can get her out here, then figure out a way to interview her. What do you guys think?"

"She's a wily one, for sure," Pat said. "I'm wondering if there's any way we could put a big money incentive in there, just for good measure."

"Money? Like pay her to come out here?" Jude said.

"No, buckshot, I'm thinking we lead her into thinking she has some money coming to her, I don't know, maybe we can say Shari had accumulated some money for Sage, but that it was still in Mike's name, or, hell, I don't know, you guys help me out here, too!"

"That could actually work," Jamie pondered. "Let me see what I can figure out, ok?"

All along, I knew Grandma Mina hadn't exactly been forthcoming on Mama's investigation. Even though she'd promised Aunt Penny that she'd help however she could, she was never quite available to actually *really* help.

I once asked Aunt Penny about her, just to kind of get an idea of her first impression when her and Uncle Doug had gone out to Emmit to pick up Sage.

"Well, she seemed nice enough," Aunt Penny said. "A little snobbish, though. I don't know, there was just this feeling I got that she wasn't telling us everything, you know? You know how sometimes people just tell you only what they want you to hear?"

I nodded, thinking of Sage. "Yes, I actually do."

"Doug thought she was kind of pushy, too," she continued. "He got a little worked up when she said something to him about an old girlfriend of his, Veronica Valdez."

"What? Uncle Doug used to date Rico's mom?" Wow, I thought to myself, now this is interesting. "Is that why he's so angry at Rico?" I asked.

"Doug's mad at Rico Baca? Why?"

"I don't know, I thought maybe you did."

"No! I don't have the foggiest idea why he would be."

186

25 EL CABRON

Doug Stevenson sighed as he rolled over to the side of the bed and got up. "I gotta get going," he said, looking back at the tangled bedsheets barely covering Veronica's voluptuous body.

"Why? I thought you had till tomorrow?" she pouted, pulling the sheets around her as she sat up.

"I've got three more stops on my route then I still need to go into Albuquerque and pick up that new coin changer. Sorry, sugar." He headed into the motel's bathroom and closed the door.

"Well," she said loudly, trying to be heard above the shower. "It's not like this is a one-stop-shop, mister! I've got things to do, too!"

"So, get your ass out of bed and come join me then!" he shouted through the wall.

She smiled.

Ever since Doug and Penny moved to Lona after Shari's murder, Veronica Valdez made it a point to quietly follow him from a distance whenever she saw him around town. That first year was really just hit and miss; she knew how preoccupied he was with the funeral, the move, his nieces, and the investigation and she wasn't even completely sure herself that she wanted to talk to him if she did happen to run into him.

But after secretly observing his comings and goings, she started to recognize his routine. Mondays were Smith's and Walgreens, Wednesdays were the Chuck E Cheese's on 4th Street, then Fridays were set aside for Chelsea's out in El Rio, so she started to plot how she might just coincidentally run into him.

One particular Friday Rico had gone into Albuquerque to take care of an outstanding parking ticket so she called into the clinic to let them know she wasn't feeling that hot and wasn't going to make it in today. The Lona Clinic would just have to make do with one less vampire today, she thought, anxious to finally get a chance to meet up with Doug Stevenson. Taking particular care with her hair and makeup, she wondered what she was going to say to him.

It didn't even occur to her that he might not want to talk to her. After all, they did leave things in a pretty crappy state years all those years ago but, nonetheless, she felt a small thrill at the prospect of seeing him again. As she drove down Main Street, she immediately spied his truck parked outside the market so she pulled in next to it. Ten minutes later he walked out the door, pushing a large empty dolly towards the curb.

"Hey handsome," she said through her open car window.

"Well, lookie here!" he said, clearly surprised to see her. Coming over to her side door, she got out and gave him a small hug. "Heard you were back home. Doug, what happened with Shari, we're all reeling from that. I'm so sorry."

"Thanks. These past couple of years have been one helluva shitstorm, that's for sure."

"So," she said casually changing the subject, "What're you up to today? I mean, do you have any free time? Maybe we can go somewhere for a cup of coffee and catch up?"

He looked at his watch and nodded. "Well, I actually have to run out to El Rio right now to drop off a contract. Wanna tag along?"

"Sure!" She said, hoping she didn't sound too enthusiastic. She took a quick peek in the side-view mirror to check her lipstick, locked her car, then went around to the passenger side of Doug's truck. They drove out to El Rio, talking all the way, mostly about old friends, what they'd been up to since high school, and Doug's business. Neither mentioned Penny, Shari's death, or him and Penny moving back to take care of the girls. As they were pulling into the parking lot of El Rio's only gas station, she looked down at her pinging phone, frowning.

"What is it?" Doug asked, seeing her perplexed look.

"My son, Rico. Hold on a sec while I answer this, ok?

"Sure, take your time. I'll just be a minute in here," he said, turning off the engine and starting to get out.

"Wait." She held up her hand. "Shit. Rico's been in an accident."

"What? Is he okay?"

"Yeah, no injuries, but I need to go into Albuquerque to help him. Doesn't that just figure? He goes to pay a crummy parking ticket and now he's in a frickin' fender bender. That kid! I'll tell ya, just be glad you don't have any of your own!"

Seeing the pained look immediately wash over Doug's face, she quickly backpedaled, "I'm so sorry, Doug. I know you've got the girls now. I plain just wasn't thinking." She reached for his hand, then searched his face, realizing he wasn't too upset with her.

"It's ok," he said just a bit more gruffly than she would've liked. "I'll just be a minute then I'll get you back to your car."

"Sure, thanks. And hey, maybe we can do this again next week?" she offered. "Same place, same time, and I'll try not to have any interruptions next time?"

It became a weekly routine for them. Veronica would leave the clinic around noon and drive to a secluded area of El Rio and Doug would be waiting there for her. It didn't take long for their meetings to turn into more and soon their steamy nights at the motel in Los Mancos,

just outside Albuquerque, landed them right back into the relationship
they'd had all those years ago.

After showering one particular morning and heading out the door
to their separate vehicles, Veronica stopped, gasped, and quickly pushed
Doug back into the room.

"What? What is it?" he said, craning his neck. trying to see past
her shoulder.

"I'll be GODDAMNED but I think I see Rico out in the parking
lot!" she hissed back to him.

"What? Do you think he knows?" Doug was clearly upset.

"How could he? I'm sure he doesn't! Oh God, I hope not!

They shut the door and both peeked through the heavy curtains,
trying to see where Rico was heading.

"There! There he is!" Doug pointed. "He's going into that room
down at the end!"

"What? What's he doing *here*? I mean, he's alone, right? What
the *hell*?"

Just then, Penny's truck came around the corner and parked
close to the small motel's front office. He couldn't quite make out who
was driving, but now he was visibly shaking.

"Shit! Penny's out there! *SHIT*! How'd *she* find out? Shit, shit,
SHIT!"

"But wait! Why would Penny AND Rico be here?" Scenarios
were flying through her mind and she was getting more and more upset.
Penny and Rico? What the hell?

"No, wait, wait, I see someone getting out. No, it's not Penny,"
he breathed a sigh of relief as he saw Sage leave the truck and head
toward the room at the end of the building.

"Looks like we're not the only two lovebirds in the family," he said, feeling her sharp nails dig into his arm.

After Mama died, I couldn't even look at the photo album I'd been so excited to share with Sage that fateful day. I'd shoved it into a pillowcase and buried it in the bottom of my dresser drawer, the one where I kept all the things I never wore anymore, but I came across it when I was cleaning a while back. I gently took it out and sat it on the bed, sliding it out of the pillowcase and stared at it, just as Sage walked into our bedroom.

"What's that?" she asked.

"Oh, just a book of photos I made a long time ago," I said, cautiously eyeing the album in my lap. If I said anything more, I felt it just might burst open on its own, each page laying bare all the guilt I still carried around with me.

"It's nothing," I said, starting to put it away. But Sage stopped me, reaching for the book. "What's in in it? Can I see it?"

"Um, well, it's just that, well..." I didn't want to explain that day, the day Mama and I were headed to Texas to pick her up. Or how it all changed because of me and this stupid book.

I sighed, knowing Sage wouldn't let it go. "It's pictures of me and Mama, and all the stuff before.... I mean, before..." I trailed off.

"How about we go for a walk? We can take it with us and then you can show it to me if you're comfortable, ok?" She was being kind.

We walked down the driveway and down the road before we found ourselves at the old bridge and sat down on the wooden planks at the edge because I didn't want to get too close. It seemed that, even after all this time, I still felt a pang, being so close to this place that brought

Mama so much worry back then, not to mention Sage's bad luck on this very bridge.

"Mama had some trouble here," I explained as I gently directed Sage to an area closer to the bank.

"What kind of trouble?"

"I guess when she was in high school, her and some of her friends were inner-tubing and Mama got sucked in under that culvert over there," I pointed to the wide dark hole. "She didn't get stuck or anything, but was just really scared and I guess Veronica Valdez was there and didn't help her get out or anything."

"Rico's mom? Well, that's not surprising," Sage said.

"Aunt Penny told me Uncle Doug used to date Veronica in high school."

"What? Wow. That's crazy. I wonder if Rico knows that. I'll have to ask him."

I was curious so welcomed her bringing his name up. "So things are going pretty good with you two?" I asked.

"Pretty good. I like having a boyfriend. And I'm really happy with him, KC. Really."

"Ok," I said somewhat dubiously. "It's just that you never really talk too much about him." In fact, I often wondered if she was just making more of their relationship than it really was, she so rarely talked about him.

"Look," she said, "let's not get into all that with him, ok? I'd really rather just take a look at these pictures."

We spent the next twenty minutes or so going through the album. I'd tried to include things I thought she'd be interested in, explaining photos of people and places that had made up mine and Mama's lives.

There weren't a lot of photos of Mama, but Sage spent a long time looking at each she was in.

"She sure was pretty."

"I think you look exactly like her."

Sage looked sidewise at me, hearing the slight tinge of sadness in my voice.

"I know how much you miss her, KC. I really do." She turned the last page of the book over and closed it, sighing. "I just wish I could've known her. I was so little I barely remember anything about her."

"Didn't Grandma Mina have photos of her?"

"Hell no! I don't think she *wanted* me to remember Mom. She had photos of Dad all around the house but none of Mom. It was weird, because as I got older, I'd ask about Mom and Dad and Grandma would always change the subject or something else would always come up. I guess I just got used to knowing they weren't part of my life."

"But don't you think it's even weirder that Dad died?"

"You know, I get this feeling he's still out there somewhere. Even after all this time, I can't put my finger on it and I also believe Grandma knows it, too. Something happened that he had to leave back then. I just don't know what."

"Well, maybe there'll come a time when you can ask her, you know, now that you're an adult. Do you think she'd even talk to you about it?"

"Probably not. She's going to be pissed at me forever since I chose to come out here."

"Well, lucky for me you made the right decision," I smiled. "You know she'll be here next week, remember? Maybe you can talk to her then."

I was starting to believe that Mama's murder was never going to be solved, it'd been so long. The latest I'd heard was that our grandmother was scheduled to come to Lona for an interview with Pat and Jamie.

"Are you nervous?" I asked Sage of our grandmother's impending visit.

"No, not really. I don't even plan on seeing her."

"Really? What if she wants to see you?" She just shrugged and got up. "I'm not worried about it. Hey, I need to get back. I've got a handsome guy picking me up in about an hour so I need to get ready."

I was secretly hoping it would work out that I, too, would finally get to at least get a peek at this woman I'd only ever heard about. I knew from what Aunt Penny was able to find out that she was supposed to meet with Pat and Jamie early next week. So when we got back home and Sage had gone into the bedroom and closed the door, I dialed the phone on the off-chance Jude would be out at the ranch and might be able to work it so I could somehow be in on the visit too. Miss M answered immediately, happy to hear my voice.

"Hey there," I said, genuinely happy to hear her, "How are you?"

"Oh good, sweetie, just trying to beat the heat. You?"

"Fine, nothing new. Planning to start at UNM this fall."

"Oh, that's wonderful! And will you be studying art, or writing?"

"Hopefully both, but I'm just going to take two classes to get my feet wet, then we'll see how it goes. Hey, would Jude happen to be around?"

"No, honey, he took Tucker and Salva into town. Maybe he's going in to watch the Lona Days Parade, I don't know. But he should be back in a few hours or so." The annual parade pretty much closed down the entire main street of our small town, where everyone, old and young alike, brought their dogs, cats, chickens or whatever pet they wanted to walk the mile or so down main street. "I don't think they plan to be in it, he just wanted to sit and watch it. Then he has that meeting with Pat and Jamie to talk about that big hoo-hah lady," she sniffed. "Oh, dangit, honey, I'm sorry. I know she's your gramma and all, I just don't think I even like her a bit."

I laughed. "No worries, Miss M. Her reputation isn't the best in my family, either. Ok, so will you just let him know I called?"

"Sure will, hon. And, KC, don't be such a stranger, ok?"

"I won't, I promise."

Well, I thought to myself, that didn't go how I'd hoped. I asked Aunt Penny if I could take the truck into town on the premise of watching the parade myself, hoping I'd possibly run into Jude.

"Sure, maybe take Sage with you?"

"Oh, I thought you knew. Sage said that Rico was going to come by and pick her up. She said she left you a message; that was about an hour or so ago. I was in the shower when they left so I didn't actually see them, but she said she'd be home by dinnertime."

"Hm, no, I didn't know that. I thought she mentioned yesterday that Rico was in Las Cruces with his dad for the week. Oh, wait, look, here's a message on my phone. Dang it, I need to turn the volume up or something. I'm always missing calls. Yup, it's from Sage. Well, ok, then, just be careful, ok?"

"Will do," I said as I snagged the truck keys off the peg by the kitchen door. "See ya later. Is there anything you need?"

"A way to get rid of twenty pounds?" she asked hopefully, grabbing her hips and swaying around in a circle, laughing. "Actually, I could use a few groceries if you don't mind stopping in at Markie's on your way home? Or maybe even the Safeway in town. They've got all that good Hatch green chile now."

"Sure, just give me a list. And by the way, Aunt Penny. I love you just the way you are."

"Right backatcha, kiddo."

I took my time driving into town, happy to have an afternoon to myself. I watched for Jude's truck parked along Main Street but I didn't see him anywhere, not when I drove (twice) by the feed store, nor outside the post office/bank building or parked anywhere along our one long main street. I stopped at the end of the feed lot and waited for the little parade to pass by, growing more and more dejected. After it was over, I looked around one more time, then headed over to the grocery store.

Sighing, I loaded the last of the groceries into the truck. As I came around to the driver's side, I heard a familiar loud engine and looked up just in time to see the tail end of Jude's truck passing by.

I quickly threw my purse onto the seat, started up the truck and pulled out of the parking lot, thinking if I hurried, I could catch up to him at the light. I could see his truck turning onto a side road just past the light but, of course, with my luck, the light turned yellow, then red as I slowed to a stop.

Impatiently, I willed the light to finally turn green and, after what seemed like minutes dragging by, I quickly drove to the next road and put on my turn signal. Weird, I thought, looking around the area. Where would he be going here? The road wasn't actually a residential street, more of a side road that was paved for about twenty-five feet then turned into gravel. Then I remembered it was the back way to get out to Escobar Lake without having to jump up on the highway and go the long way around. He's going fishing again, I smiled to myself. I could see the cloud of dust kicked up by his truck tires way up in the distance and eagerly anticipated catching up with him.

Escobar Lake wasn't big, it was actually more of a little dam the Middle Rio Grande Conservancy District had set up over fifty years ago to alleviate the over-used irrigation canals at the time. Mama and I came out here several times when I was younger, though neither of us ever fished. Even though it was small, it was always pretty and serene, although occasionally we'd see a big black tarantula scuttle across the road. We both squealed the first time that happened, Mama stomping on the brakes just as the huge spider disappeared in the sagebrush at the side of the road.

"What *was* that, Mama?" I implored her, peeking over the dashboard, worried that whatever it was might be coming back.

"Just a really, really big spider, honey, it's called a tarantula and they're all around here."

"Is it poisonous?" I asked, worried.

"I don't think so. But I sure wouldn't want to be the one to find out!" she smiled.

Mama would put together a basket of peanut butter and jelly sandwiches, a couple of apples and a big thermos of iced tea, sweetened just perfectly. Then, once we got to the lake, she would spread out that big denim patchwork quilt she'd painstakingly pieced together out of all our old jeans, square by square, then backed by bright red bandana-print flannel. I loved that blanket and we'd sit there, swatting the flies away and eating our lunch, sometimes not talking at all.

Mama used to let me draw on the quilt with my collection of fabric paint pens, so every few squares there would be a bunch of pink and purple flowers, another had a big red and white heart, yet another a checkerboard pattern of greens and yellows. I could sit there for hours, Mama reading her book and me painting on that dang old quilt. Once I'd even drawn a picture of Mama, her dark brown eyes huge and her long white hair twirling around her shoulders. She looked like those paintings you used to see in the back of the magazine, the ones where the little waif-like girl was standing in an ally with her kitten and she was all eyes with a real sorrowful look. I hadn't intentionally made her look like that, but she did and, from then on, Mama always would set the picnic basket over that square. I never said anything about it.

I came around a small bend and could see the still lake stretched out in front of me, parts hidden by a high canopy of old cottonwood trees. I couldn't immediately see Jude's truck, so I parked the truck and got out, walking over to the ridge overlooking the lake to get a better view.

Just as I crested the hill, I looked down and could see his truck in the distance. I could just make out Jude's silhouette sitting inside, his arm casually draped across the back of his seat. I squinted so I could see better and just then, my mouth fell open as I realized he wasn't alone.

Sage's unmistakable white-blonde hair was shining through the back window, resting on Jude's broad shoulder, the image flying up to me and stabbing me in the heart.

I opened the kitchen shade to what was promising to be another rainy Denver morning. Nevertheless, I dutifully moved the small cactus to the east side of the window, hoping it might eventually absorb even the smallest bit of light coming in. It was the one piece of home I brought with me to Denver, a defiant badge of greenery in an otherwise concrete-laden world. Standing with a certain sense of authority in its small, brightly painted ceramic pot, I realized it was a lot like me, trying to fit into a surrounding that wasn't optimal for either of us, certain we would wither and die if put out of our safe enclosures for too long.

I looked down at the neatly laid out breakfast table. As he had every morning for the past three months since I'd been here, Mannie Marquez set a small glass of orange juice next to a bowl and spoon, coffee cup filled and cream and sugar sitting next to it.

"Mr. Marquez, you don't have to do this every morning," I insisted. "You and Mrs. Marquez are far too kind to me."

"KC! Please! Call me Mannie! Every time you say Mr. Marquez, I feel like I should look around for my dad!"

I laughed. "Ok, Mannie. But I wish you wouldn't wait so much on me."

I remember announcing to Aunt Penny and Uncle Doug that I was moving to Denver.

"What do you mean, move? Move where? Why?" Aunt Penny was dumbfounded.

I didn't tell her what had happened with Jude and Sage; it was still as painful as that day I saw them out by the lake and I couldn't bring myself to even think about it, much less explain to them what I was feeling.

"I just need to get away," I said. "Nothing's wrong or anything, it's just that, well, I applied to the Community College of Denver and I was accepted. I thought I'd go ahead and take advantage of the money grandpa left Mama and see if I can start studying design."

"But you told us you wanted to go UNM this fall! Why did you change your mind?"

I couldn't tell them that Jude and Sage changed my mind. "I guess I just want to get out of New Mexico, you know, just see what else is out there. It'll be fine, I promise."

"But where will you live? I can't let you just go to Denver alone, KC!" Turning to Doug, she pleaded, "Doug, help me here! We can't just let her go!"

"Well, I don't see any problem, Pen. She's old enough, and it sounds like she's thought this through. And I was just thinking, you know Mannie and Denise still live up there. They're good people and I guarantee they'll help you out. Maybe I can give them a call and see if they can keep an eye on her when she gets up there."

Aunt Penny stared at him; her eyes steely in determination. "No! I think this is all wrong!" Then, turning back to me, she pleaded "KC, honey, have you truly thought this through? I mean, do you already have an apartment? Do you have any friends up there?"

"Um, no, not actually, but I know I can find something close to school. Don't worry, Aunt Penny. It's only six hours away! Besides, I'm almost nineteen and it's something I've been wanting to do for a long time," I said, not entirely true.

It turned out that I was able to quickly enroll for the classes I needed and, as he had thought, Uncle Doug's friends were more than helpful. They insisted I stay with them until I could find a decent place to rent and I figured I'd be better off doing that than trying to live out of a hotel room until I could get my feet on even ground. Ever since their daughter, Melinda, had moved to Austin with her boyfriend, the Marquezs had been feeling the throes of empty-nest syndrome. I was staying in her old room and I think I was fulfilling a wishful hole in both their hearts, so I didn't protest too much. Mannie and Uncle Doug were high school buddies and they had stayed close friends ever since.

The evening before I left for my new venture, I was laying on my bed, thinking about my plans when I heard a light knock on the door.

"KC? Do you mind if I come in?" Sage asked quietly.

I sat up. "It's your room, too, Sage."

"I know, but, well, you've just been so quiet this past several weeks and I get the feeling you'd rather not have me around."

"No, I'm just trying to work some things out."

"What sort of things? Is there something I can help you with?"

I felt the muscles tighten around my heart. Her help me? I couldn't even begin to process my feelings at that moment, the pain of seeing her and Jude together was still so raw in my mind.

"No, it's fine. Really. I guess Aunt Penny told you I'm leaving tomorrow."

She immediately came to the bed and sat down beside me; her eyes full of concern.

"She did, but I still don't understand. You were so excited about going to UNM this fall. What happened to change your mind?"

"I think I need to get out of Lona for a while. I just want a change of scenery, I guess. Besides, Denver's not that far."

"I know, but what will I do? I mean, everything's been going so well, and now, well, now with you leaving and all, I'm going to be all alone."

I had to quickly bite back my anger. Alone? She's not alone at *all*, I thought. Not with Jude around.

"I mean," she added hastily, "I've got Rico here, of course. But now I won't have my sister!"

I couldn't bear looking into her eyes right then. Part of me wanted to confront her blatant betrayal, and the other part wanted to scream deep inside myself, chastising my jealousy over the one dearest person in my life.

I got up quickly and went to the kitchen to clean up the breakfast dishes, the conversation with Sage as painful and fresh in my mind as it had been weeks ago. How can this be so difficult? Why can't I get over this? It was going to be a long year.

Fall in Denver is always kind of a hit and miss affair. Fair days promised a pair of shorts and a t-shirt; but the weather could easily turn by afternoon, requiring a hoodie and jeans. Judging by today's heavy, low clouds, this was proving to be somewhere in between so I quickly showered, slipped into jeans and a top, then moved tidily through my morning routine before heading out into the near-freezing rain.

I hadn't met many people yet; it seemed as though everyone here was always in some kind of a hurry. Hurry to get on the bus, hurry to their classes, hurry to get out of class, hurry back to the bus. But it was ok for the time being since I wasn't really even looking to make friends.

I missed Aunt Penny tremendously and this particular morning I felt the sharp pain of distance. "I'll call her tonight," I promised myself.

Aunt Penny was easily the strongest person I knew. Well, along with Mama. And Sage, too, I guess. I think Aunt Penny understood me the best, though, so it was easy later that evening when I called her, crying, gushing it all out over what happened that day at the lake.

"KC, I think you should call Sage and tell her everything you're telling me right now. She's so sad all the time and she just mopes around the house. She's not even spending much time with Rico anymore and I can see how terribly unhappy she's been since you've been gone. Can't you maybe give her a chance to tell her side? There's got to be some kind of explanation."

I knew I should try to see Sage's side of the story, or at least hear her out, but it just hurt me too much to even try and figure out what had happened.

"Her side? Aunt Penny! She *knows* how much I care for Jude! And that didn't stop her from crawling all over him every time he'd come out to the house, or whenever she'd see him in town! I'm just sick knowing that they were going behind my back all that time!"

It wasn't like she didn't know how much I cared for Jude, even if it was unrequited. But Sage didn't have to go after him! And Jude, what was HE thinking? Oh, hell, I was just working myself up again. He wasn't ever "mine" to begin with so maybe I didn't really have a leg to stand on in this fight. Or was it a fight? I looked at it as the most supreme betrayal on earth. And here I had thought Sage and I were getting closer and closer to common ground. How could she have done this to me? Why?

"But honey, I seriously don't think that's what was happening. Sage has always been upfront with us. I mean, I know there was a time when she first got here that she was pretty unpredictable in her feelings and all, and I don't deny her that. But you and her have come so far these last few years, KC. I just can't let you throw that all away."

"Me throw it all away? Me?" I couldn't believe what I was hearing. "Aunt Penny, it's *always* been what Sage wants! Sage gets upset and everyone has to run to her side and make sure she's ok! But me? Ha! I'm the one who saw my mother murdered and NO ONE ever came running to MY side!"

The line was quiet and I knew I had overstepped my boundaries.

"God, I'm sorry, Aunt Penny. I'm really sorry. I don't know what just got into me."

"Well, you know, KC, I love you more than life itself. Both of you. And if there's ever been a time where I've made you feel less than that, well, I'm sorry too."

"No, no, it's just me. I'm just feeling sorry for myself. I know how much you love me, and you've *always* been there for me. I'll get over all this, I promise."

"I know you will, honey. But I also want you to know I'm right here and I will always be right here for you."

"I know. Love you." I hung up the phone, then looked around my little surrogate room. "I really do need to pull myself together," I thought morosely, heading to bed. The next morning, I slogged my way to the bus station and waited in the chilly morning rain, our conversation still stinging my consciousness. I knew how lucky I was to have people around me who cared so much about my welfare, my well-being, my happiness.

I just wish Jude were one of them.

Fairly quickly my routine became, well, routine, and that suited me fine. The months came and went and it wasn't long before the holidays were less than a month away. The thought of going back home for Thanksgiving and Christmas made my heart yearn even more, but my mind was made up. I was here for the long haul and if I was ever going to make it on my own, I had to sever myself from everything in Lona. At least for the time being, I convinced myself.

My classes were interesting and I actually started enjoying my life up in the beautiful Rocky Mountains of Denver. Of course, I wasn't used to the sheer number of people, and cars, and buildings everywhere you looked, but there was also something almost therapeutic about allowing myself to become so totally immersed in the sheer enormity of my surroundings and life.

Jamie kept me up to date as best he could since Mama's death. Every couple of weeks I'd get an email from him, but there was rarely any news. After three years, they had reached the point where it had become a "cold case" since they had no leads and nothing had materialized to give them any movement towards a resolution.

And I knew that Aunt Penny was still as voracious in her quest to resolve this as anyone. I always looked forward to what had become our weekly phone calls so, one Friday when it was my turn to call, I must've caught her crying because she was sniffling when she answered the phone. I could hear it in her voice.

"Hey, Aunt Pen! Are you okay?" I asked immediately.

"Oh, hi, honey," she sniffled. "I'm fine. How're things up in Denver? How's school?"

"Everything's fine. I'm taking on-line classes this semester so I've been doing a lot of painting. But...wait...Aunt Penny, why are you crying?"

"Not crying, ha! Well, not unless they're tears of relief!" she laughed. "I've just got a little cold is all."

"What do you mean, 'tears of relief?' Has something happened?"

"Well, it's nothing that I didn't already suspect a long time ago, KC. And he still hasn't admitted it to me, but I'm certain your Uncle Doug's having an affair."

"An affair? Uncle Doug? With who?" I tried to sound incredulous.

"We'll talk later, hon. I know it's a lot on your plate, and I wasn't going to say anything, but you'd find out soon enough, I reckon."

"Gosh! Are you ok? Do you need anything?"

"Oh, I'm fine. Heck, I should be asking *you* that! But no worries here on my end. You see, Doug and I had an agreement before we got married. Sort of like a prenup, if you will. My money, which, by the way is a lot more than his, would stay "my money" and his money would stay his. He tried to get me to leave this house, though. Can you imagine that? He said that technically it was *his* house, since it was your Mama's to begin with and I wasn't any kind of blood relation or anything."

"No! I'll stand up for you and insist you get to stay in the house!" I said adamantly.

"No, you don't have to worry a bit about that. I just told him if he wanted me to move out, then I just might want to let all his business contacts know what he'd been up to. Small town, you know how people talk and all..."

"Well, just so you know, you will always have a home there, Aunt Penny. Always." I said emphatically.

"Thanks, honey. I know that. I'll be fine so don't you even give it a second thought, okay?"

"Ok. But you let me know if you need anything at all."

"I will. Do you mind if I ask you something?"

"Of course not! You can ask me anything, you know that."

"Well, I know this isn't my business and I know how sensitive you are about this, but did you ever think any more on contacting Sage? She misses you so much, honey."

"I told you I don't want to talk to Sage. Or, well, I mean, I'm not *ready* to talk to Sage right now. I just don't even know what I'd even say to her, Aunt Pen."

"It's just that she's so, well, she's got a lot of things going on right now, and I know this thing between the two of you is weighing heavy on her. I guess I'm just hoping one of you can make the first move."

"What kind of things?" I asked skeptically.

"Oh, I'm not going to get in between this. I'm sure she'll tell you in her own time."

"Tell me what?" I was genuinely concerned now.

"Oh, shoot, honey, there's someone at the door. Can I call you later?"

"Sure. I'll be here."

When her call didn't come in until 11:17 p.m., I'd already been up and down for a couple of hours, worrying. I've never been a good sleeper, anyway, not because I don't want to, it's just something that I've not been for a long time. So, after pacing around my bed for the tenth time, I sat down on the edge, considering my next move. I stared at the dim glow from Mama's old alarm clock as it reflected off the rounded glass of my treasured snow globe from Mrs. Chavez. I picked it up and shook it, the tiny flakes soundlessly floating down.

Aunt Penny was decidedly vague but I knew from her voice that something was wrong. What was Sage up to this time? I stewed it all over in my mind and when I finally decided I should just lie down, I stared at the clock again until I just gave up and started pacing again.

Sage's life was often a storm. Sometimes just a few little flakes, others more often a blizzard. But, if truth be told, so was mine. I've always tried to believe my lack of a good night's sleep was because I was afraid of the dark, but deep down, I know better. Sometimes at night, I'll be dreaming and think I see that dark shadow of a person again. Not by the tree, but on the riverbank, standing next to the old bridge, clothed in black, just looking down into the fast-flowing water, a big black dog by its side. Guess a psychiatrist would have a field day with me.

I decided to just head down to Lona and the drive down two days later had been fairly uninteresting. Mr. Marquez insisted I use his car, saying he and his wife would be just fine with hers and it took just under seven hours to get to Lona. I made my way through Albuquerque and drove down I-25 towards home. Turning left onto the lone two-lane blacktop, I gritted my teeth as tiny pellets of snow and ice pelted the small car like a swarm of angry soldier gnats, making it even harder to see in the waning light of the day. It rarely snowed here this time of the year so this unwelcomed weather shifted my already sour mood three gears lower. I expected it in Denver, but not here. Not now of all places or times.

Even though it was not yet even 6 p.m., I didn't want to chance the icy and snowy roads out to the house so I left Aunt Penny a message that I got in late and that I'd call her tomorrow when I got up. As I finally made my way into Lona, past the first of its four main street corners, I peered through the ice-crusted windshield for a place to spend the night and realized with annoyance my mood wasn't getting any better. Was it this place or was it the weather that was getting me down?

The approaching nightfall brought me right back. All I really wanted was a glass of wine and a warm bed, so when the soft lights of the Zia Hotel sign at Juniper and 1st Street finally came into view, I sighed and pulled into the near-empty parking lot. Coasting to a stop near the front office with the blinking neon vacancy sign, I went in, paid for a room and got settled.

"Hey, it's me." I said when Aunt Penny answered the phone the following morning.

"KC, honey! Omigosh you're here! I'm so glad! I got your message last night! When did you finally get in? Where are you?"

"I got a room at the Zia because I got in pretty late, what with the weather and all," I lied, my head still a little fuzzy. The night before I'd figured reading a few chapters of my homework would've put me right to sleep, but it didn't work out that way. So by 8 p.m. I wandered down toward the little motel bar right off the side of the lobby, knowing that probably no one in our small town would ask me for an ID.

"Well, I'm so dang happy you're home! When will you get out here? Quite a little storm that moved through last night, huh? I've got fresh banana bread in the oven and your room's all made up and waiting for you!"

"I guess maybe in an hour or so? I just need to finish packing up here then check out, ok?" Then, I had to ask the unenviable question. "So, is Sage ok with me taking over half her room again?"

"Oh, honey, well, first off, I want to apologize for waking you up at o'dark thirty the other morning. I get so dang worried about stuff and then I get to the point where I just have to talk to someone, and I wasn't even thinking about what time it was. I'm sorry."

"You can call me any time, night or day, Aunt Penny. You know that, right?"

"Well, I guess there's something you should probably know right up front before you get here. Sage asked me not to say anything earlier to you but you'll find out soon enough."

"What?" A familiar pang shot through my heart. "What's wrong?"

"Nothing's really wrong, exactly. It's just that, well, first of all, Sage has moved out."

"Moved out? Where to? What happened?"

"Well, she moved out a couple of weeks ago. Her and Rico did. They moved in with Rico's dad and sister in Albuquerque."

This didn't make any sense to me. Why would Sage move in with Rico when she was in love with Jude, I thought to myself? Did her and Jude break up?

"Wow, I never thought Sage would do something like that. I mean, she was just getting so used to family and us, and..." I had to stop, suddenly realizing I was probably the reason Sage left.

"It's my fault, right?" I asked sadly. "Oh, Aunt Penny! Now you're all alone out there!"

Uncle Doug and Aunt Penny had come to an understanding that things weren't working out. It wasn't actually a mutual decision, but Penny had had it with his late nights, being gone for entire weekends, and the ridiculously transparent excuses he gave her. He was petulant and angry, saying that it was his family's house and he shouldn't have to be the one to move, but she stood her ground, giving him an ultimatum of either coming clean to her what was going on or the next time he took off, she was going to throw everything he owned out in the middle of the road.

"Of *course* it's not your fault, honey! None of this even remotely has anything to do with you. Listen, I'll fill you in on everything else once you get here, ok?"

I finished up and got checked out as quickly as I could. Aunt Penny met me as I drove up the driveway. I noticed she had changed her haircut from her normal shoulder-length to a short, highlighted pixie cut that made her look ten years younger.

"Wow! Look at you!" I said as I got out of the car. "You look fabulous!"

She blushed as she nervously ran her fingers across her scalp. "Pretty short, huh? I just had it done a couple days ago down at Miranda's. Do you really like it?"

"Like it? I LOVE it! What made you cut it?"

"Shoot, I don't know. Maybe just wanted a change, I guess. Doug's not crazy about it, but I kind of like it myself."

"But I thought...you and Uncle Doug... I mean, er..." I said awkwardly, looking towards the house.

"Oh, he's still gone! And good riddance, I say. But he had to come out yesterday and pick up a few things he'd left here. You know, he had the gall to tell me I should've left it long. Can you even believe that? The nerve of that man! I wanted to say, yeah, and you should've left your wanger in your pants, too, but I didn't!"

Blushing, I had to laugh, but I inwardly cringed hearing Uncle Doug's name. After how he treated me and Sage, I didn't have much interest in his opinion, anyway.

"Who *cares* what he thinks? He's a jerk for saying that. Besides, I'm kind of glad it's just us girls!" I said emphatically.

She just sighed, picked up my bag and headed toward the porch. I felt bad, hoping I hadn't overstepped the boundaries with my comment.

"I mean, I don't want to say his opinion doesn't matter," I said, following her. "I know you care and all, but you're the one who gets to make the decision on your hair. And after he, well, after the …. Well, good grief, right?"

"There's a little more to that story, too," she said, turning back toward me.

"What do you mean? Is everything ok?" Now I was all sorts of curious, but could see she was already through the door.

"I know this sounds crazy, but I'm pretty sure he's picked up with Veronica Valdez again where they left off all those years ago."

I was speechless. Veronica Valdez? The one who had written all those mean letters to Mama? I couldn't wrap my head around what I was hearing. I'd always had some suspicions, but actually hearing it threw me for a loop.

"Oh, Aunt Penny, I'm so sorry!" I didn't know what to say.

"We'll get to that part later, ok?" she said, opening the screen door and going inside.

"Well, you look like a twenty-five-year-old!" I called out to her enthusiastically, meaning every word.

"Ha! You always were a pretty good little liar," she called back. "Let's get you unpacked. Did you have a good evening?"

"Oh, sure. Just hit the sack as soon as I got in... long trip and all, you know?" She had me pegged.

I brought my other suitcase into the house and followed her back to my old room. Mine and Sage's old room, I thought. Though I hadn't actually been away long, it seemed like it had been forever since I'd laid on my bed, on my side of the room, Sage and I whispering about this or that, or listening to music, or, well. Sage. Her absence draped itself over me like a heavy blanket.

"I'll give you a few minutes to unpack, ok?" Aunt Penny smiled, standing in the doorway then turning away, leaving me alone. It took all of five minutes to put the few things I'd brought away. Mostly everything stayed in the suitcase.

"So!" I said brightly, coming back down the hall and into the kitchen. "Mmm, smells good!"

Aunt Penny placed a generous slice of warm banana bread on a plate and slid it in front of me. "Coffee?"

"Sure, I can get it. You don't need to wait on me!"

"Heck, I'm so happy you're here, darlin'! I don't mind waiting on you a bit!"

"Ok, well, if you insist then." I smiled, taking a big bite of bread.

"Yummy! This is so good!" I hadn't eaten the evening before and I was hungrier than I had realized. "Aunt Penny, I have to admit, I'm completely shocked about all this. You *have* to tell me everything. What happened? There's so much I've missed! And, hey, what's been going on with Mama's case? Any news at all?" Although I knew she would've called me in Denver if there had been any.

"Well, I'll get to Sage in a bit. I do want to tell you the little I found out just yesterday about your Mama. I told you Mina finally came out, I guess it was just maybe a few weeks after you left. Jamie says she wasn't all that helpful and had a water-tight alibi, but while she was here, she asked to see you and Sage. Sage was pretty reluctant at first, but she finally agreed Mina could come out here to the house for a visit before she left to go back to Emmit."

"Wow. How'd *that* go?"

"She's still kind of a cold fish if you ask me. I just kept getting weird vibes from her. I don't know why, other than she doesn't particularly like the fact that Doug and I took her granddaughter away." She saw my face fall. "Oh, honey, I didn't mean it like that. I know she's your grandmother, too. It's just that, well, shoot, I'm sorry."

"No, don't worry, Aunt Penny. Seriously! I don't even know her! I shouldn't be feeling bad at all, I guess. Different time, different people. It's ok."

"Anyway, she came out on a Tuesday afternoon and only stayed about twenty minutes or so. Her and Sage sat out on the front porch and I tried my best not to eavesdrop."

"How well did that go?" I asked her teasingly.

"Not good at all. I couldn't hear a thing." She smiled back at me.

"Well, I'm sure Sage told you everything once she left, right?"

"I asked her, without sounding too, you know, snoopy, or anything, but I could tell she was a little reluctant."

"Why? Man, I'd be all *over* that if it were me!" I was slightly irritated with myself because if I had stayed here, I might have finally gotten to meet my grandmother.

"I don't know. Maybe she was feeling protective or something. I know Mina always had a sort of hold over Sage. But I do know one really good thing came of it."

"What's that?"

"She left her a check for $20,000."

"WHAT??? $20,000 dollars?"

"Yup, and she also said there's $20,000 dollars waiting for you, too."

I sucked in my breath, speechless.

She continued, "Evidently it had something to do with a trust they had set up years ago for Sage. She didn't know about you back then, of course, so you aren't on the official documentation. But she must've had a change of heart or something because she told Sage, who told me, that you get the same amount, too. There's some sort of clause that says once you two turned twenty, you'd get the full amount."

I was still in shock.

"KC! Are you ok? You're as pale as a ghost!"

"Aunt Penny! Are you *sure*? I mean, I can't believe this! So you're saying in less than one year I'm going to get $20,000? Now I can help you pay for the detective!"

"No, don't even think about it. Jamie isn't even charging us for any of this. Just as long as he and Pat get an occasional meal and a beer or two, they both said they're good on the money situation."

I hadn't known this, although I often wondered how that all worked, money-wise. I was liking Pat and Jamie more and more.

I wanted to ask about Jude, but Mama was more important. "So, what's going on with the case? Anything at all? Has something happened?"

"Not really, although I spoke with them a couple days ago and all Pat said was that they're "tightening the noose," whatever that means. You remember Pat Lassiter, the police investigator working your mom's case? I guess he's the one who finally got Mina Davenport out here to talk."

"But what did they talk about? What did they think she could tell them?"

"Pat and Jamie both have been pretty mum on everything. I don't know if they really don't know anything or if Mina really didn't have anything to add."

"Well, it sounds like they have a pretty good suspect, I hope?" I asked, intrigued. But deep inside I was sick at the thought that a grandmother I never even knew could ever be even remotely involved in Mama's murder. It just didn't make any sense to me and I made a mental note to discuss it with Sage if we ever got back on speaking terms.

"Did they give you any idea when we'd know anything?" I asked impatiently. "I mean, what does that mean, 'tightening the noose?' If they know something, they need to tell us!"

"Jamie promised me he'd keep us all in the loop, honey. He said the minute they knew anything, we'd know. Let's just keep our hopes up that something turns up sooner than later, okay?"

Unmollified, I really didn't have an answer. But I also knew that what Aunt Penny was saying was the truth. I knew it was just a matter of time before this all got figured out.

"So, Aunt Penny," I said, changing the subject to something a little less discouraging. "Tell me about Sage and Rico living in Albuquerque. I'm still so surprised she moved out. Do you think it's something I did?"

"No! I mean, I know she's been really unhappy how you two left things when you moved to Denver, KC. It nearly broke her heart. But, no, she had other reasons for leaving."

"Like what?" I couldn't imagine Sage moving to Albuquerque, especially moving in with Rico's family.

"Is Rico working? Is Sage?"

"Well, yes and no, but there's another thing, hon."

Oh God, what more? I thought.

"She's pregnant."

"Pregnant? PREGNANT?" I could hardly believe it.

"Yes. Four months to be exact."

"Oh, Aunt Penny! Sage is pregnant? I mean, I'm thrilled for her, right? Are you? Is she? I can only imagine how Rico's mom feels about that!"

I remembered Veronica's distaste toward Rico and Sage's relationship.

"I haven't talked to her about that, nor would I have any reason to yet," Aunt Penny said. "But I'm sure you're right. No love lost there."

Thoughts were spinning through my head. Sage? Pregnant? Wow, just wow.

"It's taking some getting used to for all of us."

"Is she ok, though? I mean, is the baby ok and all that?"

"I think so, honey. She hasn't come back since she left except to visit Dr. Mora, her obstetrician here. She's more stubborn than you are, refuses to go to the OB clinic in Albuquerque, only wants to see Dr.

Mora. Anyhoo, she comes up once a month for now, and the last time we met for lunch she promised next visit she'd stay longer. I hope that's the case. She did promise that she'd keep me up to date on everything, but since she's so early in her pregnancy, there's really not much to report."

Sage, pregnant? Uncle Doug having an affair with Veronica Valdez? Mina giving me $20,000?

My head was spinning and nothing made sense.

28 HOW TO UNBREAK A HEART

The house phone rang early that afternoon and I felt an instant flip in my heart. Even though it'd been months, I couldn't stop thinking about him.

"Hey, KC, it's Jude. Heard you were back in town."

"Oh, gosh, hey, Jude," my heart was racing, hearing his voice. "I was just thinking about you."

"Really? Well, my ears weren't burning or anything," he teased. "How's life in the big city? What ya been up to since you've been home?"

"Oh, you know, ok, I guess. Just school and all." I didn't even want to begin to try and explain what all was happening in our little household.

"Um, so how're you doing? How's Miss M? And the pups?"

"Same ol', same ol'. Nothing really ever changes around here. Well, except you remember Salva isn't a pup anymore, not by any stretch of the imagination. But hey, I do have some news. Was wondering if you might want to come out to the ranch some afternoon?"

"News? What kind? Something with Mama's case?"

"Well, yes and no. How about you come out and I'll tell you all about it. Or I can come get you and we can go have lunch or something, if you'd rather?"

"No, no, I'd love to come out to the ranch and see Miss M and the pups....er...dogs," I said. And you, I didn't say.

"Great! Is tomorrow ok? I can swing by around noon?"

"Noon's fine, but I'll drive out there. You don't need to pick me up."

"Oh, right, gosh, I keep forgetting you're old enough to drive."

That stung, but I didn't say anything but "Ok, well, see ya tomorrow, then."

The next day I met him at the ranch. It was a beautiful late fall day in New Mexico, with its crisp mornings and warm afternoons. I marveled at the beauty the land offered, instantly forgetting the concrete jungle of Denver. I hadn't realized how much I missed home.

Jude and Miss M met me as I drove up. "New car?" Jude said eyeing Mr. Marquez's car with curiosity.

"No, just a loaner. I still haven't bought a car since I can usually just take a bus to and from school in Denver. Don't really need one."

"Oh, I guess I was just hoping maybe you've come home for good." Did I detect a wistful note to his voice? Now, KC, don't let yourself go there, I admonished myself.

After chatting a bit with Miss M and playing around with Tucker and Salva, Miss M discretely disappeared and left Jude and I alone on the long veranda overlooking the expansive yard.

"So, tell me, what's going on with the case?" I asked. "Is it good news?"

"Pat and Jamie were finally able to pin down Mina Davenport. You remember she kept getting out of our appointments with her? Well, Jamie devised a sort of "plan" that she needed to come out to Lona to wrap up some paperwork involving Sage."

My heart tightened at the mention of her name, especially coming from him.

"Really? What kind of paperwork?"

"He had to improvise, you know, legally speaking and all, but he worked it so she couldn't sign them in Texas; had to be specifically done in New Mexico under a New Mexico judge with Sage present. I talked with Sage and she agreed to meet. So, anyway, that's why Mina came out here."

"Aunt Penny told me a little bit about it. I guess you heard about the money." I added.

"Yes, that was crazy generous, huh? I mean, that was pretty out of the blue, coming from her."

"What do you mean? Wasn't it part of a trust, or deal or something anyway? I mean, I thought she *had* to give it to us, you know, like legally, or something."

"She does, I guess, but I don't know what the specifics are. Jamie'd probably be better at explaining all that. Anyway, while she was here, we sort of tracked her."

"Tracked her? What do you mean? Like tailed her? What? Why?"

Jude got quiet, and I could tell he was thinking how much he should divulge to me.

"Come on, Jude! You've *got* to tell me now!" I insisted.

"Ok, look, and this is all still under the hat, as Pat would say, but he's got a guy staking her out, both when she was here and also back in Texas."

"Why on earth is he tailing her?" I was incredulous.

Jude went on to explain how, initially, all the meager evidence put them at a dead end. The bullet casing couldn't be linked to anyone locally who owned that caliber of gun and the shoe imprint could've been made by anyone.

"So, what, what do you have?"

222

"Well, Jamie thinks he might have found something. Do you remember that stack of notes and letters your aunt found in your mom's closet?"

"Yes, the ones from Veronica Valdez?" I asked, unsure where this was leading.

"Stuck in the pile was a copy of an email addressed to Veronica from an unidentified sender, but Pat's guy was able to decipher the IP address. It was the same address as belonging to an account held by Mina Davenport."

"What? Mina? Jude, this doesn't make any sense!"

"I know. It's complicated and his guys are working it. All we know for sure right now is there was an email from Mina's account that was linked to a receipt for $2,000."

"Receipt for what?"

"A 9mm Glock."

I felt sick to my stomach. "Jude! Do you think she killed Mama?"

"No, wait, wait, KC! No one knows WHO did it at this point. God knows I didn't mean to upset you like this. I probably should've just kept my mouth shut. I'm so sorry, please, please forgive me, ok? There's just so much we don't know at this point."

"But a receipt for a gun? An email between Mina and Veronica? Jude! Isn't it obvious?"

"Here's the plan, KC. And this is just between us, ok? I mean, I just feel like you should be part of this but I need complete silence; no one, not even your aunt and uncle, need to know yet, ok?"

"I can't keep this from Aunt Penny, Jude," I said firmly. "She's been the one person through all this that I can trust completely and I know she wouldn't keep it from me. So, she's in on it, too, ok?"

He shook his head, but finally agreed. "Ok, but KC there's so much involved right now. I'll tell you what, we'll bring your aunt in on one condition and that's if she gives you and us her word that she won't whisper a word to anyone yet."

"I vouch for her, Jude. I promise she won't say a word. So, can you tell me any details right now? I mean, is this happening, or is it going to happen, or what's the plan?" I was on the edge of my seat.

"After zeroing in on the IP address and confirming it belonged to Mina Davenport, we began the painstaking process of developing a reason to search her computer," Jude explained. "It's not going to be an easy task, especially since there was no clear motive nor evidence leading anyone to think she was even involved."

"What size shoe does Mina wear?" I asked, suddenly.

"Right. Sorry but we already figured out she's a size 9."

"Oh," I said, somewhat deflated. "How'd you find that out?"

"Sage told us, months ago. She said she used to sneak into her grandmother's closet when she was gone and try on her vast array of shoes and boots. She said they fit her perfectly, and she's a perfect size 9."

"Oh," I said, disappointed. "And what about the gun? What about that? Is there any more information on that?"

"Again, we'd need a search warrant to search her house to get access to her computer or search for a gun. All we have is the bullet casing. But if we can find the gun, we can have the experts test fire it and they'll be able to match the striations on the test bullet to the one found in your mom's…um…in her…. oh, I'm sorry, KC," he stopped, seeing the tears well up in my eyes.

"No, that's ok," I sniffled. "I want this finally solved more than anyone. Please, just keep going." He moved closer to me and put his arm around my shoulders.

"Are you sure you want to hear all this?" he asked, his eyes searching mine, genuine concern on his face.

"Yes, yes. I'm fine, keep going," I said, moving away from his embrace, uncomfortable at the closeness.

"So, ok then. Jamie says that until we can make an evidence connection strong enough that the District Attorney will grant us a subpoena to search her house, Mina's off the hook for now."

"Ok, well, so where does Veronica fit in all this?"

"Well, that's the sixty-four-dollar question, for sure. We know the email with the receipt for the gun attached was sent to Veronica's email address. But when the Lona detective originally interviewed Veronica when they were trying to eliminate people, she was incredulous and adamant that she'd never even seen that email."

"Well, of course she's going to deny it!" I said emphatically. "She's not going to incriminate herself! I should've *known* she had something in it for Mama! It all makes sense now! Veronica was the woman in our driveway! How could I have missed it? Jude, do you think *she* came back and shot Mama?"

"No, KC. Veronica was in Albuquerque the day your mom was shot. We've proven that through her cell phone records."

"No! I've already told the police all this! She *wasn't* in Albuquerque, Jude! At least not during that morning! She was in our driveway just minutes before we left for Texas!"

"But that's impossible, KC. I mean, you were pretty upset, rightly so, of course, but could it have maybe been the day before that you saw her instead?"

"I *know* what I saw, Jude! She came in her car and she was yelling at Mama and then Mama told her to get off our property and then she got mad and went tearing off down the road! Then we got in the truck and left for Texas. Then I forgot that stupid album and made Mama drive back home and then I went inside and then, and then......" I couldn't go on; I was so spun up. Jude again put his arm around me and I didn't push him away this time.

"Shhhh, KC, it's ok, we'll get this figured out, ok?"

"Jude, I know what I saw," I sniffled. "She was right there. In our driveway."

"I'm going to get ahold of Jamie and Pat this afternoon and see if we can go back through the police records that day, ok? Maybe they just forgot to include that part, although that'd be pretty shoddy investigating, for sure."

"But if Veronica was in Lona, why was her phone in Albuquerque?" I asked.

"Good question, one we'll get to the bottom of, I promise, KC."

I finally settled down. Embarrassed, I told Jude I probably needed to get going back home.

"No! Mom asked me to make sure you stay for dinner. Please? She'd kill me if I didn't keep you here. She's making chile rellenos, your favorite..." he encouraged.

"Oh, you're tempting me! Ok, tell her I'll stay, but only because of her rellenos!"

He laughed, "Right, I'm sure that's why. I'll go tell her now."

"So, um, so how is Sage, anyway?" I asked cautiously, not even sure I wanted to know his answer. I wondered if he knew she was pregnant. I wondered if he was the father. I'd driven myself crazy at the thought of the two of them out by the lake that one afternoon more times than I cared to admit. Even after all this time, it still hurt inside, just thinking of the two of them together.

"Sage?" he asked, surprised. "I guess she's ok. Heck, KC, you'd know better than I would. I've only talked to her on the phone once when I called to talk to your aunt. I haven't actually seen her since I sold her boyfriend my old truck."

"Oh?" I said, trying to sound disinterested, but something seemed a bit off. "So, Rico bought your truck, huh?"

"Yeah, good kid. I was glad to sell it to someone who'd appreciate the fact that it only had 120,000 miles on it. Ha!"

"Rico's a nice guy. I always liked him. I know Sage really liked him at one time, too," I ventured further. "You know they used to be a couple, right?"

"Still are! I used to see them toodling around town all the time, not so much lately though. Heck, the day I sold it to him he told me him and Sage were on their way to have a picnic out at Escobar Lake."

"Wait a minute," my heart was beating fast. "When... when exactly did you sell him your truck?"

"Gosh I thought Sage would've told you all about it, KC. It was the same day of the Lona Days Parade, maybe four months or so ago?"

I had to steady myself on the edge of the table.

"Wait a minute. So, you're telling me *Rico* was with Sage out at the lake?" I asked, incredulous.

"Um, well, I guess so, if we're talking about the same thing here? When they were leaving after he bought the truck, that's what he told me they were planning to do. I don't know that for a fact, though. Why are you asking, anyway?"

"I, uh…" how was I ever going to explain this?

"I guess I just thought, I mean, I didn't know it was Rico. I mean, I had seen you drive by that day and then you headed out to the lake and then I followed you and then I… I…."

Jude was laughing. I wasn't sure if I should be offended or not, then he said, "Oh, *now* I get it! You thought it was *me*? Me and Sage? Oh, good Lord, KC! She's not even my type! No, I'm sure that was Rico you saw with Sage, not me."

I was so embarrassed. And confused. And supremely happy.

"I don't mean to laugh, KC, it's just that, well, I…. wait a minute. Why were you following me? I mean my truck? Did you need to talk to me?"

"Um, well, sort of. I mean, I saw you and thought I'd just say hi, and then I couldn't catch up to you at the light, and then I saw you drive away, so I just sort of followed you and …." I was rambling miserably and he knew it.

He put his finger under my chin and gently lifted my chin as he looked into my eyes, "KC, we need to talk."

Jude, Jamie and Pat came to the same conclusion immediately after raking through the incomplete report taken by the police the day Shari was killed. There was more to Veronica's denial than they had thought.

"Ain't doing much for me, no sireebob," Pat admonished the police remotely.

"What we've got here is a gal who has motive, wherewithal, and now a shaky alibi after all."

"What if someone else was using her phone?" Jamie offered. I mean, just because it's her number doesn't mean she actually used it, right?"

"Now you're using yer noodle, son. Ok, so why *wouldn't* she be using it? I mean, why would she give it, or lend it to someone else that particular day?"

"I don't know, Pat. I'm still thinking Mina is the one. I just have this feeling she's better for it than Veronica. One. Motive. Getting Sage back or getting revenge for Shari taking Sage away. Two. Money. She has more than God. Three. Connections. I'll bet she's smarter than most and has more ties to whatever she needs "done" than anyone."

"True," Jamie agreed. "And we have to remember the email to Veronica originated from Mina's address."

"Dang it I just wish we had something more to go on," Jude said. Just then his cell phone buzzed. "Well, speak of the devil," he said, smiling as he answered the call. "Hey there, Miss Sage! How ya doing?"

After a few minutes, Jude got off the phone and turned to Pat and Jamie, their faces expectant.

"So, what was that all about?" Jamie asked.

"Gentlemen, we may have some progress here after all," Jude winked.

It took them another week to finalize their plan. Jude called me to explain what they had in mind.

The plan was first, to get Veronica to admit, this time on record, that she had written the letters and notes to Shari and what her plan had been. If they could get her to do that, then the DA said she could go forward with offering Veronica a plea deal.

If Veronica agreed to it, then the next step in the plan was to set up Mina and get her to admit she bought the gun that killed Shari. That would involve Veronica meeting with Mina and wearing her own wire. Once that was all on record, it was just a matter of an arrest and eventual conviction. But I was sick to my stomach over everything we were discussing.

"Wow," I said, still trying to absorb all Jude was telling me. "It sounds so complicated on one hand, but, on the other, so simple. Do you think this will work?"

"We're all hoping so, KC," Jude said. "Really hoping, because we don't have much to go on anymore and our prospects don't look very good for the future."

"It's just that, well, you're always saying how devious Mina is," I continued. "What if she figures it out and it all falls apart? I mean, it's a great idea and all, don't get me wrong. It's just that…well, I don' know. A wire? Do you think Veronica will actually wear a wire?"

"She will if she wants a plea deal. Once we have Veronica, then we go after Mina, so her fate is up to her."

"Well, I hope it works out, Jude. You have a great idea."

"It wasn't mine."

"Who's was it?"

"Sage's."

Sage called me from Albuquerque the day before I was scheduled to drive back to Denver. I was surprised to hear her voice, but sad and somewhat skeptical, too.

"Hey, there," she said when I answered the phone.

"Hey," I said. "How are you? Aunt Penny told me about the baby. I'm so happy for you and Rico, Sage. I really am."

"Well, thanks. We're thinking of making it official, not the baby, I mean getting married next October. She'll be here by then, and...."

"It's a GIRL? Oh my gosh, Sage! That's wonderful! A little baby girl! I'm going to be an aunt! I just don't even know what to say!" I gushed.

Clearly surprised and happy by my response, she said "Thanks! I mean, really! I was afraid to tell you anything after, well, you know after you left so quickly and then you wouldn't answer any of my phone calls, and then I've been having horrible morning sickness, and then all this with the detectives and mom's case, and then Rico's mom HATES me and, oh, KC, I've missed you so much! I'm so sorry for whatever I did!" she sobbed.

"No, Sage," I said, serious. "I'm the one who's sorry. This is on me, not you. It was my pig-headed stubborn defensiveness and it wasn't anything you did at all. I promise you. I am the one who's sorry."

"What, what happened then? I mean, KC, what happened that made you leave?"

"Can we talk about it in person sometime? Maybe not real soon, I mean I want to see you real soon, I just don't know if I'm ready to talk about it yet. Is that ok?"

"Of course! You know I'm coming down to Lona next week, right? I mean, I assume Jude and them told you about Mina?"

"Yes, and I have to admit I'm a little worried about all this, Sage. What if Veronica doesn't tell you anything?"

"She will, KC. She's got too much at stake here to screw it up. I just want to be around when they arrest her."

"What about Rico, though? I mean, his mother and all?"

"Rico's behind this all the way. He's so furious at his mother for what she's done and how she's treated him and me and how upset she is that I'm pregnant, and, well, just everything. She's tried everything she can to sabotage this and, you know, KC, it's so sad because Rico is so happy right now. She got all mad at him and took away his keys to his new truck, well, not new, new, it's the truck he bought from Jude. But it was too funny, because Jude had an extra set of keys, so he gave them to Rico. We drove by the clinic and honked the horn when she was going in. Made her even more angry."

"Sage! I can't believe you did that!" I laughed, but really could.

"She deserves it. But I am a little worried about this wire thing. It's serious shit, KC."

"What about his sister, what's her name?"

"Ronni. She's ok, but she's never around anyways. She's in school for some kind of nursing degree or something like that. We rarely even see her. Hey, so when are you leaving? I thought I'd come up next Tuesday and maybe we can hang out for a while?"

I didn't tell her I was driving back to Denver in the morning and ruin our genuinely sweet conversation but I didn't really have a choice. "Um, actually, I leave tomorrow."

"NO, KC!" she cried. "Change your plans! Can you do that? I mean, just change them to next week instead? Pleeeeaaaase?"

It was hard to deny her, so I smiled and said I'd see what I could do. Luckily this semester's online classes gave me a lot of latitude.

"I told Aunt Penny I'd be there Monday, but I'll try and come sooner, ok? I'm sure she won't mind if I spend a few extra days. I'll go ahead and see if I can change my OB appointment to Friday afternoon. If I can, I'll just go there, then come out to the house after I'm done, ok?"

"Sounds like a plan," I smiled into the receiver.

I hung up, feeling better than I had in months. It wasn't hard to reschedule a few things at school for a week or so and I took care of that in a matter of minutes.

Aunt Penny came in just then. "Well, aren't you all smiley, today! Who was that on the phone?"

"Oh, just Sage," I smiled tentatively up at her.

"Oh KC!!!! I'm so glad she called! Is everything ok? I mean, did you two make up? I mean, *are* you going to make up? Or, oh gosh, listen to me ramble on. Are things ok between you two?"

"Hold on, Aunt Penny!" I laughed. "I think so. We talked a little. Did you know she's having a girl? A GIRL! I'm so excited for her! And yes, we sort of made up, I mean, kinda sorta. We still want to get together and talk more. Hey, I was wondering, is it ok if I stay another week?"

"Mind? KC! This is your home! Of course, you can stay, as long as you want!"

"Well, there's a little more to it, though," I ventured.

"What do you mean? Is Sage all right? Is the baby all right?"

"Yes! Everything's all right that way. It's just that, well, there've been a couple developments in Mama's case that you might not know about yet."

"What kind of developments?" She eyed me, immediately cautious.

I went on to explain how Jamie, Pat and Jude had devised a plan to trap Veronica into admitting she sent the letters to Mama. Once they had that on record, they believed they could use that to push Veronica into trapping Mina.

"Trapping Mina? Trapping her how? KC, this is getting scary."

"I know," I admitted. I wasn't sure about anything either, but I also knew we didn't have anything to go on unless we could get Veronica's assistance.

"Jamie says once she commits to it, on the record, then the DA will have sufficient reason to issue a subpoena to search Mina's property. If Mina had anything to do with this, Aunt Penny, he says they'll find it."

"What if Veronica backs out? She's not the most reliable person on earth," Aunt Penny said. "And the fact she's sleeping with my husband."

I wasn't sure what to say, but looking at her face, I could feel her sadness. "I know. I think everyone's thinking that, too. I mean, not the affair part, the Veronica part. Does Sage even know about that?"

"I've only told you."

"Well, I won't say anything. Besides, and I'm not sure, but I think all of them believe Veronica knows more that she's letting on. Pat says he doesn't trust her, but he also feels like she'll turn in a heartbeat to save her own ass....er...skin, sorry about that."

"What about the police? Where do they stand in all this?"

"I don't know. I only know that the guys are pushing to get this going early next week."

"Well, as long as you girls are as far away from the fray when it happens, I guess we can only hope for the best," she surmised.

"Um, well, you see, that's kind of the tricky part, Aunt Penny," I said, wincing. "See, Sage is the one who's going to be wired and will try to get Veronica's confession on tape."

"OVER MY DEAD BODY!" she was already reaching for the phone.

I quickly snatched the receiver away from her. "Aunt Penny! Please! Wait! *Please* just hear them out. It was actually Sage's idea. She sees Veronica now and then when she goes in for her OB appointment, so she suggested that since she has more at stake here with Rico, and the baby and all, that Veronica might be more vocal, or forthcoming to Sage than she would anyone else. She'd be suspicious if anyone else approached her on any of this, so it kinda makes sense."

"But what will Sage say? 'Oh, by the way Veronica, I hear you were involved in my mother's murder?' KC, Veronica's not going to buy that and you know it! I'm surprised Jamie would even *think* this cockamamie idea would work. I don't like this one bit, KC. Not one tiny bit."

I sighed, knowing I felt the same way, but also knowing I had full trust in what Jude had told me. "If there is any way that Sage can get Veronica to admit to even the tiniest little thing, I think they can move forward with getting to Mina, then maybe we can figure out what really happened to Mama."

Her anxious eyes just stared at me.

Sage and Rico got into Lona Saturday morning. I ran out to the front porch just as they were coming up the driveway, wrapping Sage in a big hug.

"Oh my god! Look at you!" as I held her out for inspection. "May I?" I said, pointing to the slight swelling of her belly.

"Of course," she laughed. "Not much there yet, but I already feel like a cow."

"Well, that's the last thing you'll ever be like, I guarantee that! You are simply glowing, Sage! And look at your leg! You're perfect!"

Rico, standing off to the side, coughed slightly to get our attention.

"Oh, Rico! Oh, gosh! And look at you!" I gave him a big hug too. "I'm just so happy for you two! Come on, come on in!"

I helped them get settled into our bedroom. Aunt Penny and I had pushed the twin beds together to make one big bed and she pulled out Mama's large denim patchwork quilt to make it homier looking.

Sage turned towards me. "Are you sure you're ok with sleeping on the couch for the time being?"

I assured her I was fine with that arrangement; I was just happy we were all together again.

Later that afternoon, Jude called. "Hey, there, how's it going?"

"Good, you?" I answered, hopefully thinking he was going to mention something about the last thing he said to me during our last conversation: "KC, we need to talk." I had replayed that over and over in my head for the last few days and my heart sank when he said that he needed to talk to Sage.

I handed her the phone, but waited anxiously next to her, hoping I could tell what they were talking about.

"Uh-huh, yes, ok. Ok, that'll work. Sure, uh-huh. Ok, see you then."

As soon as she hung up, she turned to see three pairs of eyes expectantly waiting to hear what she had to say.

"Ok, here's the plan. I'm meeting with Jamie on Monday morning to go over everything, kind of a dry run, if you will. You know, just to make sure I know what to do." She smiled nervously at Rico.

"I'll be right next to you, babe," he squeezed her hand.

"That's good, honey, but only on Monday. On Tuesday, I'm meeting with them again so they can place the wire and all."

"I don't like this, Sage," Aunt Penny said. "I'm just totally against it, and I wish you would change your mind."

"I think this is the best thing, Aunt Penny. And don't worry, Jamie, Jude and Pat are going to be out in Pat's RV so they'll be right there in case anything goes wrong."

"Anything goes *wrong*? What's that supposed to mean? What could go wrong?" Aunt Penny was beside herself now. "I'm calling Jamie. I just can't let this happen, Sage. Not without some sort of guarantee that you'll be safe."

"It'll be fine, I promise," she soothed.

"My mom won't do anything stupid," Rico stated. "She may be full of herself, but she won't do anything to hurt Sage...or her granddaughter."

The remainder of the weekend went by fairly quietly, each of us enjoying the other's company, but still holding our private thoughts about the upcoming Tuesday morning plan. Once Sage was wired, she was to go into her obstetrician's waiting room and sit down. Veronica only worked Mondays, Tuesdays and Thursdays and the doctor's office where she worked was directly next to Sage's obstetrician's office. In fact, there was actually just a hallway that separated them. Sage was to go in at least 45 minutes earlier and check in on the premise that she had written the appointment time down incorrectly but because she was already there, she'd offer to just wait in the waiting room.

Once she saw Veronica come in, she'd casually go to her office and ask if she could talk to her.

"What if she says no?" I asked.

"If she says no, or if she says she's busy, or whatever, then I'll just stay there and tell her directly, "I think you're going to want to hear what I have to say."

She turned towards me. "Will you be there, too? I mean, at least out in the truck or something?"

"Of course," I assured her, not looking Aunt Penny's way. "I'll be wherever you need me."

We were all on pins and needles Tuesday morning, especially me, thinking about how it was all going to go down.

"What are you talking about, Sage?" Veronica was indignant, closing the office door behind them. "I don't know anyone named Mina Davenport!"

"I think you do, Veronica, or, should I say *Mother*?" Sage said sweetly.

"What the hell are you up to? This is bullshit. You need to leave my office right now or I'll call security!" she said reaching back for the just-closed door.

"Go ahead," Sage said. "I'll just wait for them to get here so I can tell them about your secret little affair with my uncle."

Veronica's jaw nearly dropped. "Wha...what do you mean?"

"Oh, yes, everyone will know *exactly* what a home wrecker you are. Is that what you want? Is that how you want your granddaughter to know you as? Is that what you want Rico to have to explain to his friends and coworkers? I think not."

She stopped and turned toward her office door, quickly turning the lock. "Ok, Sage, just what is it you want?" her eyes slit in anger.

"I just want to know how you know Mina Davenport, my grandmother. I know you do because I saw you talking with her a couple of weeks ago outside this very office. I'm pretty sure if we needed to get the security camera footage, we'd be able to."

"So, what, I was talking to her! That means nothing!"

"So, you *do* know her, then?"

"I might have run into her. There's tons of people who come through here to have their blood drawn."

239

"From Texas? Hmmm, I don't think so...."

"Sage, what the hell do you want? Why are you even asking about Mina Davenport?"

"I think my grandmother killed my mother and I think you know something about it."

Veronica's face paled and she had to sit down.

"I'm not saying any more to you. You don't know who you're dealing with, Sage."

"Meaning you, or my grandmother?"

"Sage, believe me, your grandmother will stop at NOTHING to get what she wants. Nothing."

"Oh, I've known that for years. So, what exactly is it she wants this time?"

"This is blackmail, Sage and you know it."

"No, this is you telling the truth for once."

Veronica, defeated, slumped into her chair. "I was only supposed to take her cell phone to Texas."

"Why?"

"She didn't tell me why! She met me and gave me her cell phone and told me to drive to Emmit and make a few phone calls. She gave me the numbers and times I was supposed to do it."

"And then what?"

"What do you mean? Nothing is what! I did what she asked me to! I think we're done here."

"Just like that? Just out of the kindness of your heart? Or were you threatened over something? Or, wait, better yet, did she *pay* you?"

Veronica cast her eyes downward, silent.

"Well, what was, it, *Mom*? Money?"

"Two thousand dollars."

"That's it? Someone pays you to take a cell phone to Texas, make a few phone calls, and you don't ask why? I think *someone's* not telling the whole truth here, am I right?"

"I've told you everything I know."

"Not the part about you being in Lona when you just said you were in Texas making phone calls. So why didn't Mina have her phone that day? Was she here in Lona? What was it? Tell me!"

"Honestly, that's all I know! I don't know about any kind of plot to kill Shari! I was only supposed to threaten her so she'd get scared!"

"Scared? Scared of what?"

"She...Mina wanted me to threaten Shari that she was going to take away *both* you and KC if she didn't restore full custody of you back to her."

Sage sucked in her breath, trying to remain calm. "So that's why you drove out to my mom's house that morning? The day her and KC were supposed to be coming to Emmit to pick me up?"

"I guess that was the plan. She didn't fill me in on everything. I was supposed to talk to your mom earlier that week, to, you know, try and change her mind, but of course that didn't happen. So, I decided to just drive out to your house and so I did. I went out, talked to your mom, then I left. I don't know what happened after that!"

"So, if *you* weren't in Texas, and *Mina* was here in Lona, *who* was making the phone calls on Mina's phone? And why was Mina here in Lona just a few weeks ago?"

"I'm not saying anymore to you Sage. You need to leave right now."

Just then, Pat and Jamie walked in the front doors to the office, coming down the hallway and Pat rapped loudly on Veronica's door. "Open the door, Veronica!" he boomed.

Veronica whipped her head back towards Sage, furious. "What the *hell* have you done?"

"Sage, Sage! Are you ok?" Rico ran up to her as the police were leading Veronica out of the office and to a waiting police car.

"I think so," she was visibly shaken and fell into Rico's outstretched arms.

"Oh, Rico, I'm so sorry it had to come to this! I feel terrible that I put your mom... I mean her, I mean..." she started sobbing uncontrollably.

"Shh, shh, it's ok, babe. It's all going to be okay, I promise you."

Jude and Jamie spent a few minutes talking with the arresting officer then came back in to talk to Sage.

"You did great, Sage," Jamie was the first to speak.

"Yep," Pat added. "I reckon we got her right where we want her. Once she knows she's been exposed, she'll cut a deal quicker than a jackrabbit havin' babies!"

Pat, accompanied by the District Attorney, came into the interrogation room, setting a cup of coffee in front of Veronica. "So, it looks like *someone* didn't tell us the whole story," She turned her head toward the policeman standing in the corner of the room and said nothing. Jamie and Detective Alvarez stood behind the one-way glass, watching as the conversation unfolded.

"Yeah, I'd probably not want to drink it myself," he smiled.

"Ok, let's get right to the point, here, why don't we? As it stands right now, you are an accessory to a murder, Veronica, and you're looking at twenty years in the state penitentiary, do you understand?"

She remained silent, not looking his way.

"So, let me make sure I've got this straight. Mina Davenport hired you to threaten Shari Stevenson that she was going to take away her girls. So, you drove out to Shari's house, threatened her, threatened her with what? I mean, what did you tell her was going to happen if she didn't revoke her custody of Sage? Did you tell her you were going to hurt her? Kill her?"

Veronica slammed her fist onto the table, "I don't know ANYTHING about killing her! I've told you this a thousand times! Nothing! No one! There was no plan to kill *anyone!*"

"Yet someone killed her," Pat said quietly, uncharacteristically gentle. "Someone walked out of that vacant lot, pulled out a 9mm gun and shot her right through her heart. And you know nothin' about it? I'm finding this all pretty hard to believe."

"Believe what you want," she said sullenly. "I don't really give a shit."

"But you will, Veronica. You will give a BIG shit when you're sitting in a jail cell for something you didn't do. Is that what you want?"

"I DIDN'T DO ANYTHING!"

"Heard that line too many times before, Veronica. Besides, you already admitted you did. You already told us, and we have it recorded, that Mina Davenport paid you to threaten Shari to give up custody. We got motive. We got intent. So, what exactly *was* the deal, Veronica? What did Mina say was going to happen to Shari if she didn't knuckle under to your threat?"

"I don't know! Mina never told me she was planning to *kill* her! I wouldn't have gone through with it if I thought so. I *swear!*"

"And what about those letters? Did Mina make you write them, too? Did she have that much control over you?"

Veronica grew silent.

"What is it, Veronica? Why'd you send those letters?"

"It was stupid," she began, then stopped. "Look, if I tell you about the letters will you cut me some slack?"

"Might. Might not," Pat said. "Depends on what you have to say."

Encouraged, Veronica continued. "Shari found out something about Greg." Mistaking the surprised look on all their faces for a way out, she continued, encouraged. "Greg had, well, he had been taking some money, sorta on the illegal side, from the clinic where he worked and Shari figured it out when she was working for that accounting company. I just didn't want her to take it to the police."

She looked around the table pleadingly. "You've got to understand. That money is what Greg paid me in alimony each month. The more she dug into it, the more I knew he wasn't going to be able to pay me, and...and...well, you see?"

No one said anything so she continued. "The letters weren't like some death wishes or anything. I was just trying to scare her, to get her to back off from exposing Greg."

"Well, it looks like you're pretty good at trying to scare folks," Pat interjected, though he was somewhat let down that her excuse for writing the letters was so nonproductive. He had been so sure that the letters were somehow involved with Shari's murder.

"Ok, so let's forget the letters for now, and I'm not saying I even believe you, to be honest. But I want to swing this back to Mina. You took her money, played her game, whatever it was, then left the scene just in time for her to pop out of the trees and shoot Shari, am I right?"

"No! There wasn't any game! I didn't know Mina was over there in the vacant lot waiting! How was I supposed to know that? All I did was drive out there and, and.... Jesus, HOW MANY TIMES DO I HAVE TO REPEAT THIS?"

This time it was Pat who slammed his hand down on the table. "ENOUGH TIMES 'TIL YOU GET IT RIGHT! GET TO THE TRUTH, VERONICA!!!"

"I'm telling you the truth," she started to cry. "I'm so sick of all this! It wasn't supposed to be this way! We were just supposed to ...." She stopped herself short.

"We? Who's we?" Pat immediately interrupted her.

"No, no one. I... I meant me, just me."

"You said *we*, Veronica. I heard it, sure as shit. So, I'll repeat the question, who the hell's we?"

"I want a deal. If I say anything more, I want a deal."

It didn't take long for her to fold and request a lawyer. Together with her and the DA she admitted her part in Mina's scheme, although when Pat pressed for what Veronica had meant by the "we" in their last conversation, her lawyer told her to remain silent and that she didn't have to answer.

Frustrated by what he was observing, Jamie pushed forward with the plan to have Veronica trap Mina, or at least to have Mina admit to something, anything, that would merit a search warrant of her house and property. Sage and Rico were already back in Albuquerque and no one thought Sage should have to get any more involved that she already was. She did her part catching Veronica and Veronica was still furious with her. Best to keep them both away today.

I had insisted that I be in on the operation, but Jamie said that would be impossible, so Jude and I spent our time sitting out in the police department's small lounge area, just waiting for the door to open.

A little more than 20 minutes later, Pat and Jamie came out, talking between themselves.

"Well?" I demanded. "What happened?"

"She's going to do it," Jamie said.

I sucked in my breath. "She is? What does that mean? Did she admit to anything? I knew it. I just *knew* she was involved." I got up, intent on going in to confront her myself.

"KC," Jude gently put his hand on my arm. "We don't know all the details yet. Let's wait and see what Pat and Jamie have to say, ok?"

I wanted to be in on that phone call. I wanted to hear my grandmother say the words that were going to send her to prison for killing Mama. My heart beating fast, I wrestled away from him and started marching into the interrogation room. Jude caught up with me and locked his arm through mine.

"KC, please. Please wait and let this work out how it's supposed to." I looked at his beautiful warm eyes holding steady with mine, and I realized he was right. I sat down on the nearest bench and put my head in my hands.

"It's going to be ok," he promised. "We just have to wait to see what they have to say."

Once everything was fleshed out and set up, Veronica stayed in the interrogation room, surrounded by her lawyer, Pat, and Jaime, plus the District Attorney and two technical specialists. She made the call to Texas on her cell phone, which was being recorded.

But Mina Davenport was suspicious from the very first word.

"*Why are you calling here?*" she hissed into the phone. "I told you never to call here. We have nothing to say to each other, do you understand? It's over."

"No! Wait, wait, Mina. I... I... don't know who else to call. I'm in real trouble here."

Silence.

Then, "What do you mean, trouble? What kind of trouble?"

"I got an anonymous call yesterday from a guy who said I had to come up with five grand by this weekend or he was going to spill the beans to the Feds."

"Spill what beans?" Mina asked.

"You know, Mina, the *plan*."

"There is no plan you silly twit. I have no idea what you're talking about. It sounds like it's something you need to go figure out yourself."

"But, Mina, *you're* the one who got me involved in this. If you hadn't made me do that to Shari, I wouldn't even be involved in the first place. You've got to help me out." Veronica started to cry into her phone.

"And how do you suppose I'm going to do that? Get myself involved in some stupid situation you've gotten yourself involved in? Jesus, Veronica, pull yourself together!" she snapped.

"I just don't know what to do, I'm so scared, Mina. And I don't know what that guy's going to do if I don't come up with the money. You've got to help me. Please, just lend me the money. I promise I'll pay it back. I can drive to Emmit and be there by noon tomorrow. Please, Mina!"

"I don't have to help you do anything, Veronica. I don't have a clue what you're talking about." And she hung up.

"Well, that didn't go as planned," Jamie said, defeated. Everyone around the table let out a resigned sigh, not sure what to do next.

"Ok, my client has done her part," Veronica's lawyer said. "We're out of here."

"Not so fast, lil lady," Pat interjected. "The plan was for Veronica to get Mina on tape fessin' up to setting this all up. She didn't get nowhere close to that."

"But you heard her!" Veronica complained. "She's not going to implicate herself in anything."

"She's slippery, I'll give her that," Pat commented. "But we're better. Just gotta put a bigger worm on the hook for ol' Mina to bite."

The District Attorney turned toward Veronica's lawyer. "Keep her in Lona."

"Like I said," her lawyer got up, pulling up Veronica's arm. "Until you have something on the table that my client has agreed to do, we're out of here." They both left the room, Veronica casting a side glance towards me as she left the building with her lawyer at her side. I could feel the chill from twenty feet away.

Pat and Jamie came out next and walked up to Jude and I. Jamie turned to Pat and asked, "Ok, Pat, what now?"

Pat turned and looked directly at me. "KC and Sage. That's what's gonna work."

I didn't know what to say. I mean, I of course was going to do all I could to help find what happened to Mama, but this wasn't something I saw coming.

"What do you mean? Me? So, I'd be the... you know, the bait?"

Jamie looked at me thoughtfully. "It could work, KC. If we set it up so that it is completely natural and non-confrontational, something that maybe we make Mina think was even her idea to begin with, this could work."

"But why on earth would Mina confess *anything* to Sage or I? That doesn't make any sense."

"I think," Jamie interrupted, "that what Pat is saying is if we can get Mina out here, this time on the premise of seeing you and Sage, and then somehow we work it that Veronica shows up, I don't know. Maybe it'd get her just riled up enough that she'd get mad at Veronica and say something. What're ya thinking, Pat?"

"Well," I interrupted, shaking my head at the prospect of putting Sage in another sticky situation. "I don't know what anyone else thinks, but I for one don't want to involve Sage anymore. This can't be good for the baby, either."

Heads nodded in agreement. "We'll work on setting up Plan B," Pat nodded enthusiastically. "We'll hook 'er and cook 'er quicker 'n you can say it!"

32 A TRIP UP NORTH

Jamie, Pat and Jude sat together at the long table in the ranch's large dining room, all three of them immersed in the various stacks of papers surrounding them. No one spoke as they pored over everything, trying to find a way to get to the bottom of this. I sat near the large stone fireplace; an autumn chill had seeped into our warm little town and the fire was just enough to keep us all comfortable. Tucker and Salva were stationed at my feet and I was only half-listening to the conversation.

Just then Jamie frowned down at the paper in his hand. "Whoa, what's this?"

"Got somethin' there, amigo?" Pat asked, leaning back in his chair and stretching his long legs out in front of him. It'd been a long three days and none of them had found anything that was bringing them any closer to finding out who killed Mama.

"Well, I'm not sure," Jamie said. "But I've been going over these files from Detective Alvarez and I'm not seeing any mention of Shari turning in the notes and letters she said were from Veronica. I wonder why. Didn't Penny talk with Alvarez and he told her they already knew about the letters? That Shari had contacted them a few years ago when she first started getting them? Something's not tracking here. Let me do some more digging."

"Jude," Jaime asked, "slide me over the ones that we've verified the IP address on those emails, will you?"

"I've gone over and over them, Jamie. I don't see anything out of the ordinary, at least nothing that's a red flag or anything."

"Ok, let's look at it from another angle, ok? So, we've figured out the original email was from Veronica's computer, right? But Veronica swears she didn't write them. Is it possible someone else hijacked her email address and sent them to Shari to make it look like they were from Veronica? Who would have access to Veronica's computer?"

I said kind of off-handedly, "well, maybe Uncle Doug? They spent a lot of time together and all…"

"Yeah, but what reason would he have? I mean, why would he want to stir up trouble between Shari and Veronica all over again? Let me take a closer look, ok?"

He spent the better part of the day analyzing the notes and letters. One he took a second look at, not because it was necessarily threatening, but it was different from all the others in that it had some nondescript information from what looked like an ad from a hospital of some kind, then some hand-writing scrawled across the bottom. It was clearly a photo-copy and not an original printed email. The advertisement wasn't of interest to him, it was the handwritten scrawl with the words "AL 10/19 3347 that caught his attention.

"What do you make of this?" he showed it around the table. "Do these numbers mean anything to you?" They each inspected the paper, then passed it on, shaking their heads in the negative.

I was curious so asked if I could also see it, and Jude brought it over to where I was sitting.

"I know what they are," I said, as soon as I saw them.

"What???" Jamie jumped up and came over to me. "What do they mean, KC?"

"Well, I'm not 100% positive, but I'm pretty sure that AL is for Alaskan Airlines and 3347 is a flight number. The only way I know is that I remember seeing Aunt Penny and Uncle Doug's flight information from when they first flew down to Lona after Mama died. I'm pretty sure it's the same flight number. I remember writing it on the calendar in the kitchen."

"Ok," Jamie said excitedly, "this could be something. KC could you help us out?"

I was more than thrilled to be part of the investigation, in whatever small part I could, so this was perfect. "Of course, what do you want me to do?"

"Get on the internet and go to Alaska Airlines. See how often they use that particular flight number, ok?"

I did so in a matter of minutes and came back to them. "It's their standard flight, once a week, every Monday from Anchorage to Seattle."

"Ok, is there a different one going back to Anchorage? Will you try and find out all you can about it? Thanks so much, KC, this is really a big help."

I smiled as all their eyes were on me, but the only ones that mattered were Jude's.

It turned out that particular flight was on Monday, October 19, so, in going back over the past several years to find which years had a Monday falling on October 19, Jamie was able to figure out that in the three years before Mama's death, there was just one year in which that occurred, the year before she died. Pat said he would get with his buddies up in Washington State and see if they could find out any kind of manifest, or flight passenger list, or anything that could determine who, or if, was on that flight that might be connected with Mama's case. We knew it wasn't Uncle Doug or Aunt Penny, so the question we were all left with was, "Who?"

Jamie was getting that old familiar tingly feeling that told him he was on to something as he dialed Penny's phone.

"Hello?"

"Hi, Mrs. Stevenson? This is Jamie Martinez. How're you doing?"

"Oh, Mr. Martinez! Er, Jamie! I'm fine! How are you doing? Do you have any news?"

"Well, not sure. Just a hunch on a couple things. Was wondering if you would mind me coming out to talk with you a bit. Maybe this afternoon?"

"Of course, I don't mind! Is everything okay? I mean, well, I guess everything's not okay. I just meant, well...I mean, of course you can come out. Any time. And please, call me Penny."

"No worries, Penny. I've just come across a couple things, well, actually KC helped me figure out a couple things and I think you might be able to shed some light on them. Is two o'clock okay?"

"That'll be fine. I'll be here."

Penny Stevenson had never been one to shy away from controversy. Even when she was a little girl, her mother would constantly admonish her for always seeming to be in the thick of trouble whenever and wherever it happened in their small neat neighborhood just on the edge of Eagle River, Alaska. She grew up the third child with two older brothers whom she adored, Timothy died in the Vietnam War in 1968 and Jessie fell victim to a heart attack when he was only 37 years old.

When she met Doug Stevenson, it wasn't exactly a match made in heaven. In fact, she thought he was probably one of the most arrogant men she had ever met when he came into the grocery store she managed in Rogers Park, near Anchorage, Alaska.

"Are you in charge here?" a man's voice asked her as she was pulling the sales reports from the side of the printer.

She turned to see a tall, interestingly handsome man looking directly at her chest.

"Up here," she said, pointing to her eyes. "Up here."

"Oh, sorry, just admiring the scenery," he grinned.

She turned back to the paperwork, ignoring him.

"Well?" he pressed.

She turned back around, glaring at him. "Yes, I'm the manager, what is it you need?"

"Well, sorry, I didn't mean to offend you. It's just that I've never, I mean, you, er, those are *great* glasses!" he said, pointing to her bright purple specs perched on the end of her nose.

"What is it you need," she said again, now clearly irritated.

"Look, I'm sorry, truly. I just haven't met too many beautiful women up here and you just kind of surprised me."

"I surprised you or these surprised you?" pointing to her chest, then turning back to the printer. "I think you best leave now."

"No! Seriously, let me start over, ok? I'm Doug, Doug Stevenson from the states. Just moved up here about a month ago and I own SnackCity Vending, I'm sure you've heard of it?"

Sighing, she turned back to him, "I think so, but aren't you only in the Fairbanks market?"

"Trying to expand a bit, ma'am. Was wondering if you'd be interested in me putting a machine in your store," he winked at her.

Not missing the inuendo, she put her hands on her hips and said, "Look, if, and that's a pretty big *if*, I choose to put anyone's machine in my store, it'd better be worth it."

"Oh, it'll be worth it, I promise."

Penny smiled to herself at the memory. Where had it all gone so wrong?

33 SAID AND DONE

We went into town Saturday morning to get our nails done and I drove carefully, as a light snowstorm had passed through during the night and the roads were a little icy, the skies gray with the threat of more. But I was okay with going slow; I knew this would probably be one of the last times that Sage and I would be able to get together before I headed back up to Denver next week and we were both a little excited to just spend some time alone.

As we drove into town to the Lucky Nails Salon, we had to pass by the old feed lot on Elm Street. I slowed the truck down to a crawl, pulled over to the edge of the curb and came to a stop. It had been so long since we'd been here, our special, and, yes, still somewhat simple, little place. Turning off the engine, we were both silent as we gazed across the littered and weed-filled lot. We could just make out the large rectangular pieces of plywood that were covered with a light layer of snow.

It's funny how we outgrow things. I mean, not like when my favorite pair of jeans got too small and I had to toss them, or when I realized I really didn't like lima beans after all. It's more like we get so used to doing something one way, or listening over and over to a song that reminds us of something sad, or just living our normal life and then, one day, we realize we've moved on. We've outgrown it. Like something bigger, or wider, or more interesting, softly floated onto the horizon and that all old stuff just lost its urgency and faded away without even so much as a whisper.

After Connie moved, I figured I'd pretty much outgrown that old fort, so I just stopped going there. I didn't really miss it or anything, well, maybe once in a while, but for the most part, I didn't even think about it.

257

But then when Sage came into our lives, that worn-out, dusty old hollow in the ground was somehow new all over again.

"What are you thinking?" she asked quietly.

"Oh, nothing, really," I sighed. I stretched my hand out toward our fort. "It just seems like yesterday, though, huh?"

"Sure does." She turned suddenly towards me. "You know, KC, I've said this a hundred times. I'm not the easiest person to live with and I know that."

"Well, I'm no piece of cake myself," I began. "But who cares? We're good, right?"

"I guess I just never wanted to talk about Mom."

"We don't have to now, either." I felt a pain in my heart.

"It's just that, well, I think after all this time I want you to know something. I think it's all my fault. Everything."

"How can you even *say* that?" I was incredulous.

"If I hadn't decided to come live with you and Mom, you guys would've never decided to make the trip to come get me and then she, and then…." She trailed off, her voice hitching.

"Sage! Don't *ever* think that!" I instinctively took her hand in mine and squeezed it. "No one could've known what was going to happen. None of us. I would never, ever, blame you and I sure hope you don't blame me."

"Of course, I don't. It's just that, well, I think about her all the time and…" I put my finger up to her lips to quiet her. "Let's just remember Mama the way we do now, ok? She wouldn't want us to feel that either of us had anything to do with what happened. I know that for a fact."

"Ok. I know you're right. It's just. Well, hell, ok, let's not even talk about it. Hey, you know, something just occurred to me! We never cleaned out our stuff! Dammit! The snow houses! All of it! We've got to go get it KC!" She was already decisively pulling up the door's handle.

"Wait, Sage!" I pulled her arm back. "Wait a minute, ok? Um... well, look, I didn't tell you but, well, when I saw you and Jude... back then, at the lake, I was so angry I went down to the fort and cleaned everything out. It's all in boxes in the garage at home. There's nothing left down there now." I couldn't look at her.

"Why? I mean, good thing you did, because I sure wouldn't want anyone else to find our stuff and..." her eyes suddenly opened wide. "Wait... what... what do you mean 'when you saw me and Jude?' What do you mean, KC? You saw us at what lake? I don't understand!"

I knew we had never finished our talk about why I had left so abruptly for Denver. It wasn't that I didn't want to, I just didn't know how to bring it up without sounding so jealous and immature and, to be truthful, the more time that went by, the easier it became to just not say anything at all.

But sitting there in Mama's old truck on the side of the road that cold morning, I knew the time had come. We sat there for the next twenty minutes as more snow fluttered quietly around us. I explained everything to her, about how I'd followed Jude's truck out to Escobar Lake, how excited I was that I was going to see him and then how upset I'd gotten when I thought I saw her with Jude.

"But, KC" she pleaded, "You know I'd never, *ever* do something like that to you!"

"I do, now. I'm so sorry, Sage. I feel so awful. Jude told me all about him selling Rico his truck. And I'm an idiot for even *thinking* you would do that to me. I'm sorry I didn't trust you more. I know this whole rift between us was my fault and I, well, I can't even begin to tell you how bad I feel about it. Do you hate me?"

"Of course, not KC! I'm just so happy you told me! I've just wanted things to be back to normal like forever! I could never hate you!"

I smiled tentatively at her. "Ok," I said a little shyly, "So, we probably ought to get going before the snow gets any worse. Still on for nails?"

"Of course!" she beamed.

We drove into town, parked the truck, and we made our way inside, chatting amiably. Before I even sat down, I heard my phone ping and I knew something was up as I read Aunt Penny's text.

"Sage," I said. "Jamie is coming out this afternoon! I wonder what's going on?"

We headed home right after our appointments were over and Jamie was just pulling into the driveway as we got out of the truck. Sage and I joined Aunt Penny as she came out to greet him.

"Well, this is a nice reception," he smiled. "You all look beautiful."

Aunt Penny blushed and said, "Oh go on. I mean, come in; the girls just got back from town and I can tell you, we're all insanely curious as to what's going on."

Once we all got settled at the kitchen table and Aunt Penny had poured him a cup of coffee, Jamie recapped the conversation I'd been part of regarding the scrap of paper with the Alaskan Airlines flight information.

"Yes, KC and I were was just talking about that last night. How can I help?"

"Well, we're trying to piece this all together so maybe you can fill us in on a few things. So this gal, Ronni Baca, Veronica's daughter. She was on a flight to Alaska back on October 19 the year before Shari died. What do you know about her?" He eyed Aunt Penny carefully, noting her surprised look.

"Well," she sighed, putting her cup down and sitting back in her chair. "I know a lot, I guess, but before I begin telling the story, please remember that neither Doug nor I had even the foggiest idea of who she was back then. It was so out of the blue and, now, well, now after all these years I look back and it all kinda makes sense."

Sage and I watched Aunt Penny intensely. This was news to us, too.

"Just do your best, Penny," Jamie encouraged. "I'll make notes where I need to, but I'd prefer if you just put it in your own words and let's see where we go with it, ok?"

Aunt Penny sighed as her mind floated back in time.

Back in the early 1980s, Doug Stevenson's business, SnackCity Vending, was fast-growing and hugely popular, so much so that by the time he and Penny got married, he was able to secure three additional stores in the Anchorage area. Penny quit her job as store manager to help him and his growing enterprise. Over the next fifteen years, she became the accountant, human resources manager and publicity manager for the business and was used to dealing with all sorts of different people. So it wasn't any surprise to her when she pulled into their driveway coming home from work one day and saw a young, dark-haired woman sitting on the front porch step.

She stopped the car, getting out as the woman stood up, shielding her eyes against the late afternoon sun. Penny thought she was

261

vaguely familiar but couldn't place where she might have seen her or known her from.

She took off her wide-brimmed hat and, squinting, called out "Hey there, can I help you?"

As she got closer, she realized that she was really no more than a teenager, maybe 17 or 18 years old, but with the air of someone much older. Possibly a new job recruit? She couldn't remember any recent resumes coming in, so she waited for her to speak.

"Hi," the young woman began. "Um, I know you don't know me or anything, and I'm sorry to just drop in on you like this, so I'll just get to the point. I'm Doug's Stevenson's daughter, Ronni."

Penny was speechless.

"I, I...um, know this is all probably a shock to you, but, well, is he around?"

Finding her voice and her manners, Penny motioned for her to come into the house. "Please, I'm Penny, Doug's wife. Would you like to come in?"

"I know who you are," she said, her voice tinged with what Penny noted was a note of sadness. "But I was really hoping to talk directly to him. Will he be home anytime soon?"

"He should be here in about an hour. Um, you're, you're welcome to sit a spell if you want. I can call him and let him know you, let him know his...I mean, I can call him if you'd like."

"Well, no, I'd rather meet him face to face, if that's ok. I'll just wait in my car."

"There's no need to do that. I don't mind you waiting inside."

"No, I'd rather wait out here."

As soon as she got inside the house, Penny immediately grabbed the phone and dialed Doug's number.

"Come on, come on," she urged him to pick up.

She let it ring six times before it went to voice mail.

"Hey hon, it's me. Um, it's not an emergency, but I think you need to come home as soon as you can. There's someone here you'll want to meet."

Doug pulled up into the driveway twenty minutes later, pulling in behind the car parked in the driveway, curious.

"Hello?" he said uneasily to the young woman getting out of the car and turning to face him.

"Hi. I'm Ronni. It's me, Dad, your daughter," she said, a tentative, expectant smile on her face.

Doug paled as he looked from Ronni to Penny then quickly back again to Ronni.

"I, I, um... I think you might be mistaken?"

Ronni's face immediately fell into a dark cloud.

"No! It's me, Dad! Ronni!" she repeated.

"Now I'm sure you must be mistaken because I don't know any Ronni," Doug stated firmly.

"No, I'm definitely *not* mistaken" she said, clearly angry now. "I *am* your daughter! Veronica Valdez is my mother. Oh, don't remember her? Well, she's the one you screwed and got pregnant and then took off to Alaska, leaving her to fend for herself!"

"I...I...what makes you think I'm your father? I'm s-s-sorry, young lady, but there seems to be some kind of misunderstanding here. I'm going to have to ask you to leave," he said abruptly, attempting to move around her side towards the front steps where Penny stood, glued to the porch.

"No, no, I can guarantee you there's no *misunderstanding*," she was a mask of anger.

Penny found her voice and spoke up just then. "Miss, is it possible you might have the wrong person?" she asked gently. "I mean, that stuff happens all the time. What makes you think Doug is your father, honey?"

"Don't call me *honey*!" she spit out as she thrust a legal-looking paper at her. "This. This is what makes me think it!"

Penny cautiously took the paper from her hand and her and Doug both looked down at it, reading it while glancing up at her as they did.

"Oh! Well, this doesn't really prove anything. This could be all made up!" Doug said confidently.

Now furious, Ronni snatched the paper from Penny's hand, turned around and walked quickly back to her car. Before opening the door, she turned back to both of them, saying, "You know, I should've known my dad was a loser. Why am I not even surprised?"

"He's not a loser! You've got him all wrong!" Penny helplessly called back to her.

"And you're a loser too, married to an asshole who would run off and leave his pregnant girlfriend all by herself! Shame on you!"

"Now, wait a minute! You have no right to come onto our property and accuse us of these things!" Penny was visibly upset now.

Doug grabbed her shoulder, trying to calm her down. "Shh, shh, don't worry honey." Then loudly, towards Ronni, "If you don't leave immediately, I'm calling the police!"

"Fuck both of you," she said flatly, getting back into the car and backing down the driveway.

Both Penny and Doug were silent, but Penny could see the young woman furiously wiping her eyes as she drove off.

As soon as she was gone, Penny turned accusingly toward Doug, seething with anger.

"She's your *daughter*, Doug? You have a *daughter*?"

"Pen, look, we don't know that."

"That paper, Doug. It was a birth certificate. You saw that. It was as clear as black and white. Do you think she would've come all the way up here from New Mexico if she *didn't* think you were really her father?"

"I just don't believe it, Pen. Hell, anyone could trump up a piece of paper to say anything they wanted. I'm not doing anything unless I have more proof."

"Proof, Doug?" Penny was incredulous. "What more proof do you need?"

"Nothing," he said, his eyes flat and cold. "End of story."

After Aunt Penny finished speaking, she looked apologetically at all of us sitting silently around the kitchen table. "I'm sorry. I didn't think any of that was important until KC mentioned the flight number and stuff yesterday. And now that I think about it, it's all coming into focus, Doug, the other woman, their past..." she trailed off.

"So, Ronni is our cousin?" Sage asked incredulously. "Oh my GOD! Is Rico...?"

"No, honey, no he's not. Greg Baca is Rico's father. This happened right before Uncle Doug left for Alaska. He didn't know Veronica was pregnant and Veronica never told him." She turned toward

Jamie. "I guess I should've put two and two together before this. I'm sorry."

"No! This is all good, Penny. Really, so thank you for sharing what you know."

"Well, I'm glad I can help, in any little way. But, here's one thing, though," Penny ventured. "Thinking about it all now, I can't help but wonder what happened when Ronni got back home when she left Alaska...that poor girl."

34 PERFECT STORM

Ronni flew back to New Mexico from Alaska in a sour mood. Should she tell her mother about travelling to Alaska, only to be spurned by her father? Should she tell her about finding the birth certificate buried in the box of old papers in the closet? And, God! Shari Stevenson is her *aunt*?

Angry and heartbroken, she sat on the couch at her father's house, her *stepfather's* house, she reminded herself, planning her next move. She had no one to talk to, especially not him. Knowing this would surely kill him, she thought, and he's the one person on this earth I love.

'I'll just go to Lona and tell mom,' she thought. 'I mean, what can she do? Deny it?" But she was frightened now, frightened that her mother would also deny the facts. The more time that went by, the angrier she became. All her life. All her life and no one had the respect or love to let her know, hey, by the way, your father isn't your real father. Your real dad's some jerk who lives up in Alaska with his wife. You're not wanted. You're a nobody in this family.'

A few weeks later Ronni finally told her close friend, Jackie, about what she had found out.

"Girl! You've known this for *how* long and didn't tell me?" Jackie was floored.

"Well, I just thought I'd be able to figure out what to do by now. Each time I got up the courage to confront my mom, I chickened out. But I swear this is eating me alive."

"I say go for it. Let your mom know you know what you found. I mean, what's the worst that could happen? I sure can't figure out, though, why she hasn't told you after all this time."

It didn't take long for Ronni to make the decision. She was going to confront her mother and get it over with.

She drove to the clinic where her mother worked, only to find out Veronica wasn't in that day. Sitting out on the stoop of the clinic, she felt more lost and alone than she ever had in her life.

Just then, a silver Mercedes pulled into the parking lot and parked. An older, beautiful woman, maybe in her late sixties, got out and looked around. She spotted Ronni sitting there on the pavement.

"Are you ok?"

"Yeah, what's it to you?"

"Oh, no reason. I'm sorry. You're Ronni Baca, aren't you?"

"How do you know that?"

"Well, let's just say there's a *lot* I know. On that note, do you by any chance know where your mom is? I was told she worked here at this clinic."

"I might. Why?" Ronni was intensely curious now.

"I have some business with her."

"What kind of business?"

"Nothing that concerns you, I'm sure."

"Well, it might. Besides, she's not in today."

Mina scrutinized her carefully, pretending not to be interested. "Oh, well then, maybe you can give her a message for me?"

"What would that be?"

"Just let her know Texas is calling."

"What the hell is that supposed to mean?"

"She'll know what I'm talking about."

"I'm not telling her shit unless you tell me what you're talking about, lady."

Mina looked at her calculatingly, thinking. "Are you two close?"

"Close?" Ronni said sweetly. "She's my mother. I love her more than life itself."

"Ok, then, I need you to give her this message. Let her know Mina Davenport is in town and that I have a proposition for her. Tell her I know about her and Doug Stevenson and she'll be more than interested in meeting with me."

"Wait. Doug Stevenson?"

"Yes, so do you know him?"

"Actually, he's my father, he just hasn't accepted that little piece of information yet."

"What about your mother? What does she say?"

"Well, she knows, of course. She just doesn't know that *I* know."

Hmm, Mina thought to herself, A wrinkle in my plan, she thought, but this just might work to my advantage. "Ok. Well, I'm sorry for what you're going through. I find it hard to believe your mother hasn't told you about your real father. I personally couldn't do that to my own child," she waited for her words to have the impact she was going for, pleased seeing the obvious resentment written all over Ronni's face.

She continued "As you know, Doug is Shari's brother. And now it looks like she is your aunt and KC and Sage are your cousins. I am their grandmother. If it helps at all, I didn't know anything about KC. Shari left Texas without telling any of us she was pregnant. The only way I even found out was when my petition for custody was denied this last time around. My man was able to do a little digging and it appears Shari isn't the only one keeping secrets in this family. Anyway, I know that's a lot to process, especially what you've been through, but it's a long story. The real problem is Sage is *my* granddaughter, the granddaughter Shari is trying to steal from me."

"I don't understand."

"There's a lot you don't need to understand. Just suffice it to say that I want my granddaughter back and I was hoping your mother could help me do that."

"How could my mother possibly help you?" Ronni asked.

"I think the question now is, how can *you* and your mother help me?"

Now that Mina realized the deep resentment Ronni was harboring, it was easy to convince her to set up a meeting with the three of them. "I promise this will benefit everyone involved," Mina said.

"I'll see what I can do," Ronni said, "but I'm not promising anything.

"You will once you know what I have to offer," Mina explained. "I'm not a woman with a lot of patience, you see. But I am a woman with a lot of money."

That was all Ronni needed to hear. "Ok, so what's the plan?"

"Get your mother to meet me and you, if you're interested, tomorrow at noon. I'll be in the Dos Hermanos café and we can talk about what I have in mind."

Ronni excused herself to make a phone call. "I need to talk to you, Mom," Ronni said quietly into the receiver.

"Oh my God, it's been so long!" Veronica was ecstatic.

Ronni felt a quick jab in her heart but kept her emotions in check, her mind intent on the matters at hand. Part of her was hoping this would be her chance to "out" her mom with her knowledge about Doug. She'd been harboring her little secret for a couple of months now and had never found just the right time to say anything to anyone. She wasn't sure if this was still even the right time to confront her.

Trying to balance the two competing situations, she went about enticing Veronica into meeting with Mina in the most delicate way she could. She knew how suspicious her mother was so she proceeded carefully, so she detailed the little she knew from Mina had told her.

"What do you mean, Ron? This woman, who, by the way, you don't know from Shinola, approaches you with some crazy scheme? What am I supposed to think?"

"You always told me to take advantage of a situation when it's given to you on a silver platter, Mom. You never liked Shari, anyway, from what I remember."

"No, she really screwed me over in high school."

"What happened? You've never really told me the details," Ronni wasn't sure she wanted to press further, but her heart was beating fast. "I mean what did she do?"

"Just passed around a big fat ol' lie about me, is what," Veronica sniffed.

Oh, and you don't know anything about big fat ol' lies, Ronni thought to herself. "I mean, isn't she that guy, what's his name, Doug, or something like that, isn't she his sister?"

"She is, and I really don't want to discuss her any further, ok?"

"Well, this whole thing that Mina Davenport is setting up kind of revolves around Shari, Mom, and so I think you'll be discussing her a lot from now on. Besides, this might be your chance to get back at her for her big fat ol' lies." She imagined her mother's wince.

"Well, I'm not on a vendetta or anything against Shari Stevenson. That's all in the past and that's where it needs to stay. But this woman, Ron. You say she wants to meet with us and pay us money for *what* again?"

Veronica walked into the café and looked casually around, trying to look disinterested. When she spotted Ronni sitting in a booth across from a well-dressed woman, she walked up to them and stood there, not saying anything.

"Mom, um, this is Mina. Mina Davenport."

"Pleased to meet you, Veronica, please sit down."

Over the next hour, in hushed tones, Mina laid out her plan. She explained how Sage had been taken from her in the custody suit and that she merely wanted her back. She needed someone to "shake Shari up a bit," as she put it and she couldn't do it herself because Shari had a restraining order against her in place.

"I'll need two things," she outlined. "One, I need someone to have my phone out in Emmit and make sufficient phone calls to give me an alibi. Second, I need someone to go to Shari's house and threaten her."

"Threaten her to do what?" Ronni asked.

"I need her to know that she will be sorry if she doesn't reverse her stand on keeping my granddaughter away from me. I want it to scare her so badly that she will have no choice but to comply. I have a gun."

"WHAT?" Ronni shouted, then, quickly looking around the café, she quieted and hissed, "what are you saying? We are not going to have anything to do with a gun!"

"Hold on, hold on. There's not going to be any shooting or anything. It's just to scare her."

"Well, that'll scare the shit out of anyone," Veronica injected. "I don't want Ronni having anything to do with a gun."

"Need I remind you it's worth four grand and you two divide it however you want." Mina said.

Ronni immediately thought how that could get her out of debt so turned toward her mother, "I could really use the money, mom. Seriously. Let me be the one who drives to Texas and then you go scare Shari. It could work, really. I'll be careful. I'll be safe."

Veronica couldn't believe what she was hearing, but nonetheless was intrigued by Mina's proposition.

"Ok, now let me get this straight. That's it? That's all we have to do? I just have to go out to Shari's house, point a gun at her and tell her to give up custody of Sage? And what do I say when she tells me to fuck off, huh? Do I just say, oh, I'm sorry, my mistake? I'll just be heading on home now?"

"Of course not," Mina said, "You're not going to *shoot* the gun, Veronica! All you have to do is point it at her. And say that 'this is a message from Mina Davenport and she means business. Follow it or suffer the consequences.' You know, something like that. I'm sure you'll improvise and make a compelling argument. Once it's done and I get custody of Sage *and* KC, you two get your money."

"No, we'll get half now, half later," Veronica said defiantly.

Mina smiled at both of them, knowing they had taken the bait. "So that's it, I just need to make sure Shari knows I mean business," she said coolly, then added "I am going to get my granddaughters back, *both* of them."

Jude and I were the last ones left sitting at the big table that next afternoon after going over all Aunt Penny had talked about. Miss M had already come and gone, feeding us all, clearing the table, then went off to sit with Pat out on the porch while he had his nightly cocktail. They'd become somewhat close, and she was happy. Since Pat had made the ranch his temporary home of sorts, Miss M made sure she made her best meals, had the freshest bed made up for him each day, anything she thought would maybe entice him to stick around a little longer.

"Jude, do you think we're ever going to find out what really happened?" I ventured.

"You know, I actually do. I think there's something right out there, right past our line of sight, but I just can't see it. None of us can. It's like we have a bunch of puzzle pieces, and most of them fit together, then there's one big piece missing."

I sighed in resignation. "I hope so, I just wish we could find something."

"We will, KC. Jamie and Pat are the best in the business."

"Well, you're no sack of potatoes, yourself, Mr. Lightfoot." I came around his chair and sat close to him, surprising both of us by my boldness.

"We're meeting again tomorrow at Jamie's office at one. Wanna come?" Jamie had set up his own temporary digs in the small office next to the post office. Mr. Buchner had given him a huge discount on the rent, knowing his affection for my Mama and wanting to help out where he could.

"I can't. I promised Aunt Penny I'd help clear out the last of the garden, tomorrow. We've been planning it for a while now," I said dejectedly. "But you'll have to come by afterwards and let us know what happened, ok?"

"Sure, but right now, I've got to get you back home before she calls me a crib-robber," he laughed. We both knew how fond Aunt Penny was of him, but we also both knew how much she worried about pretty much everything.

The next day was fairly warm for November so it was probably a good thing we got started early on the garden.

Aunt Penny had taken the hose and was soaking the ground, starting from the completely overgrown back section, then working towards the front where the majority of what was left of the wilted and spent vegetables was. I put on some gardening gloves and a hat and went out to find she was already on her knees, digging and pulling up years' old brush and weeds. She sat back and looked up at me, smiling.

"I think I'm getting too old to do this by hand. Go grab that hoe for me, will you?"

I did, saying "I guess if we're going to have even a prayer of having a garden next year, it won't probably won't hurt to really clean this out. No offense to you, Mama, of course," I smiled up into the blue, cloudless sky.

We were lucky if Mama was able to coax even a couple carrots each season, so I'm sure she was smiling right along with me from heaven. It had always been a standing joke between us so being here with Aunt Penny in the garden, Mama's sanctuary, just felt right somehow. "Here, let me help you," I offered, bending to start pulling up the offending menagerie of weeds.

"Why don't you start up front, over there," she said, pointing to the only area of the garden that was even close to being neat.

"I don't mind, really."

"No, seriously, KC, I've kind of gotten into a groove here. Besides, I can use the exercise, ha!"

I went back up toward the front part and started cleaning up that section. We worked quietly for about an hour, the only sound the occasional cicada in the sagebrush, the lonesome cooing of our resident mourning doves, and the scrape, scrape, scrape of Aunt Penny attacking the weeds with the old hoe.

All of a sudden, I heard her shriek "WHAT THE HELL?!!!"

I instantly craned my neck around to see her, standing up now, holding something in her hand.

"Are you ok?" I called, running over to where she was standing.

"Oh my god, KC, look at this!"

I could see her holding a small black object at arm's length, laced through her fingertips and pointing down.

"What? What is it?" I said, a little out of breath from the short sprint to where she stood.

She turned toward me and we both stared in awe at the mud-caked, black gun hanging gingerly from her fingers.

Detective Alvarez and two policemen from Lona came out immediately and secured the garden area. They put the gun into a plastic evidence bag, sealing it, and cased the area for any other evidence. We'd just gotten through our monsoon season, which happened like clockwork every summer here, so there was no evidence that could help them. The detective stayed on to interview Aunt Penny and me for about an hour.

Once they had all the information they needed, they left, leaving us to wait for Jude, Jamie and Pat to arrive at the house.

"Well, this sure puts a new spin on things," Jamie surmised. "I'm hoping the ballistics will come back to match that gun to the bullet that killed your mom, KC. We've been waiting a heck of a long time for a break like this. Once we find out who it's registered to, it's all downhill from there on. Downhill for Mina, I mean."

"What happens now?" I asked Jamie.

"Well, the next steps are pretty routine," he answered. "They'll run ballistics, the registration will be matched to the owner, and any fingerprints will be matched, though that's pretty unlikely given the conditions. Anyway, that's when we'll get our guy... or girl."

"Also," Pat interjected, "once we get all the reports back, I think we might have to just pay a little visit to Emmit, Texas and ol' Miss Mina Davenport. But first I think we maybe just start out with a little fishing expedition, if you will. Somethin' to make her squirm a little bit. Lemme think on that one and see if I can come up with somethin.' But, boy howdy, for now, I sure hope I'm in on that collar when it happens. Would love to see her face when she opens the door to a pair of handcuffs."

It took almost two weeks for the lab tests on the bullet to come back conclusive as a match to the gun. The technicians were able to lift a partial, but it didn't match any in CODIS, and the gun's registration, as everyone already figured, was registered to one Tom Davenport, Mina's dead husband.

But still, for the first time, there seemed to be a faint light at the end of the tunnel.

Doug sat in his Suburban on the back side of Markie's where the deliveries were made. Soon he saw Veronica's black sedan pull up next to him and she quickly got out, looked around then slid into the passenger side of his truck.

"How'd it go at the police station?" he asked before she'd even settled into her seat.

"No, how are *you*? Are *you* ok?" she asked petulantly.

"Sorry, just in a hurry. I've got three guys waiting on me up in Santa Fe to deliver the new coin changer, so…."

"God, Doug, a little compassion here? I just went through hell and you're worried about a damn coin changer?" She moved to open the door and get out.

He caught her arm, pulling her back in. "I'm sorry. Really. Tell me what happened."

"Well," she sniffed, sitting back into the seat. "They had my phone tracing the whole conversation but Mina acted like she didn't know a *thing*! She made me look like a complete idiot, Doug! Then they took me down to the police station and booked me! They think I'm a criminal! Thank God for my lawyer, by the way. No thanks to you but I'd be sitting in a jail cell right now. I'm just waiting for the other shoe to fall. I know that detective, James, or Jamie or whatever his name is, he looks and sounds all nice and charming, but I tell you, he's vicious."

"You've got to remember what's at stake here, you know that, right? You can't let yourself be the fall guy for Mina Davenport. You just can't. I don't know how she did it, or even why, but my sister's dead because of her. And I'm *not* going to let you go down for it. So what about Ronni?" he asked anxiously.

"Nothing, and I'm keeping it that way."

"I mean, you didn't say anything to them, right?"

"Of course not, Doug! Do you think I'd really implicate her? All she did was take that stupid phone to Emmit and make some stupid calls. She hasn't really done anything terribly wrong but I'm still not leading any of them down her path."

"I just don't get it, though," he said, exasperated. "Why would Mina want to kill Shari? I mean, I know she thought with Shari out of the picture, she'd get Sage back, but doesn't she realize I'm her legal next of kin? Shit! You two did exactly what Mina asked you to do, no questions, and now she's acting all high and mighty? Something's wrong here, something's just plain fishy. I mean, I know she isn't going to say anything to put herself in this, but doesn't she realize *you* have a little control over this, too? You'd think she'd be kissing your ass right now to make sure you don't say anything."

"Well, she doesn't know about the plea deal, of course. If she knew I'd said even a peep to anyone and that the cops know that she paid me and Ronni, shit, it'd be over for me. I don't trust that woman, Doug. If she can kill Shari in cold blood, what do you think she'd do to me?"

"Have you talked to Ronni yet?"

"I've tried calling her all day yesterday and this morning but she's either not answering her phone or the battery died. I'll try again in a little while."

"Ok, well, I'm worried about her, I mean, I'm worried about both of you. Maybe try her again now?"

"Doug, what's all this concern about Ronni? You know she barely even talks to me on a good day. Hell, if it wasn't for this chance for her to get her credit card bills taken care of thanks to Mina's grand plan, she would still be in Albuquerque with her dad, not paying a lick of attention to me. Seriously, don't worry. I know how to handle her."

"I guess I just want to make sure you two don't get caught up so deep in this bullshit that you can't get out, is all. Hey, look, I've got to get going. Are you going to be ok?" he asked, clearly wanting to end the conversation.

"I'll be fine, don't worry. I just wish this was all over and we could move on with things, Doug. I'm sick of all this slinking around, hiding from everyone, I just want it to be done and you be free."

"I wish it was that easy," he said irritably. "You don't have to worry about Penny!"

"What's to worry about? God, we've been over this a million times! Divorce her ass already!

37 GRANDMA NEEDS A BRAND-NEW GUN

Mina Davenport pushed open the heavy drapes in her bedroom, letting in the bright morning sunshine. She stood there for a moment, admiring the snowy white roses which were so big and beautiful this year, she thought to herself. Turning, she bent to fill her coffee cup from the pot Sondra had brought in earlier, noticing a small sealed envelope propped in between the sugar and creamer. Frowning, she picked it up, turning it over.

Blank, how odd, she thought to herself. She went to her writing desk and pulled out a letter opener, slitting open the flap of the heavy cream envelope. She slid out a single matching notecard and opened it, her eyes flying wide as she read the single sentence, dropping her cup as coffee splashed all over the expensive Persian wool rug.

We found the gun.

"What the hell?" She quickly crumpled the note and threw it onto her dresser, recoiling as if it were a loaded gun pointed at her. She stared at it for a minute then gripped the dresser's edge as she stared into the mirror. "What the *hell?*" she repeated, her dark and furious eyes glaring back at her.

I stopped by the ranch to drop off a book I had borrowed from Miss M and found Pat, Jude and Jaime sitting at the big table just finishing breakfast. They were getting ready to leave for their trip to Emmit today to confront Mina and I could tell Pat was in an exceptionally good mood as he looked up when I walked into the expansive dining room. "Well, hey there, lil' lady! Come on in and have a seat... I was just tellin' the boys here I guess I owe the Lona PD a big ol' pat on the back for their cooperation."

"Yeah, Mina's sure gonna be surprised when she sees all of us standing there, for sure," Jude chimed in, happy this entire saga was finally coming to an end. Jude stood up and pulled a chair out for me, right next to him, I noticed happily.

"Well, I for one don't think there'd even be a case if you hadn't been here," Miss M smiled toward Pat. Rarely one to blush, his face was a bright red beacon. She poured another round of coffee and was just putting the breakfast dishes in the sink when Tucker and Salva tore barking toward the front doorbell's chime.

"I wonder who that could be? Is anyone expecting visitors this morning?" she asked as she went to the entryway and opened the heavy front door.

Mina Davenport stood staring into the room. It had taken her all of two hours to pack, arrange a flight on a private jet, fly to Albuquerque, then find her way out to El Rio.

"Good morning, gentlemen," she smiled benevolently into the room. "I believe you have something that belongs to me."

No one said a word, just stared at Mina's imposing height in the doorframe.

Miss M, immediately realizing who Mina was and clearly upset, said "I don't think you belong here," she said as she moved to close the door.

"Hold on, Marion," Pat called out to her, getting up and moved closer to the door. He came up beside Miss M and lightly touched her on the shoulder. He turned toward the rest of us, and, with a small wink in our direction said, "I think we all just might want to hear what this lady has to say."

"Lady," Miss M sniffed, but took her hand off the door and moved to Pat's other side, making room.

Mina walked in and stood in the foyer, looking around. "This is certainly as beautiful as I've heard."

I heard Jude's quick intake of breath as he took my hand under the table, squeezing it hard, staring at her with angry eyes. I couldn't believe I was sitting there, looking at my grandmother, the person responsible for my Mama's death.

Jamie got up and came up to where the three were standing.

"Miss Davenport, exactly what *are* you doing here?" he asked her, genuinely curious.

"It's been months now so I thought I'd give you the chance to hear me out before I find myself arrested as I'm sure those idiots from the Lona Police Department are going to do if they know I'm here."

"Well, *I* sure know you're here and can arrest you quicker than a jackrabbit if I need to."

"I realize that. But I also want you to know," she said, turning to me directly and staring at me intently, "that I did not do this thing you think I did. I'm not a killer. **I did not kill your mother**. It's simple and not too hard to understand. Yes, they found my gun. But that gun wasn't in *my* hands the day she was shot. Yes, I gave my phone to Ronni Baca to give me an alibi that day. She did her part. Yes, I paid Veronica Valdez a substantial amount of money to threaten Shari to give up custody of Sage. Veronica did as she was instructed."

"You're horrible! You killed my Mama!" I lunged at her, Jude stopping me by grabbing my arm.

"No, KC, I did not," she said, then looking at me appraisingly up and down, "You favor your father."

I wanted to spit at her.

"Mina, this is highly unconventional. What is it you expect us to do?" Jamie interrupted.

"I told you. I want to clear my name, and I want to take Sage back home," she turned toward Pat. "And Patrick, I want you to ensure to me that the Lona Police don't go off half-cocked here and arrest me for something I didn't do."

"Well," Pat said, "Miss Mina, now's your chance to take a seat and tell us all what really happened."

Over the next forty-five minutes, Mina divulged her ill-fated plan.

"I only wanted to scare some sense into her," Mina began, looking around the table but finding no sympathy. "After my son, Michael, went...went...left us, Sage was all I had left of family. I didn't know about you, of course, at the time," she nodded at me. I instantly turned away. Ignoring me, she continued. "So, I worked hard to ensure that Sage stayed with me in Texas. It wasn't easy, and, yes, I guess it does pay to know people. But I was a good stand-in as a parent to Sage.

284

She never worried about money or anything. Over the years, I made sure she was happy, and she *was*, until the courts ruled she was old enough to decide for herself. But, then, I found out the other little piece of information that no one thought even the least bit important to tell me," she said turning towards me. "And that was the fact I had yet *another* granddaughter. How could Shari have kept you from me all these years?"

I could hardly breathe, much less look at her so just stared at my hands on the table in front of me.

"Anyway, I guess that's when I started hatching my plan. I didn't really know what I was going to do, I just knew I had to do something to bring Sage home, and, eventually KC, too. I always felt like Shari's custody case was pretty shaky. I think she did, too, so I knew it wouldn't be hard to shake her up a bit. She only wanted what was best for Sage, I'll give her that. But I also knew she was doing everything possible not to let me know about KC and if she took this all up to a higher court, that'd for sure come out eventually. So, I figured if I could make it difficult enough for her, she'd just eventually cave in and give up her plan to come and take Sage away from me in the first place. I thought if I could just prove to her how much it was going to break Sage's heart to leave the only home she ever knew, if she could see how much damage was going to occur because of her taking Sage away from the only family and friends she'd ever known, well... and I knew that once she knew KC would come in to play, Shari would eventually see things my way."

"Where did the gun come into your plan?" Jamie asked.

Mina turned toward him "I only thought that would be a scare tactic, but I scrapped the idea after talking with that bimbo Veronica and her basket case of a daughter. Jesus, Veronica was so nervous about a little ol' gun, she wouldn't have been able to even hold it, much less point it to scare someone. No, I realized it wasn't going to work, regardless. And I told Veronica that."

"So did Veronica have the gun in her possession?" Jamie asked.

"Yes, I'd given it to her when we met before, well, before the...." She looked at me apologetically.

"So, Veronica had the gun the day Shari died?"

"I'm assuming so. And Ronni drove out to Emmit, just like she was supposed to and made a few phone calls from my phone, you know, just to make it look like I was there."

"So, you were here? Here in Lona that morning? Why?" Pat asked.

"I thought I'd better be close by in case Veronica chickened out, which of course she did."

"How do you know that?"

"She was supposed to call me after she'd driven out to Shari's house and confronted her to tell me if Shari agreed to my terms. That way, I could go back to Emmit and make the necessary arrangements for Sage to just stay there with me. But Veronica didn't ever call, so after a few hours, I called her. She told me what she'd heard from that police dispatcher friend of hers that Shari had been shot and killed, she just freaked out and drove back home."

It was hard for me to listen to, but I was somewhat wary now.

"So, what did you do next?" Jaime continued.

"Well, I knew the first thing I needed to do was get my gun back from Veronica. At one point, I even entertained the thought that she'd gone off her rocker and actually did pull the trigger. But when I went to her house, she swore that she never even took the gun with her, that she'd just hidden it in her office."

"Her office? You mean here in Lona at the clinic? But how did *your* gun end up in *Shari's* garden?" he asked.

"Your guess is as good as mine, I'm afraid. I asked Veronica to go to her office and get it and call me as soon as she did. Then I get a call from her and she's crying and upset, telling me the gun was missing from her desk drawer. That's all I know. I'm going to repeat this to you and it will be the last time I say it. *I did not kill Shari Stevenson.* I don't know who did and I frankly don't care. All I care about is walking out this door, getting into my car and driving as far away from this crappy little town as possible, so I'd appreciate you telling me where Sage is so I can at least talk to her before I go."

"No can do, Mina Lou," Pat said, trying to sound conversational, but I could hear the steely tone inflected in his voice. "Things don't work here like they do in West Texas. And right now, you're still not out of the woods. You know we can't just let you leave."

"What do you mean?" Mina asked.

"I mean, you're going on a little trip down to the station right now. Plus, we'll need to talk with Veronica and Ronni and see what they have to say 'bout what you had to say. We've got a couple Smokeys going to pick them up as we speak."

"He's right," Jamie told her. "Do you understand, that at the very least, you will be considered an accessory to murder?"

"I've done nothing illegal and you know it, dammit! Now, like I said to begin with. You have something that belongs to me and I want her back."

"Mina, first of all, you don't even have custody of Sage anymore! She's over 18 years old and she can do whatever she wants to! Secondly, what makes you think we even know where she is?" Jamie asked.

"Because she's not at Penny's house, she's not in town, and no one in Lona has seen her."

Jude gave me a sideways glance which Mina caught immediately, quickly turning toward me.

"You! You've got her hiding somewhere, don't you?" she turned, pointing directly at me. I shrunk back against Jude.

"She's done no such thing, Mina," Jude said unwaveringly. "Besides, Sage doesn't even live..." I kicked him. Hard. He looked at me, immediately apologetic.

"She doesn't live here?" Mina asked, incredulous. "Where is she? Where does she live?"

No one said a word as Mina fumed, walking in a circle, shaking her head, thinking to herself. "If she's not here, then that means I can't get to her."

She pulled her phone out of her purse and dialed a number. "Max? I need you to come to New Mexico immediately. Yes, meet me at the Lona Police Station," she said, glaring at all of us.

39 MORE IMPORTANT THINGS TO WORRY ABOUT

I'd had a day to process my grandmother's sudden visit to the ranch. Even though I couldn't bear to think anything positive about her, I could feel the tickling of realization in the back of my mind that there might, just might, be a remote possibility she was telling the truth.

Jude said he'd call me as soon as he heard anything, so when the house phone rang early the next morning, I jumped up, eager to talk to him. But when I answered, I was alarmed to hear Sage's desperate voice.

"KC? KC! I'm sorry, but I just don't know what to do! It's been almost thirteen hours now and it's just not like Rico to not call me or return my texts!" I could hear the anxiety in her voice.

"Wait a minute! Slow down, Sage! What do you mean? When did you last see him? I mean, was he going somewhere? School?"

"No! Yesterday afternoon all he said what that he was going to the mall and he'd be back in a couple hours. That's all I know. I figured I'd just see him at dinner. But we always talk two or three times a day, no matter where we are, so when I called him an hour or so later, it went straight to his voice mail. Then I kept trying and nothing. And he never came home! Nothing, KC! Nothing all night! It's like he just disappeared!"

My first thought was that my grandma had something to do with it, but that didn't make any sense, either, because I was pretty sure she was still being held down at the police department.

"Did you try and call his dad? Or mom? Or Ronni? Surely one of them have heard from him?"

"Ronni probably was in class all day and I couldn't get ahold of his dad. Which is weird, too because he usually gets home from work around five or so. Nor his mom. Neither one of them answered their phones."

"Look, I'd call the police and at least report him missing, ok? I mean, Sage, I'm sure he's fine but it can't hurt to at least call them, ok? Then call me back as soon as you know anything," I said calmingly, but I was worried as I hung up the phone.

Sage called the precinct and spoke to the desk sergeant who told her he would get her information out to the appropriate personnel immediately. She pressed him for when, but he couldn't give her a precise timeframe so she called me back, more frantic than ever.

"Sage, hold on. Wait! Just listen, let them do their job, ok? They know what they're doing." I said. I didn't want to distress her, but I also knew she was getting desperate and it couldn't be good for the baby. "Look, I'm going to come and pick you up, okay? There's no reason for you to be alone there when you could be out here with me and Aunt Penny. Maybe there's someone Aunt Penny could call here, or maybe we could get ahold of Jamie or something, ok?"

"It's just that it's not like Rico not to return my calls, KC!" she cried. "What do you think has happened?"

"I don't know, honey, but sit tight. I'm on my way, ok? Just don't do anything until I get there." I grabbed the truck keys and ran out to the driveway. Aunt Penny was just coming in from the garden.

"Where're you going in such a hurry?"

"Rico's gone and Sage is really upset so I think I need to just get into Albuquerque and see what's going on," I said, rushing past her.

"KC! Wait! You're not making any sense! What do you mean, Rico's gone? Gone where?"

"I'm sorry, Aunt Penny, I don't know anything yet. But I can't talk right now! I'll call you as soon as I get to Albuquerque and find out what's up, ok?"

"Just be careful, KC! Don't drive too fast. I'll try and get ahold of Doug then we'll head that way, too, ok?" she called out after me, but I couldn't hear her as I was already tearing down and out the driveway.

Within minutes, Doug's Suburban stormed up the driveway and Penny ran out.

"Where is she?" Doug barked, getting out of the truck and slamming the door.

"Who, Doug? KC? Sage? Who do you mean?"

"You *know* who! Veronica! She's been gone all day and she was supposed to be back at work by noon!"

"Doug, why on earth do you think I have anything to do with that? I don't keep tabs on where Veronica Valdez is! Besides," adding wryly, "I thought that was more your job these days."

"Dammit, Penny! I know you know! I saw the message she left this morning next to the phone in our apartment! 'Penny no help. Headed to see her. Will call when I get there.' But I haven't heard from her all day and she never showed up to work!"

"Doug, the only thing I know about Veronica is that she called yesterday looking for Ronni. I don't know why she thinks Ronni would be out here anyway. Why?" she eyed him curiously. "Is there something going on here I should know about?"

"The note said specifically "Penny no help. Headed to see her." he fumed.

"But that could mean *anything*, Doug. She could be meeting her girlfriend! Or Ronni! I'm telling you; she hasn't been out here! You've got to calm down. Besides," she said, pushing past him, "we've got more important things to worry about right now than where your lover is. Sage just called from Albuquerque because she can't get ahold of Rico and he isn't returning her phone calls. I think something's wrong. She's really worried so I'm going to go get her calmed down. KC left a little while ago too."

He softened his tone. "I'm sorry, Pen. I know I shouldn't be taking this out on you. This whole thing has been hard. I mean, the whole Shari thing, then with Veronica, and..." he stopped, seeing the pain spring into Penny's eyes. "Look, I'll go with you if you want me to."

Even though the mere mention of Veronica's name made her heart tighten, his genuine concern surprised her. "I'll tell ya what, Doug, it hasn't been a cakewalk for me, either," then, abruptly changing the conversation she said, "Hey, do you think Rico not contacting Sage and then Veronica not showing up at work today have anything do with each other?"

"I don't know. Sounds suspicious. Maybe a little too much. Are you okay with me going with you to Albuquerque?" he asked again.

Penny grabbed her purse and extra set of keys from the rack and headed out the door.

"I guess I don't have a choice," she said doubtfully.

"I'll be on my best behavior," he teased. Same old Doug, she thought.

"Let's go, I'll drive," she said, reaching into the glove box and pulling out the small revolver she knew he kept there, tucking it into her purse.

"Insurance," she responded to Doug's surprised look.

40 ONE MORE TEQUILA

Pick up, Ronni, just pick up the damn phone, Veronica willed her daughter. After the seventh ring it went to voice mail. Ten minutes later her phone rang and she was flooded with relief when she realized it was Ronni.

"Ronni! God... God, why haven't you been answering my calls?"

"Why should I? Sheesher...wha... what ya' need, Mamacita?"

"I need you to..." she paused. "Wait a minute! Are you *drunk*?" Veronica was incredulous.

"I mighta had one or two, or four," Ronni giggled.

"Where are you? I'm coming to get you. Right now."

"Don't bother, Mamarita. I don't need you. N' I don' need daddy either, I mean, whas' his name again? Doug? Dougie? Is that right Mom? Ya' know, I been meanin' to chat with you 'bout that...."

Veronica's heart fell. She was speechless. She had no idea Ronni knew. What had she done? How long had she known? "Ronni, baby, listen to me. We could be in a lot, and I mean a LOT of trouble if we don't get out of here in the next thirty minutes. Do you understand? Ronni, *listen*! Mina caved on us, the backstabbing bitch! But honey, I need to come and get you now, ok? Tell me where you are!"

"I don' care an' more," Ronni slurred. "Jus' plain ol' don' care." Then the line went dead.

Veronica grabbed her keys and ran out of the house. She had to find Ronni. She knew she wasn't supposed to leave Lona, but she was desperate. Please, please, please let her be home, she said over and over to herself as she drove into Albuquerque.

Finally pulling into the driveway of Greg's house, she realized Ronni's car wasn't there. Dammit! She thought to herself. Just as she started to back out, a young couple passing by on the sidewalk had to stop or get hit.

"Hey! Watch where you're going, lady!" the guy yelled at her, as they continued past the car.

She slammed on the brake, realizing she recognized the woman. She turned off the ignition and jumped out of the car, running to catch up with them.

"You!" she pointed to the girl, "Yes, you! You're Ronni's neighbor, aren't you? My daughter, Ronni Baca?" she pointed back to the house, then turned to her, pleading.

"I am. Is everything ok? Is Ronni ok?"

"I…I don't know…I can't find her and, and, I… I think she may be in trouble."

"You know, hon," the guy said, turning toward his wife, "I think I saw her over at the park about a little while ago." He turned back toward Veronica. "She was sitting on the park bench, just watching a group of people playing with their dogs."

"Which way?" Veronica began running in the direction he pointed.

She prayed the entire way to the park and was dizzy with relief as she came around the corner and saw Ronni still sitting on a bench. She ran up to her, calling out "Ron, honey! Oh honey!" and wrapped her arms around her.

The smell of alcohol was strong and Ronni could barely speak.

"Why're ya here, mom? Why do you even care?" she eyed Veronica suspiciously.

"Honey, look, we don't have a lot of time to…" Veronica took her arm and tried to pull her up to a stand.

Ronni wrenched her arm away, "Leave me 'lone! You don't give a *shit* about me! You *never* did!"

"Please, Ronni, please, let me help you."

"Help me? Help me *what*, Mom? You lost tha' chance years ago."

Veronica knew she had to act fast.

"Ronni, listen to me. I will make this all up to you. I promise. God KNOWS I promise. But here's the thing, sweetie. And you've got to listen to me, ok? She took Ronni's hand and placed it over her heart. "I love you more than life itself. I know I've done some bad things. And I know your dad and I were wrong to have lied to you. Ron, I love you. But we've got to go right now because we are in trouble. A *lot* of trouble."

Ronni eyed her suspiciously. "Whadda ya mean?"

"Honey, I need to know something. The day before Shari Stevenson died, the day before you drove to Emmit. You remember that day? You came by my office and I wasn't there. Savera says she let you in and you stayed for several minutes. Ronni, I have to ask you this. Did you take the gun?"

Ronni was silent, looking at her mother sullenly.

"Why?" she asked cautiously, more alert now.

"Because the police found it, Ronni. Well, actually Penny Stevenson found it. It had been buried in a corner of her garden. God, Ronni! Please tell me you didn't do this!"

"What? Do what? Wait, ya' think I *killed* her? Are you even fuckin' *serious*, Mom? I was the one who drove all the way to Texas! I wasn't even in Lona tha' day!"

Veronica was mentally trying to figure this all out. Ronni was right. She was in Texas that day, doing just what Mina had set her up to do.

"Ron, listen to me, something's not making sense here. I need you to concentrate really hard right now. The gun. Do you remember the gun?"

"I might."

"You *MIGHT*? What do you mean? Ronni!" She wrenched her arm towards her, her hand moving within two inches from Ronni's frightened face. "Did you take the gun from my office?"

"Ok, ok! Geez! Let go, you're hurting me!"

Veronica realized she was squeezing Ronni's forearm tightly and immediately dropped it, apologetic. "I'm sorry, Ron, look, just tell me what you know, ok?"

"I took the gun. 'K? Satisfied? You weren't in your office and I was gonna jus' snoop around to see if I could find anything, ya know, anything more about my dad." She looked at Veronica accusingly. Veronica didn't say a word.

Continuing, Ronni said "then when I opened tha' bottom drawer, there it was, and I was all like, whoa, wha's this? Then I heard Savera coming down the hall so I kinda panicked and jus' threw it in my purse."

"What did you do with it after you left?" Veronica asked quietly.

"I wasn't sure *what* to do. I really jus' wanted to talk to you, mom." Her eyes suddenly filled with tears as she looked up mournfully. "I jus'.... I just wanted you to tell me what happened with you and dad.

My dad, Mom. I wanted you to explain things to me. But I couldn't find you and everything was goin' to crap, so I just went home and hid it in the top of my closet. I swear, Mom, I haven't seen it since then."

He remembered the day she died; how warm the sun was on his neck as the first few beads of sweat started to roll down the side of his face. He had arrived before dawn that morning and parked his truck on the far side of the old bridge, knowing no one would see it there. The shadows and darkness afforded him enough time to make his way to the lot and settle into a makeshift hideout. Not knowing when or even if Shari would be out, he settled in for the duration, the chickadees and cooing mourning doves the only sounds in the quiet morning. Around 8 a.m., he finally heard the screen door squeak open and he watched as she came out, carrying a small cooler. He stared as she opened the truck door and placed it behind the seat, then tucked something underneath the seat.

It hadn't been easy for him, killing her. In truth, he immediately thought to end this crazy revenge the minute he saw her walk out from her house into the driveway. She seemed to sense something was off, or wrong as she looked around, then toward where he sat perfectly still, crouched behind a gnarled old cottonwood tree in the vacant lot next to her house. She was as beautiful as the first day he'd met her, the sun glinting off her white-blonde mane as it curved its way down her slender back, just as it was way back in school, way back when he was a nobody and she was a goddess from heaven.

Shari didn't return his admiration back then, regardless of how many times he had tried to get her attention. On the first and last time he had asked her if she might want to go out some time, she turned him down. She was nice about it and all, but he felt the sting to this day. Making matters worse, she must have said something to her jackass, full-of-himself, jock-jerk of a brother because, from then on and all through the next few years, he had been the object of constant bullying and teasing from Doug and his equally full-of-themselves football idiots.

"Watch where you're goin' dope-ass!" Doug yelled at him one afternoon as he opened the door a little too quickly coming out of Chemistry lab and ran into him. He hadn't been paying attention and when he lost his balance and fell, splayed out amongst his books and notes, he laid there, too embarrassed to even look up. Doug and his friends just laughed, then walked away, snickering and punching each other as if they were congratulating themselves for some huge accomplishment.

He finally got up, brushed himself off and collected his papers and books. Just then he felt the hot breath of someone standing directly behind him. He turned and saw the smirking face of Doug Stevenson again, this time just inches from his.

"And don't EVER think you're gonna get a date with my sister, asshole. She thinks you're the biggest loser in school."

When Shari left Lona in tenth grade to go live in Texas, he felt robbed of the only girl he'd ever had feelings for. She didn't even say goodbye and that stung more than anything. Not that she should have, he knew, especially given that she had no idea how much he cared for her, but a small token of affection would've at least taken the sting out of her leaving. The only bright side of the whole affair was Doug's unrelenting harassment subsided. No more legs sticking out in the aisle to trip over. No more feeling the thud of mashed potatoes stuck to the back of his head. No more crap. He eventually receded back into the same old nobody he always was before. But he welcomed the change, even if it meant literally no one paid him any attention now. He moved on to other friends, occasionally dating, but never found anyone he thought of as highly as Shari Stevenson. And he knew, from the moment she walked out to the school parking lot for the last time that warm spring day, he never would.

He knew marrying Veronica wasn't the perfect life he'd envisioned, nor even the perfect girl he wanted, but when he found out she was pregnant, he didn't really have a choice. Babies, kids, teenagers, divorce. He thought back at all he'd been through in his life and realized how alone he really was.

Then, of all things, of all people, *Shari Stevenson* had to be the one to get that job with JB Associates. It had all been so perfect before she started snooping into things. "And that asshole Mario just wouldn't let it go," he simmered, his anger so bright he could taste it. "Well, I showed him. And now I'll show her."

He and Mario had met their first year of nursing school, Mario was a transplant from Alamogordo and he lived in the small housing section next to the campus. At first, they just exchanged casual greetings during their walks to and from classes, but when their individual rotations put them together at the clinic all hours of the day, they became fast friends. Mario was four years older, but they had similar interests and quickly found their common ground.

One night, after an exceptionally long and grueling shift, he was changing from his scrubs and prepping to head home. As he was on his way out, his supervisor came up to him and told him they were short two nurses and if he could stay on for a few more hours until the graveyard shift came on.

Sighing, he realized he didn't have much choice in the situation and went about suiting back up. Just then Mario came into the locker room, his face flushed and obviously agitated.

"What the hell! I'm not staying on tonight! Shit! We've been at this shit for thirteen hours! Thirteen hours and now they want us to stay four more?"

"We don't have much of a vote, bro. It's not like we get to call the shots here. Besides, we only have one more year of this shit then we're clear."

"Well, this sucks big time and you know it."

"Yeah, but what'da ya do? I'm exhausted too, but I can't take any more caffeine tonight or I'll explode."

Mario's eyes squinted as if in concentration. "I do have one suggestion," he said. "Meet me out back in ten minutes."

"Why?"

"You'll see."

He was hesitant at first. It was the first time he had ever done any kind of drug. But Mario was insistent that he just "take a sniff to get you perked up a bit" and, exhausted at the prospect of working through the night ahead, discreetly accepted his outstretched hand holding a small mirror with one long line of white powder. Not knowing what to expect, he was unsure what to do and paused as he held the flat glass in his hand, looking at Mario apprehensively.

"Seriously, dude, you want to get through this night? Just snort it up your nose. All at once. Here, use this straw." Sensing his reluctance, he added "Don't you want to see what this lovely lady'll do for you? Give her a few minutes and she'll have you dancing right into tomorrow morning."

He did. She did.

Before long, he was using cocaine on a regular basis. Mario called it "snow" or "white lady" and he never once questioned where it came from, willingly slipping him a couple twenties in anticipation each time their schedules put them together on the same shift.

He was hooked. He thought about the white lady upon wakening each morning. His mind yearned for her at noon. He sweated in anticipation each evening when he couldn't contact Mario. It became too much for him and so, one slow evening at the clinic, he pulled Mario aside.

"Where do you get this stuff?" he asked innocently.

"The snow? Who wants to know?" Mario asked, immediately suspicious.

"Me, I mean, I do. I just don't want to always have to wait around for you to show up. I mean, I guess I want to have it more available to me without havin' to go through you all the time."

"Well, it's not that easy, dude. I mean, I have a guy, you know, who can get stuff and all, but I don't even know his name or anything. I just make a call; I leave the money next to the dumpster and he drops it off. I've never even seen him."

"Where does he get it?"

"Dude! I told you I don't know! Just leave it, ok?"

He wasn't about to leave it, routinely taking his breaks in the wash station room which had a small window looking out towards the dumpster, hoping to catch whoever was leaving the drugs there. One early morning before dawn, just as he was turning back from his perch by the window overlooking the alley, he caught a flitting shadow of movement. He tensed, quickly coming to stand by the side of the wall, watching.

Just then, he saw a slight figure, dressed all in black with a black hoodie covering their head bend down and place a thick envelope between the metal hinges that anchored the back of the dumpster to the concrete wall. He watched as the figure quickly turned around and jogged down the alley in the dark of the morning.

He immediately went out to the alley, looking all around to make sure he was alone as he reached into the crevice and pulled out the envelope. He quickly tucked it into the waistband of his scrubs and went back inside, retrieved his keys and went out to his car. Once inside, he opened the envelope and saw stack after stack of small cellophane bags, each no more than the size of a playing card, all carefully sealed and rubber-banded together. There had to be enough here to last for six months, he thought, his mind racing.

It didn't take long before Mario was on the warpath. Three days later, as he pushed open the heavy glass doors into the clinic, Mario came up to him, red-faced and fuming.

"So, dude, what'da ya know?"

"Know?" he asked innocently. "What're you talking about?"

"You know, dude," Mario's voice got so low he had to lean closer to hear him. "The snow, dude," he said quietly. "What'd you do with it?"

"I'm not following you. What the hell are you even talking about?"

"You sure as *fuck* know what I'm talking about and you're not getting away with it, asshole," he said menacingly. "And you're fucking with the wrong guy if you think you will."

But he did get away with it.

Mario tried as he could but couldn't prove anything and it wasn't long before he just disappeared. He got to work one morning and Mario's locker had been cleaned out and his name erased from the big dry-erase appointment board above the nurse's station. Savera, the head day-shift nurse, saw him looking at the board and came up to stand behind him, placing one hand lightly on his shoulder.

"Sad, isn't it?" she motioned to the board." I still can't believe what happened. I mean, such a crazy accident. Too bad, he was one of the good guys."

"Yeah, he was," he nodded toward her, remembering the night before out by the old dam, the screeching tires, the grinding metal against guardrail, the glass shattering, the violent explosion. He smiled to himself secretly. Mario wasn't coming back.

It wasn't long before he established himself as the go-to guy in Lona's little medical clinic. And not just for his competency in nursing. A natural at math and organization, he offered to help out Betty, their office assistant, by taking on the labor-intensive areas of monitoring and ordering supplies, verifying shipments and several other of the more mundane parts of her job.

Everything was cool, he'd assure himself, satisfied how he had been so successful setting up the phony account through the clinic. It was so easy. Everyone thought he had such a knack at numbers, always had a great attitude about taking on the boring details of requisitioning supplies, tracking shipments, and making sure everything was diligently accounted for. They were all happy he had so easily taken on the drudgery of the task that no one thought to ask any questions. He made sure the little clinic's business ran as smoothly as anyone and, as time went by, Betty was more than willing to offload much of those duties to him.

He tested the water at first to see if he set off any alarms. No one noticed anything amiss so the following month the billing reports again sailed smoothly past Savera's desk. Month after profitable month went by, then year after year, and he continued his deceit, even though, he always told himself, it was just a little bit bad.

The problem, though, was that the little bit bad became a big bit bad when one sunny morning he went into the locker room to change and saw a sheet of paper taped to his locker.

"Please report to Dr. Carson's office asap." It was signed by Savera.

Perplexed, he knocked on the office door of the clinic's head physician.

"Come in," then," oh, hi there, thanks for stopping by. First off, I just wanted to thank you for all your hard work you've been doing for us on this accounting situation. I know that's not part of your training or anything, but you've sure been a big help these past years. I don't know what Betty would've done without you."

"Situation? What do you mean?"

"Oh, well, didn't Savera tell you? We had our bi-annual review come up last month and it showed some discrepancies, little things you probably wouldn't have even noticed."

"What kind of discrepancies?" he felt a small vein starting to thrum above his brow.

"Oh, just a few things. A missed payment for some bathroom supplies, the transposition of a couple numbers on some plastic plasma bottles, stuff like that. Nothing we can't get figured out. But I know all this was never even in your job description to begin with so I've turned over all our books to JB Associates here in town. They'll get it all figured out and sewn up. Looks like you're out of a job," he teased.

But he wasn't laughing. JB Associates? Hell, they were only the best accounting firm in the region. He'd heard about their reputation and he was getting nervous.

"Um, sir, so this accounting firm, so, are they here, local?"

"Actually, no. Well, and yes. They run most of their business out of Albuquerque nowadays, but a goodly portion in still here in Lona and up and down the valley. They've got a gal here, Shari, I think her name is, doing their business from her house. Kinda like that telecommuting thing everyone's so excited about these days. But I hear she's super-efficient, so don't worry. I know she'll have everything back on track in a matter of weeks."

It only took Shari four days to uncover his deceit.

"Hey, Dennis. It's Shari," she said into the phone. "I've found something I think you need to see."

"Is it important? I mean, can it wait til next week? I've got Marie's folks coming in this weekend and a boatload of work to finish."

"Um, well, I don't think so. I mean, well, I've found something I think you'll *want* to see.

"Ok. When can we meet?"

"I can be to your office within fifteen minutes."

Sitting before his desk, she pulled out a thick folder and laid it in front of him. He opened it and began to read.

"Can you give me an idea at what I'm looking at here? I mean, I see this is the Lona Medical Clinic's file, right?"

"Yes, and Dennis, this is weird, but I think I've uncovered something big."

"What do you mean?" he asked, curious, inspecting the pages in front of him.

"Well, a few days ago when I first started on this, I was seeing a few small discrepancies that just weren't adding up to the various invoices and billing statements. So I started keeping a separate file that noted each problem. I mean, I categorized and showed the errors on the spreadsheets, and all, but I still wanted to keep a separate list of the weird stuff."

"Weird how?"

"Ok, well, for instance, you know how the clinic has always billed MedEx for all its lab supplies? If you look on the second page there, you can see that as of March 31, the bills started going to Carson's Medical in Albuquerque. I hadn't heard of them before so I looked them up online and couldn't find any such company. But for each bill logged since then, there was always a receipt for the supplies once they were delivered to the clinic, so at first, I didn't see any problem. Once I started on my final tally, though, I started noticing that each time Carson's was billed, and I mean each and every single time, the bill was always a little more than what was actually paid. Somewhere that money was disappearing. It wasn't much each time, $50 here, $80 there, and on transactions where we're talking a thousand dollars or more each time, it was small enough no one would probably even notice it."

"Well, no one but you," he smiled. "So, what kind of money are we talking about?"

"I'd have to do one more analysis comparing this current month's billings, but from what I've found so far, over the past eight years the loss is in the neighborhood of about $131,000."

"Whew," he whistled. "That ain't small potatoes, no matter how you slice em', huh? Well, great job, Shari. This is outstanding work."

"I do have one more thing to tell you though, Dennis. It's not just the money that's the problem. I've also figured out *who* was doing it."

"You have? Who?"

"His name is Greg Baca."

42 ANGEL, ANGEL, DOWN YOU GO

Shifting his weight, he moved slowly to the other side of the tree, hoping to get a better angle. Just as he started to raise the gun, he heard a car slow down on the road and he realized it was turning into Shari's driveway. Panicked, he immediately fell down to hide in the green cushion of grass and weeds, startled at the intrusion. As the familiar black car made its way up the driveway and stopped behind Shari's truck, he slowly peered up, dumbfounded as he saw Veronica just getting out of her car.

"What the hell is *she* doing here?" he frowned to himself, his eyes scanning the road in both directions.

He couldn't hear the words exchanged, but, carefully peeking out from his vantage point, he could see that Veronica was extremely upset as she waved her arms and pointed her finger at Shari. Craning his neck, he watched the two women standing face to face, Shari's clouded with anger and Veronica's red with frustration. From the corner of his eye, he caught the image of Shari's daughter, KC, coming towards the front of the house from the side.

Just then he heard Veronica shout "I don't give a SHIT what you think, Shari Stevenson!" "Leave us ALONE!" then saw her jump back into her car and speed back down and out the driveway as he again crouched in hiding. His heart beating fast, he leaned back against the far side of the tree, completely out of sight of Shari and KC. "What the hell, what the *hell?*" he repeated to himself. What could Veronica mean by 'leave us alone?' Who's we? What could make Veronica so mad about Shari that she... that she would...

309

He stood up suddenly, brazenly aware that she would see him, but he just didn't care anymore. Just then, KC moved over to her mother's side, blocking his view and, after a quick exchange, they both got into the truck. Shari started it up, and they drove down and out the driveway, the old truck rumbling loudly into the distance and out of sight.

When they were gone, he slammed his fist into the side of the tree, furious he had just missed his one and only chance at what he believed was the perfect reprisal for everything that had gone wrong in his life. "You were nothing but a coward back then and you're an even bigger quitter today," he simmered, loathing himself and his situation.

He didn't know how long he sat there in the lot, his thoughts ricocheting inside his head, trying to find a way to calm down. He realized how much he had lost in his life, all because of his vain love for Shari Stevenson. Even Veronica had never been able to completely take that away. He knew he was wrong in how he'd handled the clinic's books, but it had just been too easy and accessible. Then after the divorce, he had to come up with child support payment. Year after year he kept telling himself he was going to stop, but Veronica would always come up with something else the kids needed. Money for a car. School expenses. It was always something. Then Shari The Fucking Accountant had to go and uncover his plan that he had spent years cultivating. He finally realized it was all over, there was nothing more he could do. Just as he resignedly stood up and got ready to leave, he heard a low rumble. It got louder and louder until, incredulously, he realized that Shari had come back. She pulled into her driveway and stopped, the truck still idling as her daughter jumped out and ran into the house.

He slowly began walking toward her, the gun held down to his side, taking a grim satisfaction as she noticed him, her dark brown eyes immediately filling with suspicion.

As he got to the edge of the lot, she finally recognized him and smiled hesitantly, opening the truck's door and stepping out. A small wave of her uplifted hand, then her eyes flew wide in terror as she saw him lift his arm and point the gun.

"No! Greg!" She held her hands out to him. "No, please. Please, Greg, don't....."

One shot was all it took. She crumpled to the ground as he quickly disappeared back into the shadows of the old cottonwood tree.

Sage was waiting for me on her front porch when I drove up and got out of the truck. "Oh, KC! What are we going to do?" she cried, throwing herself into my outstretched arms.

"Shhhh, shhh, it'll be ok," I consoled her.

She looked at me, her eyes filled with tears. I noticed the small tightening of worry lines that creased across her forehead and knitted her brow.

"There's something really wrong, KC. I just feel it."

"Let's go inside, ok?" I said, gently steering her back towards the front door. "So still no word from anyone?"

"Nothing," she murmured, quieting down a little. "It's just that I know something's wrong, but I don't have even one clue what it could be, KC. Nothing. I mean, it's not like we had a fight, or that he was getting weird phone calls, or anything at all like that. It's like he just simply disappeared into thin air."

"We're going to find him," I said emphatically. "Please, Sage, you've got to have faith in that. It's going to turn out to be some simple misunderstanding, or some message got missed, or whatever," I said bravely. "You just wait, you'll see." Then, "so, is there anything around here that seems different, or out of place? I mean, not that it means anything, but maybe a note, or anything we could go on?"

"Actually, while I was waiting for you to get here, I thought I'd look around to see if I could find anything, any kind of clue, or something that might help."

"Any luck?" I ventured as we made our way into the kitchen.

312

"Not really," she said, waving her arm toward some papers scattered across the counter. "Just these, a dentist appointment reminder for Rico, a copy of Ronni's fall class schedule and the bill for her classes, oh, and then there's this credit card receipt of Greg's from Walmart for some stuff. Nothing that means anything."

"What kind of stuff?" I said, reaching for the receipt. I read the receipt that showed a plastic bucket, two rolls of silver duct tape, a package of white nylon rope and a tin of breath mints.

"What's he need all this stuff for? Is he building something?"

"Who knows? He's always tinkering with something or other. Him and Rico both putter around a lot so he could've also gotten it all for Rico. I don't know. He must have put all that stuff out in the shed, I think. I haven't seen any of it laying around inside here."

"Ok, well, that's a start. Hey, sweetie, are you doing okay?" I asked her cautiously. "I mean, do you think maybe you should go lie down for a while or do you want to head back to Lona now? Aunt Penny is really worried about you, too. I know she'd rather you come out and stay with us while we get this all figured out."

"You know, KC, maybe I will lie down, just for a few minutes. It seems like I'm tired all the time anymore."

"Well, you do have a good reason," I smiled, patting her rounded abdomen. "Go lie down and I'll wake you up in thirty minutes or so, ok? Then I'll make us something to eat and we'll head home."

"Ok, but promise me only thirty minutes, ok?" she yawned.

"Promise. I'm just going to poke around a bit, ok?"

She was already closing her eyes so I took an afghan blanket off the edge of the couch and covered her. I brushed her beautiful white hair from her face and stared at her for a moment, amazed at the rush of love

I felt for her just then. We'd come so far, the two of us, and as I watched the slight fluttering of her snowy lashes against her cheek, I fiercely vowed to myself that I would never let us find ourselves apart again.

The splintering glass caught me by surprise and I instinctively covered my eyes as it shattered into a wide arc. The small shed's door was a lot stronger than my weight against it so I figured the next best thing without a key would be to break the small window in the door itself. I thought if I could just get it open enough, I might be able to reach the lock from the inside.

I didn't really know what I was looking for, other than what Sage had found in the kitchen and I thought the things on the receipt seemed like an odd combination. Anyway, Sage said she hadn't looked out here yet, so the shed seemed like the logical place to start.

Once I was able to get my hand inside and turn the lock, I opened the creaky door. It was dark so I felt around for a light switch and turned on the small incandescent bulb hanging in the center of the shed. Its light was barely enough to see, but once my eyes adjusted, I could make out stacks of old magazines, cardboard boxes, an old set of golf-clubs, a pile of shoe boxes, and an array of dingy, worn garden tools. I didn't see anything out of the ordinary, but, dismayed, I didn't see any rope, bucket, or tape, either. Just as I finished up my inspection and was heading back out, something on the floor caught my eye. It was a medium-sized cardboard box, just as dusty and worn as everything else in the shed, but what was different is that this one had been recently moved, as there was a darker square on the floor where the box had been sitting, showing no dust or dirt.

I bent down and opened the top flap of the box, not knowing what to expect. A bunch of old rags, I thought, pawing through them. Just then, I felt a stiff paper, or something like it, and dug a little further, pulling out a large manila file folder. I opened it up and began reading, my eyes wide in terror as I first pulled out a map of Mama's house and driveway, then a wider map of the vacant lot next door. There was an insurance bill for a doctor's visit, then also a handwritten note that just said 'gun, Ronni, morning'. I couldn't believe what I was reading. 'My God, I've got to get out of here' I thought, closing the folder and quickly standing up.

Just then, a bright beam shined on me and I heard a man's voice say "Don't move."

I froze, looking up just as an unfamiliar man walked slowly into the shed, a large metal flashlight in his hand.

"Oh...um, hey, I mean, y-y-you...." I stuttered, realizing this must be Rico's father. "Um...I...uh, what are you doing here?"

"No, I think the better question is what are *you* doing here?" he said mildly.

"I...I...I was looking for Sage and Rico, and....."

"You were looking for them in *here*? I doubt that," he said, eyeing the folder in my hand.

"Let me have that," he held out his hand.

"I...I..." I clutched the folder tighter to my chest, looking wildly towards the door.

"I said *give* it to me."

I backed as far to his left as I could, trying to gauge the distance.

His eyes followed mine, his body tensed like a tiger ready to pounce.

"Listen to me," he purred, "There's no reason for you to even be involved in any of this."

Then it all dawned on me.

"YOU KILLED MY MOTHER!" I screamed, attempting to rush past him.

The heavy flashlight hit the side of my jaw with such force I was slung backwards, hitting the edge of the tool chest and falling to my knees. The folder splayed open, spilling its contents across the shed's dirty and oil-stained floor.

We both grappled for the scattered papers, but Greg was quicker, raising his heavy boot-clad foot and kicking me, hard, in the side. I flipped over with a loud *oomph*, landing against the wall, and curled into a tight ball, my eyes blurring in stars with the impact.

45 WAITING ON THE RAINBOW

Mina got there first.

Once Max got to New Mexico and posted her bail, the first thing she did was head out to find Sage, figuring she was probably at Rico's dad's house where they were staying in Albuquerque. She wasn't even sure what she was going to say as she walked up the front steps, her mind weighed down by all the drama, sadness and trouble she knew she had created. She needed to, no, *had* to explain everything so it made some kind of sense to Sage, anything that would help her understand she always only had her best intentions in mind.

I know she'll understand if she'll just give me a chance to explain, she thought to herself. All I need is for her to listen to me and my side of this entire show, she said, trying to convince herself as she rapped lightly on the door.

No one answered her second knocking, so she waited a minute or so before going back down the steps and around the side of the house. As she walked into the back yard, intent on finding another way into the house, she briefly acknowledged the small shed standing in the far corner with its door wide open. Just as she was going to rap on the wide sliding glass door, she heard voices, and turned her attention back toward the shed.

"Hello?" she ventured, taking a few tentative steps back down the small paved walkway and across the unkempt lawn. "Hello, is someone there? Sage, is that you?" she called out again, just as she heard a woman's scream.

She quickly ducked behind a large juniper by the fence, searching through her purse for her small revolver, the one she had finally purchased to replace Tom's. Carefully peeking through the branches, she saw a man she didn't recognize appear in the door of the shed. He looked around suspiciously and she slid even further into the heavy cover of the bush.

Just as he was turning back to pull the shed door closed, she heard a muffled voice moaning "Stop, Greg! Wait! Please!"

Greg? She thought to herself. Isn't that Sage's boyfriend's dad? What the hell was going on here?

She boldly stepped out from her hiding place and leveled the gun at him. As he turned and saw her, his eyes grew wide with fury and disbelief.

"Who the hell are *you*?" he hissed, walking slowly towards her, his eyes never leaving the barrel of the gun.

"Stay right where you are," she hissed back. As he menacingly started toward her, she fired a warning shot into the ground close to his feet. He arched up as if he had been hit then stopped, frozen in place.

"I said stay where you are," she repeated, staring him down as his eyes darted back to the shed then to her gun.

"What have you done with my granddaughter?"

Silence.

"Sage?" she called out loudly towards the shed her eyes never leaving Greg, "Sage, honey, it's me, Grandma. Can you hear me, Sage? Are you okay, honey?"

"Grandma?" came a tremulous voice from behind her.

Just as she turned to see Sage standing there on the back porch, her face pale and her eyes wide with panic as she took in the scene before her, Greg took advantage of the interruption and lunged at Mina. He threw his body at her and they both tumbled backwards, her kicking and twisting and him fighting her every move. He grabbed for the gun just as she flung it towards the house.

Furious, he kicked her, hard, as she lay immobilized, then lunged for the gun.

"NO!" Sage screamed, running from the porch, grabbing for the gun just as Greg's hand closed around its handle first. He twisted around and stood up, pointing it first at Sage, then back to where Mina lay, not noticing as I crept up behind him and swung the golf club, hitting him squarely on the side of his head. He fell to the ground, moaning. I carefully stepped around him, then rushed to Sage's side, I folded her into my arms, crying, "Sage, oh Sage! Oh my God! Are you okay?"

"I'm...I'm fine... I don't know...I don't...." she suddenly wrenched herself away from my arms and ran over to where Mina still lay, unmoving. "Grandma?" she quickly knelt beside her, Grandma? Grandma, can you hear me?"

Sobbing, she propped her up into to a sitting position. I came up to them and gently knelt beside them, just as Grandma opened her eyes.

"My girls," she whispered, then, looking towards where Greg lay, "go grab that gun for me."

Aunt Penny and Uncle Doug arrived at Greg's house just minutes after I had swung the club. Hearing screams, they both came running into the back yard, alarmed at the scene as they found Sage and I standing over an immobile, but conscious, Greg. We had already helped Grandma over to the edge of the porch, where she sat, silently watching everything, her gun leveled at Greg's head.

"KC! Sage!" Oh my God! Are you alright?" she ran up to us and wrapped her arms around both of us at the same time. Uncle Doug went and stood guard over Greg, who was attempting to sit up.

"Not so fast, Greg," he held his foot on him, calling 911 as he spoke.

"WHERE'S RICO?" Sage demanded, pointing directly at Greg.

"You'll never find them," he said levelly, his eyes never leaving Doug's face. "They'll all be gone in the next few days, anyway."

Sage tried to kick at him, but I immediately grabbed her arm. "Sage! No! We need him to tell us where they are! Or what he's done with them!"

I looked down at him in contempt, wanting to kick him, too, but Uncle Doug's warning look kept me at a distance.

The police came within minutes and Aunt Penny and Uncle Doug stood next to them, talking quietly, Aunt Penny casting quick, encouraging looks our way every so often.

After the paramedics looked Greg over, Officer Daniels read him his rights and he was promptly arrested and taken away in handcuffs. Later that evening he was booked into the county jail.

"KC, what about Rico?" she asked mournfully, turning her dark sad eyes toward me as we sat side by side on the porch. "Do you think…"

"Shh, no, I don't think anything right now. Sage, I'm sure there's an explanation. We're going to find him. Let's see what the police have to say first, ok?"

The officer sat beside us at the kitchen table, Aunt Penny between us and Grandma Mina propped up on the couch, a paramedic taking her vitals.

"Ok, ladies, I know this has been one hell of an afternoon." He began. "What can you tell me?"

We spent the next thirty minutes recounting the last harrowing hour. I filled him in on everything I knew about the entire investigation.

"But I think you should probably contact Pat Lassiter and Jaime Roybal, first," realizing their professional opinions might hold more weight than mine. I turned to Sage for encouragement and realized her face was wooden.

"Sage," I went over to her. "Are you alright?" She nodded, then defiantly marched up to the officer.

"Sir, my fiancée is gone. I mean, he's missing. He hasn't answered his phone in almost a day and a half now. And his mother and sister aren't answering theirs, either. Something must be done *immediately*."

"We are working on this, ma'am, I promise you. When was the last time you spoke to them?"

"In the evening, day before yesterday. It's been too long!" she broke down and began to sob, leaning into my shoulder.

I looked beseechingly at the police officer. "Is there anything we can do? I mean, don't you think it's suspicious that they're all missing and they're all related to Greg?"

"Look, I'll need to get ahold of my boss, but in the meantime, I can hand this over to my desk sergeant and see what he says. What'd you say their names are? And I'll need their cell phone numbers, too."

"But they're not *answering* their phones!" Sage sobbed.

"I realize that, miss. But I'm going to need each of their phone numbers and each of their providers, you know, like AT&T or Verizon, or whoever they're with, ok?"

"What good will that do if they're not answering their phones?" I asked him.

"We'll get a warrant and have the providers give us the last location that their phone numbers were pinged, or used. That will at least give us the closest cell tower location where their phones were last active."

"Then we'll be able to find them?" I wasn't sure about all this.

"Well, we sure will be able to be closer to them than we are right now."

"How long will it take to get a warrant and then get all that done through the providers?" Aunt Penny asked.

"I can do that in a matter of a couple hours."

Sage and I looked at each other, terrified.

Sage, myself, Grandma Mina, Aunt Penny, and Uncle Doug went to the police substation. It took exactly two hours and forty-seven minutes for the warrant to come through and the cell phone provider to give them the last-known cell tower location for Rico's phone. It also showed the same location for both Veronica's and Ronni's phones.

Once the coordinates of the cell phone tower were identified, the police were able to cross-reference the phone numbers to an actual map location, which was in a remote area off NM 47, not far from El Rio. He then contacted the New Mexico State Police and they dispatched two officers to the area. They searched the surrounding area and identified an abandoned silo on the edge of a pasture and, as they approached, they noticed a locked metal shipping container next to the silo. Getting closer, they could hear banging coming from inside.

Sage, myself, Grandma Mina, Aunt Penny and Uncle Doug all sat at the police station's long conference room table, eyeing the door, waiting for any word on our little family's whereabouts.

After what seemed an eternity, the door swung open and Officer Daniels walked in, a big smile spread over his face. "We've found them! Officers are with them right now."

"Where? Where are they?" Sage pleaded.

"Well, it looks like Mr. Baca had them locked in a metal storage container of some sort, just out past El Rio on the edge of that old abandoned construction site. It's a good thing, too. Can't last long in those old containers."

"I'm going out there!" Sage shouted, clumsily trying to get up from the table.

"No, no, miss you can't go. We'll bring them all back here safe and sound, I promise."

"Sage, he's right. Let them go. We're better off here, especially you and the baby," I said gently. "But I'm going to call Jude right now. Maybe he and Pat are home and they can go look to see what they can find."

Jude answered on the second ring. It only took me all of five minutes to breathlessly explain what had happened.

"Oh, God, KC! Are you alright? I wish you would've called me earlier! And Sage? Is she ok?"

"We're all fine, Jude, I promise. Even Grandma Mina."

"Mina? Mina's there?"

"Yes, and, actually, she's the one who saved us, Jude. I'll explain it all when I see you, ok?"

"I'm coming in now. And, KC?"

"Yes?"

"I'm so happy you're ok."

My heart pounded in my chest as I hung up the phone.

As soon as the police van pulled up, Sage ran out and threw herself into Rico's arms before he was barely out.

"Rico! Rico, baby! Oh my God I'm so happy you're here!"

"I'm ok, honey, I'm ok. We're all ok," he said, holding her in a tight embrace. "Are you ok? Oh, God, this has all been such a nightmare! I'm so sorry, babe!" They both turned as Veronica and Ronni made their way out of the van's side door. All three of them were clearly disheveled and tired, but the relief on their faces was unmistakable.

The rest of us moved awkwardly to the side as Rico, Sage, Veronica and Ronni made their way past us. Veronica smiled tentatively at me as she passed, holding out her hand to Sage. Sage clasped it in hers briefly as the four of them went into the police station.

Sage looked at Mina, her eyes brimming with grateful tears. "Thank you, Grandma."

It took less than twenty minutes for Jude to get there and I was sure he broke every speed record doing so. As he pulled up, I saw the concern on his face so immediately ran over to his truck.

"Are you okay?" his anxious eyes were fixed on mine.

"Yes, everyone's ok. I'm so glad you're here," as I gave him a small hug then quickly stepped back, embarrassed. "I am, too, KC," he said reaching for my hand. "I guess there's not much we can do for now," Jude said, turning to our little group, just as Pat and Miss M pulled up. They had been out for an early dinner and a movie, and had come as soon as Pat received the call from the State Police.

"Well, dang if this ain't one fancy bunch, huh?" he said, smiling around at all of us.

Miss M ran over to Sage and I, hugging us both. "Girls! Oh, I can hardly believe all this!"

325

"We're all fine, Miss M," I assured her. "It has been one hell of a day, though, that's for sure."

Grandma Mina was standing awkwardly apart from us, so I immediately went over to her, holding out my arms.

"Oh, KC, what have I done?" she cried as she grabbed my hand and pulled me close to her in a tight embrace. I could feel her body shaking with her sobs as I gently pulled back from her.

"Grandma, you've saved us."

"But, before... I mean, I've been so horrible to everyone and to your... to your... mother.... I was so awful and... how can I ever..." she broke down, unable to continue.

"Shhhhh, don't talk right now, okay? It's all going to be fine." I held her close. "We're going to find a way, I promise, Grandma. Please, please don't cry."

She looked up, her tear-filled eyes full of gratitude. And just then, I could see her grandmother's love shining right back at me.

Greg had lawyered up so there wasn't a confession of any sort, but the pieces of the puzzle were slowly falling into place.

According to Veronica, the morning before, Greg had called both Rico and Ronni, telling them that their mom had been in a car accident out in El Rio and that they needed to go out there right away. He simultaneously contacted her, saying that Ronni and Rico had been in an accident in El Rio. Veronica arrived first. Seeing Greg's car parked on the side of the road, she jumped out and ran up to him.

"Greg! My God! What happened? Where are the kids?"

He casually pulled out his gun and levelled it at her. Her eyes opened in astonishment.

"What are you doing? Greg! Why do you have that gun? *Where are the kids?*" She started to move towards him.

"Give me your phone and get in the car, Veronica." His voice was stony as he held out his hand. "Do it or I swear, I will shoot you right now."

She silently held out her phone as he took it and then moved hesitantly towards the car, her eyes darting back and forth.

"Don't try anything, I mean every word I say," he pushed her forward and into the open back door of his car, just as he heard another vehicle approaching.

"If you make a sound, I will kill both of them," he directed at her. She was mute, tears rolling down her cheeks, as she saw her two children pull up to where Greg was standing and jump out, running towards him.

"Dad! What...." Rico skidded to a stop, grabbing Ronni's arm as he realized Greg was pointing a gun at them.

"Dad, I don't understand! Where's mom? Where's..."

"Hands behind you!" he barked, as he cinched plastic zip ties on each of their wrists. "Get in the car, both of you. And give me your phones!"

Just then Ronni saw her mom sitting in the car. "Mom!" She screamed as she ran over to the door. "Mom, are you okay?"

"What did I *SAY*?" Greg bellowed out to them and Ronni turned, her eyes wild with fear.

"Get in the car like he says, Ron," Rico's dark eyes never left his father's flat ones staring at him. "Just do what he says."

Greg kept the gun trained on them as he got in and drove behind the grain elevator to a small, older and unused storage container. He stopped the car and ordered them out.

"Greg! Are you out of your *mind*? Why are you doing this?" Veronica pleaded. "Please, Greg, please just talk to us!"

"Too late. That time has come and gone. There won't be any more talking. From anyone. Now get in there." He corralled them into the narrow opening, then slammed it shut and slid the heavy metal bar across the door.

After everything was over, and on Veronica's coaxing, Ronni agreed to make a statement. She didn't have a lawyer but was more than willing to discuss how she came about to having Mina's gun, how she took it from Veronica's drawer at work, how she hid it in her closet. Throughout, Veronica sat protectively by her side, nodding and smiling encouragingly.

Much of the evidence up to this point had been based on three things: one, Mina's gun which Greg had taken, two, the bullet casing, and three, the tennis shoe imprint.

But it was Greg himself who struck the final blow regarding the imprint. Evidently, he had purchased new tennis shoes and had put his old ones, the ones he wore the day he killed my Mama, in a box out in the shed, forgetting about them. The cops found the box and were able to trace the treads on the shoes as an exact match to the plaster cast they'd made of the shoe imprint found in the vacant lot.

Greg had been denied bond and was remanded to jail. As he was being led out of the courtroom, he nodded once toward where Rico and Sage were sitting, then gave Veronica a long and pleading look, which she just turned away from and stared forward.

Once we made our way outside of the courthouse, we stood in a small group, all of us relieved and exhausted. Finally knowing who killed Mama left me sad but strangely consoled. It was almost as if the long fight had come to an end and she could, well, we all could, now rest in peace.

Veronica and Ronni decided to head back to Lona and Grandma Mina announced she just wanted to get a hotel room and turn in for the evening.

Before she left, I went over to her and took her hand in mine, holding it up to my cheek.

"There's so much I wish I could tell you, Grandma. So many things about Mama, and me and Sage, and, well, everything, I guess."

"We have lots of time, my dear," she smiled at me. "In fact, we've only just begun. How about I call you tomorrow and we can decide just how wonderful the rest of our lives will be, ok? Maybe we'll start with a grand shopping spree!"

I smiled at her, just as Jude came over to me and casually draped his arm over my shoulders.

"Everything ok?" he said, watching me expectantly.

I hugged Grandma goodbye then turned back towards him. "It's all perfect."

"So, what's the plan, everyone?" Pat asked. "Lunch on me? I actually have some news I want to share with all of you."

We all agreed to meet at the diner around the corner from the courthouse and, once we were settled into the two tables the waitress had pushed together, Pat stood up, lightly clinking the rim of his iced tea glass.

"Well, folks," he began, "I wanted to tell you that the New Mexico State Attorney General and the State Police Commissioner paid me a visit out at the ranch last week."

I looked curiously over at Jude, and noticed a small twinkle in his eye. But before I could question him, Pat continued.

"They said they were *extremely* satisfied with the work we've done on your Mama's case," he said, nodding at Sage and I. "Fact is, they're so dang pleased, they want to know if they could replicate our model, you know, capture and document how we did what we did, all that, and then maybe set it up so we could provide some assistance to some of the smaller communities here in New Mexico in helping them solve their own cold cases." He looked around happily.

"And I want each and every one of you to know I couldn't have done any of this without you amigos. I mean that."

You could hear a small sniffle from Miss M and when I looked her way, she was smiling at him through her tears.

It turned out the Commissioner offered to set up Pat and Jaime in their own office in Lona, one that would in turn service all of central New Mexico.

"Wow, what an opportunity," I whispered to Jude. "So, do you think you might want to get in on it, too? I mean, if they ask, that is."

"I don't know, KC. I've never really thought of myself much of a detective. It seems like all this work we did to find out what happened to your mom was just the natural way to go about doing it. I don't know if I'm cut out for it as a profession, though."

"Well, you're an *absolute* natural, if you ask me," I said, quickly dropping my gaze as I read the clear surprise in his eyes. I was embarrassed but wanted him to know how much he meant to me, so I continued, unsure of exactly how to say it.

"I mean, everything you did, Jude, it's like, well, you're so smart, and so caring and, I, well, I..."

He took my hand under the table and squeezed it.

"Let's just wait and see what happens, ok?" I didn't know who was blushing more now, him or me.

We all ordered our meals and as I looked around at the faces of all the people I knew and loved, I couldn't help but smile as I realized we all finally had a real reason to celebrate, one that gave us the opportunity to cast off the heavy sad blanket that had been wrapped too tightly around us for too long. Miss M chatted amiably with Pat and Jaime while Uncle Doug, though still keeping his distance, listened intently to Rico's recollection of the day's events.

I hesitated as I saw Aunt Penny and Sage huddled together at the end of their table, talking in hushed tones. I motioned to Sage, trying to get her attention behind Aunt Penny's back and, when she finally looked up and noticed me, she just mouthed back to me "...tell ya later."

That evening after we got back to Lona, Sage and I finally had some time to talk. I asked about what they had been talking about earlier.

Evidently, and much to Aunt Penny's chagrin, Sage and Rico had made the decision to stay on at his dad's house in Albuquerque and Aunt Penny wanted to change their minds. "I'd just feel better if you were out in Lona with me," she worried. "I can help take care of the baby, and you and Rico won't have to pay rent or anything, plus I know you love your doctor here. Please won't you stay with me?"

"I know, Aunt Penny, and we love you for that," Sage said sincerely. "It's just that, well, with the eventual trial, and the baby, and, well, everything, we just feel it's better for us to make a go for it in Albuquerque. Besides, Rico IS hoping to eventually get into UNM's Law School."

Aunt Penny was able to convince us to stay on for a couple more days until Sage and Rico had to get back to Albuquerque. Uncle Doug had a few runs to catch up on out near Clayton, and asked if she wanted to go with him. It surprised us all, especially Aunt Penny, but she declined, saying she wanted to spend some time with Sage and I.

Knowing both Sage and Aunt Penny were light sleepers, I crept into the kitchen early the next morning, not wanting to waken anyone. I was surprised to see Sage sitting there, alone in the semi-darkness without any lights on.

"I'm going to name her after you," Sage whispered to me from where she sat at the kitchen table, the dawn just beginning to shed its pink and purple light over the nearby Sandia mountains through the front window. I reached for her hand and held it.

"You remember my real name," I whispered back, surprised. "I mean, I'm so happy that you want to name her after me and all, it's just that, well, I think Karalyn Celeste is a lot for a little one to handle."

"Actually, I've decided to just name her Angel. Did you know that your name means beloved angel?"

I could've cried.

We had about an hour before Aunt Penny had to go into Albuquerque Friday afternoon to help Sage and Rico get settled so I poured us both a cup of coffee and we sat at the kitchen table, sipping silently.

"Aunt Penny, are you happy?" I asked finally, watching her closely. Of all the people in the world who deserved to be, it was her, but of all those same people, she was also the one most adept at hiding her feelings.

She set her cup down, looking at me, a slight smile just hinting at the curve of her lips.

"Happy is as happy does, right? Actually, KC, I'm pretty content right now. Seriously. Especially not having to deal with so much after all that's happened, you know?"

I nodded my head in agreement. It had been a crazy roller-coaster of a ride over the past few years and I didn't know how I could've gotten through them without Aunt Penny by my side.

"Well, at least it sounds like things are going a little better between you and Uncle Doug," I ventured.

"Oh, he's as contrite as ever, of course, and I have absolutely zero long-term plans with him, but..." Her voice trailed off and she got quiet. I could see a little light of hope shining in her eyes when she spoke and that made me more than happy.

"Have you two had much time to talk about things?" I knew she knew what I meant so I didn't have to explain.

"He met with Ronni a few days ago. And Veronica was there, too."

"Wow, how'd that go?" I was genuinely curious, Ronni being mine and Sage's new-found cousin and all.

"I think there's a lot of repair work to do after everything that's happened between them, but there seems to be some hope at the end of this old tunnel," she said. "And, just so you know, and don't go getting all excited or anything, but I've decided to go to Clayton for the weekend with him after all. We're going to leave right after I get back from Albuquerque tonight. I hope you don't mind fending for yourself for a couple days." I just smiled.

I had the entire weekend to myself so I slept in a little later than usual Saturday morning, then busied myself straightening up the kitchen. I had been planning to later just snuggle up by the fireplace with an accounting book I'd been needing to get into and a glass of wine I probably didn't, so was surprised when Jude called around noon and asked if he could stop by to talk.

"Hey, I know you've got a lot going on right now, and you're probably exhausted," he said, "but I was wondering. Do you mind if I stop by later on this evening for a bit? Maybe I can pick us up some dinner?"

"Of *course* I don't mind," I answered, probably too quickly, but my heart was racing and my mind was doing its best trying to keep up. "I'd love to see you before I go."

"Oh, so you're still planning on going back to Denver?" I could hear a slight catch in his voice and my heart stammered again.

"Well, that's the plan, anyway. I can't stay mooching off Aunt Penny for too much longer. Besides, I'll be as big as a house if she keeps feeding me like she does!"

"So, is that a no on dinner with this old guy, then?" he said teasingly.

"No! I mean yes…I mean, yes, dinner would be nice. But I don't want you to go to any trouble. I can probably pull something together from the fridge." A small part of me wanted to remind him he wasn't *that* much older, but I kept quiet.

"Actually," he said, "I was thinking, if you don't mind, that is, that I could bring a canteen of Miss M's green chile stew and some tortillas and maybe we could take a ride out to the lake. There's a storm supposed to be moving in this weekend so I thought maybe we'd take advantage of the evening before it does."

"Ok, sure, I'd like that." I could barely breathe. Stop it, I admonished myself, trying to convince myself this wasn't a date or anything. He's just trying to be nice before I leave, I reasoned.

Nonetheless, after brushing my hair for the tenth time and frowning yet again into the mirror, I realized there wasn't a lot I could do to change the reflection looking back at me. I changed into a dark blue sweater that I felt complimented my hair, but then changed my mind, taking it off and slipping on a tan one with shorter sleeves and lace around the neckline. Frustrated, I yanked it off too and tossed it on the bed. I opened the closet door, my old closet, where Aunt Penny had stored a lot of Mama's clothes. Looking over the array of colors that Mama so loved, I finally pulled out a soft red tee shirt, one I remembered was her favorite, and slipped it over my head. I held it there, breathing in deeply. I could still smell her, the faint, soft flowery scent of her light perfume, or maybe it was just my imagination because I missed her so much, but my eyes quickly filled with tears and I had to sit down on the edge of the bed.

After a few minutes, I got up, pulled on a pair of old faded jeans and boots and didn't look in the mirror again. Jude Lightfoot was just going to have to accept me for who and what I was and that was that.

While I sat in the kitchen listening for his truck, I thought back to the day Mama died. Jude was as frightened then as I was, yet his instinct was to shield me and care for me. I didn't know it then, but he was as scared as the day he lost his wife. He'd never really talked about it and I'd, of course, never brought it up, even after all these years. I could only imagine the pain he'd surely gone through, what he still carried to this day, and my heart ached for him.

We were so much alike, he and I. Two victims of such unendurable pain, yet still two souls on the path to a more hopeful life. I don't know what I would've done if he hadn't found me there back then, standing in the middle of the road, screaming for Mama.

His truck's low hum and the crunch of gravel pulled me out of my thoughts. I jumped up from the table and went out the screen door, just as he pulled up. God, he's so beautiful, I thought, then looked quickly away before he could see the blush creeping up my cheeks.

"Hey, there! Wow! You look great!" he said, getting out of the truck and coming up to where I was standing. He put one boot on the first step of the porch and just stood there, staring directly at me, hands on his hips and a pirate smile on his lips.

After a couple seconds, I forced myself to breathe, then smiled tentatively down at him. "Thanks, and, er, thanks for the invite. I'm really, I mean, I'm happy to see you."

"Heck, I've been looking forward to this all afternoon," he smiled. He offered his hand to me and led me down the porch. I climbed into the passenger side of his truck as he quickly brushed off a couple papers and a tangled dog's leash.

"Sorry about that, I don't ever have any passengers in here 'cept for Tucker and Salva. Guess I should've brushed that seat off a little better. Do you mind sitting in the middle? I mean, I don't really have a way to lock down the cooler and stuff in the back so I can pack it in next to you if you don't mind."

I was thinking he could've also just packed it all in the middle, too, but I smiled at his one-way logic and happily scooted closer toward the driver's side. He got in and I felt the warm strength of his thigh against mine. It made me self-conscious and I didn't want to move away from him. But there was no good reason, I figured, for me to be that close, so I slid back toward the middle, but just a little.

He leaned over and adjusted the dial on the radio to a western station and left it there. "Waylon Jennings," he said.

"Mama used to love listening to him," I said. "Her favorite was always *Good-hearted Woman.* She would sing that, and *Luckenbach, Texas.* She knew the words to all his songs."

"I would've liked to have met your mom, KC, especially since she had such good taste in music." he smiled over at me and I could've hugged him right then.

I felt good. Happy and light and warm inside as we drove out past rolling chile and alfalfa fields, all harvested and brown now, but the rows were nonetheless mesmerizing. I wanted the road to go on forever, just the two of us, the windows down and a light breeze wafting through the cool air.

"Don't you just love the smell of country?" he said, almost reverently.

I hadn't realized how very much I did and felt a small pang that interrupted my musing. Right then I realized just how very much I was going to miss New Mexico. Its unassuming simplicity, its endless warm sunshine, its crystal-clear blue skies, the canopy of shimmering cottonwoods, the majestic silhouette of the stunning Sandia Mountains rising up in the distance.

"Reminds me of home," I said. "I mean, this home. Denver doesn't have much on Lona, that's for sure."

"Do you think you'll stay? In Denver, I mean?"

"I don't know," I said, seriously. "I'm just getting used to it up there and starting to make a few friends. It's a big city. I don't know, I guess Colorado's ok, just nothing like here."

I didn't want to say it used to be the only place I could escape.

"Well, Denver's a big city, KC. And you can sure get lost in a place like that," he said, putting on his turn signal and heading down the small, familiar dirt road.

I wondered if he was talking about me or remembering when he lived in Los Angeles so long ago. I didn't say anything.

We travelled in silence, both of us deep in our own thoughts. Finally pulling up to the edge of the lake, I realized he had chosen the exact same spot I had seen Rico and Sage so long ago. I didn't say anything, but my heart ached for a second as I remembered that day. But of course, he already knew they had been here, I reminded myself, and smiled as he parked and pulled out the cooler. I noticed he also grabbed a thick blanket and a bottle of wine that he had stashed behind the seat.

"Can I help?" I offered.

"Sure. Do you mind opening the wine? I mean, well, is that ok? The wine, I mean?"

"Yes," I said. I had to smile to myself.

Once he had spread out the blanket and unpacked the cooler with the small feast that Miss M had put together, we filled our canteen cups with stew and he poured us each a glass of wine into small paper cups.

"Mmmm, this is really good," I said, taking a big spoonful of the divine concoction. "You'll have to thank Miss M. She always made the best stew."

"Well, I remember your Aunt Penny makes a pretty mean one herself."

"She does. I'll have to remember to take that recipe up to Denver. They don't do green chile like New Mexico does," I laughed.

"So," he said, subtly changing the subject. "How's Sage and Rico doing?"

"They're doing good," I said, looking out over the still lake. I turned to face him, "and you know, after all that's happened, it turns out they really *are* good for each other, Jude. I wouldn't have thought it at first. I mean, Sage can be, well, difficult at times, you know that. And yet they've held together so well. I think they were just meant to be."

"Yeah, I get that," he said, taking a sip of his wine. He held my gaze over the rim of the cup.

I shifted uncomfortably, not wanting to look at him but not wanting to look away, either.

"What?" I said after several seconds of him staring at me. I swiped at my cheek, feigning irritation. "Do I have something on my face?"

"No, I don't see anything. Nothing but the pretty woman sitting next to me," he smiled.

I was blushing furiously, not knowing what to say or how to react, so just looked out at the lake again, keeping my eyes focused on some distant point, trying my best to breathe normally.

"You know," he continued, "we never really finished our discussion from before."

So much had passed between then and now. I had been certain he hadn't even remembered saying anything to me, so I listened attentively as he spoke, still staring out across the lake.

"I'm not very good at showing my feelings, KC. I probably never really was, according to my, my..." he hesitated and I gently touched his arm. He smiled gratefully and continued. "But, you know, I've learned that there's so much more out there than feeling sorry for yourself."

I winced and he immediately caught it. "No! I'm not directing that at you at all! If anything, it points towards me. I've spent so much time worrying and thinking and feeling bad about what's happened in my life that I think I've missed out on a lot of the good stuff, too. It's probably time for me to just put away a lot of that stuff, though. I mean, I look at you right now and I think I couldn't be in a better place than right now, right here, you, and this place."

He abstractedly reached for a strand of my hair, twirling it around his finger and tucking it behind my ear.

"I feel the same, Jude, about Mama, I mean. Sometimes it hurts so much I just want to scream. And then other times, I want to pinch myself because I'm afraid there'll come a day when I can't even remember what she looks like."

"I'm sorry you had to go through all that, KC. I really am, and I wish there was some way to change the past, you know? But you'll always remember your mom, don't worry."

Without realizing it, we had moved closer together, the air cooler now, the previous clear blue skies turning a dark, heavy gray. I could feel his warmth and it felt good. I wanted this moment to last forever, but I also wanted to, no, *needed* to, explain the whole Sage/Jude/lake/Rico confusion I'd had that one day. I took another sip of wine, and, turning to say something, met his finger lightly touching my lips.

"Shhh, we don't need to talk anymore," he whispered.

I could feel myself falling into him, and as I moved my cheek away and looked up, he kissed me and I kissed him back, long and soft and searchingly.

I pulled away from him, and stood up. We packed up the remainder of our dinner and stowed the blanket behind the truck seat, driving back to Aunt Penny's house in silence.

Light snow began floating down in little flurries as we made our way along the winding road. As Jude pulled off and headed up the driveway, for just an instant I felt that old aching stab, heard the crack of the gunshot, saw my sweet Mama laying there. But, just as quickly, I pushed those thoughts from my mind. It was time to move on from all the sadness.

I wondered what she would think right now, seeing me all grown up. How so much had changed since she's been gone. I know she'd be happy, loving how Sage and I have grown so close, not only as sisters but as real friends. She'd be grateful knowing that Aunt Penny and Uncle Doug will always be here for us and she'd be content to see how Mina finally became the grandmother Sage and I need. And I'm pretty sure she'd have loved Jude, too, especially with his taste in music.

I know how she'd say this was just how it was supposed to be. Mama was good that way.

That night, for the first time in years, I slept like a baby. Waking up, I could barely make out the faint light starting to poke around the edges of the bedroom curtains. It seemed brighter than usual, and I realized with quiet satisfaction that it was still snowing.

Jude lay still next to me, lightly snoring, so I propped myself up on one elbow, watching him as the muted morning shadows played across his beautiful features, loving every breath, every tiny movement of his eyelids, every single thing about him.

I don't know how long I lay there, watching him. Soon his eyes fluttered open and he smiled his endearing, crooked smile and I caught my breath, the moment was so quiet, so content.

I could almost hear the snow fall.

THE END

ABOUT THE AUTHOR

Linda L. Cecil is a writer, photographer and life-long resident of the beautiful southwest. She graduated from the University of New Mexico with a B.A. in English with a concentration in Technical Writing, and followed that up with a Master's in Business. Her career spanned 28 years in both technical writing and editing, where she spent the last several years managing a publications department for a major U.S. defense contractor. Linda and her daughter, Brenna, also conceptualized, created, and now successfully manage their own creative photography website, Imagiframes Photo Letter Art.

Linda, her husband, and their beloved cocker spaniel live in Albuquerque, New Mexico. This is her first novel.

THE SNOW HOUSES

THE SNOW HOUSES

Made in the USA
Las Vegas, NV
13 April 2022